Yellow STAR

a novel

Yellow Star
Judy A. King

Tate Publishing & *Enterprises*

Yellow Star
Copyright © 2011 by Judy A. King. All rights reserved.

No part of this publication may be reproduced, stored in a retrieval system or transmitted in any way by any means, electronic, mechanical, photocopy, recording or otherwise without the prior permission of the author except as provided by USA copyright law.

This novel is a work of fiction. Names, descriptions, entities, and incidents included in the story are products of the author's imagination. Any resemblance to actual persons, events, and entities is entirely coincidental.

The opinions expressed by the author are not necessarily those of Tate Publishing, LLC.

Published by Tate Publishing & Enterprises, LLC
127 E. Trade Center Terrace | Mustang, Oklahoma 73064 USA
1.888.361.9473 | www.tatepublishing.com

Tate Publishing is committed to excellence in the publishing industry. The company reflects the philosophy established by the founders, based on Psalm 68:11,
"*The Lord gave the word and great was the company of those who published it.*"

Book design copyright © 2011 by Tate Publishing, LLC. All rights reserved.
Cover design by Kellie Southerland
Interior design by Christina Hicks

Published in the United States of America
ISBN: 978-1-61777-043-2
1. Fiction / Historical
2. Fiction / Coming of Age
11.03.24

Dedication

To my loving and patient husband, Bob; and to my daughter, Debbie, who inspired me.

>If He brings you to it...
>He will see you through it

Acknowledgments

A special thanks to my friends, Alice and Cheryl, for their help and input.

Farewell to Philadelphia

As Promise stood in the middle of the Union Methodist Church graveyard, a slight breeze was lifting the early morning fog off the Delaware River. Those passing by on North Fourth Street might have been curious about a lone figure amidst the gravestones, but mourners were not a novelty anymore. The Civil War was leaving fresh scars in many graveyards in the North and in the South.

Promise stared down at the new grave at her feet. A tear slipped down her cheek and dropped to glisten on a blood-red petal of the potted geranium she held. The cool breeze, as if trying to comfort her, caressed her face with strands of her hair and the long, dark blue ribbon from her straw bonnet. She wanted to cry out loud, to scream, to release the anguish that painfully churned inside her over the loss of her mother.

Instead, she said shakily, "Mama, we are leaving today. I don't want to go. Aunt Hattie said moving is the only choice we have. We sold all we could. We have enough for our needed travel. So many questions I need to ask you. Since your tragic death, Aunt Hattie had to tell me your hidden secret."

Promise swallowed the sob that was choking her. "Mama, why could you not tell me? I would've kept your secret. I am not a child. I will be fourteen soon. Aunt Hattie, bless her heart, tried explaining to me. But I still don't understand. I do understand why you'd rather be known as a widow than a…" The words Promise was trying to say were foreign to her lips. She took a deep breath and whispered, "A *divorced woman*. Aunt Hattie said the good women of Philadelphia wouldn't have accepted you in their homes. Mama, we knew you were not a fallen woman. Mama, we love you so much, and I already miss you and I don't know what I am to do without you."

Tears flowed down Promise's cheeks, and her body shook with sobs.

"Mama," she said between sobs, "my father, who I thought was dead, is alive. Now his sister, Aunt Hattie, and me, his daughter, are going to live with him. Mama, if he never kept in touch with me, how do I know he'd want me now? I am scared, Mama. I am trying to be brave for Aunt Hattie. To leave the States to go into Indian Territory to a man I didn't know was alive fills me with terror."

"Promise," her aunt called from the waiting horse-drawn cab. "We must be going. We mustn't miss our train, dear."

Yes, I could. I could miss the train. I could stomp my feet and refuse to leave. But I cannot bring more distress to my aunt. It's too much already.

She kneeled and set the flowerpot down. "Here is your favorite flower, Mama." Lightly, she ran her gloved fingertips over the engraved lettering on the small gravestone and whispered, "Carolyn Ann Amrose, August 2, 1833–May 5, 1864. Mama, I don't want to leave you." A choking sob caught in her throat again. "Everything has happened so fast I cannot think."

"Promise, come dear. We must depart," said her aunt again.

Reluctantly, the young girl stood. Taking a handkerchief from her reticule, a beaded bag hanging on her wrist, she blew her nose and wiped her eyes. She gazed longingly upon her mother's grave. Chilled, she pulled her wool cloak more tightly to her person. Her shoulders felt too weak to carry it and her feet were leaden.

Feeling a hand on her shoulder, Promise shook her head. "I cannot leave my mother here alone, Aunt Hattie, and abandon her. I cannot! I will find a place to stay, get work in a factory, anything. She is alone in the cold ground. Alone! I cannot bear the thought of that." Promise dropped her face in her gloved hands and sobbed.

Pulling her close, Hattie said, "Your mother's form is in the ground but not her spirit. Her spirit is where it is warm. Promise, child, your mother isn't here, she isn't alone. She is with loved ones. She is with her Lord. We can mourn for ourselves, but we cannot mourn for her. Listen. Do you hear that?"

Promise lifted her head and felt a flutter in her heart. She heard what her aunt heard. Squeezing her aunt's hand, she searched the fog-bound treetops. Up there, somewhere, a bird whistled and twittered so cheerfully and loudly on such a dreary, cheerless morning that it brought a smile to Promise's sober face. It brought back a saying of her mama: "A bird sings to remind us we are not alone."

"I won't forget it again, Mama."

The cab swayed, and as they stepped up into it, Promise settled across from her aunt.

"Wasn't that the sweetest sound you ever heard, Aunt Hattie?"

Hattie's eyes were red and damp, and her mourning dress rustled as she reached for her niece's hand. Squeezing it, she said, "Yes, Promise. It was as if your mother was speaking, telling us not to worry."

Both leaned back in their seats as the cab wheels rumbled over cobblestone streets to Thirtieth Street Station. With sadness, Promise looked at the familiar sights passing by, and her thoughts drifted over what her aunt had told her after her mother's death.

After her divorce, Carolyn, with a baby bundled in one arm and her sewing basket in the other, had stubbornly made her way from Ohio to Philadelphia, Pennsylvania. Hattie, not only her sister-in-law but also a dear friend, had gone along with Carolyn to Philadelphia. Carolyn, passing herself off as a widow with a baby and a sister-in-law to provide for, knew there was only one place for them to live.

In Philadelphia, the rich resided in grand houses with lawns and trees behind decorative fences. The middle-class families lived in row houses facing each other across narrow streets. The working men and women dwelt with their families in more restrictive quarters, often only narrow alleys. Two blocks from the waterfront, Carolyn joined the residents in Elfreth's Alley. She rented one of the narrow, red brick federal houses that lined the brick-paved alley.

Carolyn set up shop in the parlor. Her artistic fingers proceeded from alterations to dressmaking. Hattie took care of the house and baby and did piecework for Carolyn. Promise grew up with spools of thread, fabrics, lace, and ribbons. Later, Carolyn had to turn their second-floor bedroom into another workroom, moving their sleeping quarters into the attic.

Nostalgia filtered into Promise's thoughts as she remembered how she had entertained herself while her mother and aunt were busy. She'd dress up in garments way too big for her small form and pretend she was a grand lady having tea. Or she'd wrap yards of gauzy fabric about her and run up and down the open stairways, the cloth flowing behind her like fairy wings. If she really got bored, she'd creep down the stairs, her back pressed against the faded, green-print, papered wall like she was invisible and sneak up on her mama or aunt. How close could she get before getting caught? Her aunt enjoyed the sneaking game; but if Mama was with a patron, she'd scold and push a giggling Promise back up the stairs to rest and read a book or into the kitchen, where Promise hid behind the wall, her hands over her mouth to suppress her giggles while her mother apologized for her mischievous daughter. The patron, usually amused, would remark, "No harm done," or, "How cute she is playing dress-up," or, "How clever she is to be able to sneak up on us without being caught sooner."

As Promise grew, Aunt Hattie was her companion and teacher. They explored the city together, shopped for fresh produce and staples on Market Street and selected fresh catch from the docks by Delaware Avenue, and traveled around the world by using the library on Fifth Street. Or, arm and arm, their parasols tilted slightly over their shoulders, they strolled under the elm trees in Independence Square. But it was evenings Promise liked best, when her mother joined them at the kitchen table. Nibbling toasted bread spread with berry preserves and sipping freshly ground coffee or hot cocoa, they'd share their day.

It was on those evenings that they talked about the terrible war. The larger, private homes had opened their doors to help shelter and aid the endless flow of injured soldiers. Carolyn did her turn at the side of the wounded and shared that sad task with her family.

Promise didn't think her family was different than any other. Sundays though, at church, she sometimes felt something was missing from their lives. Everyone at church was pleasant to them, but the Amroses never settled into the small groups that gathered on the walk in front of the church. Aunt Hattie said Carolyn didn't encourage friendships because of questions that were sure to be asked.

Never knowing a father, Promise couldn't say she missed one. Her curiosity about her father ceased when she was very young. She had been told he was in the army, met with an accident, and that he had loved her very much. Sadly, she now knew that wasn't true. If he loved her, he wouldn't have deserted her.

The rocking of the cab halted, bringing her out of her thoughts. In front of the train station, Hattie and Promise stood by their baggage in puzzlement. How would they get the baggage from the road's edge to the platform and onto the train?

"You'd think," said Hattie, her cheeks flushed, "that the train people hired men to assist passengers with their baggage. We cannot carry the trunk and valises by ourselves. A fine kettle of fish this is!" She kicked the trunk.

Hattie, always calm and in control, seldom lost her temper. Shocked, Promise said, "Aunt Hattie, you will hurt yourself. I am sure someone will help us."

"I am sorry, dear. I guess I am tired. I am glad we sent the rest of our belongings ahead."

After much frustration, Hattie did find a kindly gentleman to aid them. Promise carried what she could. She lagged behind and stopped to study the much-acclaimed locomotive called *The Tiger*, No. 134, which had been built for the Pennsylvania Railroad. It was brightly painted red and green, with ornate scroll and polished, mirrored brass trimmings. On its side cab panel, a colorful painted desert scene revealed a ferocious tiger ready to spring from amid swaying palm trees and tall, green grass.

Hissing steam blasted out from the side of the locomotive. Startled, Promise stumbled back from the bellowing cloud. Quickly, she glanced around to see if anyone had noticed her silly reaction and blushed when she saw a Union soldier smiling at her. Although feeling foolish, she pointed her chin up and hurried on. On the platform, she became aware of the distressing line of wooden coffins. An elderly couple slumped by one coffin; and a woman dressed in black, her face veiled, leaned over another. Her black-gloved hand moved over the wooden box as if she was petting it. The scene brought back mournful memories for Promise, and her eyes moistened. Just days ago, she also had stood over a loved one's coffin.

Turning her eyes away from that sadness, she viewed a different dispiriting sight: the immigrants' cars. Not wanting to stare but wanting to see, Promise looked out of the corner of her eyes as she passed by. Her nose twitched from the stale and sour odors emanating from the boxcars. Bored men lingered in the open boxcars' doors. Exhausted looking women with dirty children hanging onto their limp skirts stood next to the men.

Through the wooden plank siding, pale sunrays streaked across the benches, covered with bedding, giving a touch of color to the murky boxcars. Promise found the train station fascinating. Gray and black mourning clothes highlighted the spring pastel dresses and blue uniforms. She heard swishing of dresses and the clicking of boots. Sabers clanked as soldiers strutted about in their new uniforms, and their polished brass buttons shimmered like so many bright suns. She viewed women and girls sobbing in their hankies or burying their faces in the shoulders of loved ones. It was heartbreaking to watch.

Although the *Philadelphia Inquirer* ran articles and images of bloody battlefields and death in the Civil War, Promise wasn't prepared for what she was now seeing. The information that came to her about the terrible war had not seemed possible. Not even in her wildest imagination could she fathom the bloody battlefields nor the death cries, the echoing voices of the wounded in pain and scared and crying out for help.

Things that horrid couldn't be real.

As if her breath had been taken from her, she suddenly felt and smelled the smoky battlefields and heard the screams of downed soldiers. Right in front of her, she observed those who had seen battles. Soldiers in dirty and, some bloody, bandages wrapped around their heads, over eyes, or around their stumps where a limb had once been. An elegant, white-haired man and a little boy led a blind soldier through the station, skirting the mixed cluster of civilians and soldiers. On a bench by himself, another soldier twitched uncontrollably. Few were whole, their uniforms patched and worn. All of them had one thing in common: their glazed eyes held a faraway look. Her heart filled with pity for all soldiers and for the families they had left behind. She prayed the war would soon be over.

But she also heard sounds of happiness as joyful people met and laughter rang out, as loved ones were swung around and then held tightly. Children jumped up and down in excitement. It all was very emotional, and Promise felt tears in her eyes.

Their baggage loaded and seats found in the crowded car, Promise and Hattie settled in for the journey to St. Joseph, Missouri, a good three days or more depending on what delays were encountered. From there to Fort Laramie should be a thousand or so miles by stagecoach, about twenty or more days depending on the weather.

As she sat next to the window, the only country she had ever known rushed past. Dark smoke from factories faded out over the farmlands. The farmlands rushed by, rolling into the woods. The ground and foliage was beginning to green up after its heavy, white winter coat of snow.

Hattie handed Promise a sour pickle, a sandwich filled with strawberry preserves, and a ginger cake and then returned the cloth sack holding their food under the wooden seat. Promise nibbled and thought. She couldn't visualize the future. All that came to her mind was a darkened figure next to a darkened fort. However, the rails that were carrying her into the unknown could also take her back; and she could see clearly their brick house, the cracked Liberty Bell in the State House, the Olympic Theatre, and the ships docked at the wharf.

"Promise," said her aunt, interrupting her thoughts, "try to rest."

The car was settling in for the night. Already, snoring could be heard. A man walked through the car, dimming the swaying oil lamps. It wasn't uncommon for them to work loose from the walls, falling and spilling oil and fire on those beneath them. The lamp above Promise was the least of her worries. Sorrow and pain filled her mind.

Tired, Promise's shoulders drooped, and her head weighed heavily upon her neck. She rested her head against the dark window by her seat, staring into the darkness.

St. Joseph

The first thing Hattie did after signing the guest register at the Missouri Breaks Hotel was to ask for a broom now and hot water for bathing later to be delivered to their room on the third story. Promise helped her aunt strip the bedding off the iron bedstead. Hattie beat the thin mattress with the broom and then shook the bedstead while Promise shook out the bedding through the open window. Hearing pounding at the door and a man yelling, "Open up!" they each stopped what they were doing. Hattie opened the door. The desk clerk, his face flushed, stood there, his thin lips pressed under his mustache.

"What in dear heaven are you doing in there?"

"Why, getting rid of any bedbugs," Hattie responded calmly.

"I'll have you know, ma'am, this hotel doesn't have"—he cleared his throat—"bedbugs!"

"I assure you, sir, this room won't have them tonight," said Hattie with a sweep over the floor. "Please, sir, you may have our hot water sent up now. Thank you." Hattie smiled as the desk clerk turned sharply on his heels and walked away.

Refreshed from her bath, Promise draped a flannel sheet over her shoulders, covering the chemise she wore, and rubbed her wet hair with a huck towel. Its rough, knotty weave had been softened from many launderings. Ruffled petticoats over her cotton pantalets and long, white, wool stockings flared out behind her as she kneeled at the window. It was late afternoon, the sun beginning its decline, leaving wide yellow and pink stripes in the violet-blue western sky.

Below, St. Joseph Street bustled with activity. Those preparing for the long, treacherous trip west were speaking languages from many countries. Men wearing floppy wool hats, loose flannel shirts, and stout trousers repaired harnesses and wagons and shod their draft animals in front of the blacksmith's shop. Women in calico dresses and shawls busily replenished supplies and under white canvasses rearranged their ten-by-four-foot traveling homes, the prairie schooners. Children played and yelled alongside excited, barking dogs. Mules, horses, oxen, and crated chickens were everywhere. Promise heard mooing from cattle outside of the town.

Freight wagons, loaded with timber and supplies, rolled noisily under the window, stirring up dust. A teamster cracked his whip, sending chills up Promise's back, making her want to run up and down the dusty streets, pet a dog, greet strangers, and say, "I'm going west!" Promise wanted to embrace everyone at that moment.

Hattie, soaking in the bathing tub, sighed. "I didn't know a train trip could be so dirty and bruising to one's person."

Promise agreed. Days and nights sitting on hard, straight-backed benches had bruised her bones too. "Hopefully, the stagecoach will be more comfortable and cleaner and surely not as crowded."

The tired lines etched on Hattie's face were fading. The maddening efforts of transporting their baggage from one train to another after Pittsburgh were hair-pulling, along with the hassle of purchasing new tickets with each change of trains.

While Hattie's hair was drying, she redecorated Promise's straw bonnet. She removed the dark blue ribbon for a brown, velvet ribbon and added dainty, yellow cloth flowers into the brown band.

Promise studied herself in the mirror above the dressing table. Her pale hair was done in one long braid down her back. Stubborn new hairs curled about her face. She licked her fingers to wet them back, only for them to bounce forward with more curl. Under the white collar of the brown-and-yellow gingham dress she had put on lay a brown bow.

"I wish I could find Mama's cameo locket," she said. "It would look nice hanging from my neck on a brown ribbon."

The locket, when opened, revealed a likeness of a younger Promise on one side and a young likeness of her mother on the other side.

Hattie wearing the matching cameo locket's earbobs, said, "Your mother always wore that locket. She once told me after she came home from doing her Christian duty of caring for convalescing soldiers that showing the likeness of you to them brought smiles to their otherwise sad faces and made writing letters easier for them. One of us must have packed it," said Hattie. "We were so distraught at the time we hardly remember where we packed anything. I do remember putting the oval gilt frame in a pocket of one of the trunks. The locket must be there too. When we arrive at your father's and unpack, we'll find it."

Giving her niece a confident smile, Hattie buttoned up the red, braided loops called frogs on her gray jacket. The jacket fit snugly over the tightly laced corset, bestowing her with a tiny waist and an ample bosom. The scalloped hem of her full, gray skirt revealed the red ruffles attached to her crinoline petticoat of horsehair and stiffened lining.

"Your mother did wonders with this costume. She had more talent in her little finger than all the seamstresses of Philadelphia put together." Hattie smoothed her dark hair over her ears and patted the coil at the back of her neck. On her head she pinned a hat trimmed with scarlet velvet, white feathers, and a scarlet bird with spread wings perched on the crown. She then tied a neat bow at the side of Promise's neck, securing her straw bonnet.

Their eyes met in the mirror, and Hattie said, "You look mighty pretty, dear. Your mother would be so proud of you. I know this move has been hard on you. You have been very grownup about it. Your father will be proud to know you and have you for his daughter."

Promise hugged her aunt and said, "Thanks, Auntie. Let's go eat. I am famished!"

Walking into the hotel's dining room, Promise was impressed. Under the high, copper tin ceiling were tables covered with snow-white linen; and the print of the papered walls were of flowers with long, curvy stems and flowing leaves in pale reds, greens, and tans on a background of dark green. Heavy, red drapes tied back with gold tassels adorned the large windows, and the fading sunlight danced prism colors off the chandeliers. Promise and Hattie took a table. Servers in black dresses and long, white aprons hustled around the tables, serving customers.

"Oh, Aunt Hattie," whispered Promise, "are you sure we really can afford this? I mean, we have a hotel room. To think we can sleep lying down and be motionless, and bathing in a bathing tub was a dream in itself. But"—Promise glanced over her shoulder—"taking a meal in here?"

A server came to take their order and shortly returned with the evening special. The food set before them smelled and looked delicious.

Cutting her generous slice of beef roast, Hattie said, "I planned for at least one special meal. I anticipated our trip being long and tiring. "Besides,"—she smiled at her niece—"it's your fourteenth birthday today."

Promise dropped her flaky baking powdered biscuit into the brown gravy on her plate.

"This is May twenty-first. My, oh my! I forgot all about my birthday."

"Before, dear, you didn't have events to push your day from your mind as you have had this year. Hattie reached into her reticule and handed a small box to Promise.

Anxiously, Promise lifted the lid. "Oh, Auntie," she said, as slipped a hair bracelet on her wrist, "It's Mama's and my hair." She ran her fingers over her light yellow hair twined with her mother's copper hair. "It's beautiful!" She slipped it over her slim wrist, admiring it.

"I had planned on making two hair bracelets, one for you and one for your"—Hattie choked and took a sip of coffee—"dear mother for her birthday too. Ah, but I have something else for you." Hattie pushed a narrow red box across the table.

"Oh, Aunt Hattie, is it from?"

"Open it and see."

Promise just gazed at the box before her. She blinked her eyes, fighting the dampness threatening to spill from them. The clinking dishes and the chattering of the other diners faded away as she slowly opened the box. Carefully, she lifted out a fan. It was white, edged with gold thread, and had a gold tassel. As she spread the silken folds out, delicate embroidered gold roses caught the flickering flames from the overhead chandelier and sparkled. Promise's eyes widened. "It's beautiful!" She lifted a card from the box and read it out loud. "'Promise, fan your dreams toward the morrows, to a brighter future. Happy Birthday. Love, Mama.'"

Hattie reached for her niece's hand. "Your mother had a captain of one of the clipper ships pick that fan up for you in the Orient. Don't cry, dear."

Promise brushed away her tears. "I wonder what she meant, Aunt Hattie, about a brighter future?"

"Her reputation as a seamstress was spreading, and she was acquiring more work." Hattie got a faraway look in her hazel eyes. "Over these last months, I had walked in on her, and she'd be sitting by the window, staring out, and her work idle on her lap and a slight smile on her lips. I'd say, 'Carolyn, what are you wool-gathering about?' She'd jump as if I had pinched her. She blushed and stammered and gave me a nervous laugh like she was a young lass in love. Foolish thought, I know. But she had a bounce in her step and laughed more easily. Did she have a beau without us knowing?

"Unlikely. Usually one or both of us accompanied her when she delivered her work, an outing for us and company for her. Of course, we stayed home when she went to do her duty at a convalescent home. She took the chance of being recognized if any of the wounded had been from our hometown in Ohio. A brave and giving woman, your mother ..."

Hattie choked, dabbed her eyes with her linen napkin, and said, "Your mother's happiness has helped me through this trying time. She was strong-willed." Hattie grabbed Promise's hand across the table. "That is what we have to be: strong and brave. Remember, we are adventurous women now, traveling into God only knows what. But it's a new life for us. We must give it a chance. Like your mama wrote, 'Fan your dreams toward the morrow.'"

"I do miss her, Aunt Hattie. But I am thankful I have you. You deserve children of your own. I'd love to teach them as you have done for me. I wouldn't be surprised, my dear aunt, if a handsome officer at the fort fell under your charm and wooed you and won your hand."

"Pooh, pooh, child, I have lived this long without a man. I believe I am too old for one now. Now, hold the fan under your eyes."

Hesitating with shyness, Promise opened the fan across her nose.

"Yes, your mother was right! The fan's gold makes the gold flecks in your eyes dance. The soldiers at Fort Laramie will flock around a welcome prospect like you. You will cause an uprising right there in the fort. I will have my hands full."

"Stop, Aunt Hattie," Promise said, laughing. She fondled the fan. Her eyes downcast, she asked, "Do I resemble him, my father?"

Pushing her empty plate back and lifting her coffee cup up, Hattie said, "No. You are your mother more and more every day. Your mother's beautiful hair was copper red while yours is the color of a sun drenched wheat field. You have her blue-gray eyes, high cheekbones, and full lips but, to her dismay, not her fair, transparent complexion.

"Remember how your mother tried to whiten your skin? You, however, inherited your father's and my dusty complexion. No matter how many different ointments your mother used, she couldn't change it. It's preposterous how our society thinks fair skin signifies being a lady. My actions show I am a lady, not my skin! Silly, silly people!"

Promise gazed lovingly at the beautiful fan in her hand, with fondest thoughts of her mother. She remembered some of the awful smells she had to endure, and she was laughing when they left the dining room. After walking up the stairs and away from other's eyes she put on an air of elegance. Lifting her head up and squaring her shoulders, she linked arms with her aunt. Fanning her face with the golden fan, in a high voice, she said, "Every summer, Mama bought lemons, but not for lemonade but for me to bleach my skin."

Hattie leaned against the wall, laughing so hard the scarlet bird on her hat bobbed. "You poor girl, yearning for a refreshing glass of lemonade, but instead, you had to rub cut lemons over your face, neck, arms, and hands day and night."

"Oh, Aunt Hattie," Promise said, trying to control her laughter, "I must have smelled peculiar."

"You smelled very refreshing, dear," Hattie gasped out as they stumbled into their room. Once snuggled in the iron bed, Hattie said with a chuckle, "Don't let the bedbugs bite."

Tired as Promise was, she couldn't fall sleep. Spontaneous laughter drifted up from the saloon next to the dining room. Faint sounds of creaking wagons and the clopping of horses made their way to her. Though Hattie's easy breathing beside Promise comforted her, her aunt Hattie, her companion, teacher, playmate, and friend couldn't fill the gaping void she felt.

Tears slipped down Promise's face and dampened her pillow.

Oh, Mama, I miss you! Mama, if he, my father, had answered Aunt Hattie's telegram, I'd feel better about this trip. I have heard Indians cut down the telegraph wires frequently. Or he might have been away from the fort. Perhaps an answer came after we departed. I pray it might have been a welcoming reply.

After her imagined conversation, she whispered, "I love you, Mama," and, with her head resting on the hair bracelet, drifted off to sleep.

The following morning, Hattie had a row with the Wells Fargo stagecoach ticket agent, and as she doled out greenbacks for every pound their baggage was overweight, she glared at the agent and then slammed down a half dime. His face red, he stared down at the paperwork before him.

Hattie pulled tight the cord of her reticule. Turning, she mumbled, "This is a fine kettle of fish."

Standing on the lower steps in front of the hotel, Promise pulled her cloak closer. She didn't know if the morning air caused her to shiver or the thought of not knowing what lay ahead. Promise wished she still wore the hair bracelet, for it gave her comfort; but it was safely tucked into the trunk. She watched her aunt, who had recovered her humor, sharing lighthearted pleasantries with a portly gentleman on the upper steps. His salt-and-pepper mutton sideburns puffed out from his pink cheeks when he smiled. The scarred, battered case at his feet identified him as a drummer.

Hattie, like Promise, wore last evening's attire. She was warming up to the conversation, and the scarlet bird perched on her hat bobbed up and down as if it wanted to take flight but was trapped. Hattie clapped her hands and laughed at something the drummer had said.

"Promise! Promise," Hattie happily called to her niece, "I want you to meet Mr. Clem Potts. He is from New York. He has traveled to Denver, Salt Lake, and California many times selling his wares."

Mr. Potts's checkered frock coat was frayed at the collar and cuffs. His tight, trousers were tucked into worn, blackened boots. He smiled at Promise, tipped his top hat, and slightly bowed.

"My pleasure, I am sure. What an unusual name, child. May I inquire how you came by it?"

Before Promise had a chance to say she was named after her mother's mother, her aunt bubbled forth. "While crossing the ocean from the old country," Hattie said, "my niece's great grandmother gave birth. Her husband, laying his hand upon the baby's brow, said, 'The new land is a *promise* for a new life. This child is the start of our new beginning, hence, the name."

"What a charming story," said the drummer.

A team of six glossy horses being held by a stock tender shook their manes, stomped the hard ground, and flicked their tails, displaying their impatience at the loading of the stagecoach. Promise felt butterflies in her stomach. She was nervous like the restless horses, yet anxious. She was doing a daring thing leaving the States.

A tall, slim man strolled to the stagecoach. His trousers were tucked inside knee-high black boots, a slouched hat was pulled low on his brow, and hair curled on his shoulders. He easily swung himself up onto the lofty seat on top of the stage. Another man, similar dressed and carrying a rifle, climbed up next to the driver.

The driver shouted, "All aboard!"

The passengers hastily obeyed his command.

Promise and Hattie hastened inside and settled back on the smooth leather seat facing backward. Mr. Potts had commented that they'd ride easier there than sitting on the forward seat and it would be more comfortable than the bench between the seats. Promise could see how the coach could seat nine passengers inside. But it would be like wearing shoes that were too small and clamping one's toes uncomfortably together.

Mr. Potts sat next to a fashionably dressed young lady, Miss Penelope Rogers. She had a touch of rouge on her cheeks and lips. A fluffy, pink plume arched from the purple hat that sat smartly on her red hair, and her blue eyes sparkled.

Private Thomas Boyd straddled the bench as if it was rude of him to give his backside to the ladies. He quickly gripped the leather loop hanging above him for balance as a whip snapped loudly and a yell, "Giddy-up!" came from up top. The coach jerked, and they were off only to stop again to wait their turn to be loaded onto the ferry to take them across the Big Muddy, the Missouri River. The brown water foamed as cattle bellowed in fear while being driven to swim across and struggled for foothold on the opposite slick bank. On wild-eyed horses, wagon masters yelled and teamsters cracked whips.

Those who couldn't or wouldn't pay the ferryman's fee floated their wagons. Women on the riverbank, waiting to cross on the ferry, watched their men folk urge their teams into the churning river and moaned as they witnessed their wagons, carrying all they owned, being pulled in the frothy, dirty water, struggling to keep upright and float.

The Road West

It was a relief for the stagecoach passengers to reach the other side of the river; once the horses touched ground, they were off again at an easy gait. The coach rocked ceaselessly, comparable to the motion of a rowboat riding waves.

While they traveled over the rolling prairie, stirring up dust behind them, Promise learned more about her traveling companions. Miss Penelope Rogers was on her way to meet her brother in Denver, in Colorado Territory. "We had had a song and dance routine in the States before my brother went in search of gold. Now he wants to resume our routine." Her friendly face broke into a pleasant smile, and she laughed. "I really think I'll be doing the performance alone and grubstaking him. I'm sure he still has the gold fever, for he had mentioned venturing into Montana Territory.

Promise guessed Private Thomas Boyd to be only a few years older than she. Swaying with the coach's rhythm, he still grasped the loop above him. He shyly told them he was joining his new company at Fort Kearney. He reddened each time Miss Rogers spoke to him and ducked his head, lifting up adoring eyes at her before he stammered a reply.

Mr. Potts, sitting where he could see ahead, pointed out a wagon train they'd soon pass. Promise tried looking out her side window as the stage swung wide to pass. The dust was so thick that all she could see was shadows. She had to pull down the leather curtain against the gritty fog. Already, the coach's dark wood paneling was under a layer of fine dust.

Promise thought of the emigrants: What a long trek ahead of them! What brave people they are, venturing into only God knows. She felt a kinship with them, for was she not doing the same? Her heart swelled knowing she was sharing an adventure with them in saying good-bye to the States.

Promise peeked under the leather curtain. The dust had lessened. For a moment, she envied the women strolling alongside their wagons. Her limbs ached for a good, fast walk. In this vast, open prairie, she could run and run. Promise glanced at her aunt and guessed that even out here she'd be told to act like a lady. Then she realized it wasn't an idle or pleasant stroll for these women. Their heads were covered with wide-brimmed sunbonnets, bowed against the sun and wind. Without petticoats, hoops, or crinolines to tangle in snaggy scrub branches or to hold their long skirts out to catch in a wagon wheel, their skirts flopped about their ankles.

Promise was thankful they had the means for better, faster, and more comfortable traveling arrangements. Suddenly, she became overwhelmed with compassion. In an unladylike manner, she leaned far out the window, ignoring her aunt's tugging on her skirt. She squinted her eyes from the gritty dust and stretched her arm forth in a wide wave, wanting her wave to say, "Good luck. God bless. Good-bye."

The stage rolled atop a hill; and the wagon train took on a resemblance of a long, dirty, white caterpillar crawling its way west.

Before the first stage station came into view, a terrible racket from above caused Promise's heart to double beat, and Hattie gasped out in alarm. Mr. Potts smiled and assured the passengers they were not under attack. He told them the driver and his companion were hailing and blowing a bugle to alert the stage station of their arrival.

Promise felt the coach pick up speed. She gripped the window ledge and braced herself back into the leather seat. Still, she was roughly bounced by the sudden stopping jolt. Poor Hattie slid half out of the slick seat. Her hatpin tore loose from her hair, and her hat with the scarlet bird took a nosedive down her face to rest on her bosom, its tail feathers under her nose. Promise covered her mouth to suppress a giggle, for it was a funny sight.

Mr. Potts and Private Boyd assisted the ladies from the stage. Promise's limbs quivered as she helped her aunt to stand and walk. Hattie moaned and pressed her hand to the middle of her back while they stretched their limbs a bit. Before entering the long, low Lancaster Station house, they brushed dust off their clothing and washed their faces and hands at the washbasin sitting on a stand next to the door.

The small group, settled at one end of the long, wooden table. Chicken stew, thick-sliced bread, freshly churned butter; and dried apple pie served with thick, black coffee sufficed their ravenous appetites. In forty minutes, they were back on the stagecoach and off again.

Mr. Potts patted his full stomach and twirled his mustache in contentment and began to entertain the passengers with his knowledge. Promise settled back to listen, her mind always curious.

He asked Private Boyd what regiment he was joining at Fort Kearney. When the private said the Eleventh Ohio, Mr. Potts asked if he knew much about the Eleventh Ohio. The private shook his head no.

Mr. Potts said, "The Eleventh Ohio Volunteer Cavalry is mostly made up with what is called the Galvanized Yankees. Galvanized Yankees are Confederate prisoners who have agreed to serve in the western forts. The South forced Union prisoners to fight for the South but couldn't force them to shoot their own in battle. The North picked up on this recruiting method. But instead of forcing prisoners to fight their own, the North put them in the undermanned western forts to help control the Indians. You will be one of our escorts, Private Boyd. It's the Eleventh Ohio US Volunteers and veteran cavalrymen from Fort Kearny escorting stagecoaches and wagon trains through troubled areas."

"I do believe it was our congressman from Philadelphia who brought that suggestion up in front of the Congress," replied Hattie proudly.

Mr. Potts pulled his display case from under his seat and opened it on the bench, revealing his wares: samples of ladies and men's garments, small household items, and a catalog for larger merchandise. Also, he carried a variety of small items to be sold from his case, from hairpins to whetstones. Miss Rogers chose a pair of earbobs while Hattie found a tortoise hair comb she just had to have. Promise selected a pretty, red, narrow ribbon as her aunt gave coins to Mr. Potts in payment.

Mr. Potts spread out a diagram for a new style hat for men. Pointing at the design, he explained, "It's called the Stetson, the boss of the plains. This will take over the west. Its wide brim will keep rain and sun off a man's face and neck, and water can be carried in the crown to water his horse. It will hold up under all weather, not like the slouch hats that are worn now. The Stetson will become as important to a man as his horse."

Promise, becoming bored and tired, thought: *That silly-looking hat won't take over the west. It will cause a horse to bolt!*

The image of a horse bolting from a man who was wearing a hat that reached to his knees was too much for her. She had to turn her face to the window and pull her cloak up to her cheeks to suppress her giggles.

The receding sun was leaving a bright and beautiful sunset-spreading crimson hue over the rolling prairie. When the stage pulled into Kennebunk home station, the fading sunset reflected orange, red, and pink on the windows of the few buildings surrounding the station. The passengers were anxious to alight and stretch their limbs, eat, and go to bed.

It was a surprise to hear lively music drifting from the station and a bigger surprise to walk into a hoedown. The fiddler and accordionist's off-key music didn't discourage the dancers. There were more men than women, so men danced together. The men who wore a band tied around their arms took the woman's part;

and there was some high-kicking going on, making more marks on the low ceiling and causing lots of hooting and shouting.

Once spotted by the men, Promise, Hattie, and Penelope were quickly dragged out on the dusty floor to the tune of "Buffalo Gals." Promise was thrown, tossed, and spun until she was dizzy. Dancing was a new experience for her; and she didn't care for it, especially being in the arms of a shaggy, bearded, smelly man. Promise managed to escape from the dance floor and made herself useful behind the table laden with food. Mr. Potts and poor, shy Private Boyd weren't so lucky. The few women who were there were thrilled to see fresh faces, and they grabbed and pulled Mr. Potts and Private Boyd out to dance.

When the time came to rest and eat, Promise found out the women traveled far to come to the station for the company of other women while their husbands were away to the war, or the silver mines in Montana Territory, or the gold mines in Colorado Territory.

Hattie dozed over her plate of food. Promise needed to get her to a bed. As the musicians were tuning up, someone began singing. "Come home to me my darling man, let there be healing across the land." The words, so light and airy, floated across the room, not a clinking spoon or a slurp from a cup could be heard. A sound of any sort dared not to interfere with the heavenly voice of Miss Rogers. No one danced. They just listened.

A small room with one bed was found for the ladies from the stagecoach .They didn't' care as long as they were able to lie down to sleep. Hattie didn't mention bedbugs as she flopped onto the bed. Promise was put in the middle, and in spite of the lumpy mattress, was soon asleep.

After a late night, the morning came too quickly. It wasn't a sunny morning either. Dull and dreary, it reflected the mood of the passengers. After a hot morning meal of skillet cakes served with dark, golden molasses and fried eggs and ham, humor was restored—until they left the station under raining skies.

The leather curtains were inept in keeping the rain from leaking into the coach. Although Promise had a sponge bath at the basin in their room that morning, she still felt gritty. She watched the rain run down inside the coach.

If only she could catch it, she'd have a good wash. And her hair, it would feel so good to have it clean again. Her clothes were soiled, like everyone else's. Her aunt had told her when they were closer to Fort Laramie they'd clean up and put on clean garments. They wouldn't enter the fort looking like ragamuffins and embarrass Steward Amrose.

The stagecoach skidded and slipped over muddy roads. Would the rain ever stop? The roads went on and on, as did Mr. Potts. The station's meals were becoming poorly, the overnight stays more uncomfortable. The conversations at the stations were about the war. It was depressing to hear the news of General Grant losing the battles in the wilderness to General Lee. It didn't bode well for the Federals.

When the sun did shine, it brought out the best in the prairie. Wildflowers in every color beckoned to the travelers. Promise wished she could run out and pick them and smell their sweet aroma.

It was after the Three Mile Station and about fifteen miles from Fort Kearney when trouble struck. Mr. Potts was the first to realize something was wrong when the coach stopped.

Hattie wondered out loud, "Who is the driver talking to?"

Mr. Potts got a glimpse of the men the driver was talking to and frowned. His voice low, he informed the rest. "It's the Squirrelly Girly Brothers."

"The what?" asked Hattie. "Are they dangerous? What do they want with us? Promise, get your head back in here. Don't let them see you!"

"Ever been around skunks, Miss Hattie?" asked Mr. Potts. "It depends on the mood of the skunk whether it will raise its tail or not. If the tail rises, you best get out of the way. These brothers are like skunks! Their mother wanted girls, but all she got were boys. So she gave them girl names, and those boys had to grow up with that hanging over them. They have been trying to prove their manhood in all the wrong ways. Nothing so bad yet to keep them in jail long, but their every stunt is getting more daring."

The stagecoach door jerked opened. "Out now!" said a squatty, little man. "Stand in front of the door, and no funny stuff! Hey, Bernie, lookie what we got here."

A big man on a big horse growled, "Find the strongbox, fool!"

The driver spoke up and told them there was no payroll on this stage.

"Ain't believin' ya, man. Army payroll is supposed to be on this stage, so where be it?"

"Told you," said the driver, "we just have passengers. No payroll."

"This here's a Wells Fargo! And Wells Fargo carries payrolls!"

The driver took his bandanna off his neck and, wiping dust from his face, spoke. "Wells Fargo also carries passengers now on this run instead of the Overland stages."

The big man's face darkened with anger and growled to another brother, "Drat it, Max! Ya told me this was a payroll stage! Sometimes I think ya ain't got no more brains than yer younger brother over yonder. Look at him gawkin' at 'em women like he ain't never saw one before."

"Hey," said the squatty little brother through pouty lips, "have, too. These ones are purty."

"They may be purty, Baby Duck, but no better than yer ma."

"Don't call me that, Bernie! My name ain't Baby Duck, its Reen!"

"Reen? Ha," said the skinny one called Max. "Ma must've hated ya most of all, Bethel Doreen!" Max sneered. "Givin' you two girly names. But to me and Bernie yer a baby duck 'cause ya act like one. Ya waddle like one when ya walk and yer mouth always open for somethin' to eat or just quackin' 'bout nothin.'"

"Taint fair," the younger brother said. "I ain't goin' around callings' ya guys Bernice and Maxine."

Before he could say any more, Bernie swatted him with his hat loosening the dust on it to form a dirty cloud over the younger brother. "Told ya never call us by those girly names. And shut up, both of ya! I gotta think."

If the situation wasn't so serious, Promise would've broken out in giggles. She had seen clowns once at a circus, and these men reminded her of them. The short, fat one did waddle when he walked. The big one had a long nose that just about touched his chin, and the skinny one had no chin and just skin over bones.

Mr. Potts whispered to Hattie and the others to stay calm. "Since there wasn't a payroll, perhaps the thieves will move on and leave us be."

Bernie, who seemed to be the leader stared at the passengers and growled, "Not goin' without somethin.' Max, pass yer hat 'round and see what valuables it'll hold."

Max took off his soiled hat and, with an evil grin, held it out to the nervous passengers. Mr. Potts dropped his gold eagles and smaller coins into the hat and then showed his empty pockets to the thief standing before him. Private Boyd threw in the few coins he had. Miss Rogers pulled greenbacks out of her reticule and then held open the bag to show Max that was all she had. Hattie wasn't giving up so easily.

She held her reticule close to her bosom, "You cannot take our funds. It's all my niece and I have to our name!"

"Let him have it, Miss Hattie," said Mr. Potts.

Before Hattie could respond, Max tore the bag from her. He dumped the contents into his hat and scowled.

"Yer willin' to get kilt over this," he held up a handful of coins. He threw the empty bag back at Hattie and dropped her handkerchief, a few hairpins, some ribbon, and her empty coin bag on the dusty ground. Max turned to the older brother and spat, "Ain't enough for the three of us to travel far!"

Bernie, on his big horse, surveyed those standing on the ground and said, "Guess we better ante up the pot. Max, grab those young gals. Takin' 'em with us."

"To Mexico, Bernie?" asked Reen. "We'd get a lot of pesos for 'em there, huh, Bernie? Could live like kings in Mexico, huh, Bernie?"

"Now ya know why yer called Baby Duck! Why not get on top of the stage and yell fur all to hear our plans! Ya dumb chowder head! Be useful. Unhook the horses from the stage, and keep yer yap shut!"

No one paid any more attention to the fat brother as he waddled off to unhitch the horses. Concentration was on the stage travelers. Promise hung onto to her aunt, Mr. Potts had his arm protectively around Miss Rogers, and Private Boyd stood there with his hands hanging down. The driver and his companion were trying to talk sense to the Squirrelly Girly Brothers, trying to convince the brothers this was a serious crime and they'd have the army after them and spend a long time behind bars for kidnapping.

"No!" shouted Hattie. "You cannot take my niece and Miss Rogers! You must not!"

"Somebody shut that woman up," yelled Bernie, "before I hafta hurt her. Reen, get two of those horses over here!"

"What horses?" asked Reen. "I unhooked 'em like ya told me to and shooed 'em away so the stage and the rest hafta stay here—"

"How dumb can ya get? Hafta ride double on our horses now!" growled Max.

"'Nuff talk," said Bernie, holding a pistol in each hand pointed at the Wells Fargo employees. "Get those gals on yer horses," he ordered his brothers.

"You cannot," cried Hattie, her hands pressed on her chest. "Promise must not be on a horse. Please, sirs, don't do this. I beg you—"

Hattie was roughly pushed aside, and Promise was torn from her arms.

"Help me, Aunt Hattie! Don't let them take me!" begged Promise, reaching for her aunt.

Reen twisted Promise's arm behind her back and again pushed Hattie away. Max grabbed Miss Rogers, putting an arm around her neck, holding a pistol on Mr. Potts. He backed away. While Promise and her aunt tried talking to each other through their sobbing, Miss Rogers's lips were pressed tightly. Only the tears on her pale face showed her emotion.

Promise was tossed onto a saddle, and Reen crawled on behind her. His fat arms circled her, holding her tight. Miss Rogers was put on in front of Max. Bernie backed his horse up, his pistols still on the rest at the stage. Hattie broke from the group, her arms reaching out. She called for Promise. A deafening shot rang out. Promise turned her head in time to see the scarlet bird fly up from her aunt's hat, and her aunt slumped down.

"Aunt Hattie! No!" Promise screamed and tried to squirm out of Reen's hold on her as he kicked his horse into a gallop.

Over the thundering in her head and over the beating of her heart, Promise heard Mr. Potts call out, "She just swooned, Promise."

Promise lowered her head and gave thanks her aunt was alive. *But what is going to happen to Penelope and me?*

A Changed Life

The horse's black mane flowed like underwater seaweed, and its ears were laid back as it labored carrying two riders. Promise held tightly to the saddle horn. She had a glimpse of Penelope. *Penelope knows how to ride,* thought Promise. Penelope wasn't bouncing about like she was. Penelope, hair askew and her pretty hat missing and her clothes bunched up about her frame, held her chin up. She seemed in control of her dire situation. Promise thought, *If only I was strong like her. If I was brave, I'd break out of Baby Duck's hold and jump to the ground. Oh, Mama, I am weak and so afraid.*

Coming upon a rain-swollen river, the brothers pushed their laboring horses into it. Promise gasped as the cold water sprayed her. The water mixed with her tears of fear.

If only I could throw myself into the river and drown, it would be better than being sold.

After reaching the opposite bank, the brothers stopped to rest the horses. Promise was roughly pulled off and dumped onto the ground. Penelope was pushed down beside her. Max tied them to a tree.

"Don't get too comfy," he said with a sneer and then laughed.

The brothers stepped out of hearing and kept looking over at their captives as they talked.

Promise was so scared she was shivering, and her cloak was unable to give warmth. Penelope tried to comfort her with soothing words.

"The cavalry will find us," she told Promise. "The horses cannot keep taking the abuse of double riders at the pace we have been traveling."

Before she could say more, Max came and untied them and pushed them to the horses. Promise began sneezing.

"Hey, ya better stop that!" said Max as he tried putting Promise on Reen's horse.

Her sneezing caused the horse to pull back on the reins and prance, jerking Max around.

"Hey, yer spookin' the horse!" he yelled.

"I am sorry," said Promise. "This happens to me when I get to close to horses. I don't know why." She cried out in pain as she was cruelly thrown on the hard saddle. She used the hem of her soiled and torn dress and held it over her nose, using it to wipe her watering eyes caused by the sneezing and the sudden pain she just received.

Back into the river, the horses were forced to swim against the moving current. The horse Promise and Reen rode began to leap in the water, unbalancing Reen, causing him to fall, dragging Promise off with him.

Max yelled, "Grab the horse, Bernie, and fish the gal and Reen out of the drink!"

I will drown, thought Promise.

"Be careful of what you wish for," her mama would say. She didn't know how to swim. Her clothing dragging her under, she frantically beat the roiling water with her hands. She gasped for air, swallowed water, and choked. She realized she wanted to live. So when Bernie reached down for her, she reached up for his hand.

They pulled out near a cluster of trees. "We stay here tonight. No fire. Rummage yer saddle bags and see what ya have fur grub," ordered Bernie.

"I need a fire," whined Reen. "That water's cold, Bernie, and that gal needs to dry off, too. Hot coffee be good, Bernie. I could even warm up some tinned beans."

"Are ya deaf as well as ya can't set a horse?" yelled Bernie. "Fire! Smoke! Cavalry! Do you get the image, Baby Duck? Now get those gals tied up and find us somethin' to chow down."

Penelope leaned over to Promise and said, "If he can keep yelling, he can lead the cavalry to us." Then Penelope turned to Bernie and said, "Mr. Bernie, if Promise catches her death, what good will she be to you?"

Bernie hit his leg with his hat and scowled. "Baby Duck, do what ya hafta!"

Penelope spoke up again, "Mr. Bernie, Promise needs to get out of her wet garments and get warm. May we have a blanket and move closer to the fire?"

Shaking his head in disgust, Bernie retrieved his bedroll from his saddle and threw it at Penelope. She stood in front of Promise and helped her shed her wet outer clothes under the dingy blanket and then took the wet garments and laid them across brushes close to the fire. They cuddled together in the shadows of the firelight, trying to keep warm.

"Guess we ain't got to worry 'bout 'em tryin' to escape, huh, brother?" said Max and laughed. He had a cruel laugh that sent a shiver through Promise.

A tin plate and a cup of coffee were given to them to share.

"You eat, Penelope. I'm not hungry," said Promise and sneezed.

"Hungry or not, you must eat. Have to keep your strength up. Never know when a chance to escape might come our way," replied Penelope as she took a bite of warm beans.

Promise wiped her runny eyes and took the spoon from Penelope and forced down a few bites. She was exhausted and cold. She laid her head back against a tree and said, "I feel terrible. I had a chance to drown. I could have let my clothes drag me under and let the current take me downstream, let death take me out of this despair. But I am not brave, Penelope. I want to live. I want to see Aunt Hattie again and meet my father. What are they going to do with us? Are they really going to sell us in Mexico?"

"That is what they said. If they can get us there, they will. But remember we are in Indian country now. I don't know what would be worse, being sold to some old, fat, slobbering man in Mexico or being taken by Indians."

"What do you mean?" Promise asked.

"If we are sold in Mexico, there isn't much chance of us ever returning home. If the Indians seize us, there is a chance for us to return home but we wouldn't be welcome," Penelope replied sadly. "The white people are not very forgiving in many ways. I have been performing on stage all over in the States. The audiences love me on stage but don't know me off the stage. People who come and pay money to be entertained didn't welcome the same performers in their home or in their company. They see entertainers as wanton people, especially the women. Can you imagine how you and I would be received if we came from an Indian camp? Families have shunned their own daughters who have been captured and taken from them and months or years later are found and returned to their families, and some with children.

"You'd think it would be a happy time. Instead, it caused embarrassment for family and friends. Their loved ones had lived with heathens. Why didn't they try to escape or kill themselves instead of becoming slaves to the heathens' customs? Rather than live in a society that avoided them, the returned captive escaped from the white society and rejoined the so-called heathens, as they had no other place to go. Some married into the tribe and loved their husbands and had children and didn't want to leave. Some were slaves and couldn't live again with their families. You said earlier you wanted to drown, believing that's a brave thing to do. Promise, it takes bravery to live, especially in situations like ours, not knowing what tomorrow holds. No one knows what tomorrow holds."

Promise sighed. "I think I understand about what the war is being fought over. It's not so much being a slave as it is being forced into a situation you have no control over, being taken from your home and family, being sold like a cow, like you're not a person but a thing without feelings." Then Promise sneezed.

"God bless you," Penelope said.

"God bless you too, Penelope," replied Promise.

"But I didn't sneeze," Penelope replied back.

"I know," answered Promise, "but God bless you anyway."

She snuggled next to Penelope, feeling warmer, and Penelope laid her head on top of Promise's blond head.

Stars sparkled in the blue-black sky. The full moon seemed to be looking down on them. Embers from the fire lifted up sparks and glowed, and frogs sang in harmony. Anyone looking on would see a serene sight. But the snoring and mumbling from the Squirrelly Girly Brothers sleeping broke the spell; and the firelight on their scruffy faces showed unkindness on one, hatred on another, and a little boy's face on another.

Promise's eyes were heavy with sleep. She was in turmoil and misery in mind and body. The loss of her mother was still heartbreaking, especially at night when her thoughts were her own. Since leaving the States, she had been so tired by the time rest came that her private conversations to her mother were short. Now she had been torn from her aunt's arms to be taken to Mexico to be sold. It was all so unreal to her, yet she knew it wasn't a nightmare because she hurt all over. Straddling a saddle caused her limbs to be sore. She was also getting the reaction she always got if she was too close to horses: the burning and swollen eyes, the runny nose, and the sneezing.

Promise drifted off to sleep, thinking, *Mother, if only I could be brave and have your courage.*

The scurrying of the brothers abruptly awakened the girls.

"What's going on, Penelope? What's the racket about?" asked Promise.

"The brothers are anxious to leave. They are tossing saddles on the horses, and they are not even looking at us."

Excited, Promise asked, "Do you think soldiers have found us?"

"I don't know," whispered Penelope in Promise's ear, "but can you dress quickly? Here is our chance to get away. And if soldiers are close, they will find us!"

"Yes," said Promise. "Help me to my clothes."

"Promise, your clothes are right in front of you. Promise, what is wrong with your eyes?"

Promise looked at Penelope, who was a blur, "I'm sorry. This happens to me when I am around horses. My eyes swell and itch, my nose runs, and I do a lot of sneezing. You guide me, Penelope. I will follow. What are the brothers saying? Who is this Father Fox they speak of? Penelope, there must be a priest somewhere close. Do you suppose? The brothers are trying to get away before they are caught with us. That must be it. Quickly! My clothes! I must not be standing here to greet a priest in a blanket!"

"Adios, gals," said Max as he went riding past. "Ya may be out of the pot, but yer right in the fire now!" His laughter echoed behind him.

"Sorry, gals," said Bernie, riding up. "Ain't what we planned, but we ain't hangin' 'round to see who's all with Father Fox. We can't outrun them riding double. To show ya our heart is in the right place, we're leavin' him you."

As Reen rode up, he just looked at the girls and rode on.

The brothers splashed into the river and headed to the opposite bank.

"What is going on, Penelope? Are they gone? Are we safe now?" Promise asked, reaching out to touch Penelope.

"I don't know," whispered Penelope. Penelope took Promise's hand. "Come. I will help you dress and then we'll wait for Father Fox. No sense in us trying to run, we don't know where to go." Penelope ripped a piece off of her petticoat ruffle, wetted it at the river, and then laid the cold, wet cloth over Promise's swollen eyes.

"That feels good," Promise said with a sigh. "Thanks. Do you see anything? I wonder why a priest caused such fear in the Squirrelly Girly Brothers. What a mess I must be." Promise ran her fingers through her tangled hair. "My dress is dirty and torn, my slippers are falling apart. Do you think we could go to the river and wash our faces?"

"Yes," said Penelope. "I need to wash up a bit also."

After the girls did what they could to clean themselves, they went back to wait by the fire.

"Listen. What do you hear?" said Penelope.

Promise again had the wet cloth on her eyes. She removed it and turned her head about. "I don't hear a thing, not even a bird. My mother always said a bird sings to let us know we are not alone."

"I don't hear a bird either, and I don't think we are alone," Penelope said, inspecting the trees and bushes.

"Why do you say that?" asked Promise, trying to see through her blurred eyes.

"I feel like there are eyes staring at us," answered Penelope.

"Perhaps an animal?" asked Promise.

"Perhaps," said Penelope, putting more wood on the fire.

The girls sat by the fire, their hair wild and unkempt, their clothes ragged and soiled, but their faces and hands washed in preparation to greet a priest.

Promise asked, "Do you think the brothers left any food behind in their haste to flee?"

"They left the coffee pot but no coffee. I could look for berries," said Penelope, standing.

"No! Please don't leave me alone! If I could see better I wouldn't fret about being alone," said Promise, hanging onto Penelope's skirt and looking up trying to see Penelope's face. "It's too quiet, is it not?"

"Yes, Promise, It's too quiet. Don't you think Fox is an odd name for a priest?"

"I don't know," answered Promise with a shiver.

Penelope draped the blanket over their shoulders and threw more twigs into the fire; and they sat there huddled together, watching the flames dance until their eyes slowly closed.

Promise dreamt. Her hair was in two long braids, and she was wearing her brown and yellow gingham dress, which was whole and clean. And she had her mother's locket around her neck. She was so glad it had been found.

She was running in a green meadow with a creek weaving its way back and forth, her limbs stretched out to jump the creek and to glide over the tall grass. She was close to flying. Her mother was running beside her. She wanted to ask her mother why she was wearing Penelope's purple and pink dress but did not. It wasn't important.

"Look, Mama. There is Aunt Hattie sitting under a tree with a basket of food. I am so hungry. Hurry, Mama." She looked back, and her mother was falling behind. She waved to her mother to come on, and her mother said, "Keep going, Promise. Keep going."

She kept running but wasn't getting any closer to her aunt. It seemed she was jumping across the creek more and more as she ran. Her mother was farther and farther behind her, and she kept saying, "Keep going. Keep going." Aunt Hattie waved at her. The scarlet bird nodded its head at her like it too was saying, "Faster! Faster!" She flew over the grass and jumped the creek but was still not getting any closer to her aunt.

The sun was warm on her. It felt so good. The creek had sun drops that looked like rainbows. Then she saw Private Boyd on a big horse. He had the Squirrelly Girly Brothers tied to a rope walking behind him. She ran alongside them and said, "I was raised with manners and taught to be obedient to my elders. As not to bring shame to my mother or my aunt, I will show my manners. I shall ask if you, Maxine, Bernice, and Bethel Doreen, would partake a meal with us? Oh, I am sorry. I see you are all tied up!"

She and Private Boyd laughed at her wit. A bird flying overhead chirped with laughter also.

Promise slowly came awake with her head lying on a lap. She didn't open her eyes. She felt rested. Her eyes weren't burning, and her nose wasn't running. She could hear birds: *That is a good sign*, she thought. "Penelope," she said, "I am famished. What about you? Do you think we could try to catch some fish or find some berries?"

A hand touched Promise's forehead and brushed hair from her face. Promise turned her head and opened her eyes to look up at Penelope. It wasn't Penelope she saw but an Indian girl. Promise quickly rolled to her feet. She felt lightheaded and dizzy, but that didn't stop her from screaming, "Penelope, where are you?"

From Gingham to Doeskin

Frightened and panicky, Promise tightened her cloak around her shoulders and asked, "What have you done with my friend? Who are you? What do you want?"

A young girl about the age of Promise stood up from the ground. It was on her lap that Promise's head had rested. The girl held out her reddish brown hand in friendship. Promise backed away. She looked about and saw an older girl and two men. The girls wore long, doeskin dresses and short leggings; and the men wore long, buckskin shirts over leggings. The young girl took Promise's limp hand and spoke in English.

"Don't be afraid. We not hurt you. Your friend with my uncle, Chief Spotted Tail. She safe. I am called Squirrel. My cousin"—she pointed at the other girl—"called Brings Water, Chief Spotted Tail's daughter. My father had eyes on this camp. He not know if white women were in trouble or with their men. He let himself be seen to see what the dirty men do. When they ran like coyotes with their tails between their legs and left you, he knew they were no-good, bad white men." She led Promise closer to the fire. "You sit."

Feeling numb, Promise sat on a rock by the fire. She couldn't understand what had happened. Why did Penelope go without her? These people in front of her were Indians.

Am I still in my dream, and did it turn into a nightmare?

The one called Brings Water spoke to the men and pointed to the trees. They shook their heads in refusal, and she put her hand on the big knife in her belt. She pointed at Squirrel and at Promise and then at herself. More angry words were spoken. Brings Water pulled out her knife and waved it in the men's faces and the men threw up their hands and walked into the trees.

Brings Water sat close to Promise, staring at her. She pointed at herself and said, "Brings Water." Then she poked Promise in her chest.

Promise looked over at Squirrel for help. But the Indian girl's attention was on something in a pouch she carried. Brings Water again pointed at herself and said, "Brings Water," and again poked Promise.

"What do you want?" Promise nervously asked the older girl. "You want me to give you water?"

Squirrel handed Promise a piece of dried meat and told her to eat. As the starving Promise chewed the dried meat with its strange taste, Squirrel explained what the other girl was saying.

"She tell you her name, Brings Water; in your tongue. Only English words she knows and want to know your name. What do your people call you?"

"Oh, that's her name. My name is Promise. Thank you for the food. I was hungry. Forgive me for screaming, but you did startle me. My friend not being here scared me, and I was expecting to see a priest. Is my friend really safe?" Promise asked again, looking deep into Squirrel's dark eyes as if the truth could be seen in them. She saw kindness in the Indian girl's eyes. "Why was I not taken with my friend? Why was I left behind with you and Brings Water?"

Squirrel pulled Promise to her feet and said, "I tell you soon. First, we wash. Then meet my father."

Brings Water stood and picked up a bundle that they had brought with them. They walked along the river's edge until they came to a quiet spot in the river concealed by crowded trees and bushes. The sun revealed a nice, sandy pool of clear water.

The Indian girls began to undress. Brings Water motioned to Promise to take off her clothes.

Nervous, Promise shook her head no and knew she was blushing. "I can wash from the shore," she said. She looked about and asked, "Where are the men who were with you?"

Squirrel said, "Brings Water told the braves to return to our camp. We take care of you."

The Indian girls stood up, chucked their dresses, and ran into the water with a splash. Surprise and shocked at their lack of modesty, Promise gaped at them. Giggling, Squirrel beckoned the white girl to join them. Promise looked down at herself. Her dress was ripped and dirty. She looked at the Indian girls again, and she looked around, seeing nobody. She knew there was no place for her to go without these girls. She dropped her cloak, squared her shoulders, and walked into the water.

Promise gasped from the coldness that slapped against her limbs. In a blink of an eye, the girls grabbed her and dunked her, and she came up sputtering but she felt warmer.

"Brings Water stretched out and began to swim smoothly and easily around the white girl, and she motioned for Promise to do the same.

Promise shook her head and said, "No. I never learned to swim."

Between Brings Water and Squirrel, Promise learned a few strokes. Her dress and petticoats kept pulling her under. Finally, she took Squirrel's advice and removed her sodden dress and petticoats, throwing them on the dry ground.

Practice was now easier for her. She made sure her feet were able to touch bottom. When she sank, she could get her footing, but she still swallowed water and got water up her nose and sputtered and spit and gasped for air and tried again. She didn't want to repeat the ordeal she had had in the river when she had thought she'd drown. She wanted to at least learn to keep afloat.

Squirrel and Brings Water splashed each other and laughed. Promise smiled at their frolicking. Though she wasn't comfortable with them being unclothed, she felt safe with them: But why? She had just met them, and this wasn't what she expected from Indians. From what she had heard and read, they were savages, heathens, and uncivilized.

Squirrel came closer to Promise and said, "We wash your hair."

Before Promise could do or say anything, Brings Water brought up sand from the bottom of the pool and gently rubbed it into Promise's wet scalp and hair. After rinsing the sand out, she rubbed sage in her hair and rinsed again and it felt wonderful. Promise watched the girls use sand to wash themselves, and she did the same. She rubbed the sand on herself, and it felt like it was grinding the dirt off her skin. It felt good.

When it came time to get out of the water, Promise held back. The girls, clothed again in their doeskin dresses and short leggings, held out the same style dress for her. It was plain like theirs, with long fringe at the bottom and on the sleeves. Brings Water held up an attractive pair of beaded moccasins from a bundle, holding them out like she was enticing Promise to come out of the water. Promise knew she'd have to leave the river sooner than later.

She couldn't look at the Indian girls looking at her. She picked up her cloak from where she had dropped it and held it against her frame. Her eyes to the ground, watching water drip off her, she made her way to Brings Water. Holding her arms up, the cloak fell, and the doeskin dress slipped easily over her head. It was soft and not binding, and she felt clean from her head to her toes. Her ankles and shinbones were exposed. She felt indecent.

Both girls wanted to brush Promise's long hair with the porcupine-tail brush brought from their bundle. They took turns. Promise's hair was snarled and tangled, and she was teased about having mice living in her hair. Squirrel shared with Promise what Brings Water said, and Promise laughed with them in between hollering, "Ouch," when her hair was pulled. She was surprised to realize she enjoyed being with the Indian girls. She knew they'd be going to their camp and the reception she received there she couldn't comprehend. She felt confident and safe with Brings Water and her big knife.

Squirrel searched the bundle until she found what she was looking for: a small, rawhide container holding grease, bear grease Promise found out later. Both girls dipped their fingers into the grease and spread it on their long, brushed, black hair, smoothing it down and making it manageable and glossy. Squirrel offered to grease Promise's hair. Promise turned her down. The grease smell wasn't pleasant to her nose. Squirrel respected her wish this time. The Indian girls braided their hair and left Promise's long hair to hang freely except for the hair hanging down next to Promise's cheeks. This hair was pulled back off her face and tied behind her head with a leather string.

Brings Water sprinkled red powder from a rawhide pouch into a small turtle shell, added a little water and grease to mix with, and painted the part in her hair. Squirrel followed suit and then offered the vermilion to Promise. Promise didn't know the custom for the red paint. There were a lot of things for Promise to learn and to find out while she waited to be rescued. Until then, she felt perhaps she should adapt to some of their customs and allowed her part to be painted red, also.

Promise made a bundle of her tattered, muddied, and stained clothing and wrapped it in her cloak. She felt hope within her, and where she was now was more promising than what it was when she was held by the Squirrelly Girly Brothers. Wearing the comfortable new moccasins, she followed Squirrel, and Brings Water followed behind her on an animal path weaving through the dense woods.

They broke through to a clearing. Under the cloudless blue sky, a sparkling river appeared, revealing green willows dipping their limbs into it. At the river's bend stood a circle of decorated tepees. Outside the circle, horses grazed. It made a pretty picture. Promise took a deep breath and wondered: *What does that ring of tepees hold for me?*

Barking dogs loped toward the girls and growled and yipped at them. One spotted dog in the pack hopped around and seemed to enjoy itself without making any of the noise. Indians appeared to see what excited the dogs.

When they saw two of their own, they waved and hurried toward them, kicking the dogs out of their way as they came to meet the girls.

Promise thought the waving seemed friendly, so she shyly waved. As they got closer, she tried to see if a priest was among them. She became fidgety when Indians of all ages crowded around, touching her hair. One Indian brave, carrying a spear, grabbed a handful of Promise's long yellow hair and laughingly held it against the black hair hanging from his spear.

Scalps!

Promise thought she was going to be sick. She tried to move on, but he held her hair. Brings Water pulled her wicked knife and poked it at the brave along with harsh-sounding words until the brave backed off, his face darkening from anger. Like a curtain pulled against the sun, the mood quickly changed. An uneasy hush filled the air.

Squirrel took Promise completely by surprise when she reached down and lifted Promise's doeskin dress, revealing her pantalets. Promise was already feeling uncomfortable about her dress being too short; and now all these unknown people, these Indians, were looking at her limbs and underclothes. Embarrassed, Promise thought of her mother.

Thank goodness my pantalets are clean now from the river!

Laughter brought Promise out of her trance. Looking about her, she saw the Indians pointing and giggling at her undergarment. Their black eyes sparkled in merriment. Promise knew she must appear ridiculous to them. She imagined herself as they saw her: a white girl with long, yellow hair dressed in doeskin wearing white man's clothes underneath. She started giggling and then broke into laughter. The three new friends hung onto each other to keep from falling down and laughed until tears came.

The whole tribe that was there laughed just as hard. Men and children rolled on the ground like dogs scratching their backs, stirring up dust clouds.

A long, wide shadow appeared, creeping over the grass, silencing the laughter. Brings Water and Squirrel broke apart and stepped back from Promise. Promise, filled with terror, thought her knees would buckle if she tried to turn around. Squirrel touched Promise and whispered for her to turn and meet Father Fox. Relieved, Promise sighed and rested a hand on her chest. She gladly turned to meet the priest who had cast the big shadow. Her mouth fell open in shock at what she saw.

The big, wide shadow came from a man just a head taller than she. He wore not a robe of priesthood but one made of buffalo over a beaded tunic; and around his neck hung not a cross but a necklace of long, yellow bear claws. His long, black hair wrapped in fur lay over each shoulder, and behind an ear were three feathers. Father Fox strolled over to Promise and stood before her, his arms folded across his chest, his stance making him look bigger than he was. She stood there like a fool, gawking, until Squirrel nudged her.

Promise, not knowing what to say, said, "Greetings, Father Fox. Thank you for taking me under your care."

After Squirrel repeated in Lakota what the white girl said, his dark eyes widened, and he nodded his approval.

Squirrel beamed; and Brings Water, her hand on her big knife, nodded to all who were looking on. Her nod said, "He has accepted the white girl in his Oglala band, and so will all of you."

Promise was taken to Father Fox's lodge.

The tepee was larger inside than it appeared from the outside.

It's clean and neat. Aunt Hattie would approve of this dwelling, thought Promise. She put her bundle down where Squirrel pointed, under rawhide bags hanging from a pole.

The young Indian girl rolled out a bedroll of a buffalo robe and Hudson's Bay blankets and said, "Rest, Promise."

Promise slumped down on the buffalo robes as if her blood had drained from her and left her limp. Squirrel covered her with a blanket and backed out of the tepee, closing the flap to give her new friend privacy.

Promise, her eyes closed, mutely spoke to her mother. *Mama, can you believe where I am? Who'd thought that by just leaving one's home to go to another that so much could happen so fast? I am so thankful that Aunt Hattie didn't get hurt, and I am sure the army will be looking for me as they will be looking for Penelope. I'm not as scared as I was with the Squirrelly Girly Brothers. I felt they were evil. I don't feel that here among the Indians, not these Indians anyway. Squirrel said Penelope is safe. I hope we meet again, soon."*

Sometime during the night, Promise woke. She smelled smoke from the small fire on the tepee's floor, and snoring could be heard. She could see a shape of someone sleeping above her head and someone across from her. Feeling a body next to her startled her until she recognized Squirrel in the dim firelight. Promise went back to sleep.

The sun breaking in the east cast a golden glow through the tepee's opened flap, giving light that woke Promise. Gathering her wits about her and remembering where she was, she decided it was time to meet her new world. She stepped outside.

Squirrel brought a wooden bowl of stew to Promise, along with a horn spoon. Promise was ravenous.

Squirrel sat beside Promise and pointed out what was in the stew. "Deer meat, turnips, onions, herbs, and berries."

The taste was different than what Promise was used to, but it was good and filling. She went back into the tepee with Squirrel and helped her roll up the bedrolls. They put items back into the different-sized, painted rawhide bags called parfleches. These bags held anything from clothes to dried food. They were of different lengths, and their four sides folded in and then tied shut and stacked neatly. Round-shaped bags and pouches hung from the tepee poles.

The inner tepee lining was decorated with painted pictures.

Not much different than a white man's home, thought Promise.

There was much work to be done by the women of the village. Being the daughter of a chief, Squirrel had a lot of duties to perform. Still retaining some misgivings about the Indians, Promise followed Squirrel wherever she went. She carried bundles of firewood and hurried to keep up with her friend. She toted water from the river. She saw how hard her friend labored to keep Father Fox's lodge. She went into the meadow and trees with the Indian girl in search of plants, roots, and berries used for food and medicine.

One evening, tired as they were, Squirrel took Promise's hand and they walked to the river to a big, flat rock and settled themselves down on it. The moon was high, and stars reflected off the water as if there were thousands of burning candles in the river.

Promise stretched her aching muscles, gave a slight moan, and rolled her shoulders.

Squirrel turned to her and said, "I thank you for all the work you do. Much help for me. Time for answers to your many questions. We saw your friend looking for berries while you slept. Didn't mean to scare either of you. She told us why she and you were there. She told us you couldn't see. Horses blind you when you are around them." Squirrel paused and looked at Promise. "Horses make your eyes go blind?"

"Can," Promise answered back.

"Too bad," said Squirrel. Then she gazed back at the river. "Chief Spotted Tail moving his band north. Said he not take you but take your friend. That was good. I wanted you to stay with us. My people already camped. You and I be friends, and you help me in my father's lodge."

Her heart beating and her back stiffened, Promise said, "I am your slave, a captive?

"No," said Squirrel, a look of shock over her face.

Promise, close to tears, said, "Brings Water's is your cousin and stays in your lodge, and I don't see her helping you. So I am a slave."

With a slight laugh and a wave of her hand, Squirrel said, "No woman work for Brings Water. No carry firewood or carry water or cook or make clothes. All beneath her. She rides with the braves on raids. Even her father, Spotted Tail, boast of her daring and her bravery. My cousin's minds set on marrying a white officer and live in white man's lodge. She tells her father to accept white man ways. He no like that. They fight. You and me friends, I hope. I teach you and you teach me, like sisters. I have sister and mother no more. Sister I knew not. She died in having child many winters ago before me. Mother died of white man's pox two winters past. I said to my father, the chief, to do right by him I want him to take another woman or wife into his lodge. 'Not yet' he says. Lot of duties on me to do. You much help. You carry water, search for food to help feed our lodge. You no complain. I like you. You no slave or captive. When Bluecoats come, you go with them. I will miss you already."

In the moonlight, Squirrel looked so sad that Promise reached over and put her arm around her thin shoulders and thought: Squirrel is pretty young to take on overseeing Father Fox's lodge. He being the chief of the band, everything had to be done with the utmost care in his lodge.

"I am sorry to hear about losing your sister and mother. I know the sadness and pain that comes with loss of loved ones. I also lost my mother."

Squirrel laid her head on Promise's shoulder, and they gazed at the starry sky, the night sounds surrounding the girls. Crickets and frogs sang a night song, and the lulling of the river calmed their thoughts.

"I wished I had Mother's locket with me to show you the likeness of her and me. She was so pretty." Promise laid back on the rock, stars flickering above her. "Before my last birthday and her death, Mother had purchased a beautiful, delicate, gold fan for me. My aunt gave it to me before we left the States. It seems like my mother is still with me. Do you think we'll see our mothers again?"

"Yes," said Squirrel. "My people say the Great Spirit takes us to the great hunting grounds in the sky. We'll see the ones who went before us. They will be waiting for us. Yes, I will see my mother again and meet my sister."

"My aunt said about the same thing. She said God takes His people home to heaven, and we here on earth will see them again when our time comes."

That night, under the robes, Promise spoke to her mother mutely in her mind.

Mama, I believe I thought all this was a game I was playing at and it would go away. Promise found the work hard. She was sorry that she bickered when asked to do tasks around their home. She didn't know what chores were until she arrived here. But she was learning more here than she'd learned from library books. She had her mother and Aunt Hattie to look out for her, then just Aunt Hattie. It was time for her to take care of herself and help Squirrel all she could. Promise thought of Penelope often and felt sure she was being treated well. She wondered if Aunt Hattie had made it to Fort Laramie and if her father was there. If so, would he send out soldiers for her? And what would he think finding her with Indians and not in Mexico? Would he accept her? Aunt Hattie had made remarks about how they dare not be an embarrassment to him when they arrived at the fort.

Promise had hoped to be the first one up to start the fire under the cooking pot. But Squirrel's side of the robe was empty. Promise tied on the short leggings that her friend had given her. She slipped on her moccasins and ducked through the flap, closing it behind her, shutting out the heavy breathing of Father Fox and the soft breathing of Brings Water.

The crisp air gave her reason to shiver in the early false dawn. The early morning reminded Promise of going to the wharf with her aunt for fresh fish that came in on the fishing boats.

"Greetings," said Promise to Squirrel. "Looks like another nice day."

Squirrel, stirring up embers in the smoldering campfire nodded her head and said, "Yes."

"Let's eat fish for our early morning meal," said Promise.

Squirrel's dark eyes widened, "Yes," then she frowned. "Catch fish with what? Need sharp spear like the men when they fish? Not have one."

Promise was set on fish, and fish they shall have. They just needed hooks, bait, and string. "Did I not see steel needles in your sewing bag? What can be used for string?"

"Sinew," said Squirrel as she slipped into the lodge and came out with her sewing bag.

The wide end of two needles were wedged into sticks and held into the fire until the pointed ends glowed red. Using a small, flat, round rock, Promise bent the glowing pointed ends into hooks and then quickly dipped the new fishing hooks into cold water.

"Where you learn this?" asked Squirrel.

"I read it in a book in a library." Promise giggled. She was happy because it worked. She noticed an inquiring look cross Squirrel's brown face. "A big lodge in the States with many books," she added.

Running upstream, followed by dogs, the girls found a likely spot. Squirrel cut two long, slim willow limbs. Promise dug in the earth with a sharp stick for worms. Not wanting to touch the muddy, slimy-looking creatures, she used the stick to flip them into one of the baskets they had brought along.

Wetting the stiff coil of sinew in the water to soften it, the girls were able to tie one end of it to their willow pole and thread the other end through the needle's eye. Only then did Promise realize she'd have to touch those slimy, wiggly worms. Squirrel giggled as she watched the different disgusting faces that her friend made as she tried to put and keep a worm on her hook.

As quickly as she had started laughing, Squirrel stopped. She raised her arms to the sky. Then she spread her arms over the river and thanked the river spirit for bounty of fish. And to the fish she gave thanks for giving up their lives to feed the People.

After unhooking her first few wiggly, slippery fish, Promise got over being squeamish about touching them, and the dogs became a menace to the fishing girls. They no sooner caught a fish than the dogs began fighting for it before it was released from the hook and Squirrel had to beat them off with a stick. One dog, the spotted one, didn't mix with the others. It sat off by itself, watching. When Promise noticed that dog, she threw a fish to it. It jumped high to catch the food and took off before the other dogs ran after it.

Washing their hands and cleaning themselves up before going back to camp, Promise, giggling, asked, "Do you think we got carried away with fishing?"

"We do as the hunters do and share with lodges that don't have hunters," replied Squirrel.

"It's good we can do that," said Promise, feeling noble about sharing their bounty with others. It even made the slimy, wiggly worms worth it. "We had fun, yes?"

"Yes," agreed Squirrel with a smiled.

As the rising sunbeams streaked through the trees, the girls hurried back to camp with their basket full of fish. Every once in a while, one giggled; then the other giggled.

So this is what it is like to have a friend around my age, thought Promise.

The sun had warmed the air by the time they arrived back at camp. Women were at their fires, and those in need were happy to receive the fish. They thanked Squirrel, the chief's daughter, and smiled and nodded at the white girl.

At a tattered-looking tepee, the fire had not been stirred to bring up the flames. Squirrel held Promise back as she stepped forward. The flap was closed on the lodge, and there wasn't a wood block to knock on. Squirrel stood beside the flap and spoke in Lakota.

The flap slowly opened, and a hand flipped at her to go away.

Again Squirrel spoke in Lakota. The woman stepped out of the lodge, a thin blanket covering her head. The woman saw Promise and began to cry as she turned away, but not before Promise saw pale blue eyes. Squirrel tried to comfort the woman, but the woman grabbed the fish and hurried back into her lodge.

In between stopping at other lodges, Squirrel told Promise the story of the white woman called Crying Woman.

"Winters ago, she was a captive of the Pawnees. A trader had a horse that the Indian who owned Crying Woman wanted, so he traded with the trader. The trader took the white woman back to her family. They not know her. She had no place to go but back to the Indians. Stone Face, her man now, found her and brought her here to his lodge. Stone Face mean. Dogs live better than her."

Back at their lodge, Father Fox was waiting. Using green sticks because they didn't burn, Squirrel whittled points on them. She slipped the fish over the sticks, and propped them over the fire. Father Fox's black eyes followed Promise as she helped his daughter. Promise glanced at him and saw him viewing her, and she smiled nervously at him. She knew it was her fault that the morning meal wasn't ready when he arose from his robes. They had so much fun fishing that time got away from them.

She kept her head low as she set out bowls and spoons. She felt his eyes on her. *What is he thinking? Am I and Squirrel to be punished or just me?*

Squirrel said something to her father, and he answered her with a nod. She then slipped over to where Promise was and asked if she'd fix hot tea for Father. Relieved to keep busy, Promise seeped a mixture of roots and leaves in a brass pot and then added fresh berries into the tea, plus the berry hulls and seeds, like she had seen Squirrel do.

Squirrel handed her father a stick piercing a smoking fish and a bowl of corn mush. Father Fox reached past her and took a pinch of ash from the campfire edge and sprinkled it over the fish and corn mush for added flavor. Promise held a buffalo horn cup with the strained, steaming tea out to him. He still preferred his drinking horn to the traders' tin cups. He sniffed the aroma and nodded in approval. Promise let out a breath she didn't realized she was holding in.

After Father Fox had eaten, the girls sat down for their meal. To Promise, it was the tastiest meal—probably because she had helped catch the fish.

Brings Water came out of the lodge hungry. The girls waited for her to finish eating before they could gather the dirty vessels to take to the river to clean. Squirrel said some harsh words to her cousin. Brings Water's dark eyes widened in surprise at her cousin's tone, and then she laughed and brushed the words away with a wave of her hand.

At the river Squirrel told Promise what she had said to Brings Water. "Told her next time she late to eat she wash her own bowl. I not nice to my cousin. She can make me so mad. She rides out with the braves and comes back for me to wait on her. Me like her but get so tired of work. Wish father take in another woman."

"As long as I am here, my new friend, I will help you. I will try to learn fast," said Promise. She swished sand around in the dirty vessels to clean them. "See," she added, already I know how to wash dishes in the river like you," bringing a smile to her friend's sad face.

That night, the girls went to bed early. It had been a long, busy day. Promise spoke to her mother in her mind. By sharing her day with her mama, she felt better and didn't miss her so grievously.

The fishing brought back good memories with her mother and aunt. They never understood the excitement of fishing. When they strolled along the riverbanks of Schuylkill River on a nice Sunday afternoon, they saw grown men act like children when a fish was caught. Now Promise knew it was exciting to bring a fish ashore.

She also decided to apologize to her aunt for the grief she gave her when they were at the library over Promise's choice of books. Hattie told her a rounded education wouldn't hurt her and might benefit her. And reading about fish hooks proved her point.

Father Fox

One day, Squirrel asked Promise if she wanted to know why her father was called *Father* rather than *Chief*.

Squirrel began by telling about the priest, Father DeSmet, when he came to the Indians. He impressed Chief Fox with his kindness and his teaching about the Father in heaven. She pointed to the sky.

"Who loves all people, yours and mine. Father DeSmet received much honor and trust from the whites and Indians. And your Great White Father much-respected by your people and his Word obeyed. To my father, to be called Father signifies honor, respect, and trust from the whites more so than being called a chief."

"Does your father like the white people?" asked Promise.

"My father has no patience with bad men, white or red. He will punish anyone who brings harm to his family or his people. My father wants peace. His voice strong in councils. He wants to live on the land always, the land to be used by all people to share and take care of, not to own. My father, a wise man, knows what is taken off the land must be replaced. White men not do that. He takes and takes without giving back to the land. Father knows the whites are many, like ants pouring out of anthills, covering the land and want to take our way of life from us. Already buffalo hard to find. More of our people are depending on the whites for food and trade.

"We travel in a small band. Easier to feed less people than a lot of people. Chief Spotted Tail has many lodges to find food for.

He has to move a lot to follow game. He not depend on white man's word for food if he takes his people to a reservation. He thinks as my father thinks. White men not honor their word to the People."

Would Penelope move with the band, Promise wondered?

Squirrel sighed and dropped her head down. "My father fears without the buffalo our people will perish. Scary our life now. We know not if we live from sun to sun."

Promise went over and sat down by her sad friend on the rolled buffalo robes. She knew what it felt like not knowing what tomorrow would bring. But surely the future for the Indians couldn't be that bleak.

Brings Water popped through the opened flapped into the tepee greeted Squirrel and Promise.

It didn't take long for Brings Water and Promise to understand each other by picking up words or using sign language, and Squirrel was always close by to translate for them.

To free Squirrel for other duties, Promise took tasks upon herself. She tied sage in small bundles to hang inside the lodge to help freshen the air and ward off insects. She made sure firewood was on hand to feed the campfire and the lodge fire when needed. The days were busy, and Promise learned fast. She joined the other women in the trees and the meadow. She didn't know the names of many plants she picked, though some were familiar. She recognized blue flag, yarrow, and the bouncing bet from which, under Squirrel's directions, she made soap using its leaves and roots. Except for her yellow hair, she could be mistaken for an Indian maiden. Her skin had become darker; she wore shells and copper rings in her ears; and her long, pale hair wrapped with leather at the nape of her neck flowed down her back. Like many of the Indians, she had a braid called a scalp lock hanging down at her temple. To this Promise sometimes tied feathers or a string of beads.

The villagers became used to seeing the white girl. Promise seemed to run everywhere she went. She toted water and firewood for the older women. Promise picked berries and left some at Crying Woman's lodge, along with firewood in hopes of seeing the other white woman. A few times, Promise had seen footprints in front of the lodge, too big to be the white woman's.

Her man must come and go like a ghost, thought Promise.

Young boys on stick horses made a game of chasing or sneaking up on Promise wherever she was. She didn't want to discourage them and allowed them to catch her or sneak up on her more times than not. It was an honor for them to touch the white girl's yellow hair. They counted it as coup as the braves did when they made horse raids against their enemies, the Crow and Pawnee or the whites. When the older boys put themselves into the game, Promise made them work for their coup; but she didn't always outrun them. Soon, she was asked to join in their foot races. She did, and there she outran them all. She loved to run. Sometimes small crowds watched and wagered bets. Father Fox strutted, collecting bets, as if it was his own daughter who had won. It wasn't all work in the Indian camp.

Evenings when Brings Water was away and Father Fox rested against his willow-rod backrest, smoking his pipe, deep in thought, Squirrel and Promise would take a stroll, usually down to the river to the big, flat rock, and share their thoughts. Squirrel enjoyed listening to Promise talk about her life in Philadelphia. Someday, she also hoped to see a library and a museum. It was hard for her to understand why so many books were in one place, and she wanted to see the white man's paintings on museum walls. Promise had told her the paintings by her people were like a museum keeping records of what had happened in their lives and to their families from long ago.

One morning, the sun was warm, promising a hot day, Promise decided to do something special for Father Fox. Taking the water pouch, she hurried to a shady part of the river where the water was deep and cold. She lay on a rock and let the pouch down with an added strap so it could sink deep and pulled up the coldest water. Quickly, she tied the opening shut, as if that kept the coldness in. Pleased with herself, she also picked fresh mint as the Indians did to add flavor to the water.

She rushed back to the lodge. Father Fox was sitting under a tree, visiting with two elders and using a buffalo tail to swat at flies. Promise handed him his horn cup and the other men tin cups filled with fresh, cold, mint water. She was so excited and proud to show these other men how well she took care of Father Fox. Her smile was so large it made her face sore, but she was so pleased with herself she couldn't help but smile.

The men thanked her, looked into their cups, and looked at her big smile. They began talking and chuckling among themselves but not drinking the cold water.

To Promise's horror, they began laughing. *What,* she thought, *is so funny?*

Father Fox motioned her over and handed her his horn cup, offering her a drink from it.

What could I have done wrong? She wondered.

Her hands shaking, she glanced into the cup as she brought it up to her lips and her stomach came up in her throat.

Minnows! Minnows were swimming around in the cup! She could have just died of embarrassment. She wished she could crawl underground with the worms!

Squirrel came around the lodge and wanted to know what was going on. Promise, panicking, tried telling her friend how she got the cold water, even made sure there were no water bugs near to get into the pouch; but she pointed at the inside of the cup. Squirrel looked, and for her friend's sake, she tried not to laugh. Father Fox fought to keep a straight face and patted Promise on her head affectionately before turning his back to her. He and his friends couldn't subdue their tittering, and the shaking of their shoulders gave them away.

The rest of the day was uneventful, except for the snickering Promise heard behind her back. Not only did she give the fishy mint water to Father Fox but his friends, too. The whole village knew how foolish this white girl was. Now was the time for soldiers to come before tomorrow so she'd not have to show her face in the village. Was Father Fox ashamed to have her in his lodge? Had she embarrassed him in front of his peers?

That night, after everyone was in bed, the awful event replayed in Promise's mind. *How did I not see the minnows in the water pouch?* She remembered the rush she was in, and she didn't pay attention to what she was doing. She realized she was showing off and wanted everyone to again see how clever she was. The fishhooks had brought a lot of favorable notice to her, and she enjoyed the fuss made over her.

As Promise dwelt upon these thoughts, more images emerged. The expressions on Father Fox's face and on his friends' faces were not looks of horror but a more comical expression. Promise began to giggle thinking of their weathered faces wrinkling up and trying not to laugh.

What must they have thought when they saw minnows in their drinking cups and me, the white girl, with a giddy grin on her face?

Promise pulled the robe over her head to quiet her giggles. She didn't want to wake the lodge. She felt Squirrel's body begin to tremble, and buffered noises could be heard from her. Promise knew her friend was thinking the same thing, and Promise's giggles were becoming snorts as she tried to control them. But with Squirrel losing control of her laughter, Promise was losing her battle, too. Then chuckling was heard from Father Fox's bed. The lodge erupted in laughter, waking Brings Water, who had gotten in late. Angrily, she spoke.

"What you laugh at? Go to sleep," said Brings Water, and to her amazement, Promise understood most of what she said.

Father Fox arose and motioned Promise and Squirrel to follow him outside. Squirrel made a soothing tea for them, and they sat under the stars and talked and laughed as they sipped the hot brew. Promise learned that to laugh at herself was better than feeling sorry for herself. She also learned that Father Fox had a good sense of humor. He had thought she played a good joke on him until he saw the stricken look on her face when she saw the minnows. He then tried to make light of the situation, but his belly was full of chuckles.

Father Fox paid more attention to her now. Still, she didn't know what his thoughts were. When he passed her, he patted her head like he did to his daughter. He acknowledged her cooking skills. Even when she messed up, he ate it anyway. The time she closed the smoke flap before a big storm hit was a huge blunder. It put Father Fox's temperament to the test.

Everyone but her had retired that night. She had stoked the lodge fire and added more wood before she retired. When she heard raindrops hitting the lodge, she thought the smoke flap, which was open, needed to be closed to keep the rain out. So she closed it. Nestled under her blanket, she drifted off only to be awakened by choking coughs. Father Fox jumped out of his bed, his hand over his mouth, and quickly opened the smoke flap to release the smoke that was trapped inside. But to breathe, those within the lodge had to flee.

The chief of the village, his daughter, his niece, and the white girl he took under his care stood outside in the chilly rain, getting drenched while they waited for the smoke to clear out of their lodge. In a flash of lightning, Promise saw Father Fox's wet face. His mouth was drawn down, his arms were folded across his chest, and his eyes were staring at the flashing sky.

How he must be embarrassed to be standing with his family out in the rain while rest of the villagers are dry in their warm lodges, thought Promise.

Her head bent in shame, she told him how sorry she was. She'd not blame him if he cast her out of his lodge. Tears added to the rain running down her face.

When the family re-entered the lodge, Squirrel put a pot of water on the lodge's fire to brew tea. Everyone wrapped themselves in blankets and sat around the fire. Father Fox cleared his throat and said in Lakota, "Rain good. Good tea." He winked at Promise.

What joy she felt to know she was included in his family, accepted for who she was. He never said anything about that night. Nor did he stop patting her head.

Promise was at the river's edge, digging up tender cattail roots, when she heard dogs barking. She saw Squirrel running toward her from the encampment. Promise dropped her basket and ran to meet her friend.

"Come. A truth bearer from Chief Spotted Tail rode in."

The girls ran to Father Fox's lodge, where a tied pony stood. Promise couldn't wait to hear the news. Was it about Penelope? Or was it about her father inquiring about her?

"Let's go in and find out the news," Promise said, pushing Squirrel to the flap.

"Must wait! Father will tell us when he ready," said Squirrel, pulling Promise back.

By now, more of the villagers were standing around, waiting. The spotted dog worked its way to Promise and followed behind her as she paced back and forth.

"Sit," said Squirrel, patting the ground beside her.

Promise dropped down. She wondered if others saw her beating heart. She looked around at the crowd, waiting for news. When the flap opened, Promise jumped to her feet. The Indian rider swung onto his horse's back and rode like he had ridden in: fast. Promise, showing no emotion, waited for Father Fox to speak.

His arms folded across his chest, Father Fox's stern face took in all who were waiting for the news that the truth bearer brought. His dark eyes fell on Promise. He began talking, and Squirrel interpreted his message to Promise. My father says the truth bearer only speaks the truth. He came from Spotted Tail's camp. Truth Bearer said Bluecoats passing through Spotted Tail's encampment found and took the white girl. She was unharmed and told the Bluecoats so. She asked about the other white girl. The Bluecoats didn't know of her. She asked if they were going to find the other white girl. The Bluecoats said they had been ordered back to the fort so they couldn't disobey orders by backtracking."

There must be a mistake, thought Promise.

Surely they'd come for her. Not only Aunt Hattie was championing for her future, but now Penelope would also push for Promise's return. They would surely know she hadn't arrived in Mexico but was still in Indian Territory. Why hadn't her aunt insisted on the soldiers finding her? But wait. From what fort did the soldiers come from? Tears threatening to spill from her eyes, she quickly straightened her back and pulled herself together. It wasn't a good thing to show weakness in front of the Indians.

"The white man has broken another promise to our people, and our people are starving," said Father Fox. "Young braves want to wipe out all whites and have set fires to stage stations. Blood being spilled up and down the white man's trail. Our braves are not waiting for the old chiefs to speak. They are riding and delivering their show of distrust and hate for the white man. Killing the white man won't rid him from our land. More will come till we are crowded in a small corner without our brother, the buffalo. I cannot hold our warriors back, for it be like keeping a mother bear from her cubs. She will give her life to protect."

Promise heard Father Fox's speech through Squirrel, but her mind was on Penelope.

Will Penelope convince somebody to come for me? Will word of me being with Indians reach my father at Fort Laramie? And how was Penelope received at the fort? Was she scorned, or was she accepted?

At the first chance, Promise went off by herself—or so she thought. Near the river, she found shelter under a cave of willow branches. She crawled through the limp limbs until she came to a nice, little, open space. Sunrays poked through the lacey leaves above her. She put her head on her knees and cried. She missed her mother, her aunt, and her home in Philadelphia. She was so deep in her misery that she didn't see what had followed her in her hiding place.

Moon

Something cold and dry pushed against Promise's neck. Thinking, *Snake*, Promise wilted in fear but didn't move. She was nudged again. It felt too heavy for a snake, and Promise dared to open her eyes. A dog! It was the spotted one that had been hanging around her since she had fed it fish. She pushed it away.

"Go! I don't want you here!"

The dog's lips spread back over its teeth, its tail wagged. First Promise thought it was snarling at her, and then it dawned on her the silly dog was smiling at her. She couldn't keep a smile from spreading on her face. She grabbed the dog by the scruff of its neck, burying her face in its fur, and sobbed some more. The dog didn't move.

In the willow cave, Promise accepted a new friend. The short-haired dog had taffy-colored eyes and small, floppy ears. She was light brown in color with big, dark brown spots and a bushy tail.

Promise dried her eyes, and the dog licked her face and snuggled against her.

"Fiddlesticks!" she said to the dog. "Feeling sorry for myself isn't going to change anything at this time. Come, dog."

Feeling better, she crawled back out in the sunlight. Promise heard a songbird, and her hope rose. Yes! Soldiers might yet come for her. She should prepare herself to be ready to leave the Indian village.

She stopped and looked at the dog. Perhaps Father Fox would be against her claiming a dog. None of the village dogs seemed to have owners. And what about when soldiers came? Would they allow her to take a dog with her?

"Until then, dog," she said, "we'll be friends. But what am I to call you?"

The dog sat on her haunches, her head moving back and forth as if listening. Again, a big smile opened on the dog's face, showing long, white teeth.

"Name you Smiley? No, and I'm not going to call you Dog."

Promise squatted down face to face with the dog and looked into her eyes, hoping they'd reveal something special about the dog; and they did. In one eye, in the darkest circle lay a white crescent moon.

"Moon," said Promise. "I shall call you Moon."

Promise, with Moon happily at her side, went back to camp. When Father Fox saw the white girl with a dog loping beside her, he frowned and held up his hand to stop her. "You keeping dog?"

Before Squirrel could repeat the question, Promise decided to take a chance and show Father Fox what she had learned living in his village. Speaking halting Lakota, she answered him. "Only...with your permission...Father Fox."

His dark eyes widened in surprise at her speaking Lakota and the showing of respect to him. A tinkle in his eyes softened his stern look. He then asked, "Dog eat at my fire?"

Again, Promise replied, "With your permission, Father Fox."

He nodded his head and said, "Everyone who eats at my fire earns their food. Do you understand?"

Promise got lost in so many words and didn't understand what he said. She turned to Squirrel for help. Squirrel translated her father's words to Promise.

"Yes," said Promise, although she didn't know how she'd put Moon to work for her food.

Father Fox looked down at the dog and said, "No dog sleep in lodge."

Promise felt good about conversing with Father Fox and proud of herself for picking up the language as quickly as she had, although there were still many words she didn't understand.

Promise retrieved her clothing bundle from the lodge and went to the river, washed them, and laid the clean garments over bushes to dry. She borrowed a needle and trader's thread from Squirrel to mend the tears in her clothing the best she could, so her garments would be ready to wear when soldiers came for her. She didn't notice the sadness on her friend's face.

"Squirrel, how do I teach a dog to work?" asked Promise. "What can Moon do to earn her keep?"

"Hard question you ask," said Squirrel. "Before horses, dogs were used to do what horses now do. Now dogs alert camp of intruders. Hard time for dogs. Winters kill many of them either by starvation or freezing. Winter is hard on the People, too. Don't have food to feed dogs."

Promise thought of Moon. What would happen to her if she didn't learn some type of work? The outcome didn't look promising for the dog. Promise, sitting back against a rock, her sewing on her lap, asked, "What do the horses do that the dogs once did?"

"Dogs were used to haul the People's belongings when they moved from place to place. Packs were put on the dog's back or a travois was put on behind the dog, and the dog pulled it. The lodges were much smaller then. The lodge skins were rolled and put on the travois, and the lodge poles were used to make the travois so the whole lodge was pulled behind the dog. When horses came, the lodges could be bigger, for the horses could pull a larger load."

"Then that is what we'll do," said Promise, smiling. Then she frowned. "You do know how to make one, do you not, Squirrel?"

"Yes," said Squirrel, looking at the dog. "She does have a thick neck and chest to be a good puller, and I know where one is. But what will Moon pull?"

"Firewood," Promise about screamed in her excitement. "Yes. She could help me fetch firewood." When her friend didn't react in being as excited as she was, Promise asked, "Squirrel, are you unhappy?"

Squirrel, looking at the ground, rolled grass around her fingers. She nodded her head, and said, "Yes. You are preparing to leave when Bluecoats come. I understand you want to be with your people, but I will miss you. You like a sister." She buried her head in her arms and cried.

Promise dropped her sewing, put her arms around her friend, and cried with her. She knew she'd miss Squirrel. She also knew she'd miss Father Fox and Brings Water and many of the villagers. She liked it here, had made many friends and learned a lot, things she wouldn't ever learned living in Philadelphia. How could she feel so happy just thinking of seeing Aunt Hattie again and feel so miserable about leaving the Indian village where her new friends were? Why couldn't they be within distance of each other, where she could visit anytime she wanted to?

Moon wedged her long nose in between the crying girls, bringing their heads up to see her smiling face, and both girls began to laugh.

"How long has Moon been in your camp?" Promise asked.

"I don't remember seeing her till after Chief Spotted Tail and his band moved out. Ah. A trader was here then too. She had to come from one of them," Squirrel answered her friend while patting Moon.

They were sitting up at the edge of the encampment, farther back from the river, when Brings Water joined them. She was excited about more lodges joining the camp. To Brings Water, it meant she could go out on more raids.

Promise wondered, *How could soldiers come for me now with so many braves in the village?* As if Squirrel read Promise's thoughts, she leaned over and said, "Not worry. Bluecoats come. You can go no problem."

"Oh, Squirrel," cried Promise, "I want to see my aunt again, but I will miss you."

Before the girls could start crying over their upcoming separation again, Brings Water, agitated, said, "You act like lovesick prairie dogs! Promise not gone yet, I will miss her, also. Laugh now, cry later, yes?"

Promise realized Brings Water was right. She and Squirrel were wasting time crying when they could be enjoying their friendship and making good memories.

Promise and Squirrel echoed, *"Yes."* All three girls started laughing and went back to the lodge. After eating a cold meal, they decided to go to the river to bathe.

At the river, more women were there, splashing each other, enjoying the cool water. Promise's modesty had lessened, and she didn't feel embarrassed at the river with friends anymore. Nor did seeing the men wearing only breechcloth shock her anymore. She didn't think of them as being half naked, just being sensible in the hot weather.

She enjoyed the play in the water. After scrubbing themselves clean, washing their hair, and rubbing their bodies with sage, the girls were ready to turn in for the night.

Father Fox was visiting another lodge when the girls were getting ready for bed. Suddenly, Brings Water began yelling at something in the doorway and swinging her arms.

Promise looked, and there was Moon nosing her way into the lodge. "No, Moon! Out!" Promise hollered, jumping to her feet.

Moon smiled.

"Ahh!" screamed Brings Water.

Squirrel jumped to her feet and was hopping around like a rabbit and yelling.

Confused, Promise didn't understand why her friends were acting so strange. The louder they screamed, the bigger the smile on Moon. Then Promise figured it out.

"No, no. She is smiling, not snarling." Promise tried to calm her friends.

Brings Water had pulled her knife and pointed it at the dog.

"No, no!" Promise said, pushing the knife away. "Nice dog. See. She is smiling," Promise stood in front of Brings Water wearing a big smile, trying to show her friends.

At last, Squirrel knew what Promise was saying and spoke to her cousin till she calmed down. Promise finally got Moon out of the lodge and everything quieted down, but not fast enough. At a dead run Father Fox and other braves were swinging weapons over their heads and headed their way. Promise ducked back into the lodge and told Squirrel who was coming; and Squirrel quickly told Brings Water, who went outside to meet the braves. What she told them Promise never found out. But grumbling could be heard when the men left, something about a wolf.

The lodge had settled down, everyone curled in their robes. But Promise's mind was on Moon. Where did she go, and will she be back? She closed her eyes and silently thought of her mother.

Promise lay facing the taut skin covering. She heard a whine. Moon! She is becoming a pest, thought Promise. She scratched on the covering, hoping Moon knew it was her, and whispered, "Shh." She didn't want to wake up the others. Promise heard Moon plop her body down, causing the covering to bulge inward.

Promise patted the bulge and then faintly heard Father Fox say, "Wolf, ha." Promise buried her head in the crook of her arm and squeezed her eyes shut.

The following day, Squirrel and Promise borrowed the dog travois for Moon to pull. Two long, narrow poles slipped into a loop on each side of the dog harness and dragged behind the dog. Smaller poles were tied between the long poles to hold them apart at the back and also make a platform to carry things on. The preparations went to the satisfaction of the girls. They were quite pleased with the travois. But they forgot a young dog was to be involved in their plans.

Moon had watched the girls hauling in poles and even picked up a few sticks herself and lay them with the poles, smiling gleefully like, "I can play too." When Brings Water measured her chest for the harnesses, Moon, to Brings Water's disgust, licked her face playfully. Moon basked in the attention she was receiving. Finally, the time came to hook Moon up to the travois.

It started fine. The harnesses went on her, but before the poles could be slipped in the loops, Moon was gone. She didn't go far, just far enough away to say, "Catch me if you can."

"Moon," Promise yelled, "be a good dog and come here." Promise patted her knees. "Come on, girl."

Moon's tail wagged so hard she was hitting herself in the face. She danced around Promise. Squirrel made a dive for the dog and grabbed the harnesses, but the dog jumped right out of it. The noise being made in front of Father Fox's lodge brought onlookers. Soon, a crowd gathered around the dog and the girls, and they yelled out advice. Moon was enjoying herself. It was like she was putting on a one-dog circus with her antics. The girls heard children laughing and the grownups giggling, but they didn't think Moon was being that funny. They were getting discouraged.

Moon did backward flips in the air, her white belly exposed to the sun. Her feet hit the ground and bounced right back up for another flip. She teased the girls by getting close to them and then jumping out of reach. She trotted before the crowd, smiling. She did that one time too many. Father Fox grabbed her and held on as she twisted and squirmed to escape his arms. He carried Moon to the girls and held her while they hooked the travois to her harness. When he let go, Moon stood there, her head down, looking very sad. Her big eyes glanced up, and then she was gone with the travois bouncing behind her, stirring up a cloud of dust.

She wasn't gone long. When she returned, she acted tired; and surprisingly, the travois was still in one piece. Father Fox took the girls aside and told them now was the time to put the dog to work while she was too tired to play. And so they did. The three girls, with the dog pulling the travois, went into the trees to find firewood. Gathering wood was beneath Brings Water. She watched and gave advice.

Moon was strong, and she pulled effortlessly. When they returned to the village, many were watching for them. As though she was on display, Moon held her head high, her ears winged back, and proudly pulled the load of firewood past them, stopping only when Promise said, "Stop, Moon." Then Promise untied and lifted off firewood and gave it away; and Moon received pats on her head and was called, "Good dog."

Father Fox was waiting for them in front of the lodge. Promise and Squirrel took off the rest of the firewood. They released Moon from the travois, and she laid down facing Father Fox. Father Fox looked at Moon, and she stared back at him.

He said, "You earned your keep. Rest." He then looked at Promise and said, "Still no dog sleeps in tepee."

Promise agreed. She felt better knowing Moon was accepted by Father Fox, even though at times Father Fox pointed at Moon and said, "Wolf." Then he held his stomach and chuckled.

It soon became common to see the white girl and the dog going for firewood. Not only the travois carried wood, but Promise did, too. Sometimes though, she'd carry baskets holding roots, mushrooms, or berries.

Having a dog didn't hinder the village boys from chasing Promise to count coup on her. Moon ran beside her in the chase. She thought it was a game for her, too.

Early one morning, Squirrel entered the lodge with an odd look on her face. She motioned for Promise to come outside. Promise followed her friend out of the lodge. Waiting for her were two young braves who wanted to race her. They had heard she was fast, but was she faster than them? Their hair was loose and flowing, and they were only wearing breechcloths and moccasins. Promise knew they were dressed light to race. She wondered if it was proper for her to race these young braves. What would Father Fox want her to do? She didn't want to cause any more embarrassment for him.

Father Fox came at that time, and Promise told him that the young braves had challenged her to a foot race and asked what he thought. He studied Promise and the braves. He motioned her into the lodge. He asked her if she thought she could outrun them. Promise shrugged her shoulders. She didn't know. Racing the young boys was one thing, but to race with braves was different.

He asked, "Do you want to race?"

Without even thinking, Promise said, "Yes." She wanted to see how fast she could run. Father Fox nodded his head in agreement and, returning to the braves, told them to meet down by the path that led to the trees.

Squirrel entered the lodge. "Is it true you are racing the braves?"

"Yes. It is something I feel I must do," answered Promise. "I must lighten my garments, but how?"

Squirrel's dark eyes lit up. She moved quickly and pulled out a parfleche. From it, she lifted out a trader's red pullover cotton nightshirt. "Father never wore shirt. You wear it." She held it up to Promise. It came to her ankles. "Too long and sleeves too long, too. We cut sleeves off shirt at elbow. We cut nightshirt off to below your knees and slit both sides up at seams to make more leg room to run. In games and hunts, clothes vary and are acceptable. Don't be shy of your limbs showing. No one cares. You will run like an antelope. Many bets will be on this race."

The path was lined with people waiting for the race to begin. Father Fox took a double look at Promise as she, Moon, and Squirrel came forward. Promise's sun-streaked, yellow hair flowed down her back, and her limbs were long and straight and she walked with confidence. What wasn't showing was the shaking inside her. Moon must have sensed her nervousness because she didn't search for attention or pull any of her silly acts.

Promise noticed the braves she was to race. Their muscular frames glistened in the sunlight as they kidded around with others. They seemed at ease about the upcoming race. She wished she felt as confident as the braves. After all, she wasn't racing young boys now but men.

Father Fox's Secret

"Everyone from the village must be here," said Squirrel as she slipped a rawhide rope over Moon's neck.

Promise just nodded in agreement. She was trying to concentrate on the race, not on the crowd. She looked down the path to a tree tied with a cloth fluttering in the breeze. This race with the braves was farther than the races she had with the older boys. Did she even have the strength to finish it?

Yes, the braves might be strong and fast, their upper bodies long and lean, but she had been running every day. She decided not to let doubt enter her mind. She leaned down and kissed the top of Moon's head and told her to be good.

Squirrel gave Promise a hug and said, "You run like an antelope and leave them in your dust!"

Father Fox marked a line on the path where the runners were to line up. He called them over and pointed out the rules. The only rule was to run to the marked tree, go around it, and come back to the starting point. He held up a special knife for all to see, a steel knife with an elk antler handle. "Goes to the winner," he said.

That's something to win, thought Promise. She glanced at the two braves; and by their expressions, they thought so, too.

The three runners lined up. Father Fox held a cloth high. All eyes were on that cloth. Promise tried to calm her breathing. Out of the corner of her eye, she saw Moon trying to pull away from Squirrel.

Cannot think of that now, she told herself.

She focused back on the cloth, and it dropped. The runners were off. Side by side they stayed until one brave pulled ahead and then the other. Promise was trying to get into a smooth stride. She thought of the dream she had before meeting Squirrel, where her mother said, "Keep going, Promise. Keep going." And the scarlet bird on Aunt Hattie's hat said, "Faster. Faster." Promise remembered how she glided over the meadow like she was flying.

Her rhythm changed and her limbs stretched out. Her arms coordinated with her legs and propelled her forward. She was gliding now like in her dream. She felt wonderful, free, and weightless. Promise got into her stride, and her speed picked up. The braves were still ahead when she went around the marked tree. With each long stride, she closed the gap. She passed one and then the other. The next thing she knew, Father Fox caught her when she crossed the finish line the winner.

The braves crossed, breathing heavily.

The crowd yelled, "It good!"

The two braves came to her and let her know it was a good race. She told them they were very hard to catch and yes, it was a good race.

One brave took a feather from his hair, cut the top off, and gave it to Promise. He reached over and lifted Promise's scalp lock. In Lakota he said, "Someday I too win."

The other brave nodded in agreement as he too took a feather from his hair and cut of the top and gave it to Promise.

Promise could feel the smile on her face stretching and pulling until it hurt, but she couldn't stop smiling. Moon broke away from Squirrel. Promise kneeled down and hugged her four-footed friend. Father Fox tapped her shoulder and handed the knife to her. Promise was elated with the prize. The carved handle was beautifully etched, and now Promise had her own knife.

Going back to the lodge, Brings Water bragged to everyone she met about her friend, Promise. Squirrel told Promise that those who knew her bet on her but the newcomers bet on the braves.

"Look at you. You not even breathe hard."

Promise laughed. Her mind was so full of everything, she couldn't think of one thing. She was speechless.

At the lodge, Promise took off her racing clothes and dressed properly. Squirrel took the two feather tops and tied them together so Promise could display them on her scalp lock. "I think you be winning more feathers."

"You think I will be challenged again?" Promise asked.

"More will come and want to race the white girl. Be good. Take minds off of troubles."

Father Fox entered the lodge. He smiled broadly, and he was carrying a bundle of items he had won from the race. He put a string of shells around Promise's neck, and looped beaded strings over his daughter's ears. He then sat on his bedroll and sorted through pelts and trinkets he had won. He held up a fox pelt and said to Promise, "Trade you for the knife?"

Promise shook her head and laughed, saying, "No." She stopped herself from saying anything more. She was confused and felt as though the excitement of the day was playing tricks with her mind. She looked at him as he was holding up the pelt; and she said in Lakota, "Say again please, Father Fox."

"You trade for the knife?"

"But you are speaking English!" Promise said her mouth agape.

"Yes, I am," answered Father Fox. "I found out one should never tell all they know, no matter what language they speak. Someone who hears might speak the same tongue, and then they will know your secrets. I reveal my English only to those I trust. It is time I share that with you, Promise."

Promise didn't know how to react to this news. She stood and tried to speak, but she stammered and stuttered, overwhelmed by his trust in her. She didn't know how or why she had earned that trust. But she also felt privileged.

Squirrel grabbed Promise's hand and pulled her down on the bedroll. "It all right, Promise. You received a shock, but it will go away. Now my father can tell us stories at nighttime, and you will be able to understand all he says. I don't think he wants the knife either. Do you, Father? I thought not. He teased you."

Father Fox lit his pipe; and as he puffed on it to get it going, he said to Promise, "I put the knife as the prize because the braves might not give all their power in racing a girl, especially a white girl. The braves thought one of them win the knife, so they raced each other, forgetting about you until you passed them and won. You had to give your all to beat them."

Promise had a lot to talk about to her mother after she went to bed. Moon, outside the lodge, made a bulge against the covering again; and Promise patted it as her thoughts went to her mother.

There were more races in the days to come. Braves raced Promise to win her scalp lock. It was looked on as a trophy now. Promise raced for the pure joy of it. Squirrel kept the trophy feather tops in a pouch for Promise. Finally, Father Fox had enough of the footraces. Work had become slack around the village, so he said, "No more racing!"

One afternoon, the girls were sitting quietly on their favorite rock in the cool shade. Promise's back to Squirrel. Promise couldn't understand the Indians' fascination with her hair, but she loved having it brushed. It reminded her of evening with her mother. Brings Water gazed out at the river, the bare sky, and the village. The girls were not talking, each in their own thoughts.

Suddenly, Brings Water jumped to her feet. "Look!"

Holding onto each other, the other two girls leaped to their feet and looked where Brings Water pointed.

"Oh," said Squirrel, covering her mouth in surprise. Then she pointed. "There is Crazy Horse and his good friend, He-Man. And look, there is Green Raven and Touch the Clouds, Young Hump, and Dull Knife. Wonder when they came to village?" She looked at Brings Water and said, "Bet you are itching to go raiding with them."

"Yes," answered Brings Water. "Like you are itching to walk in the blanket with cousin Crazy Horse. He only wants to walk with Black Buffalo Woman."

Promise looked over the braves the girls were talking about. The one called Crazy Horse wore a blue buckskin tunic over white leggings. His long hair resembled the beaver fur that was wrapped around it over each shoulder. His hair puzzled Promise; and she asked in Lakota, "Why does the one called Crazy Horse have light hair. Was he a captive?"

"No!" both girls answered.

"More strangers ask that," said Brings Water. "Just because his hair has a wave in it, like you have, Promise and is light in color. After he had his vision, his father—who was Crazy Horse, a medicine man—gave his name to his son, and he went back to his first name, Worm. And you know your white chief wants the People to keep one name and not change it so the whites can keep track of us! How can that be, it our nature to change names. Never know when a brave deed is done, a vision is seen, and new names goes with them. To be truthful, we don't care if the white man can keep track of us or not. Just soon they not!"

Squirrel jumped in and said, "Look at Green Raven! He has grown! He was the son of my older sister, who the Great Spirit took when he was born and before I was born. He would like to walk in the blanket with you, Brings Water."

"Not with me," Brings Water grumbled. "No Indian walks in the blanket with me, only a white officer. Then I live at the fort and have white man's comforts!"

Brings Water and her cousin Crazy Horse resembled each other a little. He was a nice looking brave, his face oval with a short straight nose. She was pretty with her dark flashing eyes and white teeth. One would think with her short stature she wouldn't have the temper she had.

The brave called Touch the Clouds was seven feet tall. The one called Green Raven was Father Fox's grandson and a nephew to Squirrel. His mother died giving birth to him, and his father rode away the same night and never returned. Promise felt a kinship with him, although she hadn't met him. They both had been abandoned by their fathers. She understood from Squirrel that, from the day he was born, he was filled with fight, hate, and guilt. He believed he killed his mother and drove his father away.

That night, Promise had a lot to think about. There were many things she didn't understand.

The white people wouldn't let the Indians live their lives like they had been. They were willing to get along with the whites if the whites just let them be. Father Fox said the Lakota Indians loved each other, and when the white man came, they showed him love. And the white man took advantage of that love and turned on the Indians with untruths and hate.

The elderly ones Promise fetched firewood for gave her gifts. She didn't want to take from their meager supplies. But when she saw the look of rejection in their eyes, she graciously accepted their small baskets, pieces of soap, bundles of sage—whatever was handed to her.

Promise wished her mother was able to see the beautiful beadwork the women did. Even Squirrel, at her young age, made a sheave out of rawhide for Promise to carry her new knife in. Squirrel painted the band's emblem on it, which was a yellow circle of triangular points representing the sun and on the left of it, a blue star, usually worn on the garment's left shoulder.

Promise was saving Squirrel's and her hair from the quill hairbrush that both used, for a friendship hair bracelet for Squirrel.

Firewood getting scarce, Promise had to travel farther away to find wood. Still very playful, Moon did her job pulling the travois. Promise took into consideration that Moon was young. She liked to be petted, lick faces, and run, jump, play catch, and be chased. When she got in trouble, she smiled like that would get her out of trouble, and Promise had learned it usually did. She had said to Squirrel more than once, "It's hard to stay mad at a smiling dog."

Promise was used to seeing the early morning peaceful activities in the village: old men sitting under trees smoking their pipes, braves repairing or updating their weapons, boys with their small bows and arrows chasing each other while girls played with their dolls. Cradleboards were hung on tree limbs with babies being rocked to sleep by the breeze. Women worked by their lodges, gossiping while grinding dried meat, berries, or roots or doing sewing and beading. Always one pony was staked out near its owners' lodge, its tails swatting pesky flies.

She and Moon left for firewood. Promise wanted to crawl into her willow cave to braid on the hair bracelet. She liked getting away by herself sometimes. She wasn't used to being around people all the time. She liked to be isolated from others to do some thinking, usually about her father and what he'd be like and when the soldiers would be coming for her. She tried to keep her mother's image in her mind. Promise didn't want to lose her mother's beautiful face.

Moon brought Promise out of her thoughts by whining. They had gone far into the pines, and Promise had not put any firewood on the travois. "Sorry, Moon. My mind has been wool-gathering, and my hands haven't been gathering wood. I wanted to get back to the village early." Promise got busy picking up dried downfall. "Come over here, Moon, don't just stand there. No time for play."

Moon was moving but not pulling the travois. She was stepping side to side, sniffing the air, and whining nervously. She tried to wiggle out of the harness.

"What is wrong with you?" Promise asked as she tried to calm Moon down.

Moon kept looking up the hillside. She licked Promise's face and looked again up the hillside.

"Look, I will unhook the travois, and we'll go to the top of the hill to see what has you nervous."

Moon raced up the hill, Promise behind her. She stopped quickly when she heard talking. Grabbing Moon, Promise told her to stay and crept to the top of the hill and peered over the rocky edge. Down below was a group of Indians on horseback. At first, she thought they were another group joining Father Fox's band, but she didn't understand their language. She burrowed between the rocks and down into the grass and brush and studied them the best she could. They wore paint on their faces. Promise had learned paint didn't always mean war. Mostly, it was worn to help keep the hot sun and winds from burning their faces. Who were these Indians?

She felt something move beside her. Moon crawled next to her, staring down at the Indians, and a low growl rumbled in her throat. That surprised Promise. Moon wasn't one to growl or bark, so why was she growling now?

Promise knew the Sioux had enemies, Crow and Pawnees to name a couple. The Pawnees greased the top of their hair to stick up, and the sides of their heads were shaved. These Indians had long hair flowing freely like the Indians wore when they went out on raids or to count coup. Whoever they were, Moon didn't like them. What were they doing here?

Promise pushed herself back from the edge. She tried to think where she was compared to where the village was. If these Indians followed the curve of the hill, it would take them right into the pony herd. The herd had been moved farther from the encampment because grass was running out. Promise wiggled back from her hiding place and jumped to her feet. They are after the horses!

Moon at her side, Promise ran down the hill toward the pony herd. She had debated between the village and the ponies. The herd was closer to her and the other Indians. To go to the village would take longer, and she'd be too late. The ponies could be taken by then. She ran all out, slowing for nothing, dodging low limbs and jumping over bushes and downfall and slipping on pine needles. Moon, as if she knew where they were going, was in the lead. Promise landed on the valley floor and, without pause, headed for the pony herd, hoping one of the young guards spotted her. Promise saw one and began yelling and waving her arms to get his attention. The young guard rode over to her. Promise leaned over her knees, trying to get her breath, and pointed behind her. She described the Indians she had spotted. The young guard said, "Crow!"

They quickly discussed a strategy. Promise was to run to the village to bring back help while the guards moved the herd toward the village. It was a large herd. Promise took off again. She thought running through the herd would be faster than taking the uneven hillside. By moving the herd into a trot and the guards squeezing them together, they crowded Promise, hindering her run. She had to push ponies aside to get past them. She was bumped and jostled. It didn't stop her. She darted through any openings she saw between ponies.

Moon was running along the hillside, and Promise wished now she had done that. She finally got ahead of the horses, and her screaming brought out the villagers. Still running, she pointed and shouted, "Crows are coming!" Then she began sneezing.

In a blink of an eye, braves rode past her to surround the herd. They hollered and waved their weapons over their heads so the Crows heard and saw them and turned back. Promise sank down into the dust the braves left behind. Father Fox lifted her up and helped her back to the village. He even patted Moon a few times, who was so tired her head hung to the ground with her tongue dangling out.

Promise couldn't see. Once in the lodge Squirrel put some kind of warm, wet packs on her swollen eyes. Squirrel couldn't stop talking. She was so excited about how Promise saved the pony herd. Father Fox came into the lodge and sat by Promise on her robe.

"That was quick thinking bringing the herd closer to us so we could be quicker to meet the enemy." He gently touched her red, swollen eyes. "I see now why you cannot be around horses. It too bad. You'd make fine horse rider, like Brings Water."

"Father Fox," Promise said, "it was Moon who sensed the Indians and wouldn't stand still to be loaded with firewood. I wouldn't have known Indians were there if she hadn't made a fuss. And the young guard was quick in thinking of what to do. He will make a fine brave."

Father Fox patted her head and left. Promise's eyes burned, her head ached, her nose ran, and she sneezed and sneezed. She heard the flap open, and somebody entered the lodge.

"Who is there?" she asked.

A cold nose pushed her.

"Moon! Girl, you cannot be in here. It's good to feel you, but you must go!"

"I think," said Father Fox, "Moon can be in lodge. I think she is a spirit dog, and she belongs to you. Where you are, she will be."

Then Promise heard Father Fox leave.

"Did you hear that, Moon? You can sleep inside by me now. I think I will rest. I'm tired."

Moon pushed in closer and curled up beside Promise.

Promise woke to loud voices outside the lodge. One sounded angry. She heard a man say, "This is my best pony. Why not Father Fox take it in trade for the girl? She not worth this good pony." It was getting harder for Promise to understand the man's words. He was talking faster and louder. She caught the Lakota words, "I'm showing respect to you, Chief Father Fox, in offering this pony to you and taking the white girl off your hands.

Promise quickly sat up. *I must be dreaming!*

Yellow Star

Promise clutched Moon. Her eyes were slits, and everything was blurry. *Would Father Fox trade me for a good pony?* The thought brought tears to her swollen eyes. The flap opened, letting in light and the blur of Father Fox as he stepped into the lodge.

He stood and looked down at Promise and said, "You heard?"

"Yes," mumbled Promise, not looking at him.

"You are like a daughter to me. I don't trade my family without their consent. If you want to go with this man, I won't stop you, but I'd not be happy for you."

"Father Fox, I don't want to go with any man. Who is this man who wants to trade for me?" Promise asked in a shaky voice.

"Not a good man," replied Father Fox. "He is called Stone Face. Crying Woman lives with him."

"Never! Never!" said Promise, her hand reaching for Father Fox's hand. "I know I will have to leave someday soon, but with soldiers."

"You make an enemy of Stone Face by turning him away. I don't want you to be alone. Always someone be with you now that he has set his mind in having you."

"Why me?" asked Promise.

"You are valued by many and worth many ponies and pelts to the one who owns you. I wouldn't trade you for all the ponies that are here. You have brought smiles to my daughter, and you have helped her keep my lodge. You have brought laughter to my people and me in these uncertain times. I don't even want to see you go with the Bluecoats…like to keep you in family, but not in these times. Wouldn't be safe for you, as it isn't safe for us. I will keep the band here as long as possible. May the Great Spirit be kind to you and find you a way back to your people."

Then Father Fox did a surprising thing. He embraced Promise, and she wanted to cry. Was this having a father was like, who was caring, loving, and protective? Then she did cry, her face pressed against the bird bones of Father Fox's breastplate. She couldn't imagine Squirrel being left with enemies of her people and her father not doing all he could to find her and get her back safety. Promise couldn't imagine Father Fox deserting and ignoring his daughter all of her life either, something she hadn't want to admit, like her own father had done to her. Promise pulled back and looked up to the chief's kind, weathered face. In a steady voice, she said, "Father Fox, your camp hasn't moved since I have been here. Wait no more for soldiers. If my father was looking for me, he would've found me before now. He doesn't want to find me. My mind has been trying to tell me that, but my heart didn't listen. Be my honor to stay with your lodge and call Squirrel my sister."

Father Fox nodded in agreement, patted her head, and said, "It's good."

When Promise was up and around again, she felt better. She had come to terms that her father didn't want her. She felt sad about not seeing her aunt. Perhaps when the fighting between whites and reds stopped, she could find her. It was a relief for Promise not to feel the anxiety that she had felt every day wondering: Is this is the day soldiers will come?

As Father Fox warned, Promise didn't go out alone. She knew she was being watched. She felt eyes on her, and Moon showed nervousness. She didn't stop what she had always done, but she was careful and always with others. Sadly, she couldn't go to her quiet place, the willow cave.

Going through the big pines to where the travois had been left Promise tripped over a rock, an odd-looking rock. She loosened the soil around the odd rock and picked it up. It was a large skull. It had a high dome above the eye sockets and bony knobs along the snout and what looked like small teeth. It excited her. She had seen bones like that in magazines. They were called dinosaur bones, and statues of the huge lizard and birdlike beasts were in the magazines. Could there be dinosaur findings here? Her friends didn't want her to take it, but she insisted.

Squirrel and Brings Water kept shaking their heads and didn't look at her as she put it on the travois. Father Fox wasn't pleased to see the strange-looking skull.

That evening, a lovelorn brave sitting on a hill, blew his flute for his maiden. Soft notes fluttered on the night air. Father Fox stood in front of his lodge. The campfire danced shadows off the crowd standing and sitting in front of him. They came to hear a story.

"Once there was a wise man," said Father Fox, "so long ago that not even the oldest of the old ones can remember his name, and many have forgotten his vision. His vision revealed creatures so terrible and ferocious that their voices shook the treetops and thunder sounded when they walked. There were creatures taller than the trees we know today. That is what roamed Mother Earth before the People came. The wise man said the Great Spirit looked down from the sky at his giant beasts and thought, 'I am lonely and want people to talk to. But the giants are too big and dangerous. They will frighten and kill my people.'

"He didn't want to destroy His creations. He decided to keep the smaller creatures and have them grow to benefit the People. The giants became tiny and were adorned in feathers and flew over Mother Earth and sang pretty songs for the People. And they all lived together.

"If the People come upon the giants' bones, bones beyond man's imagination, let them lay to fade back into Mother Earth. They belong to the Great Spirit, as all things great and small belong to the Great Spirit. The giant bones are a reminder that the Great

Spirit created the giant creatures and then made them vanish from what they once were. He can do the same to the People."

The early sun found Promise and her friends taking the large skull back where it was found. They laid it to rest in the earth. Firewood on the travois, the girls hurried to return to camp. They were too busy chattering to watch where they were going. Moon's growling stopped them.

On a painted pony in front of them, a rider with slit, black eyes stared down at the girls. His painted face stretched tightly from his forehead down over his high cheekbones and tightened his narrow lips into a frown. His chest and limbs were shiny from grease.

Although the day was hot, Promise felt a chill go through her, and she shivered.

Brings Water, her hand on her knife, said to the man, "What you want?"

He pointed a spear at Promise. "Her!"

At the same time, Crying Woman came running and shouting and grabbed at the spear. She was flung to the ground, the air knocked out of her.

The rider jumped off his horse and knelt beside the fallen woman with his fist raised. Promise couldn't stand back and see Crying Woman being mistreated for coming to her aid. She rushed over and pushed herself between the Indian and white woman. He grabbed Promise by her shoulders and roughly pushed her aside, and she hit the ground hard. Brings Water jumped on the man's back, and Squirrel angrily whacked him with a stick. Moon, harnessed to the travois, stationed herself between the man and Promise. The hair on her back standing up, Moon lowered her head and showed her teeth. She wasn't smiling.

Crying Woman rolled away as the man tried to beat off the other two girls. The girls backed away and took their place next to Promise. He stood and glared at the girls. Pointing his spear at Crying Woman, he motioned her to go back to his lodge. She scrambled away in obedience. With one last hateful look at Promise, he leaped onto his pony and cruelly whipped it into a gallop.

The three bruised girls dropped to the ground; and Promise asked, "Was that the one called Stone Face?" She dropped her head onto her arms when told yes. "What will he do to Crying Woman now?"

The two Indian girls shook their heads sadly. Promise wouldn't let Stone Face mistreat Crying Woman if she could help it.

Back at the village, everyone seemed to be at their own business. If they knew of the encounter among the girls and Stone Face, they didn't show it. Promise had learned the Indians kept out of others' affairs unless they interfered with the well-being of the encampment. How Father Fox perceived this, she had no idea. But she knew it wasn't over.

Promise tried to see Crying Woman wherever she went the rest of the day. She kept their lodge in view when she could. So far, there was no sign of Stone Face. Luck didn't hold for long. He rode back into camp, leaving dust in his wake, and pulled his poor, lathered pony up hard in front of his lodge. Muffled screams could be heard coming from his lodge. As if reading Promise's mind, Squirrel held her back.

"Crying Woman is his, and he can do what he wants."

"How can anyone stand back and let him beat her?" cried Promise. She was struggling to pull away from her friend and go after Crying Woman.

"Don't, Promise. You will make matters worse. Crying Woman and we have humiliated him. Let this pass, please, Promise. We'll see what we can do to help her later. Maybe try to get her out of his lodge. But remember, she has no other place to go."

That night, with Moon curled at her feet, Promise tried talking to her mom. It was hard to put into words what was on her muddled mind.

There was so much about life and people Promise didn't understand. Brings Water had told Promise about her sister who had married a white man, and the man mistreated her. Promise had seen Crying Woman and knew her man beat her. So it wasn't men of one race or another, but all races had mean people. Promise learned something about herself, and she wasn't sure if it was good or bad. She interfered with a man abusing his woman. She didn't even think of what she was doing or what the consequences of her actions would bring. Now she thought it was foolish. Not only could she have been badly hurt, but so could her friends, who came to her aid.

The incident of that day was never spoken of. What Father Fox's thoughts were about it, Promise didn't know. Father Fox had been talking in council about moving closer to their winter home, but buffalo were spotted, and preparations for a hunt were in process. Sweat lodges were erected for the hunters to purify their bodies and to pray for a good hunt. Father Fox, smoking his pipe, discussed with the elders whether they should move with the hunt or wait until after the hunt and processing of the meat. They decided to wait till after the hunt.

The day before the hunt, Father Fox, Promise, and Squirrel took a leisurely stroll along the river. When he stopped, he lifted Promise's hair and said, "Your hair is soft like rabbit fur and the color of a hot sun shining through a cloud. The sun has touched your skin. It's like the color of Mother Earth. You are not pale and sickly looking as most white women."

Promise couldn't help but grin. She was thinking: If only Aunt Hattie could hear this!

"Ah," said Father Fox, his eyes wide, "I didn't know your eyes have specks in them like the color of the white man's yellow metal."

Promise was really grinning now.

"Ah. They grow bigger and brighter, like a star in the dark sky. They dance in your eyes and light up my old, dark heart." Then he threw his arms around a stunned Promise.

Squirrel had tears in her eyes and threw her arms around them both.

"We dance tonight for a successful hunt and our hunters to be safe from harm," said Father Fox as they walked back to camp. He leaned over and whispered something into his daughter's ear, bringing a big smile from her.

That evening, a large fire was lit. Red, blue, and yellow flames rose, licking the dark sky only to dip back onto themselves. The glow from the flames lit up the closer lodges and people at the edge of the dance circle. It flashed on and off on the painted dancers as they shuffled and stomped the ground with their feet and chanted to the beat of the drums, each singing his or her own spirit song.

Promise stood with her friends. Squirrel had insisted she wear a white doeskin dress. Promise loved the feel of its softness against her body. She was pleased the girls helped her dress properly for the dance. She felt pretty. They had bathed earlier. She was scented with rubbed wildflowers, and she allowed the girls to do her hair. Her hair part was painted red. They wrapped white doeskin around her braids. Looping her braided scalp lock, they clipped it to her hair using a very attractive hair decoration that Squirrel had surprised her with to show off her winning feather tops. It was a dark brown leather disk with the winning feather tops glued on the back, leaving the tips showing around it. Three narrow strands of leather hung down from it with blue and yellow beads on the bottom. And a yellow bird was painted in the middle of the disk.

She wore dangling white shells in her ears. The yoke of the dress and part of the sleeves were decorated in pale blue and yellow beads with white shells. The band's emblem in darker yellow and blue beads adorned the left shoulder. Long, white fringe hung down from the winged sleeves, the yoke seam, and the bottom of the dress.

Father Fox sat with the elders and chanted along with the drummers, "Heye aa aa, heye aa aa." Father Fox stood, and the dancing stopped. Dressed in his finest robe and wearing his war bonnet, he resembled a nobleman as fine as Promise had ever seen. He held his hands up and spoke. Looking over the crowd, Promise scratched Moon's head, not paying attention to what he said. She heard sounds of approval from the crowd, and then Squirrel pushed her into the glowing firelight. Promise stood alone. Embarrassed, she turned to go back, planning on hitting Squirrel in the head for pushing her. Then Squirrel and Brings Water stepped forward, one on each side of Promise, and walked her to where Father Fox stood.

The chief had a proud and satisfied expression on his weathered face. This time when he spoke, she listened. What she heard brought numbness to her limbs and shortness of breath. She was being adopted into the band and getting an Indian name.

Father Fox closed his eyes and reached his arms upward, praying to the Great Spirit. Promise heard chanting and soft drumbeats. Then he spoke to the People. "The morning star bright as Grandmother Moon welcomes Grandfather Sun in the east before a new day begins, giving life and a new start to the Great Spirit's people and his creation and creatures." The chief looked deep in Promise's eyes and said, "Yellow the color she carries in her eyes, like the white man's yellow metal they call gold. The spirit of the eagle is her guide to strength, wisdom, and vision."

Father Fox laid his hands on Promise's shoulders and said, "You now will be called Yellow Star, Giver of Light." He slipped a beaded necklace with a beaded emblem over her head. The emblem displayed the band's insignia of the sun and a star to show she belonged to Father Fox's band. Then he hugged her and kissed her check. Her friends hugged her while others shouted, "It good!" The dance began again, and Promise caught herself chanting and singing, "Heye aa aa, heye aa aa," and swaying with the other women.

That night, lying in bed, Promise couldn't sleep. She rubbed her toes in Moon's hair and enjoyed the comfort of knowing Moon was there. By Squirrel's heavy breathing, Promise knew she was sleeping. Promise wanted to talk. She wanted to relive the precious moment of being given an Indian name, Yellow Star.

Mama, you always said that to hear a bird sing means we are being looked after. Would you believe an eagle represents my Indian name? Then she told her mother about the dancers singing to the Great Spirit for skill in their hunters and speed for their ponies. She had recognized Touch the Clouds and Green Raven, though she had never seen him up close and Stone Face in the midst of dancers. She gave a sigh of relief knowing Stone Face would be going with the hunters.

The women pulling travois behind their ponies rode out behind the hunters just before daybreak. Shortly after that, riders from Spotted Tail's band rode in. They had come to escort Brings Water back to her father's encampment. It was a teary good-bye for Promise. Brings Water promised Yellow Star she'd see her again.

Squirrel wasn't happy. Before her father left, he had informed her to ready the butchering knives.

She turned to Promise and said, "Father didn't have to tell me to prepare for the hunt! I am smart enough to know how to get ready for it!"

Promise was surprised at her friend. She had never heard her speak harsh words against her father. Then Promise reasoned that Squirrel was thinking of the extra work that had to be done. Well, she was there to help. Stakes were whittled to pin the hides down, racks built to dry meat on, and preparations readied for the feast when the hunters returned.

"Brings Water good at sharpening knives," said Squirrel. "Miss her."

It felt strange to have the lodge to themselves. Squirrel took over the sleeping robes that Brings Water had used; and Promise, for the first time in her life, had a bed she didn't have to share with another. She didn't count Moon as sharing her bed.

It had been a long and busy day for Promise and for all the women who were left behind to prepare for the returning hunters and their kill. She did find time to sneak off to her willow cave and finished the hair bracelet. She was pleased how it turned out. Strands of Squirrel's black hair threaded throughout the braiding of her own yellow hair. She'd give it to Squirrel the evening of the celebration after the hunt.

It was pleasant for Promise to be able to walk where she wanted to without the worry of Stone Face lurking close by. She noticed Crying Woman had gone on the hunt also. For Crying Woman's sake, Promise hoped Stone Face downed a buffalo. Not only did they need the meat but the hide was needed for their dwelling. Promise and Squirrel readied extra stakes for Crying Woman and laid them by her lodge.

Squirrel had told Promise that, for those who didn't bring down a buffalo, others would share with them. Crazy Horse always made sure every lodge had meat before he kept any for himself. Squirrel thought that if Stone Face could provide for his own lodge, he might be easier to get along with. Promise had her doubts about that; she believed Stone Face was a mean man. Promise still feared him. Moon didn't like him either, and she thought Moon has good instincts.

Promise yawned, rubbed her toes into Moon's hair, and closed her eyes. Later, Moon woke and lifted her nose in the air and sniffed. Still sniffing, she arose and slowly went to the flap. A low growl rumbled in her throat.

"Moon, hush," mumbled Promise.

After a moment, she went back and lay down again at Promise's feet.

The Feast

Smiling, Promise stepped out of the river, slipped on her garments, and headed for a rocky knoll overlooking the shimmering river. She felt elated at not having to be guarded and being able to roam freely. As she sat on a rock running her fingers through her hair, releasing tangles and spreading it to dry, she watched the activities below.

After her romp in the river, Moon was basking in the sunlight on her back, showing off snowy-white hair from her neck and belly. Squirrel, with other friends, played in the water; and the laughter could be heard. Promise was getting used to Indian life, although it was a lot of hard work. That morning, Promise and Moon had been busy bringing in firewood for the fires needed for the upcoming feast. She was looking forward to the celebration. Squirrel told her there would be storytelling, dancing, and singing.

Promise gave her hair a shake. Suddenly, a hand pressed painfully over her mouth. Shocked, she tried pulling the hand from her mouth. Then an arm went around her throat, and she was yanked backward off the rock.

A voice whispered in her ear in Lakota, "You mine now! I wait long time so no Brings Water near. I not get sliced up like the Blackfoot she cut when he tried taking her!"

Promise stared into Stone Face's eyes. His menacing, black-and-red-painted face swept terror through her.

He held Promise tightly as she desperately struggled in his grip. Under his pressing hand, she shook her head no. He laughed at her and dragged her toward his painted pony. She had to do something! What? She couldn't leave the band this way! She was consumed with fear. Stone Face started to fling Promise onto the pony when she kicked out. Her feet hit the animal's side hard; and in doing so, she pushed herself back into Stone Face, causing him to lose his balance. Down they both went! She screamed before he could grab her again. He was faster and was on feet holding his spear point just inches above her. "Quiet or I'll kill you!" he said. He stepped back, giving her room to rise up.

Mad now, she didn't care; she'd rather be dead than go with him. Still on the ground, she scrambled backward over sharp rocks. Picking one up, she threw it at him and hit the pony instead, causing it to snort and jerk back. Stone Face's face held hatred when he threw the spear at her. As she quickly rolled over, she heard a growl, a yip, and a plop.

Looking up, she saw Moon on the ground. Blood seeped along the spear under her. "Moon, no!" she cried, reaching for her dog.

Stone Face also was reaching, but for Promise's hair, pulling her up by it. Again, Promise cried out, this time in a different type of pain.

"Quiet or I slit dog throat," snarled her abductor.

"And I put an arrow in your back, Stone Face!"

Stone Face dropped Promise and spun around to see who threatened him.

Green Raven's body turned at his narrow waist. One shoulder pointed the arrow; the other shoulder pulled back the bow taut and aimed at Stone Face. Father Fox stood by his grandson, along with the old men from the encampment, all with weapons in hand. Father Fox quickly went to Promise's aid. She was leaning over Moon, her hand on the wound, trying to stop the bleeding. Father Fox gently examined the dog's bleeding wound.

"Ah-h-h," he said, smiling. "Spear bounced off bone. Just make hole in flesh." He poked around the wound. "She be all right."

Moon whined and wagged her tail.

"I think hitting the ground hurt her more than spear. If it not her with spear, it be you with spear," he kindly said to Promise.

Then Promise realized how close she had come to death. If Moon had not come and jumped when she did... Promise didn't want to think about that.

Father Fox gently lifted Moon up and said, "Green Raven help girl."

Strong hands lifted her up. Weakly, she swayed against him and gazed into the greenest emeralds eyes. All she could do was stare into those captivating eyes: *So this,* she thought, *is why he is called Green Raven.* She felt a warm tingle run through her. She thought she was going to swoon in his arms. Taking her gaze off his before she drowned in them, searching for their depth, she slowly glanced over his sharp cheekbones, slim nose, and full lips. As her eyes traveled back up his face, she had a sobering thought. *Why are his eyes green? Except for Crying Woman and myself, everyone else has dark eyes.*

His face darkened. "White girl brings nothing but trouble to Father Fox!"

He roughly let go of her, swung away, and leaped onto his black-and-white pony. Stunned by his reaction, she realized he had looked at her with hatred. But why?

"Yellow Star, are you all right?" Father Fox asked, handing Moon to an elder.

It took a moment for Promise to realize she was being spoken to and called by her Indian name. "I think so, a little wobbly. What about Moon?" she asked and then added, "I don't know why you are here, but I am most grateful." She leaned into his chest.

Holding Promise's shaking frame, Father Fox answered her questions. "Bleeding stop. Moon is taken to lodge to rest. At hunt I saw no Stone Face, and Crying Woman said he go. I got Green Raven, and we ride back here fast. We saw Moon leap in front of the spear, turning it from you."

Squirrel was now at Promise's side, and villagers had surrounded Stone Face. Father Fox said to Stone Face, "You must go. You have attacked Yellow Star, who lives in my lodge, displayed disrespect for your chief. You be banished from this Oglala Lakota band and all Lakota tribes. Already messengers have ridden out to the four winds to deliver the message of the disgrace and banishment of you, the one called Stone Face.

Stone Face scoffed, "I leave this weak band of women." He pounded on his chest and said, "Like a panther, I will join other brave panthers and fight the whites and anyone who gets in my way. I wait for my woman to take my lodge down and ready supplies. Then I leave, showing my back to the fading sun and to this band of women!"

"No," said Father Fox. "You go. Crying Woman stay here! You take nothing but what you have now with you. Your lodge and belongings go to the one who takes Crying Woman in their care."

Something Stone Face had said came to Promise's mind. He had said he didn't want to be cut up by Brings Water. Promise spoke up and said, "It was you Moon growled at last night creeping around our lodge! Ha. You thought Brings Water was in the lodge. You are a snake slithering on the ground waiting for your prey to be alone before you strike. Brings Water, the young maiden you fear, left right after the hunting party rode out. She wasn't even here!" Then she smiled and added, "I won't be without my knife again." Promise didn't realize she just added more fuel to Stone Face's hatred by revealing his fear of Brings Water to all who were listening.

Outraged, Stone Face jumped at her, but Green Raven stopped him. Stone Face glared at Promise, venom dripping from his voice, as he told her, "I see you again. You dead and your dog, too!" He leaped onto his pony and cruelly whipped it, again leaving dust in his wake.

Back at the lodge, Moon licked her wound. Someone had stitched her up. Promise sat down beside her and rubbed the dog's head and told her what a brave dog she was. "But I think you and I have a lot to learn about protecting ourselves. I'd ask Green Raven"—again, a warm tingle ran through her, to teach me to throw a knife. But for some reason, he doesn't like me." Though feeling sad, her voice sounded more confident when she added, "Why should I care if the brave liked me or not?"

Squirrel entered and said the hunters were riding in. The girls prepared themselves for the feast. The hair-yanking Stone Face had done to Promise left her with a sore head. She didn't fuss with her hair; she just let it flow down her back with only her feather-top disk clipped to her scalp lock. Silver dangled from her ears, and the cherished beaded emblem hung from her neck. She then remembered her gift to Squirrel.

Promise retrieved the hair bracelet from its hiding place. She turned to give it to her friend when her friend turned at the same time holding out a beaded belt. Giggling, they made a fuss over their gifts. Squirrel slipped the bracelet on her wrist and admired the beauty and craftsmanship of it. She ran her fingers over the blonde hair with strands of her own black hair threaded through it.

"It was to be a going-away present," said Promise, "but since I'm staying, I thought you could have it now." Promise slipped her knife sheaf onto her new, beautiful, beaded belt and tied it around her waist. She hugged her friend and said, "I needed a belt to carry my knife. I'll cherish this belt forever, Squirrel."

"And I shall think of you when I look at my bracelet. I see our hair is intertwined as our lives are," Squirrel said, with fondness.

The girls laughed when they told how each hid when they worked on their gifts.

When Father Fox entered the lodge, they were ready; but he brought a surprise with him. Behind him came Crying Woman, carrying a bundle, her head covered as always. "Crying Woman," said Father Fox, "will be sharing this lodge and will help with the work." He turned and left the girls looking at one another and then at Crying Woman.

"Come," said Squirrel, pointing at the robes that Brings Water had used. "You are welcome."

Crying Woman nodded her head, tears streaming from her eyes as she went to the robes and sat down.

"Please forgive my crying. I am filled with a running river of tears that I cannot stop. I cry over everything, good or bad. Mostly, it has been bad. But this is good."

Promise sat next to the other white woman and said, "Crying cleanses the soul, and your soul must be the cleanest."

That brought laughter to the lodge. Promise reached for the blanket covering Crying Woman's head. Crying Woman put her hand on Promise's hand to stop her and then gave in and let the blanket drop off.

The young girls were shocked at what they saw. Now they knew why Crying Woman always had her head covered. Her hair was snarled and knotted, and she had bald spots where it had been pulled out. Neither girl had to ask who pulled out the hair. Promise took a deep breath; looked Crying Woman in the eye; and said, "Squirrel and I will fix your hair so you don't have to keep it covered, and you will look nice at the feast tonight." Squirrel gave Promise a doubtful look.

The girls worked on Crying Woman's thick, tangled mess of hair. They brought water in the lodge and washed it after they cut off knots they couldn't loosen enough to be brushed out. They worked most of the snarls downward so they wouldn't have to cut too short. After the cutting and washing, they could see that her hair was a pretty, dark brown. They covered the bald spots with hair ornaments. Crying Woman looked pretty except for her tattered garments. Squirrel handed her a doeskin dress and insisted she take it.

Even though Father Fox didn't down a buffalo, he was given the meat and hide of one. Crying Woman had been with the Indians long enough to be helpful and she went right to work. Ribs and roasts were put over fires. Meat juices sizzled and popped, filling the night air with tasty aromas, causing mouths to water. The mood of the village was carefree, and storytelling was taking place in a big circle. With Moon stiffly limping along, Squirrel hurried Promise and Crying Woman to the circle. It took moments for many to recognize Crying Woman, and they nodded in approval.

Promise had seen theatre plays but nothing as dramatic and lively as what she witnessed now. She blushed when she realized a young brave, the guard from the pony herd, was acting out the day the Crows came. He pretended to be Promise running to him, and then he jumped back to represent himself. It was quite comical. The crowd cheered him on, the drumbeat in the background giving momentum to the young brave. He portrayed Promise pushing through the ponies and Moon running on the hillside. When he imitated the braves riding from the village to meet the Crows and save the ponies, the crowd went wild.

Braves from the hunt entered the circle, relived the hunt, and showed how they downed their buffalo and how quick their ponies were. Some showed how they reached into the buffalo; ate the liver; and lifted the heart from their brother, the buffalo, up to the Great Spirit before returning it back to the earth.

One of Crazy Horse's followers entered the circle, and his story had the crowd rolling on the ground. He re-enacted a coup they had done at Fort Laramie. They had kept out of sight while following Bluecoats back to the fort. He hung his head to show how tired the Bluecoats were and panted to show how hot the day was. The Bluecoats entered the fort and halted in front of a long lodge; leaving their horses, they went inside. The hot horses, still saddled, tried rolling in the dirt. Still no Bluecoats came out. Crazy Horse and his braves rode fast across the bridge; screamed their war cry; and waved their blankets, pushing the army horses ahead of them, right across the fort's grounds. Crossing the river on the opposite side, they headed to the hills. The Bluecoats tried following them. The brave hit his chest to show they outsmarted the Bluecoats again.

Eating and dancing went on all night. Tired and full, the encounter with Stone Face finally took its toll on Promise as she felt aches and pains overtaking her. She and Moon went back to the lodge for a much-needed rest. Promise knew Moon was hurting by the way she walked. Promise also knew she'd be sharing the bed robes with her friend again. But, as she told her mother, she was used to sleeping next to someone.

She shared the celebration with her mother. She giggled a time or two, telling the stories. In her mind, she could see Crazy Horse and his followers take the soldiers horses from right under their noses.

Promise's mind drifted, and she came face to face with another fact—one she had been keeping buried because she didn't want it to come forth, not after the care and love she had received from these people. She missed her own people. Not just her mother and her Aunt Hattie, but the white world. The library with all its books the church, the leisurely strolls to the ice cream parlor on a hot day for a dish of ice cream with berries on top.

The women here worked hard preparing hides for their needs. Their ways were crude compared to the white man's way. They did beautiful, hard backbreaking work. Promise had watched hides staked out and scraped with just the right pressure so as not to cut into the pelt. The hides were laced onto wooden frames and stretched. The white traders helped ease some of the work. Before the traders, the women decorated their garments with porcupine quills flattened by being pulled between the women's teeth. The traders' pony beads were easier to use and didn't ruin the women's teeth. Sinew, a strong cord used to sew with, came from the back of the larger animals. It had to be washed, pounded, separated, dried and all done very carefully.

Promise thought about everything but what was stuck in the back of her mind: Green Raven. When Promise finally fell asleep, it was just she and Moon in the lodge; and when she awoke, it was still just she and Moon. She heard activity outside, and she went out with Moon following behind. The village women were bustling about processing hides and meat. Kettles boiled on the campfires, and some smelly odors were arising from them. Bones were boiled for fat to make soap and then broken open for the marrow. Hooves, hide shavings, and hide scraps were boiled for glue.

Squirrel gave Promise a bladder to wash out in the river so they'd have a new water pouch. Promise didn't let herself think that the water pouch she'd been drinking out of was once a bladder.

It was at the river she heard that Crazy Horse and his followers had left camp. Promise's heart felt like it dropped to her belly. She knew Green Raven was gone, too. She ignored Moon, who was poking her with her nose. She didn't look up until she saw some of the other women stand and look over her head. Standing, Promise saw a big man leading a pack mule. His sheaved rifle was visible on the side of the pack. A long-haired, black dog walked into the encampment beside him.

Promise finished her task and went back to the village. Groups had gathered, whispering back forth. In front of Father Fox's lodge stood the mule and dog. Squirrel came from the lodge and grabbed Promise, turning her away. "Promise," she said, "go to Crying Woman's lodge and wait there."

Giving her friend the cleaned bladder, Promise wanted to ask, "Why?" The concerned look on Squirrel's face told her not to argue.

Ben Reed

Promise glanced around Crying Woman's lodge. It was dark and drab, a depressing sight. She thanked the Lord that Crying Woman was out of this dreary place and away from Stone Face.

Promise couldn't be idle. She pulled old robes and tattered blankets outside to air. She swept the lodge's dirt floor with a pine branch, doing anything she could think of while she waited. She didn't want to think about the man who was at Father Fox's lodge, but it was hard not to. Was he a trapper, a trader, or someone just passing through? Why didn't Father Fox want her to see him? A thought came to her, and she sighed with relief. Father Fox didn't want the white man to see her. He might want to take her away.

So she was baffled when Squirrel came and told her to come back to the lodge.

"Why?" Promise asked.

Squirrel, her dark eyes sad, said, "My father wants you to meet the white man."

Promise got very excited and asked, "Did the white man come for me?"

Her friend shrugged her shoulders. All she knew was he was searching for someone.

The first thought that came to Promise: Was he her father? No, he couldn't be her father. He would be wearing Union blue and riding a big military horse. Perhaps the man was a trusted friend of her father who was sent to find her. With the Indian trouble, soldiers were needed elsewhere. When Promise sorted out one question, another entered her mind. Why were there no horses with the man? Aunt Hattie, of course, would've told her father about his daughter and her problem with horses. Also, Aunt Hattie knew Promise liked walking. The big question Promise had to ask herself was, did she want to go? But that also was soon answered when she turned to her friend.

"Please, Squirrel, go back and get my bundle and bring it to me. I must ready myself to meet the stranger."

While she waited for her friend to return, Promise went to the river and washed her face and smoothed her hair back. She broke a twig, flayed the end, and brushed her teeth. She then returned to meet her friend.

Sadly, Squirrel handed the bundle to Promise. Promise could hardly contain the unexpected happiness that surged through her. She didn't even notice her friend leaving.

Promise opened her bundle and retrieved the clean and mended yellow and brown gingham dress. She slipped on her frayed pantalets and camisole and was surprised nothing fit right. The pantalets were loose at the waist but tight on her hips and buttocks, and the camisole was tight at her chest. Her petticoats had been too tattered to mend, so she just pulled on the dress, which was too short to be proper and the top too tight. She could hardly breathe. This wasn't going to work. Her thought was to return to her doeskin dress and the soft calf-hide underclothes. No. She wanted to make a good impression on the stranger. But she'd wear the calf-hide underclothes since hers didn't fit.

She ripped off the dress top and wore the bottom as a skirt. Also in the bundle was the red racing nightshirt. Slipping it on, she tucked it inside the skirt. The beaded belt, with the knife sheave attached, went around her waist to help hold the skirt on. She put on leggings and moccasins and the beaded emblem she always wore. Promise secured her hair back and clipped the feather-top disk to her scalp lock. She felt like a mismatched quilt belonging to two different cultures, but it would have to do.

Entering Father Fox's lodge, her head down, Promise stepped to the left, as was custom for women to do, praying that no one could see her shaking hands. She had waited and thought about this day for far too long. She had even given up, but her father had not. Promise was given permission to sit down. Her eyes downcast, all she saw was the white man's blue Union trousers tucked into high top moccasins that were folded and fringed at the top. She couldn't hold the smile from her face as she waited in anticipation.

Father Fox said in English, "Yellow Star, this is Ben Reed, to us he is called Standing Bear. He is searching for his son, and I want you in his care."

Shocked, Promise looked at Father Fox as if she had not heard him. Then she realized what he had said. This man had not come looking for her. Her father had not sent this man for her. Her father still didn't care if she was ever found.

Dismayed that her dream of her father coming for her was destroyed again, along with Father Fox betraying her and planning on sending her away, Promise jumped to her feet, not meaning to show disrespect, but she couldn't allow this to happen.

"You said I'd stay with you, and you promised not send me away without my consent!"

Squirrel was quickly at her friend's side, trying to calm her.

The man stood and said he agreed with the girl. He couldn't take her. For the first time, the two strangers faced each other. What Promise saw shocked her. Under the man's heavy brow, above his droopy mustache were green eyes, emerald green. He looked at her, and his face paled, and as though his legs gave away, he sat down hard.

"Chief Father Fox, may I speak with you alone?" he asked.

The girls were dismissed. Outside, Promise had all kinds of questions for Squirrel.

"I not know him. He was before my time," answered Squirrel to Promise's first question. "I didn't know till now he's Green

Raven's father, the one who had left when the boy was born and my sister died."

"I don't blame Green Raven for disliking the white people," said Promise. "To be abandoned is a disgrace. Now I understand why he doesn't like me. Why is his father looking for him now? And why does your father want me to go with him?" Promise remembered that Father Fox spoke in English so at one time he trusted this man.

"I not know," Squirrel said, sadly shaking her head.

They could hear the talking in the lodge, but the words were not clear. Promise absently scratched Moon's ear, as she was again deep in thought. When they were summoned back to the lodge, Promise saw Father Fox's face. It was full of sadness. "This isn't easy for me, Yellow Star. It's not like I want you to leave.

"Then why, Father Fox, do you want me to go with this stranger?"

"While at the hunt, warriors rode up to us and shared news about what was happening. Whites killing reds, reds killing whites, the People have no use for any whites now. Keeping you, Yellow Star, with us could be dangerous to you and to the band. This white man is a good man." He pointed at Ben. "Hurt clouded his mind and his judgment many winter ago. He has aged and with that he has received wisdom. Finding his son might release the hate his son has for all white people and for himself. It's hard to be part of two bloods and only knowing one blood. I don't know where his son went. I told him when he sees his son, he will know him. It be up to you, Yellow Star, to tell where your white family is."

Promise studied the man. His sandy hair reached his shoulders, and his droopy mustache was thick. He wore a fringed buckskin shirt with the band's sun and star emblem on the left shoulder. His wide-brimmed hat was pushed back on his head.

What she made out just by looking at him was his blue trousers with the yellow stripe down the sides showed he had been in the Union army, and he acted as though he had a bad leg. He had been accepted into this band at one time, for he wore the band's emblem; and Promise was sure he spoke Lakota. He had married Father Fox's oldest daughter and had a son by her; and when she died, he was weak and fled.

Father Fox then told Ben Reed the qualities of Yellow Star. "She learned lot living here. She good worker. Her smile brings light in this trying time. She swift like antelope. Before horses, she be a runner carrying messages to other tribes. She no complains about work. Be no trouble to you, Standing Bear."

"You're askin' a lot from me," said the big man. "I have a lot of territory to walk. I don't have a horse for her to ride, and I don't want one."

"That all right," Father Fox said. "She go blind around horses. She walks, too. You do what you need to do before you take her to her own people."

"What if I don't want to go to my people? Couldn't I just stay here?" pleaded Promise.

To no avail the chief was adamant that she go with this man.

Father Fox turned to the white man and said, "Now, we agree you take Yellow Star. What you give me for her, Standing Bear?"

Promise was stunned to think Father Fox would even ask for something after she and the man were forced to accept his bidding. Squirrel whispered to her it was a show for the villagers. It wouldn't look good if the chief didn't receive gifts.

Ben Reed was quiet. Then he gave a slight laugh and said, "You sly old fox, still as crafty as your name. I have pelts. Before we leave in the morning, so all can see, you can take your pick."

Arrangements were made for the girls to stay in Crying Woman's lodge, and the man stayed with Father Fox. Promise left Squirrel and Crying Woman to tend and feed the men. She needed to be alone. She needed to think again about her father. She felt so low and was mad at herself for letting her feelings about her father run away with her to be blown down again.

Promise and Moon went back to Crying Woman's lodge. She slumped to the ground, Moon beside her, and cried. Crying

Woman entered and put her arms around Promise, and tears flowed from her eyes, too. "Promise, if you return to your people, don't tell them you lived with Indians," Crying Woman said, holding Promise's hand. What she told Promise, Promise had heard from Penelope.

Crying Woman went on to tell Promise about her abduction years ago when she was a young girl. "I was scared, but killing myself scared me more and being rescued was always a hope. So I endured, and a trader came into the Pawnee village and traded a horse for me. He was kind and helped me find my family." Crying Woman wiped her eyes. Promise put her arm around her friend's shoulders. "I was elated to see my family once again. My family was shocked to see me in my leathers and with my wild, unkempt hair. 'Any decent white girl would've killed themselves,' they said.

"I had endured the Indians but couldn't abide living with my family. Then I did start thinking about killing myself, but for what? I had a right to live as anyone else." Crying Woman's voice became stronger. "I didn't choose the path I was put on. . I made the decision to walk away one day and kept on walking. When Stone Face found me, I accepted the Indian life again and didn't realize the nightmare I entered into from that man. But I held up the best I could, and now I'm with a kind and caring family, and I can be great help to Squirrel.

"Promise, whatever happens to you, be strong. By going with this man, no one will ever have to know you've been with the Indians."

"But it's only a half truth—still a sin," said Promise, shaking her head in disagreement. "And how can I travel with a man who is a stranger to me?"

Crying Woman held the girl's hand and sincerely said, "Sometimes an untruth, or half truth, fares better than the truth for all involved. Father Fox wouldn't send you with anyone he didn't trust, and he trusts this man." Before she left, Crying Woman added, "And you trust Father Fox."

Promise thought about what Crying Woman had said: "Trust Father Fox." She couldn't go against the chief, but she didn't have to like that man who abandoned his own son like her father had abandoned her.

Squirrel brought food to Promise, and Promise fed it to Moon. There wasn't much sleeping that night. There were too many tears and too much sadness. Like Brings Water told them one day, "Save the tears until you both are separated. Laugh till then." The girls began talking of their times together, and soon they were smiling and laughing. Squirrel shared survival suggestions for Promise: look for food, pick it, and store it in the bag she'd give her; look for healing herbs; and be on the lookout for tracks not their own. Soon, both girls fell asleep. Promise's sleep was restless with strange dreams. Early the next morning, after Promise had bathed, she sat on the bank where the river ran smooth and stared down at her reflection. Her face and arms were darker than any white woman should ever be. Her eyebrows and hair, sun-bleached, appeared such a pale yellow that it looked almost white in the calm water. *Do I really look like that?*

Dressed in her Indian clothes, she walked slowly back to Father Fox's lodge.

A crowd had gathered at the lodge and parted when Promise and Moon walked through.

Friends that Promise had made handed gifts to her. Even the first brave she had met with the scalps hanging from his spear stopped her. He handed her a spear. It was smaller than his but carefully crafted to fit her hand. She accepted the spear gracefully and said, "Thank you." She was handed summer and winter high-top moccasins, plus a winter dress, leggings, and a deer cape. From Crying Woman, she received a fleshing tool, a scraper, an awl, and a bone needle plus flint and steel in a pouch to wear on her belt. Squirrel held out a beautiful beaded bag. It contained sinew, trader's thread, steel needles, dried meat, and pemmican cakes wrapped in leather. She didn't check all the small-wrapped parcels in it.

Promise hung the bag over her head and one shoulder, and it lay against her hip. She was overwhelmed by all their kindness.

She wished she had her pantalets on so she could reveal them and lift the sober faces into smiles as Squirrel had done when she revealed Promise's underclothes to the Indians when they had come out to meet the girls that first time.

Father Fox sat on the ground going through fur pelts, feeling them and nodding to the white man sitting across from him. When he came to two white weasels' tails with black tips, his eyes lit up. "Ah," he said in approval. He set them aside with other pelts he had chosen.

When he saw Promise, he stood. In Lakota, he said, "Yellow Star, you ready?" She nodded her head without looking him in the eye. "Come, Yellow Star, and stand beside me. My people, this white girl has brought much joy to us. We'll miss Yellow Star but not forget her. We want best for Yellow Star, but it not here. She must go with Standing Bear. He old, trusted friend. Great Spirit, we pray for protection on their travel. We pray someday to be together again." He turned to Promise and hugged her.

Squirrel, trying hard not to cry, hugged her, too.

Then she handed Promise a red and black Hudson Bay wool blanket. On top of it were her wooden dish, her horn spoon, and her tin cup. Squirrel also handed her a parfleche to carry her possessions in.

The travois with Promise's belongings on it was put on Moon. Promise felt that the man didn't want to take Moon. Father Fox explained that Moon was a spirit dog and goes with Yellow Star. Moon had not made a good showing when the man told his dog, Queen, to fetch Milkweed, the mule, tethered to a tree. Fascinated, Promise watched the black dog pull the rope, untying it from the tree and leading the mule back to Ben. It would've gone smoothly if Moon had not tried making friends with the mule and the other dog. Queen wanted nothing to do with the spotted dog, and Milkweed tried taking a hunk of flesh from Moon. Moon, in her playful way, thought they were playing. But after Queen turned on her snapping and snarling and Milkweed tried to stomp her, Moon slipped away with her tail between her legs. Now harnessed up, Moon ignored them.

Ben spoke to Father Fox and pointed at the travois behind the spotted dog. The chief nodded his head in agreement.

Father Fox explained to Promise that if they ran into trouble, the travois could be a hindrance slowing their getaway. As bad as she hated to admit it, Ben was probably right. She agreed to take the travois off of Moon. Ben and Squirrel, as if Promise wasn't there, sorted through the parfleche. Promise watched how he rolled an extra pair of moccasins and her eating vessels and her cloak in the Hudson Bay blanket. He wrapped the cape—as with many Indian clothing it was smoked to repel water—around the blanket. Using a rope, he tied off both ends, leaving two loops for Promise to slip over her shoulders to carry the bedroll on her back. While he added the parfleche to the mule's pack, Squirrel whispered to Promise that it was much better this way. In case she got separated, she'd have her bedroll and some of her own things and still be able to survive.

Ben had Promise put all her survival tools in the pouch and leave the eatables in the beaded bag. Squirrel helped Promise with the changes.

"My heart breaking. Miss you already." Tears swelled in her big, brown eyes, and she rubbed the hair bracelet she wore.

Promise also put her hand over the hair bracelet. "I know, my good friend, my sister. My heart is breaking also. The day will come when I will be free from the grownups and can do what I want, and I will find you. Until then, remember we'll be under the same sun and stars." Then Promise threw her arms around Squirrel. She hated leaving her friend. She hated leaving with a stranger. Then she remembered Crying Woman's words: "Trust Father Fox."

Father Fox spoke kindly to Promise. "If you leave footprints behind, be sure they go where you want them to." With a hard hug and a push, he sent her on her way, saying, "Not look back."

Ash Hollow

Promise's feelings toward the strange man were still hostile. She had never carried unkind feelings toward another and didn't like doing it now. She felt as if she was carrying a burden inside her and wished she could let it go. Father Fox might trust the big man, but she understood how Green Raven felt. Being abandoned by his father caused his distrust and hate for all white people.

Though wary of the big man, Promise had no reason to distrust him. He had shown nothing but respect for her and kept his distance. When they stopped the first night, she fetched firewood and water from the small creek they were camped by and started the campfire. Ben put a long-handled skillet over the fire and cooked bacon he retrieved from his pack. He fixed coffee, but she preferred tea and heated water in her tin cup. Squirrel had packed a bag of dried berries and herbs for her, and Promise chose to have blackberry tea. They ate the bacon and fresh berries and sipped their hot drinks in silence. He tossed both dogs thick slices of bacon, which pleased Promise. She had wondered how she'd feed Moon. Without asking, Ben took Promise's bedroll, putting the capeskin side down on the ground. When she finally put herself to rest, after cleaning the cooking and eating vessels, she lay upon the furry side and pulled the Hudson Bay blanket up to her chin. She thought the man would stand guard over them and was surprised when he lay across the fire from her. Their eyes met; and as if reading her mind, he said that between the two dogs and Milkweed, no intruders would get close.

That first day had been a long one physically and emotionally for Promise. Frogs croaking was the last thing she heard. She slept soundly with Moon at her side and her hand on the spear. The second day was a copy of the first, except Ben asked questions. Haltingly, Promise answered in shrugs or with a yes or no. Soon, Ben stopped asking. That night, he opened tinned beans to serve with the bacon. He also mixed up dough by adding salt and baking powder to the flour in the flour sack. Then he stirred in just enough water to form the amount of dough he wanted. Dividing the dough in four portions, he flattened and fried them in the bacon grease. By the time he retied the flour sack, the fry bread was ready, crispy and golden. They ate in silence again. Promise enjoyed the fry bread, scooping the beans up with it. Each dog again had a thick slice of cooked bacon and was treated with bread also.

Ben packed his pipe with tobacco out of a drawstring pouch and lit it with a flaming stick from the camp fire. He settled back against a rock and sipped his coffee. He coughed a few times then asked Promise, "What's your name?"

"Yellow Star," she answered without looking at him.

"No. I mean what's your English name?"

Promise paused then answered, "Promise Amrose." She glanced at the man under her lashes; and in the firelight, he seemed pale.

"Promise is an unusual name, isn't it?"

He was awarded with a shrug.

"Where are your people?"

Again a shrug, then Promise said, "I don't have any people."

"Come, girl. You must have family someplace. A mother? A father?"

Promise sat back on her heels, looked straight at him, and said, "My mother is dead, and I don't know where my father is." She didn't feel like she was telling an untruth about her father. But in a way, she was telling an untruth by not mentioning Aunt Hattie.

Ben seemed stunned. His mustache and lips were moving, but no words came forth. He cleared his throat a few times. Finally he asked, "Where are you from?"

Promise, shrugged her shoulders, and said, "Back East."

Ben took a deep pull off his pipe and asked, "How did your mother die?"

"I don't want to talk about it," Promise said.

Ben leaned forward and tapped the burned tobacco out of his pipe. "How did you get to be with Father Fox?"

"You ask a lot of questions. Good night!"

She would've liked to ask where they were going. Instead of answering his questions or asking her question, she turned her back to Ben and pulled the blanket over her head.

In the late afternoon, sand hills and tuff grass surrounded them. Time and again, the wind swooped up the gritty soil, stinging her eyes and face as she walked. Spotting a prickly pear cactus, Promise stopped and carefully sliced off the thorny pads to add to their evening meal.

Although sagebrush burned hot and fast, it had to be used to fuel the campfire. Promise slipped the cactus pads over sticks to singe the thorns and then peeled back the tough skin to the soft meat inside. It was a welcome, sweet dessert after their meal.

The sameness of each day was tiring to Promise's mind. The hot-to-cold-to-hot-again weather didn't help her temperament any. She shared her dried meat and pemmican cakes with Ben. Still, with all the sharing that was being done, Promise was mute towards him. When he supplied fresh meat, it was a relief from the bacon, and the break in their diet raised Promise's mood. He gave the furs from rabbits to Promise to do with what she wanted. She knew how to process them and kept them for later use. While rabbits or sage hens roasted over the fire, the dogs lay with their heads on their paws, their eyes never leaving the roasting meat. Every now and then, they lifted their noses to sniff the air and lick at the aroma floating past their noses.

The sand had become tiresome to see; so when Promise spotted a river, her spirits lifted only to drop again when she saw how wide it was. The brown water was even with the sand's edge, but small islands of grass and trees were scattered about in it. Ben told her it was the South Platte River, a mile wide and an inch deep. She didn't believe that.

She watched as he rechecked the pack on Milkweed, making sure it was secured. "The river isn't deep," he said, "but we need to be of careful of quicksand. Milkweed and I will start, and you follow. I will throw you a rope if you get in trouble. Queen, you stay with the girl."

It seemed Milkweed had a different idea. He didn't want to cross. Ben led him out a ways before the mule jerked the rope, throwing the man down into the water. Still holding the lead rope, water dripping off him, Ben shook his fist at the mule.

"You ornery, cuss! Why I didn't leave you back in the mining camp I'll never know!"

Milkweed's long ears came forward, looking innocent.

Promise wanted to laugh but thought better of it. Holding her moccasins and her doeskin up, she waded across. The cold, muddy river's soft sand sucked her feet down and gave haste to her movement. Quickly, she joined the dogs, Ben, and Milkweed on an island. While the mule nibbled grass, the others rested under a cottonwood before they started again. It might have been more than an inch deep, but it was a mile or more wide.

Later that day, heads bent to the wind, Moon began to act nervous and was underfoot, tripping Promise. Ben stopped and looked at the sky.

"We better find shelter. A storm's a-comin.'"

Promise looked upward. There wasn't a cloud in the dark blue sky.

Ben spoke again. "Animals can sense a storm long before man can."

He nudged Milkweed to move faster. He took them off the trail they had been following and went in a different direction. The blowing sand was soft underfoot, slowing them down. Over the now-howling wind, Promise got the man's attention. She had spotted a gully and thought shelter might be found there. He disagreed, shouting above the coming storm that a flash flood could drown them. They came upon an outcrop when the first raindrops began. Promise squeezed herself under a rock rim and into a wide crack, pulling Moon with her. Ben pushed Queen in and tried fitting himself in the narrow outcrop shelter. Still, he was getting the full force of wind and rain, and there was no shelter for the mule. Ben held the mule's rope, trying to keep him calm. Hail came. Large ice like rocks pounded the earth, Milkweed, and Ben. Lightning lit up the darkened sky, and thunder rumbled. Promise curled her arms around a shaking Moon, trying to soothe her. Lightning hit the rocks above them, and the noise was deafening. It took all of Promise's strength to keep Moon from bolting. Milkweed screamed and reared, tearing the rope from Ben's hands.

Ben yelled, "Milkweed! Whoa!"

Jumping up, he told Queen to stay and ran after the frightened mule.

Queen whined. Promise reached out her hand and called to her to come. Surprisingly, Queen crawled up by Moon, and Moon licked her nose. Promise sat as the terrible storm raged, holding two shaking dogs and wondering what had happened to the man. Rain dripped in on her and the dogs. She wished she could take her pack off her back and put the cape around them, but she couldn't move in the tight space. Soon, she was shivering along with the dogs.

The storm was over before Ben returned with Milkweed. He had lost his hat to the wind, and he was drenched again. He had never completely dried off from his fall in the Platte. Promise knew there wouldn't be a warm fire this night or a hot meal to warm their cold bones. They all nibbled on pemmican and dried meat. She even offered Ben her blanket or cape to add to his blanket as he tried to warm up. He declined her offer, saying he'd dry off when the sun returned. But the sun didn't return and a dreary haze covered the landscape.

The dogs closed their eyes; the mule dropped his head; and before Promise's eyes drooped, she saw the man leaning against the rocks, sleeping.

Coughing awakened Promise. Looking around, she spotted Ben by the mule, rearranging the packs. He'd lay his head against the mule and cough deeply. She could tell by the way he stood that his bad leg was hurting him. She hoped that he wasn't getting ill. Dampness lingered from the day before. She offered to build a fire to warm by, and he could rest his leg. But he insisted they go on to a place called Ash Hollow. He'd rest there.

As the day wore on, Ben's coughing seemed to worsen, and he was holding onto the mule as he walked. The sun broke through the haze as it was setting in the west, and everything was yellow. Promise saw the man stagger, and she caught him before he fell. He agreed to a short rest. Promise's thoughts went to herself as fear bubbled up inside her.

If he dies, where will I go? I don't even know where I am. Could I find my way back to Father Fox? No. The village will be moved by now to the winter camp.

Troubled by her fear, she gazed upon his feverish face. For the first time, Promise felt something besides hostility for this man. He had been kind to her. She gave him water and a piece of dried meat. He tried to eat and sip the water but couldn't swallow. For the first time, Promise noticed his hands and let out a gasp. His hands were raw and bloody from the rope burns he received when Milkweed pulled the rope from them during the storm. Using two of her rabbit furs, she wrapped them around his hands.

Helping him to his feet, Ben hooked his sore hand around the pack rope, telling Promise to lead the mule and keep going west. The mule didn't fight her, and she hoped her eyes wouldn't swell shut. She kept an eye on the man in case he fell.

Grass was beginning to take over the sand. When she came upon a steep incline, she stopped. Ben focused his red, glassy eyes to where they were.

He pointed at the wagon wheel ruts that were deeply cut into the precipitous grassy hillside and mumbled, "Windlass Hill." Then he pointed to a grove of treetops, a welcome sight farther away, and said, "Ash Hollow. Go."

Promise didn't want to travel the deep ruts down Windlass Hill. She moved her group to the side of it. As surefooted as Milkweed was, the tall, thick grass was relentless and wouldn't let him take hold. He slipped on his rump and began sliding, taking Promise with him on her backside; and Ben was being dragged as he held onto the pack rope. The dogs tumbled a few times as their pace picked up going to the bottom. It was a relief to be on somewhat level ground again. Promise checked on Ben. He was looking worse. She knew she must get him to the hollow, get a fire going, and set up camp.

She smelled smoke before she saw the tepee. It was small and had been patched many times. A spotted dog growled as an old woman stepped out. Her back was bent; her hair white; and her weathered face, as Squirrel would say, "had seen many winters." She hobbled forward to meet the strangers and was by Promise when Ben fell.

Quickly, the old woman took charge. Promise guessed her to be Cheyenne, but she did speak some Lakota; and with sign language, Promise was able to understand what she said. Between the two of them, they managed to get the big man into the tepee and on the old woman's bedroll. Promise hurried to find more firewood.

After she delivered wood into the tepee, she tended to Milkweed, who was still standing where he had been left. Promise lifted the packs off him and tethered him close to a spring where he could water and feed. She would've liked to pat him on his big nose but did not. So far, her eyes hadn't swelled. She hurried back to the old woman.

The old woman had undressed and covered Ben with a thin blanket and was rubbing him down with cool water. His hands had been treated and rewrapped. He was tossing his head back and forth and moaning, his breathing shallow. She tried to get him to drink a warm liquid but stopped when he choked. She told Promise to find a burr, a small burr, and hurry.

Promise, with Moon behind her, searched the area for cockleburs. Finding what she needed, she rushed back to the old woman, wondering what the burr was for. Smiling and showing a toothless mouth, the old woman took the burr, tied sinew around it, and heavily coated it with fat. She forced Ben to swallow the burr, holding his head as he gagged and tried to spit it out. She rubbed his throat to coach the burr to go down, watching the sinew disappearing into the man's mouth until it stopped moving.

The old woman jerked on the sinew a few times, testing it; and then she began pulling it back up. Ben, too weak to fight off the old woman, moaned and gagged and fought for breath. Promise felt sorry for him. She knew he hurt and was in misery before, and now a small pincushion was ripping up his throat. The old woman pulled till the burr came out of his mouth. The burr was a sickly sight and caused Promise to gag, but the old woman was pleased with what the burr brought up with it.

Ben's breathing was already better, and he was able to sip the warm liquid and soon fell into a restless sleep. Promise held a piece of leather over the fire to warm it as the old woman told her to. The old woman mixed up grease with herbs; and as she started to rub the mixture on Ben's hairy chest, she paused. She motioned Promise closer and pointed at a chain around his neck. The man's bare torso shocked Promise with all that hair while with the Indians she never witnessed hair anyplace but on their head. Giving herself a shake, she unclasped the chain and lifted it up; and with it came a locket, a familiar-looking locket.

It cannot be, she thought.

She opened it and let out a gasp. Looking back at her was the likeness of her and her mother.

Before the old woman could stop Promise, she was shaking Ben's shoulders and yelling at him, "How did you come by this cameo locket? Wake up! Wake up and tell me!"

The old woman grabbed Promise about the time Queen growled and bolted to her feet. Moon leaped in between Promise and Queen, but Queen quickly calmed down when the old woman dragged Promise out of the lodge, kicking at Moon, who was snapping at her heels.

"What go on here?" asked the old woman. "He sick man. You be good."

Returning to the lodge, she added, "When he heals, you can beat him up."

Stunned, Promise lay in a heap on the grass. She felt withered. The shock of seeing the locket turned her insides upside down. How had Ben Reed gotten it? It was impossible for him to have the locket, but he did. Rubbing the cherished piece of jewelry over her hot cheek, she said, "Mama, how could you have known this man? When and where? Perhaps he robbed your body after you were run over? No, I don't believe he is that kind of person. I will have to have patience until he can speak."

She pulled Moon into her arms. "You tried to protect me again. I am glad now the old woman pulled me off the man or there would've been a terrible dogfight. You can learn a lot from Queen, so you need to keep friendly with her." Standing, she brushed loose grass and twigs off her clothing and said, "I owe an apology to the old woman."

Walking back to the lodge, Promise stopped. *Now,* she thought, *I know why he looked pale when he first saw me. I resembled the likeness in the locket. And when I told him my name, I thought he looked pale again. He had heard my name somewhere sometime before. It must have been a shock to him to run into me in Indian Territory.*

But where had he gotten the locket?

Ben was sleeping quietly on the old woman's robes. His face was still flush from fever. The old woman fanned smoke over him and chanted. Promise stepped lightly and touched the woman on her shoulder. After a moment, the woman stood, turned, and steered Promise to the opened flap. Outside, Promise told the woman how sorry she was for causing an unruly scene in her home.

Relaxing under a tree, the woman said, "Call me Grandmother. I always loved this place, Ash Hollow. That why my band left me here, to wait till Great Grandfather Spirit calls me home to Him. Now I think I supposed to be here to care for the white man. The Great Spirit had more for me do to while I wait to go to Him. Tired now. You look on the white man while I rest here under the tree?"

"Yes," answered Promise, "and I am called Yellow Star."

Before she could finish talking, Grandmother touched the beaded emblem hanging from Promise's neck and spoke.

"Ah-h-h, you from Father Fox band. I know Father Fox, a great chief to his people. Heard of you, Yellow Star," she said, and she embraced the surprised girl. She touched the feather-top disk hanging from Promise's hair and asked, "These your winning trophies, yes?"

Promise could only nod yes. She was speechless that the old woman knew so much about her.

"Go," said the old woman and waved Promise away so she could rest.

Ben was moaning when Promise entered the tattered lodge. She went quickly to his side, whispering to an alert Queen that she wasn't going to harm her master. Still, Queen kept close as Promise dipped a cloth into a bowl of cool spring water and dabbed it on Ben's hot forehead.

"Mr. Reed, we are fortunate to have a Cheyenne woman to doctor you. I really hope you get well soon. I have a lot of questions to ask you."

Promise's wrist was grabbed by a hot hand. Eyes glazed over by fever stared at her.

"Carolyn!" his mumble was close to a cry. "You came! You don't know how much I've missed you. I'm lookin' for my son, like I told you I would. But...but," confusion came over his face, "somethin' is holdin' me up."

He tried sitting up. In his weak state, Promise had no problem pushing him back down. His grip was strong though. It tightened on her wrist.

"Don't go away, Carolyn." His feverish eyes began to roll back. "Don't go. I—I will find my son. We—we'll be a family."

Then he slipped into a restless sleep.

Trying to keep the man cool, Promise wouldn't let herself think of what he had said. She knew he mistook her for her mother.

A Time to Die

The old woman dipped broth from the cooking pot, and the tasty aroma floating in the air kindled hunger pains in Promise. She had picked wild onions and herbs to add to the stewed grouse Grandmother had snared.

"Broth be good for man," the old woman said.

Promise held Ben's head up while the old woman gave him sips of broth. The blanket slipped down revealing part of his chest. Before Promise averted her eyes, she saw an ugly, wide, ragged scar embedded in his side that disappeared under his pants' band. The angry, red, puckery holes along his side reminded her of someone. But who? Who did she know with scars who had a beat-up appearance? Promise sighted the light, curly hair on the man's chest. Mr. Cat! This poor man was beat up and scarred like the old, yellow cat that hung around Elfreth's Alley. Something let loose inside her, like her heart being thawed.

It was a relief to rid herself of the heavy burdens of being judgmental, hateful, and rude. After releasing all that was alien to her nature, everything seemed brighter and prettier to Promise. She enjoyed the beauty of Ash Hollow. She understood why Grandmother wanted to pass her last days here. It was like being in the Garden of Eden with its many cold, sweet-tasting springs, abundant berry bushes, and grapevines. Wildflowers brought color and fragrance to the eye and nose, and there was a slow-moving river close by. It was wonderful to bathe daily and to rub her hair and body with perfume smelling of rose and jasmine petals. She ran through the tall grass with Moon. Sometimes Queen joined in the run; and sometimes Grandmother's dog, Dog, entered into the fun.

Queen seldom showed a fun side to her demure nature. Usually, she was in charge and alert. She held her head like she was royalty and moved with confidence and elegance. Promise hoped that some of Queen's manners might rub off on Moon. Moon was full of mischief and play and liked to run with or without Promise. But she also had a serious and protective side to her like Queen and Dog.

Dog was an odd-looking animal. He was old with short legs; his mangy hair was many colors, and he had small eyes. But he was a happy dog. Promise wondered if he would've been so happy if he had known he was left behind to be a meal for Grandmother, nevertheless, he was happy. Grandmother showed him much love and attention, and he returned the affection. Promise realized that not only Moon could learn from the other dogs but that she also could learn from Grandmother and Ben.

Promise was also playful, and one day, she hid behind some bushes and whispered for Moon to come. Moon's ears perked up, and she glanced around, trying to place where the voice was coming from. Promise covered her mouth to suppress her laughter. Moon nosed around the bush and, to Promise's delight, found her. After so many times searching for Promise, Moon picked up on the game and began hiding herself. She'd give low woofs to get Promise's attention. Her tail wagged hard, and her smile was large when she was found. And Moon wasn't easy to find. She blended into wherever she was. Promise soon learned to look for the whites of her eyes. Promise had played hide and seek with her aunt, but Ash Hollow had more hiding places than their home in Elfreth's Alley. Then the young girl and her dog began sneaking up on each other, causing laughter from Grandmother and Ben. It was the game she had played by herself when she was small.

It wasn't all fun and games at the hollow. Promise added their provisions to Grandmother's meager supply, as she had shared everything she had with her visitors. Grandmother doctored Ben; kept him shaved; and, with much patience, trimmed his mustache. She entertained Promise with many stories.

One evening, Grandmother and Promise sat out under the sparkling stars. Grandmother pointed at a wide, long, milky-blue strip curving upward lighter than the darkened sky. Promise recognized it as the Milky Way. "That the Hanging Road, the trail we travel when we leave Mother Earth to meet our Great Grandfather Spirit. Be happy times again for this old Cheyenne woman. I will see my children again, my husband, my parents, great parents, and meet family I have never known except through stories. Yes. Be happy times."

Promise realized Grandmother had no family left.

The old tepee wasn't large enough to sleep all the people who were now in Ash Hollow.

Promise had put her bedroll under an ash tree alongside the tepee. With Milkweed close by, Moon at her side, and her spear in her hand, she wasn't fearful. She felt rested after her long trek through the sand dunes and was again able to visit with her mother.

Staring up at the big, bright moon under the largest night sky she'd ever seen, Promise felt peace within herself. The hollow was good for one's soul. She had many questions for Ben Reed. As anxious as she was for answers, she'd wait patiently for him to recover. Promise gathered willow bark to ease Ben's aches and pains. While Promise and Moon rested the old woman slept by Ben's side, along with Queen and Dog. One warm night, Promise saw a falling star, and Grandmother told her about the night the stars fell out of the sky. Grandmother stretched her skinny arms upward. And as she flicked her long, bony fingers, bringing her arms down, she spoke. Arms and fingers rising up and down portrayed her story. "It was many, many winters ago," she said, "in the moon of when the wolves run together, when stars fell from the sky all night." Her people thought the end of life was coming. She said she gathered her children and, with her family and others, hurried to caves for protection from the dropping fire. But no fire came upon them. A new sun rose, and all was fine. It gave the People something to talk about for many winters to come.

One day, after Grandmother had seen Moon chasing butterflies, she told a delightful story. "The Great Spirit created colorful rocks—red, blue, and yellow—and put them on hillsides. The north wind blew through and told the Great Spirit the pretty rocks should do more than just lay on hillsides. The Great Spirit turned the painted rocks into butterflies. Now all the People can enjoy the beautiful-colored butterflies when they flutter past our eyes or sit upon a flower."

Promise didn't think she'd ever look at the Milky Way or a butterfly the same way again.

Moon rose and interrupted Promise's sleep. The dog turned in a circle, around and around, until she finally flopped back down on the flat grass.

"You are a silly dog, Moon. Are you comfortable now? I must be silly too, talking to you like you are able to answer." Patting Moon's head, Promise continued talking to her dog. "Have you observed Grandmother? She seems to be slower. Even Dog has slowed down compared to what he was, and he was no rabbit chaser to begin with. You could learn a few things from that old dog. When Grandmother snared her game or downed a bird, Dog fetched it back for her. I think I best take on more tasks for her and let her rest more. I can sit with Ben and do more for him.

"Although my feeling for him has softened, I still feel myself tensing when I am near him. Perhaps the reason is there are so many unanswered questions between us. I better pick berries and dry them for Grandmother and for our use before we leave. Even you dogs seem to like berries. I think Milkweed is used to me now. Anyway, he doesn't try to bite me anymore. I think I can be around him as long as I don't touch him. So far, my eyes haven't swelled. Nor have I sneezed. But it seems like he still doesn't like you. So, Moon, you have to stay away. That means you don't try to play with him."

Soon, all that could be heard in the night were frogs, crickets, and snoring from the old tepee.

In the following days, Promise, with dogs beside her, picked berries. She laid them out on blankets to dry in the sun, turning them often. She took some of Grandmother's dried meat; and with what she still had in her bag, she ground it all using Grandmother's tools. Then Promise ground the berries and added it to the pulverized meat with fat and formed small cakes. She shared the pemmican with Grandmother to keep in a parfleche, and Promise wrapped hers and put into her beaded bag. Promise also gathered rose hips for her and Grandmother. They were used for many things and made delicious tea. She picked wild onions, wild peas, and milkweed buds to dry to be used later. She scoured the countryside for anything edible or useful.

Pleased to have her supplies built up, Grandmother insisted Promise take more, for there were two of them and only one of her. Promise pointed at Dog and said he needed to eat also and Grandmother relented.

She looked with kindness at the old dog and said, "When my people left me here at my request, they also left Dog behind. Yellow Star, do you believe Grandfather Spirit gave all creatures to the people for their use?"

Aunt Hattie had read scriptures out loud, and Promise remembered the belief the old woman spoke of. "Yes, I do."

"Dog became good company for me. Couldn't eat him." Then Grandmother laughed and said, "He be tougher than my old hide to eat. When my time comes, it be his time too."

Promise wondered how Grandmother could know Dog would die when she died. She didn't ask, for she had learned the Indians have ways of knowing things that are beyond the white man's knowledge. She did ask how long she and Dog had been in the hollow.

"My people and I wait until last white man in his tepee on wheels stopped coming through Ash Hollow. Been here only one moon. Before the white man came, we came anytime. We don't want to see the whites. We come when they go. As you see, whites cut many trees. Trees don't grow back like berries do." She halted her words and looked long at Promise. "I forget you are one of the whites. But you don't act like one. I am glad I have met you, Yellow Star, Giver of Light."

Ben was beginning to feel better, and he was getting restless. Grandmother agreed to let him sit in the sun a few hours a day, but he had to promise to rest only. When his fever was out of him for two sleeps, he then could build up his strength. Promise watched him sit quietly in the sun, slowly petting Queen, who lay at his side. Grandmother brought him rose-hip tea and whatever the cooking pot had to offer. Promise had to fight the urge to run to him and badger him with questions. She caught him watching her a few times, and she wondered if he remembered calling her Carolyn. She fingered the cameo locket that she now wore around her neck alongside her emblem.

The day came when Promise built up her courage to face Ben. His green eyes were on her when she approached him. He patted the space beside him, and she sat down. Neither spoke. They seemed to be absorbed in their surroundings. Nervously, Promise pulled up grass. When he spoke, it was about the songbirds in the trees.

"Someone once told me that to hear a bird sing means we are being looked after. Do you believe that, Promise?"

Taken by surprise by what he asked, she coughed a few times, trying to clear a sob rising in her throat. "Yes. That was a favorite saying of my mother."

Promise turned to face the man. Dirty, dull, sandy hair laid flat on his head; and his pale face was gaunt with dark circles around his sunken eyes. Chest hairs curled above his knitted undershirt, and suspenders off his shoulders lay at his side by the Union trousers he wore.

She lifted the locket to show him she was wearing it and blurted out, "How did you come by this? It belonged to my mother! Tell me true." Tears welled up in her eyes.

"When I saw you at Father Fox's village, I thought you must be a twin to my beloved's daughter. When you told me your name, my breath left me. When you told me your mother was dead, my heart died."

"But where did you—?"

"I took cannon shrapnel in my leg and side from the battle at Graveyard Ridge at Gettysburg. In a convalescent home in Philadelphia, a beautiful woman stopped by my cot. She laid her hand tenderly on my head and asked me what she could do for me. I never thought I could love again, but my heart melted. I never dreamt this beautiful creature could love me back. I had a lot of wear and tear on me, along with a bum leg and shrapnel still in me. For some reason, she took to me. She told me all about you, Promise, and your aunt Hattie. You were the apple of her eye. She told me about your father, and I told her about Fawn, my wife, daughter of Father Fox, how she died giving birth to my son. I felt I was the one who killed her. Because I loved her, she died. I couldn't face my son knowing it was my fault he'd grow up without a mother. So I ran, leaving him without a father, also. She told me how silly I was. Love doesn't bring death to another. But not acknowledging a child can bring pain to the child. She didn't mince words with me.

"When I healed and was discharged from the army, your mother and I decided I needed to get my affairs in order before I started a new life with her and her family. We talked about moving out West for a new start for everyone. I had left Queen and Milkweed with an old man in Virginia City when I joined the Union Army. I wanted to retrieve them and then search for my son and try to make amends with him.

"Before I left Philadelphia,"—Ben was able to touch the locket before Promise pulled back—"she gave me that to remember her by, as if I'd forget her." Moisture was in his eyes when he asked how she died.

Her head bent, pulling at the grass, Promise tried to control her emotions. Her mother had been in love, and she didn't know it. It didn't make her feel any better that Aunt Hattie didn't know it either. This man, Ben Reed to the whites, Standing Bear to the Indians, was to be her stepfather and Green Raven, a stepbrother. But if her mother loved him and was willing to make a new life for them all with him, then he must be a good and decent man. Now she needed to answer his question, a question she didn't like to think about, much less talk about: how her mother died.

Promise rose, brushing tears off her face. "I cannot…at this time tell you what you want to know. I need to get my wits about me."

With Moon at her side, she went down to the river. Dropping her garments, she stepped into the cold water, the coldness numbing her mind. Moon swam around her, wanting to play, but was pushed away.

The note that had come with the beautiful fan from her mother had read, "Fan your dreams toward the morrows, to a brighter future." Ben must have been the future she was speaking about. She must have had her reasons for not telling her or her aunt earlier and the note hinted she had something to share with them. Promise remembered what her aunt had said, that she didn't know why Carolyn's step was lively but was thankful that she was happy before she died.

Promise ducked her head, mixing her tears with the river water. *Mama, I miss you so!* she screamed in her head.

When Promise returned to camp, Grandmother and Ben were quietly talking. She motioned Promise to join them.

"You need to know what I say to big man."

Ben rolled his head on his shoulders and said, "I believe she's too young for this conversation."

"No!" replied Grandmother. "No one too young to know the way of the People. I say to Yellow Star what I say to you. I came to Ash Hollow to die. I here when you came to me sick. I bring you back to wellness. Now I ask a request to be done for me. I ask you to stay till my time comes and tend to my body, as my people would have if they be here. It won't be a long stay. You, big man, need to gather your strength back to your body."

She looked at the two white people sitting by her. "Don't look sad, Yellow Star. From the time we are born, we begin to die. I had good husband, good children, and long life. I am ready to walk the Hanging Road."

Promise reached for Grandmother's thin hand. "I know you came here to die, Grandmother. It's hard to lose one who you have grown close to, as I have grown close to you. You are the grandmother I never had. We'll stay with you, won't we, Ben?"

She asked before she realized she made a decision without asking permission. She glanced over at the man, and his slow nod acknowledged her decision to stay with the old woman.

One evening after the meal, Ben and the old woman sat around the campfire enjoying a smoke while Promise cleaned the cooking and eating vessels. She had supplied the evening meal and was pleased with herself. Earlier in the day, she had speared a rabbit, her first. Her face grim, she had dressed and cleaned it. She had known someday she'd have to down an animal for food. Now that she had, she hoped the next time it would be easier. It wasn't something she enjoyed doing. She stewed the rabbit with onions, rose hips, wild celery, and dried turnips from Grandmother's supplies.

She had mixed up dough, enough for the three dogs too for fry bread the way Ben did. Grandmother ate, smacking her thin lips between bites; and Ben nodded in agreement as he ate, dipping his bread into the broth.

The fading sun left a bright sunset, filling the sky with brilliant colors that man would never be able to produce. As the stars emerged in the darkening sky, Grandmother pointed at the Little Dipper.

Promise and Ben looked up when she said, "Those stars were once seven Indian brothers who climbed up a tree to escape a mad buffalo. The tree stretched and grew into the sky where the brothers couldn't be harmed, and they turned into stars."

She then turned her head, and Promise knew she was looking at the Hanging Road.

Grandmother spoke to Ben. "You are the one called Standing Bear, son-in-law of Father Fox." She didn't wait for Ben's acknowledgment. "You are searching for your son."

Ben lowered his smoke and sat up straighter. "You know my son? You know where he is?"

"I think so," Grandmother said. "He be where Crazy Horse be, on Rapid Creek where Crazy Horse family be. Lot of anger in your son, Standing Bear."

"How do you know this? Did you see him? Did you talk with him?" Ben asked a touch of excitement in his voice.

"Our paths crossed while I traveled with my people. Also, paths crossed with one named Stone Face. No good man. He wants to travel with Crazy Horse, but Crazy Horse had no time for Stone Face."

"What's my son called?" asked Ben.

"You not been told by Father Fox or by Yellow Star, I not tell you. But I tell you this. He hates all whites."

Every day Promise observed Grandmother, and she'd ask herself, "Does she look frailer today?" One day she said, "Yes, Grandmother is failing." Promise tended to her like she was a baby. She tried coaching her to sip broth or water or eat a morsel of soft food. Grandmother refused. Her feeble hands slightly brushed over Promise's hand. Promise told Ben it was like a butterfly wing touching her. Promise now slept in the tepee and Ben under the stars.

If Grandmother's head wasn't visible, one wouldn't know there was anyone under the robes. Dog lay beside her, her hand on his head. His tail wagged every now and then. One day she whispered for Ben to carry her out under the sky so she could see it once more. Ben lifted her gently, and Promise carried Dog. It was a solemn group sitting by Grandmother. Even Moon was quiet, and Queen lay at Ben's feet.

Promise wanted to thank Grandmother for taking them in and sharing her stories and all she had with strangers. She held an old, weathered, frail hand in her own and soothingly said, "Grandmother, you did our hearts good when you shared your camp with us, strangers who tumbled in on you. You didn't even blink an eye when you took us in. And you used your healing skills and charm, making us feels welcomed. I cannot thank you enough for your friendship."

Weakly, Grandmother pulled on her hand and breathlessly said, "A wise man once said, 'When you were born, you cried and the world rejoiced. Live your life in such a manner that when you die, the world cries and you rejoice.'" Her voice faded away, her eyes closed, and Dog's breathing stopped.

"Grandmother! Grandmother!" cried Promise. Moon rose and licked Promise's wet cheek and then put her nose under Promise's chin as she leaned over Grandmother.

Promise felt hands on her shoulders, and Ben spoke.

"It's over now, Promise. We have work to do to lay her out as her people would. You gather her belongings and ready her body, and I will build the scaffold."

Moving On

Promise's sun-touched hair flowed down her back, paler than the light brown doeskin dress she wore. Against her chest, she held bright, yellow sunflowers. Ben, thinner now, dressed in his Union trousers and buckskin shirt, stood next to her under the shade of an old ash tree; and they gazed upward. At their feet sat the dogs. They were a sober group. Even the mule was quiet.

Thick, green leaves cloaked the pole scaffold tied between two strong branches—at least until the snow came. Indians would respect the burial of the Cheyenne woman. But Ben's concern was with any whites who might yet pass through the hollow. That was why he didn't erect the scaffold on a hillside but in the confinement of the tree. Whites wouldn't respect a dead Indian and invade the last resting place of the old woman to steal or scatter the items that lie upon the scaffold and then destroy it.

Promise felt confident that she did right by Grandmother. She even surprised herself that she didn't bring shame to her, even though she was dead, or shame to herself by being squeamish about tending to a lifeless body. She bathed Grandmother with tenderness and washed her long, white, thin hair and carefully braided it as Grandmother had worn it. In a parfleche, Promise found a fairly new doeskin dress, beaded moccasins and earrings, and beaded and shell necklaces. She adorned the lifeless body with her findings. She then wrapped Grandmother and Dog, her companion, together in a robe. Promise gathered Grandmother's belongings to lay on the scaffold with her so she'd have them in her new life. Also pemmican, dried meat, a bowl of berries, and fresh water in the water pouch were laid with her so she and Dog wouldn't be hungry or thirsty as they traveled the Hanging Road to their new dwelling.

Turning to Ben, Promise asked if he knew the story about the sunflowers. Not waiting for his answer, she told him what Grandmother had told her.

"Once was a young warrior who loved the sun and always followed it. Since he loved the sun so much, he was turned into a sunflower. That is why sunflowers turn their faces toward the sun."

Then, before she put the stems of the sunflowers between her teeth, she asked him to boost her up into the tree, and she climbed to the scaffold where she laid them next to the Cheyenne woman. That gesture brought back memories to her. It wasn't that long—four or six months—that she placed a pot of red geraniums on her mother's grave, though it seemed like it was forever ago.

They ate a light midday meal beside the old tepee. Ben didn't want to take it down. Someone coming through the hollow might be in need of shelter.

Grandmother would like that, thought Promise.

Making sure the fire was out, and with fresh spring water in the canteens and Milkweed repacked, they were ready to go. But first Ben wanted to discuss some questions he had.

"Why did you say you had no family when I know you do? You have an aunt, your father's sister. And the last your mother knew, your father was at Fort Laramie. Why wouldn't you tell me? Wouldn't you rather go to him instead of staying with Indians or me, a man you hardly know?"

"So you knew all along who I was!" said Promise, almost snarling at him. "You knew my father was alive and probably in Fort Laramie before I did, and you didn't come forth with the truth! Besides, you didn't want me with you any more than I wanted to be with you!"

"When I saw you, Promise, that threw me a loop. I couldn't think straight. You couldn't be Carolyn's daughter; she was with her mother in Philadelphia. You were a girl who just looked like Promise, and I didn't want a tag-along. I was on my own mission. I have a son to find and apologize to and ask for his forgiveness. I had a future before me that I was anxious to fulfill. It was with Carolyn and her family and hopefully my son. You told me your name after we were on the trail. When you told me your mother had died, that crushed me. I then knew I had to do my best for you."

"I didn't know my father was alive until after Mother died. Aunt Hattie and I were traveling to Fort Laramie when another and I were taken from the stagecoach to be sold in Mexico by the Squirrelly Girly Brothers. Father Fox took me from them, and I have been waiting since for my father to come for me. He never did! The other girl who was with me went with Spotted Tail's band, and soldiers looked for her but not me."

"Thank the Lord it was Father Fox and not another. You might not have fared as well," said Ben.

"I'm going to clean the air between us. I'm heading us to Fort Laramie to your father, if he's still there. Is that agreeable with you?"

"No! I am not prepared to meet him yet. I feel very hostile toward him. Can you not just take me with you wherever you are going? I know you and I don't know him. Why didn't he search for me?" Tears filled Promise's eyes and she turned from him.

Ben studied the girl before him before he replied, "How can I force you to meet your father after all these years when I myself haven't met my own son? I planned to head north after I left you at the fort. If you want to continue on with me, you're welcome. It won't be an easy trip. We'll have to winter someplace until spring and then head on to Rapid Creek. I'm a-thinkin' that Crazy Horse will stay at Rapid Creek or close by for the winter. With any luck, our paths will cross with him sometime in the spring or early summer. And hopefully, my son will still be with him. We'll even go on to Mateo Tepee if we have to. I hope you are up to it, Promise. It will be a long journey. We have the sand dunes to cross again. Endure unpredictable weather and rivers to cross."

Promise was thinking he was trying to talk her out of going with him and guessed she'd really preferred to go to Fort Laramie. She stiffened her back. "Living with the Indians has made me strong and taught me survival! I can walk it, Mr. Ben Reed."

"Whoa," said Ben, with a chuckle. "Just call me Ben. I just want you to know what lies ahead of us. I'm not trying to scare you off." He paused and then asked, "Will you tell me about my son and what you know about him?"

"Green Raven is his name," said Promise. "When he was born, he was named Fighting Cub. As I understand it, he was mad from the time of his birth. He also blamed himself for his mother dying giving birth to him and believes that is why you left, why you couldn't lay your eyes upon him."

A shocked look covered Ben's face. "Not true! I couldn't bear to witness my son without his beloved mother.

"It was no one's fault," said Promise.

I blamed myself, and he's blaming himself. His mother dying had nothin' to do with either of us. My sorrow turned into self-pity. It was me who couldn't stay in the village without my wife. I have done him great harm! Do you think he would ever speak to me if I found him, forgive me?"

"I don't know. He carries much hate in him. He blames himself, so he must hate himself, also. We just have to find him to find out."

"You speak of my son with fondness. Do you like my son?"

Promise remembered gazing into the young brave's emerald eyes rimmed with long, black lashes and felt a rush of warmth to her face. "I have no reason not to. He did save me from the hands of one called Stone Face." Then she remembered Green Raven's eyes darkening to loathing after showing concern and added, "But he hates me along with all whites."

Ben stood and stretched his back and said, "We're packed, and the animals are ready to travel. Promise, I'll wait until you are ready to talk about your mother."

Just about the time he was reaching for Milkweed's lead rope, he stopped and turned back to Promise. "I just about forgot...Grandmother asked me to give you this," he said, reaching inside his shirt and brought out a small bundle. He handed it over to Promise.

Her hand trembled as she reached for the package. Her thoughts went back to when she had gathered Grandmother's possessions together and she was tempted to keep something small, just a token to remember Grandmother by. None of it was hers though. It would've been stealing. Opening the bundle, her eyes widened in surprise. A silver and turquoise necklace with matching earrings lay in her hand.

Ben spoke. "Grandmother said you were like a granddaughter to her, and she wanted you to have this jewelry. Her husband traded his best buffalo pony for them many, many winters ago when she was just a bride."

"Beautiful! Just beautiful!" said Promise, close to tears. "I did want something of hers." She tried to say more, but words wouldn't come. She put the small bundle in her shoulder bag.

At the North Platte River, Ben looked the mule in the eye and said, "Milkweed, behave yourself this time."

They crossed with no problems. Again, they traveled in sandy terrain. It made leaving Ash Hollow harder, going from green foliage and fresh water to lack of good water and grass. Promise harvested pear cactus for their sweet meat. Roasted or raw, they added a tasty flavor to one's mouth. She gritted her teeth when she had to gather dried buffalo chips to use for the campfires. She had to use sand to scrub out the eating and cooking vessels until they came across water again.

They wove their way around rugged buttes and sometimes rested under a shaggy tree hanging onto life. Farther north, they came upon giant sand hills being changed daily by wind. Valleys with creeks rested between hills they passed through. It was a joy to Promise when they camped in a valley and she could wash in a creek or pond and feel clean again. The dogs enjoyed lying in the water as they lapped it up. Milkweed's temperament was subdued by the abundance of grass.

Many wild animals took advantage of what the valleys had to offer. Already, the animals were growing their winter hair. Getting fresh meat was easy for Ben. The hides were scraped and rolled for later use. Meat strips were smoked over the fire, replenishing their dried meat. Promise took these resting times for mending tears and reinforcing the soles of her moccasins. She didn't want to wear the extra pair she was carrying yet.

One evening, after a long walk and a simple evening meal, Promise and Ben sat on rocks gazing into the fire. Promise had her cape over her shoulders to keep her back warm from the chilly night air. Ben took a last puff on his pipe and knocked out the tobacco ashes against his hand over the fire.

Promise didn't look at him when she said, "My mother was on her way delivering a sea-going dress when it happened." Her voice sounded far away. "It was an attractive green costume. She was quite pleased with how it turned out. A soft, white shawl fit around the shoulders, and a sash tied around the waist held the shawls pointed ends down. It was to wear on the ship's deck to ward off the cool, breezy sea air. She was able to make her own patterns. She had hoped someday to purchase one of those machines that sewed.

"The sun was out that morning, melting the slushy streets from an early spring snowfall the night before. Mama didn't want Aunt Hattie or me to walk with her to keep her company. 'Too messy a morning,' she said. She was walking down Second Street to Chestnut Street, where she would've turned to walk to Eighth Street."

Promise paused for a few moments and then continued, speaking faster. "But she didn't make it to Chestnut Street. At the corner of Market Street and Second Street, she stepped off the walk to cross. Coming from First Street and Market, a dray wagon filled high with casks appeared. Traveling too fast from the docks, it tried turning on Second Street, causing the draft horses to slip on the slushy streets. The wagon and horses began slipping and sliding, toppling the load of casks."

Again, Promise paused, taking a few deep breaths to steady her breathing. Ducking her head, she rubbed her cheeks against the cape to wipe away the moisture that was clinging to them. "My mother was in the way of it all. I was told she didn't know what hit her. It happened so fast." Promise turned away from Ben, burying her face in the cape. She didn't want him to see her tears.

She felt his hand on her shoulder. He pulled her close to his chest and held her.

"I'm sorry, Promise."

She could hear the choke in his voice.

"I loved her, too. You make me feel closer to your mother. I hope you don't mind."

Thinking it'd be nice to visit with him about her mother and enjoy her memory with another like she did with Aunt Hattie, she answered, "No. I don't mind. I know what you mean. Sharing her makes her closer."

Ben cleared his throat and said, "Not much farther and we should be coming upon on Herb Finley. He homesteaded on the White River some years back. If he isn't there, perhaps his cabin is, and we can take shelter."

One misty day, the travelers stopped early. Ben's leg was aching something awful. Promise fixed him a cup of willow bark tea and made him comfortable before she ventured out, searching for edibles to add to a stew. She had already put hunks of deer meat in the pot over the fire that was keeping the man warm. Moon with her, Queen stayed in camp along with Milkweed tethered close by.

With her cloak's hood over her head to keep her dry, Promise pushed back dried fallen grass and leaves to see what lay beneath. Moon pushed her nose in the grass, sniffed, and pawed around. Promise's thoughts were on meals she had not had since leaving the States. She closed her eyes, thinking of baking cornbread. She could almost smell it. She could see butter melting on the warm cornbread. A horse neighed, and Moon growled, causing Promise to freeze.

She didn't look up but tightly gripped her spear. Moon's head lowered, and hair stood up on her back. Panic seized Promise. She froze and neither moved nor breathed. Moon growled and pushed against her, shaking Promise out of her fearful trance. She wondered if she could leap up fast enough to aim and throw the spear or just bolt and get an arrow in her back or even get shot. She was sure she couldn't outrun a horse.

Fiddlesticks!

She scolded herself. She'll have to face her foe.

But before she turned, a deep voice boomed over her head, shocking her into stillness.

"Who are you? What are you doing here?"

Promise, not moving, her hand on Moon's head to calm her, answered back in Lakota. "My name is Yellow Star. I am with one called Standing Bear." Before she could finish speaking, the hood of her cloak slipped from her head, and she heard snapping sticks and falling pebbles coming from the butte behind her. The voice boomed again, but friendlier.

"You are white and with my good friend, Standing Bear. Where be he?"

Promise turned to meet the man face-on. Dear heavens, he was big!

The big, black man wore a buffalo robe that enlarged his broad shoulders. His black, tight, curly hair shaped like Aunt Hattie's big mixing bowl made his head larger than normal. He led a big horse down the steep embankment until they came to a halt in front of the girl. Touch the Clouds was seven feet tall, and this man seemed to be taller—perhaps because he was as wide as he was tall. Promise's mouth was dry. Her neck became stiff looking up at the man.

In a weak voice, she said, "Standing Bear is at our camp, and I am gathering food for the pot." She coughed and added, "Would you pleasure us with your company and partake of our meager fare?"

The man's laughter bounced off the buttes, scaring birds into flight, startling deer to flee, and sending shivers down Promise's spine. It caused Moon to cower; something Promise had never seen her do.

"Yeah, I'd like to see my old friend. I will follow ya, or ya want to ride on the horse with me?"

"Thank you for the offer, but I go blind around horses."

He gave her a funny look and then opened his mouth, showing white teeth next to the dark skin, and roared again in laughter.

Walking back to camp, Promise hoped that Ben really knew this man. Ben was standing against a tree when Promise walked in, followed by the man and horse.

"Stop where ya are, ya dirty polecat!" Ben commanded. "Get away from him, Promise. Now!"

Scared, Promise dropped her basket and ran with Moon beside her and watched as the two men stared each other down.

Dear heavens, she thought, trembling, *what have I done by bringing this man into our camp?*

Buffalo Warrior

Ben snarled when he said, "I've never seen a coyote as ugly as ya! Shocked at what Ben said, Promise pulled his arm to quiet him. Ben was big, but not as big as this giant he was standing up against.

The black man roared again, shaking everything that was lying loose. "Ya dare talk to me, ya runt of a boar? With one hand I'd break yer back and leave ya squirmin' on the ground like a rat a snake spit out!"

Crouched, the men pulled their knives and sidestepped, slowly circling, facing each other while the dogs whined and paced.

"Queen, stay where you are, and you too, Promise," said Ben without even looking their way. "I've a hankerin' to skin me a varmint.

Shocked, Promise heard the change in Ben's language.

Waving a big knife at Ben, the black man bellowed, "'It's pitiful that the old she dog that birthed ya kept ya alive with her sour milk to grow into the pitiful man ya are!"

"Yer a chicken-liver, yellow-belly, worthless piece of flesh. Even fish throw ya back, so ya'd not rot their water," growled Ben, waving his skinning knife at the other man.

The black man stopped. A big grin spread across his broad face, and he said, "Bad luck to ya if ya kill me."

This time, Ben roared with laughter and said, "Thought I'd never see your black hide again. Thought your scalp be hangin' from a spear by now. Ya still have the Indians fooled in thinkin' ya are a crazy old coot?"

"Still have my hair," said the big man. "Any Indian takes my fuzzy topknot brings bad luck to the whole tribe."

"Promise," said Ben, "this polecat is called Buffalo Warrior. The Indians think he's touched in the head. It's a bad omen to harm him, so he can come and go as he likes without worryin' 'bout losin' his hair."

The men laughed and chatted. Promise threw what she had found in with the boiling meat, wishing she had bad mushrooms to make them ill for playing such a mean trick on her. As she mixed up dough for fry bread, she realized the laughter she heard from Ben seeing an old friend was doing more good for his miseries than what she was able to fix for him. The dogs still didn't know what to think about the new man in camp and were cautious of him. Promise turned in for the night. The men closer to the fire's warmth, talked.

Her back to the fire, Promise opened her eyes and took in the black sky dotted with sparkling stars and a sliver of moon. She yawned and once again closed eyes.

The smells of bacon frying and boiling coffee drifted under Promise's nose. She tried to fight from awakening. She didn't want to lose the thread that held her dream together. But she lost the fight. She took a deep breath of the chilly air and shivered under her bedding. Smiling, she remembered who was in her dream: Green Raven.

"Time to rise if ya want any grub," Buffalo Warrior said in his booming voice.

Moon was no help. She nudged her nose under Promise's chin, licked her face, and then gave her a big smile.

"Moon, you are a traitor. You are supposed to be on my side. I had a sweet dream I didn't want to wake from."

The decision was made that the group would stay a while longer at this camp. As Promise went about her duties, Buffalo Warrior and Ben asked and answered questions that each wanted to know and relived the past. Ben told how he got his game leg, and Buffalo Warrior told of roaming the Plains and the Black

Hills. Only he could get away with entering the sacred hills without being staked over an anthill and left to die by the Sioux.

When night came, Promise curled up in her bedding, and Moon cuddled next to her. She gazed at the dark, sparkling sky. She had a lot to share with her mother because she had gleaned much from the men as they reminisced about their youth.

Buffalo Warrior's English name was Isaiah Jefferson. He and Ben met when they both signed on the Fremont expedition at Fort Leavenworth. The men had argued who had been the wettest behind the ears and laughed till tears came. Both had lied about their ages. Ben mentioned there were too many mouths to feed in his family, and he wanted to see and do more than being stranded on a dirt farm. One less mouth to feed would not bother his pa. Ben's hard work on the family farm built strength into his lanky body. Isaiah received his strength from wrestling other blacks for his master's entertainment. When he left the South, he wanted to go west, not north. He didn't want to be in a populated area.

Promise never did hear if Isaiah was a slave or a free man. How he spoke of the Underground Railroad, she suspected he had used it to escape from the South.

Ben and Isaiah bent their backs to the poles on the keelboats as the Fremont party traveled on the Missouri River till they reached the Platte. Kit Carson guided the party overland to the Rockies. Being with old trappers who knew how to live with the land and with educated men drawing maps and making charts with instruments the lads never heard of, they strutted about like peacocks. The first painted Indians they encountered sent chills up their spines, and the peacocks lost their strut.

The party picked up supplies at the American Fur Company post, named Fort Laramie.

A mixture of trappers and Indians induced activity in and outside the log stockade. They traded from each other, challenged hatchet and knife throws, and raced horses. Firewater flowed, provoking fights.

Their first taste of firewater inspired braveness in the lads. Before they could get themselves scalped, they passed out. Under the hot, midday sun, Ben woke, moaned, and tried to feel for his head. Someone offered him water. Through his hazy eyes, he saw a copper-skinned girl. Shaking his head to clear his eyes and mind, he groaned, putting his hands on his head again. The girl knelt and held the water to his dry lips, and he drank. When he looked again, he saw large, dark eyes staring back at him. Her lips, the color of a pale rose in a heart-shaped face, smiled at him. Her doeskin dress had a yellow, beaded sun and a blue star on one shoulder. Ben tried to speak but couldn't rid the cotton from his mouth. She spoke, but Ben didn't understand what she said. The girl rose; nodded her head; and left, her long, shiny, black braids bouncing on her back. Ben could hardly breathe. His breath went with the Indian girl. With his head ready to explode and now his lungs feeling ready to burst, his heart pounded. He thought he was dying.

The time came when Ben was able to rise up on his feet without groaning, and he went in search of the water girl. He asked around and mentioned the sun and star emblem on her shoulder. He was told she belonged to Chief Father Fox's band. When he spotted her, he watched her from afar. She saw him and lowered her head in shyness and ran away giggling, taking his heart with her.

The expedition party was ready to leave the post. Ben and Isaiah traded their clothes in for leathers. Now they resembled most of the other men they were traveling with. Ben searched the Indian faces for the young girl with no avail. She might be out of sight but not out of his mind. He took a lot of ribbing from Isaiah as they marched on.

The lads had only heard about the land they were crossing and heading for. Ben and Isaiah did whatever needed done. They became close friends. They traveled over the hot, dusty, barren desert; and game was scarce. Wearily, they crossed the Great

Divide, sand dunes and buttes. Spirits were lifted when they entered and rested in the Sweetwater Valley. They crossed the South Past to the Wind River Range. The snow-capped Rocky Mountains reigned over the rugged and beautiful country. Cold water gushed down between layered, uneven mountains; and foothills poured into Wind River. The lads had never seen anything so alive with game and birds and sounds in their weary lives. They behaved like little boys gazing at jars of candy, trying to take it all in, wanting to touch, smell, and taste. All too soon, the country's sweetness vanished under hard work and the cold as they traveled into the mountain range. But the drudgery couldn't erase the many glorious sights they encountered from their minds. Ben could see him and the Indian girl together in these mountains. Game and water was plentiful. One couldn't ask for more.

By the time the party returned to Fort Laramie, the wilderness, the bone and muscle-tearing work had toughened Ben and Isaiah. They were no longer looked upon as lads.

To Ben's disappointment, Chief Father Fox's band had moved on.

Ben knew what he was going to do. Isaiah, not wanting to go back to the States and be just another colored boy, opted to travel with Ben. They drew their pay and left the expedition. Ben had learned that to get something from the Indians, one must trade for it; and he wanted the Indian girl.

With fresh horses, supplies, and a pack mule, they headed to Colorado Territory to try their luck at gold panning. They set up camp at Cherry Creek, not far from Denver. Panning was wet, cold, hard, and miserable work. They did, however, retrieve gold flakes and some nuggets enough to cash in for traps and trinkets to trade with and use as gifts. They still trapped and hunted for furs along the way as they traveled, searching for Father Fox's band. The following year, they came upon the band.

Riding in, Ben spotted the girl, and she spotted him. Both had changed, but they recognized each other, her his emerald green eyes and him her beautiful face. She covered her mouth with her hand to show the expression of surprise and ran toward the biggest lodge.

Chief Father Fox greeted the intruders with hospitality, offering them food and drink. The young girl, Fawn, was brought in. She knew the white man's language and translated between the men. Ben's eyes were only on the girl. A young maiden now, her braids hung over her shoulders. She kept her dark eyes cast down in shyness, but he noticed that without lifting her head, she lifted her eyes to him.

Ben and Isaiah were welcomed to stay. The Indians were curious about Isaiah's black skin and tried rubbing it to see if the color came off; and when it did not, their eyes widened in surprised. The children followed him wherever he went. He'd yell, "Boo," in his booming voice, and the children would scatter, laughing.

Ben walked in the blanket with Fawn under the scrutinizing eyes of her father and mother. On a buffalo hunt, Ben showed his mettle when a young brave's pony went down among the stampeding buffalo. Ben pulled up his horse, aimed his Hawkins at the nearest buffalo to the brave, and downed it. The following rampaging buffalos veered around the downed animal and the fallen brave. It was a good hunt for everyone.

Isaiah's treated buffalo hide was made into a cape for him. With it on and his tight, curly, black hair and his height, he soon was known as Buffalo Warrior. When Ben married Fawn and was adopted into the band, he was called Standing Bear. Isaiah thought it was time for him to leave and go elsewhere. His feet were itching to see more of the West.

Ben was the happiest he had ever been. He cherished Fawn. She was his life. Their love was bright as the sun in the day and the moon at night. Her beauty matured when she became with child. Ben felt so light he thought he could fly like a hawk and soar in the air. He, a husband to the most precious woman in the land, was going to be a father. He'd have a family to adore, care for, and lavish love upon.

When Fawn died in childbirth, Ben's heart shattered in little pieces. He got on his horse and rode away, not looking back, not thinking of his son, but of his loss. He roamed the country, not caring if he lived or died. He ended up in the Montana Territory working in a silver mine. He also became owner of an abandoned pup and a mule that was going to be shot. Having others to care for was what he needed in his life, along with hard work. It helped him to not think. When the Civil War broke out, he joined up. He didn't figure being wounded at Gettysburg would give him a future to look forward to—a wife and a family. Finding Promise in Indian Territory and learning about the death of her mother, his wife to be, crashed down on him. He then realized he still had a son he wanted to find. And the girl who was going to be his step-daughter was already with him, and he felt love for her like a daughter.

Buffalo Warrior took it upon himself to show Promise how to defend herself. She wasn't good at throwing the spear or her knife accurately. She owned up to the fact that the first rabbit she downed wasn't running. Finally, Buffalo Warrior made a slingshot for her. He cut a leather patch, punched a hole on two sides, and then cut two narrow strips from leather tied one at each end of the patch. He told her to find small, round stones and to practice swinging it and letting the stone fly when she thought she could hit the target.

She did practice, and every moving thing around her was in peril. Queen and Moon hid, and Milkweed and Buffalo Warrior's horse nervously paced where they were tethered. When Promise knocked a bird, which she wasn't aiming at, off a limb and it dropped at her feet, she felt terrible. She picked it up and cradled it her in hand. Poor bird! And it was her fault! She showed the men what she did. She held the little bird up for them to see. She wasn't going to use the slingshot anymore.

Ben said, "That's why you have to practice, Promise."

Buffalo Warrior nodded in agreement. Then a wonderful thing happened. The bird lifted its head and wobbled onto its feet. It looked around and flew out of her hand back into the tree.

Her practicing did pay off. She missed more than she hit, but she was able to get in the area she was aiming at. Always seeking food, Promise now paid attention for small, round rocks for her slingshot, and she carried them in a bag she had made out of one of her rabbit hides.

One day a flock of ducks flew over, heading south; and Ben, walking, and Buffalo Warrior, on horseback, followed their direction. Promise checked the supplies, which were dwindling faster with an extra mouth to feed. She had taken over much of the meal preparations, and she welcomed advice from Ben. She wished he had advice on how to make bacon taste like fried chicken or a pot roast with potatoes, carrots, and onions. Or fresh baked bread. She could almost smell the aroma. Her mouth watered as she pictured butter dripping off a thick slice of warm bread. Or to even have preserves to spread on fry bread would be a welcome change. She tripped over Moon. "Moon, you have been underfoot all day. Why didn't you go with the men and Queen? The hair on Moon's back was up; and suddenly, Promise felt uneasy. She felt eyes on her. Looking in all directions, she didn't see anything unusual.

"Moon, you have me spooked. Oh, look. The men are back."

Ben carried three ducks.

While the men rested, she cleaned and plucked the ducks. In their gapping cavities, she sprinkled a mixture of dried herbs with extra sage. She slipped the birds on a green spit and laid it in green, forked sticks at both ends of the camp fire. In a small pot of boiling water, she added a mixture of dried berries and cuts of dried pear cactus for the sweetness it would deliver and the thick juice pulp. She was excited to have a preserves of sorts for the fry bread. Cow parsnip stems were peeled, ready to roast in the coals; and their leaves burned around the edge of the fire so their ashes were available for an added flavor to the ducks.

When the ducks were crisp and golden, they were removed, a duck for each person; and each person shared with the dogs. Ben told her what Buffalo Warrior had told him while they were hunting.

"Promise, Buffalo Warrior had been telling me about a cabin tucked away on the edge of the Black Hills past the hot springs. It's been used by trappers and hunters over the years. It's located on our way to Rapid Creek. If no one beats us to it, it would be a good place for us to winter at."

As Promise cleaned up and Ben and Buffalo Warrior led the big animals to the creek to water, she went over what Ben had told her. She thought wintering in a cabin would be good shelter for them. Tomorrow, they would part company. It was sad parting with Buffalo Warrior. Promise felt he was her friend also.

The morning came quickly with a chill in the air. Buffalo Warrior sat on his big horse, Promise had already received a bear hug from him. He learned over nodded to Ben and to her, said, "You haven't seen the last of me. Our paths will cross again, my friends."

Ben and Promise

It was late morning when the travelers came upon the White River. Ben left Promise, Moon, and Milkweed near a cluster of trees close to the water while he went to scout out the area.

Promise went to the river's edge and felt the water. It was cold. What she wanted was to clean up and wash her hair. She went back to Milkweed and retrieved her parfleche. She took out the little bit of soap she had left from Squirrel. She built up the camp fire and then grabbed her cloak. On her way back to the river, she shivered just thinking of the cold water. Checking her surroundings and seeing Moon having a nap, she felt she was safe. She laid her dry items on a bush at the river's edge and jumped in. The cold water knocked the air out of her, and she came up sputtering and gasping for air. She didn't dwindle in bathing, washing, and rinsing her hair. She was out in no time. Wrapped in the cloak, she hurried to the fire and sat as close as she dared fingering her wet hair over it.

She was dressed, had her hair pulled back into a long braid, and had stopped shivering when Ben and Queen returned. He had spotted a cabin with smoke coming out of the chimney just across the river, and he found a place to cross. Promise couldn't help but be excited. Perhaps white people were there, perhaps the people Ben was looking for.

She looked down on herself and said, "Ben, do you think I should get into different clothes? I don't want anyone to know

I've lived with the Indians. I'm not ashamed of that, but white people might look at me differently if they knew."

"You're probably right, Promise. Do you have different clothes so you won't have to wear your doeskin dress?"

"Yes, but they will be terribly wrinkled," said Promise.

"Make do," said Ben. "I'm going to take a quick dip in the river."

He gathered a few items and a blanket. Promise shook out the garments she had worn when she first met Ben: the dress bottom she wore as a skirt and the nightshirt. She wished now the shirt still had its long sleeves. Now she was dressed again the same way; and again, felt like she belonged to two different cultures. She fingered the cameo hanging from her neck. She'd have Ben conceal her knife and spear along with her bedroll and her bags in with his packs.

Ben's face was red where he shaved using his Bowie knife. "That water's cold," he said with a shiver as he looked for a clean shirt in his pack. He brushed off his pants as well as possible and tucked the pant legs into his high-top moccasins.

As he was rearranging the packs on Milkweed, Promise came up to him and said, "Ben, we might be looked on as odd, a man and a young lass traveling together in these parts. If you want to claim me as your daughter to whomever we might run into, that is all right with me. After all, you were to be my stepfather, so it's not completely an untruth."

Ben looked at Promise, smiled, and said, "That's a good suggestion. I'd be proud to acknowledge you as my daughter."

The group followed the river until they came to the crossing. The river was wider here and shallow with many rocks to step on. There was evidence of wagon wheels on the banks. They followed the tracks to the edge of some trees and paused. Ben and Promise looked around and saw a log cabin, a barn, a corral, a buckboard wagon, and a chicken coop.

Putting his hand on Promise's shoulder, he said in a low voice, "I'm sure Herb Finnely told me he had the best watch dog in the country, so why are we not hearing barking if this is his place?"

"Perhaps it isn't his place," whispered Promise.

"Perhaps not, Promise. Watch the dogs. See them sniffing the ground and squatting, leaving their scent? At one time there was a dog here."

About then, a lone, white turkey came around the corner of the barn, gobbling loudly, its feathers ruffled, and scattering squawking chickens. Moon and Queen backed up, but Milkweed went forward. The turkey came at him without pause. If it was a dog, one would say it was snorting and growling. The travelers didn't know how to respond to the attacker now flaying its wings. It caused Milkweed to turn tail. Milkweed had met his match.

The cabin door opened, and a stout woman with unruly red hair yelled out, "Who goes there?"

Loudly, Ben said, "Are you Mrs. Herb Finnely?"

"Yes. Who are you?"

"I'm a friend of Mr. Finnely, said Ben. "We met in Silver City in Montana Territory. Herb told me if I'm ever up in the area to look him up."

"Greetings to you, stranger, come on in," said the woman. "Turk. Turk, get back here and let those people be. Turk, I mean it! I will roast your old, tough hide. Get back here!"

Surprisingly, the turkey did turn around and headed back to the cabin, turning now and then, ruffling its feathers and throwing gobbles at the strangers.

Promise thought: *They don't need a dog with a crazy turkey around!*

"Tie your mule up at the hitchin' post and come on in. Herb only knows friendly people, and they all are welcome here," said the woman, standing in the doorway with two children peeking around her skirt. Their hair was as red and wild as the woman's. "The dogs can stay outside. If they don't bother Turk, Turk won't bother them. Come in, come in. Nice having company. I'll make fresh coffee, and I'll lay out some honey cakes, and we'll chew the fat and get to know each other."

Promise and Ben did as they were told. It had been so long since Promise saw the inside of a white person's home, and she just took it all in. In the south corner, a jack bed had been built in the wall; and under it was a trundle bed and clothes hung from pegs. There were two wooden rocking chairs, and a small table, between the chairs had an oil lamp and an open book on it, faced the hearth on the west wall. There was a cook stove and shelves on the east wall where the woman now stood, the children still hanging on to her skirt.

"Sit. Sit yourselves down at the table," she said with a big smile on her round face. "So nice to have company, oh," she said, wiping her hands on her long white apron. Putting a hand on the red-headed girl, she said, "This is Frieda Frances, and"—she put her other hand on the boy's red head—"this is Frederick Franklin. My name is Fanny Fay. We don't need to stand on formality out here. Just call me Fanny or Fanny Fay. And your names....?"

"My name is Ben Reed. This here"—he put his hand on Promise's shoulder—"is Promise, my daughter."

"My, what a pretty name," said Fanny, a pretty name for a pretty girl."

Soon, everybody was at the table, eating honey cakes and drinking strong coffee. Promise, not a coffee-drinker, drank it because there was fresh cream on the table; and she poured it into her cup where it was more cream than coffee. A sugar loaf was on the table, and she scraped sugar into her cup until Ben put his hand over hers. He smiled at Fanny and said, "We've been traveling for some time now, and sugar wasn't in our supplies."

"What we have, you can have," said Fanny, nodding toward Promise.

"If you don't mind, Ben, you can bunk in the barn up in the hayloft, and Promise can bunk here with me and the kids. Your mule can feed in there. Don't know what to say about the dogs. I don't mind having a dog in the house if you like to have one in.

Our old dog up and died on us. Herb doesn't know old Spot isn't here anymore. He loved that old dog."

Before Ben could answer, Promise said, "Sorry to hear about your dog. It's nice of you, Fanny, to let my dog in your cabin. Moon, and I are really close, and she'd be unhappy away from me. Thank you."

"Queen will share the barn with me and Milkweed. Works out fine for us," said Ben. "We thank you for your hospitality. If you don't mind, we'll stay around for a few days. I'd be happy to do a few repairs I noticed that could be done. I like Herb and know he's trying to make a living and is gone a lot, and I know he'd do the same for me. Herb told me about a trading post nearby called Dirty Pete's, like to trade my furs in for supplies."

"Dirty Pete's is near Fort Robinson," said Fanny. "What Pete doesn't have, the trading post at the fort will. There is also a general store there. The longer you can stay here, the better I'd like it. And an extra pair of hands comes in handy. My children are a great help and good company even at their young age but it gets lonely out here."

The children had been so quiet Promise forgot they were even there. She glanced over at the children sitting side by side on a bench. Their wild, curly, red hair gave the impression of two heads under one wild, red bush. Promise smiled at them and gave them a wink and then remembered that winking wasn't ladylike. They giggled and ducked their heads. Promise realized they were twins.

Fanny stood. "Kids, it's time to milk Betsy."

The kids jumped up, put on their jackets, and picked up the galvanized milk pail.

"Don't forget to shut the chicken up. Oh," said their mother, "bring in four potatoes from the root cellar."

"Hold up," said Ben. "I'll walk out with you, and you can show me around the barn."

"How does ham and potato soup and baking powder biscuits for supper sound to you, Promise?" asked Fanny.

"Heavenly," said Promise as she began clearing the table, keeping her head down. She knew she was drooling and licked her lips.

Over supper Fanny told her guests how Herb made things easier for her. "I have a water pump on the counter. The kids and I don't have to fetch water from the river anymore, and the cook stove has a hot water reservoir tank." She pointed, and said, "The lean-to on the north side of the cabin keeps cool, and I can store milk, butter, and eggs without worrying about the dairy souring or freezing or food spoiling." She paused to take a breath. "I feel like I'm still in the States with all of my conveniences. Oh, I almost forgot. Herb dug a trench from the river into the corral, and I can pull water out of it to water my garden."

After dishes were tended to, and dogs fed, Ben said his goodnights and picked up a lantern. He and Queen left for the barn. The boy slipped into his mother's bed, and the girl lay on the trundle bed after Promise helped her pull it out from under the big bed. Moon settled in front of the hearth, her head on her paws and her eyes on Promise.

Promise yawned and excused herself for it.

"Child, you must be tired, and me going on and on. It isn't polite to brag, but I like bragging about my husband. Why don't you get ready for bed. You sleep with Frieda."

Promise thanked her and went and lay on the bed.

"Child, don't you have a nightdress?"

"No, I don't. I sleep in what I've worn during the day."

"I have something for you," said Fanny. She went to a trunk in a corner and pulled out a white nightdress with a pink bow at the neck.

"Oh no," said Promise. "I couldn't wear that. It looks new."

"It's not new, but as you can see, my girth now isn't what it was when I wore this. Put it on. You'll be more comfortable. Look, here's a shawl you can wrap around you in the morning. There are a few more items in here that I think you could put to good use, and I'd get the extra space I need."

Turning down the lamp next to the bed, Fanny said, "I've got things I want to do yet. I'll be quiet. Good night. Sweet dreams. Oh, here. I'll open the privacy screen for you."

Moon moved from the hearth to the rag rug on floor next to the low bed, and Promise reached down and patted her head and scratched behind her ear. Promise pictured her mother and her at their kitchen table in Elfreth's Alley. Silently, she spoke to her mama.

Mama, I ate butter on light, flaky biscuits. I am in a bed for the first time since the Squirrelly Girly Brothers kidnapped me and Penelope. On the mantel over the fireplace are books. One of them is the McGuffey Reader. *Aunt Hattie taught me my numbers and letters using that book. I have missed reading. I had read most of the ones on this mantel*: Robinson Crusoe, Red Riding Hood, Ivanhoe, Cinderella *and* Sleeping Beauty. *I would like to read* Moby Dick.

Her eyes closed to the tick-tock from the clock on the mantel.

The next thing Promise knew, she was waking up under the delicious smell of baking bread, and she had to lick her lips again. She opened her eyes; and Frieda, in a white pinafore over a blue polka-dot dress, stared down at her like she had been waiting all morning for Promise to wake. Then Frederick came running over in his blue polka-dot shirt.

"Come on, Promise," he said. "Time for morning meal, we're hungry."

"I am sorry," said Promise, seeing the early sun out the window breaking through the trees. "I must have been more tired than I thought. I slept like a log. You both look so nice all dressed up. Is it Sunday?"

"No," they said together.

"Ma said since we have company we should dress nice," said Frieda

Promise stretched and reached for the shawl that Fanny loaned her and put it around her shoulders. It was long and modestly covered her. She quickly made up the trundle bed and pushed it under the big bed and then made that bed up. Fanny had told her that if she wanted the privacy screen, to just open it and step behind it to dress. Promise pulled the four-paneled screen open. It appeared to be home-built, and the panels were covered in blue polka-dot like the twins' new clothes.

Promise heard Ben in the lean-to and went in to help him tend to the fresh milk he brought in. She helped him strain the milk through a muslin cloth to keep any dirt or debris from following the milk into the big crock and then covered it. From the milk the night before, Promise used a wooden spoon and skimmed the cream that had risen to the top off into a smaller crock. The twins came in through the side door with a basket of fresh eggs they had just gathered.

Noticing a door at the back of the lean-to, Promise asked the twins what it was for. Frederick opened the door, and a blast of cool air hit Promise.

"That's the root cellar," he said. "It's dug right into the hillside behind us. That's why Pa built the cabin right next to the hill, so we don't even have to go outside. Hot summer days, Ma lets us eat in here."

"Come and get it while it's hot," said Fanny.

Steaming ham steaks; fried eggs; fried potatoes; and thick-sliced, warm bread; berry preserves, and butter graced the table top. Everyone settled around the table. Fanny said a prayer, giving thanks for the food and new friends.

Promise ate so much she was bloated; she had to loosen her belt. Perhaps after she helped Fanny clean up the morning dishes, she and Moon could go for a run. Fanny liked to talk, reminding Promise of her good friend, Squirrel. It gave her an ache inside. Fanny was wearing a blue polka-dot dress, and Promise said, "That's a pretty dress you have on, and so are the children's clothes." Fanny threw back her wild head of hair and laughed.

"Let me tell you about my husband, Herb. Herb doesn't do anything halfway. It's all or nothing with him. I asked him to pick me up a few yards of material so I could make a few clothes for the children. He brings home a whole bolt. Look around you, child. I don't think you have noticed everything."

Promise looked around, and sure enough, she did miss a few things, like the blue polka-dot curtains and the blue polka-dot dress on Frieda's rag doll."

Fanny said, "I have another dress just like this one." And she laughed some more.

Promise found Ben up in the hay loft, tossing hay down to the animals.

"Ben," she called up to him, "Moon and I are going for a run up by the river."

"You have long walks every day, and now you want to take a run?" he said, pausing on the handle of the hay fork.

"That was walking, Ben. I want to run."

Moon at her side, they ran, following the edge of the river. The sun was warm, but the air had a nip to it. The sky was a shiny blue. Spotting a large, flat rock half in and half out of the river, she climbed upon it, Moon beside her. She listened to the river slap against the rocks. Overhead she heard, Caw! Caw! Looking up, she saw an eagle circling; and it reminded her of her Indian name, Yellow Star and of her life with the Indians.

Although it was for only a short time, she learned and saw and felt the ways of the Indians. She adapted and planned on staying with them. It was a hard life, but it was meaningful. Now she was back in the white man's world and realized, again, how much she had missed it.

She petted Moon and said, "Moon, I forgot that I had not eaten at a table, slept in a bed, or tasted real sugar for months. I didn't seek firewood last night. Instead, I washed dishes in a basin with hot water and soap, enjoyed a white woman's company, and slept in a nightdress next to a little white girl. If I go to Fort Laramie now, I can still do all those things. I can understand Brings Water wanting to marry a white man and live his way. But do I want to? Do I want to give up the traveling and seeing this beautiful country? Even the barren and dull countryside has beauty when one recognizes the unique shapes and the subtle colors etched in the buttes and hills, all designed by the wind and sand and rain. Do I want to keep on traveling with Ben knowing the hardship that comes with it? Perhaps Ben had another motive for stopping at the Finnelys'? Perhaps it was to give me a taste of the world I left and change my mind and go to Fort Laramie."

Moon jumped up with a growl in her throat. The bushes rustled behind them. Promise quickly got to her feet, reaching for her knife, which wasn't with her. She heard gobbling and thought: Turk? Two heads of wild red hair poked out behind a bush.

"I told you we'd find her," said Frederick to his sister and Turk.

"You scared me, you little imps," Promise said with a laugh. "I'm glad you're here. You can walk back with me and Moon."

When Promise and her new young friends returned to the cabin, Ben was dressed in his leathers and had repacked his many prime pelts along with others that Milkweed would be carrying if he wasn't hitched to the wagon. Also, Fanny was sending along eggs in a wooden crate packed in straw and pails of cream also surrounded in straw to the trading posts to be credited to her bill.

"Don't forget to check if I have mail," she said as she handed Ben a cloth bag of vittles.

"How did you get Milkweed backed up between the shafts and get a harness on him?" Promise asked Ben.

"It weren't easy," said Ben, leaning against the wagon. He used his arm to wipe his brow and said, "Promise, I'll probably be gone three or four days. What I can't get at the trading post I'll go on in to Fort Robinson, catch up on the news. You'll be all right here."

As he pulled out with Queen sitting at his side, Fanny came running. "Ben...Ben, hold up," she said, waving at him. "Please pick me up a can of coal oil, never can have too much on hand. Have a safe trip, Ben." Milkweed's ears were laid back, and he moved slowly, as if he had a plan. When he began to pull like he was supposed to, there was a sigh of relief all around.

Fanny, the kids, and Promise watched Ben cross the river without a mishap. "I offered our horse, Nelly, to him after I saw him fighting Milkweed to hitch up," Fanny said to Promise.

Promise shared her experiences around Milkweed. "We were in a terrible storm. Lightning flashed, and thunder crashed, spooking the mule. Milkweed jerked back so hard the lease rope burned through Pa's hands, causing them to bleed. "Also," Promise said, "Milkweed pulled Pa across the South Platte River."

"I think sometimes Pa was sorry he ever saved that ornery mule from being shot by his first owner."

Fanny did retrieve Ben's soiled clothes to launder in a couple of days, and she asked for Promise's soiled garments. Promise shrugged.

"All I have is just what I have on," she said.

"Well, we'll have to do something about that, won't we?" said Fanny.

In the cabin, Fanny went right to the trunk. Promise sat at the end of the bed and watched her host pull out different items.

"Here, Promise," said Fanny. "You can have these drawers. I've made myself new ones that fit me. I'm sure there is enough blue polka-dot material on this bolt yet to at least make a skirt for you, and I think I have just the right blouse to go with it. Do you know how to sew? Herb told me when he comes back this time; he'll have one of those new machines that sew. That will be nice to have."

"My mother was a seamstress," said Promise. "She also hoped to get one of those machines. And, yes, I can sew. I can do the backstitch, the whipstitch, the hemming stitch, and the inside blind stitch. I helped my mother with the piece work."

"I am impressed," said Fanny, looking up from the trunk. "You will be a great help. And between the two of us, we'll be able to have a few items finished by the time your pa gets back. You said your mother was a seamstress. Now, I know it's none of my business, child, but I think you and your pa have had some sorrow in your lives."

"Yes, we have," said Promise. She opened up the cameo locket and showed Fanny the likeness of her and her mother. She didn't say anything more.

"A beautiful woman, your mother and you resemble her."

Fanny didn't ask any more questions.

But Fanny did say, "We who have moved here from the East and have lived here for some time have learned not to ask questions of others leaving the States. If they want us to know something, they will offer it. Moving West is a new beginning for many, a new start. We came from Indiana. The twins were born in the covered wagon coming out here."

It was a busy day for Promise. She helped Fanny cut out and stitch up a skirt out of the blue polka-dot material. Ben was getting a new shirt too. Everyone now has something to wear out of that material. Fanny thought she had enough left over for a shirt for Herb. Promise was pleased with her new skirt. It had been a long time since she had worn anything that covered her ankles. The skirt had a wide waist band and wide straps that buttoned into the front. When Fanny measured Promise's waist, she told her she didn't have an ounce of extra flesh. She gave Promise a pretty, white blouse. It was out of fashion, but Promise didn't care. She'd worn doeskin for months, and the blouse looked so good with the skirt. It had a high neck collar, and the sleeves were long and loose with wide, tight wristbands with pearl buttons. Promise also received three pairs of drawers.

When Promise retired that night after a hardy meal of ham and beans with cornbread, her only question was, *Where will I wear my new clothes?*

On laundry day, Promise wore a dress of Fanny's. It was too large for her, but she cinched it in using her beaded belt. Her red shirt and gingham skirt was in the wash. In the lean-to, two galvanized tubs sat on a bench. Over the soapy, hot water, Fanny seemed to attack the soiled clothes on the washboard. Her hands, red from the hot water, gripped the wet clothes and rubbed them up and down relentlessly over the ribs of the washboard. Promise labored over the rinse water. She dunked the washed clothes a few times and then twisted and twisted until the water was all out. She took them outside, gave them a shake, and laid them over the drying line. Then she went back to the lean-to to do it over again. With the flannel sheets, it took the two of them to twist out the water.

That evening, Promise felt like she earned her keep. Her shoulders and hands ached, and her back didn't want to straighten up. She had helped her aunt with the wash back home, but she didn't remember aching like she was now. Fanny handed Promise hot tea with a few special herbs, and she told Promise, "Drink the tea. It will help ease your aches."

Promise did have a restful sleep but a rude awakening.

Strangers at the Door

Early morning Moon was raising a ruckus in the cabin, and Promise heard Turk outside, madly gobbling.

What in the world has caused Moon and Turk to be so upset?

Promise jumped out of bed, grabbed her shawl, and went to the window.

Fanny stirred; sat up in her bed and yawned; and groggily asked, "What is all the noise about?"

"Quiet, Moon," said Promise as she tried to calm her dog. To Fanny, she said nervously, "Indians are outside! Hush, Moon!"

Moon's hair stood up, and growls kept rolling out of her.

"I'm sure, Promise, they are friendly. Some have stopped here throughout the years. Don't be scared," Fanny said, wrapping a shawl around her as she went to the door. "Maybe you better hold on to Moon."

"Don't open the door, Fanny. I can tell you now that one of them isn't friendly."

Fanny didn't hear her and said as she opened the door, "There is leftover cornbread. Get a cloth and put the cornbread in it. Tie up the ends, and I'll give it to them."

Three Indians—two fairly young and one older—sat on ponies, watching her.

"Good morning," Fanny said. "I have cornbread. I will be glad to give it to you."

Two of the Indians looked at each other, nodding their heads, but the third said in Lakota, "No. Kill!"

"No!" said the younger Indians together.

The older Indian spun his pony around, shouting at the other two. They shouted back, raising their spears and shaking them at the mad Indian.

"Ma, what's going on? Frederick asked.

"I'm scared, Ma," said Frieda.

"Don't be such a baby," said Frederick.

"Both of you hush up!" said Fanny.

Although Promise stood back from the opened door, she was able to see and hear the Indians arguing. She knew what they were saying, and a shudder went through her when she heard Stone Face angry voice. He wanted to kill the white woman and her brats. He was unable to see Promise in the shadows; but if he did spot her, no one would be able to hold him back or talk him out of attacking the cabin and all who were in it.

Stone Face cruelly kicked his pony and sped away. The younger Indians jumped off their ponies and tied them at the hitching post. Each wore a buckskin tunic and leggings. Their black hair flowed down their backs as they strolled into the cabin like they owned it.

"Sit," said Fanny as she motioned them to the long bench or the chairs at the table. To Promise, she said, "No sense wrapping the cornbread. Just put it on the table. Perhaps these braves are thirsty and like coffee. Promise, please grind some coffee beans and put on the pot." She nodded to the Indians. "Sit. Sit, please, at the table."

Promise had her back to the braves as she tended to the cornbread and the coffee beans. She loved the smell of the beans, but this morning, the aroma was lost on her as she did her best to keep her hair around her face. She feared she might be recognized. The tall, lanky one had a clipped feather in his hair. She knew where the top part of that feather was: on her feather disk.

The braves sat on the long bench at the table. Besides the oil lamp, butter, sugar loaf, a jar of molasses, and utensils were already on the table. Fanny set the platter of cornbread down on the table. The braves happily took a piece and spread butter on their cornbread and, with every bite, nodded their approval.

Fanny got busy at the cook stove. She sliced side pork and fried it until the rind was crisp, and then she sliced the cold corn mush from the morning before and slipped those slices into the hot skillet grease. The braves nudged each other and rubbed their stomachs.

Turk started up another ruckus outside.

The twins, now dressed, ran outside before Fanny or Promise was able to stop them. Frieda yelled back, "Ma, it's Ben, Queen, and Milkweed. And he brought back a little Spot!"

"Easy, child, slow down. What's a spot?"

"You know, Ma, a Spot!"

Moon raced out the door, followed by the humans. Seeing Queen and Ben, she put on one of her shows. She jumped up, twisted, and flipped over backward, landing on her feet, and raced around the wagon and Milkweed. Milkweed stomped his feet, raised his head, laid his long ears back, and bared his long teeth. Moon didn't care. She was happy to see her old friends. She kept up her jumping and twisting and back flips until Promise got her settled down; and in doing so, Promise received many wet kisses on her face. The braves seemed to enjoy the antics of the silly dog. Promise had to admit she was glad to see her old friends again too and she noticed Ben had on a new hat.

Frederick rushed to his ma, grabbed her hand, and pulled her to the wagon where Ben was sitting.

"Look, Ma! Ben brought us back a Spot!"

"I see Ben and a small, fuzzy thing on his lap. What I don't see is a spot."

"Oh, Ma! That's Spot! Don't you recognize him?" He picked up a puppy from Ben's lap and held it up to his ma. "It's Spot, Ma, but in a puppy's body."

Fanny picked up the fat, little puppy from Frederick and held it up. "Well, I do see he looks like our old dog, Spot. Ben, you never saw our old dog. How did you know to pick this one? I'm sure there was a litter to pick from."

"No," said Ben. "This one was the only one left in the crate."

"Isn't that something," said Fanny. "This little guy has the same markings as old Spot, even to the black ring around one eye and over the ear." Looking at her twins, she asked, "What are you going to name him?"

The twins said together, "Spot, of course."

Then Frieda looked into the wagon bed and said, "There's something moving in that burlap sack, and it's making little noises."

Ben stepped off the wagon and went and stood next to the girl. "I guess we better check it out," he said as he picked up the sack.

Then Frieda heard, Meow! Meow!

"Oh! Ben, you brought me a kitten! I always wanted a kitty," she said with folded hands and bouncing up and down. Soon, she was holding two gray-striped kittens.

Ben walked where the braves were standing and greeted them. He pointed at himself and said, "Ben."

The lanky brave pointed at himself and in broken English said, "Lone Horse." He pointed to the shorter, husky brave and said, "Hawk."

About then, Fanny yelled, "I have food a-cooking. Come on. Let's eat."

Everyone trotted to the cabin and surrounded the table as Fanny set the food upon it and Promise poured coffee and milk. Fanny said grace and gave thanks for their bounty and new friends, nodding her red head to the braves, and gave thanks for Ben's safe travel.

When asked what she was going to name her kittens, Frieda said, "Apple Gray and Peaches."

"Sounds liked good names to me," said Ben.

The group at the table nodded in agreement.

After stomachs were filled, it was back to work. "Would you two men help me unload the wagon?" Ben asked.

The braves looked at each other and nodded yes. Ben tipped his new hat to the ladies, and the braves followed him out.

With the men folk out of the cabin, Promise and Fanny quickly got behind the privacy screen and dressed. Promise opted to wear her new clothes, hoping she would not be recognized by Lone Horse. Fanny helped Promise put her hair up using her combs and hairpins. The cameo necklace Promise always wore now lay on a background of white, and it did look nice on the blouse with the high collar. Then the women hurriedly cleaned up after the morning meal.

Soon, wooden crates and burlap sacks were piling up on the cabin floor. Fanny thought Ben must have bought both trading posts out. There was something for them all. Small bags held peppermint sticks, black licorice, lemon drops, and horehound candy. Everyone received a piece of candy. Those who chose licorice were soon laughed at for their blackened teeth. Ben continued picking items out: lead pencils, boxes of wooden safety matches, safety pins, bottles of Tommyknockers Root Beer, a bag of corn to be popped, tins of condensed milk, peaches, oysters, beans, the green material Fanny asked for, and her coal oil. Ben handed to Promise what she thought was a blanket. Upon unfolding it, she found it to be a capote, a woolen blanket long enough to cover most of one's frame that also had a hood. "Oh, thanks. This will come in handy when the snow comes."

"That's what I thought when I spotted them," said Ben. "And I got one for myself, too."

He and the braves went back out to put the wagon away and feed and brush Milkweed. And there were more things in the wagon to tend to. But first he had some things for Fanny, all outdated but new to her—a Sears, Roebuck, & Co. catalog, *The*

Godey's Lady's Book, a *Harper's Weekly*, and a letter. With both hands, Fanny firmly clenched the letter to her bosom, said, "I'll read this later." Fanny and Promise put crates and sacks into the lean-to to be divided up later.

The twins were snitching candy every chance they had, and then blamed it on their new pets and then giggled

---

Fanny noticed smoke coming out of the smokehouse. About then, Ben and the Indians came in.

Ben had spotted a deer and downed it and brought it back to butcher it. It was hung in the barn and skinned, and hunks of venison were thinly sliced into strips and now hung in the smokehouse over cords that Ben had attached to its walls. Hawk and Lone Horse built up a fire outside to cook ribs over. Ben brought venison chops and steaks to Fanny. She fried the steaks and melted grease. It was a nice break from pork and ham. When the steaks cooled, she layered them in jars and crocks. Then she poured the melted grease over the meat and sealed the lids. She did the same with small pieces for stews, and all the filled jars were stored in the root cellar.

The evening meal consist of venison chops, ribs, fried dumplings with melted butter, canned beets from the root cellar, fried potatoes; and for dessert, Fanny served thick slices of bread spread with berry preserves with rich cream poured over it.

Hardly anyone at the table could move, being so full. "I haven't had so much fun cooking in a long time," said Fanny. She looked around and said, "What a mess we have made," and laughed.

Ben stood, stretched, looked at Frederick, and said, "Son, do you think you can find an empty burlap sack? We'll put the root beer in it and put the sack in the river to get really cold, and tomorrow night after supper we'll have cold Tommyknockers

Root Beer and pop some corn." Spirits were raised all around again. They were going to have a party.

"And about you men," he said to the braves. "You're welcome to share the hayloft with me. I'm sure Fanny wouldn't mind your ponies in the barn with Nelly. Nelly probably enjoys the ponies more than she does Milkweed. Have to say the mule was pretty good on this trip. He only nipped at one dog."

"I'm pleased to have them stay, and of course their ponies are welcome in the barn," said Fanny.

"We can sort rest of the crates and sacks tomorrow," said Ben. He turned to Promise and said, "You looked mighty pretty in your new clothes." Then he did something that was out of character for him: he hugged Promise. He whispered in her ear, "Hawk told me Stone Face is around. We all are going to be all right. Don't worry."

Promise wanted to put her head on his shoulder and cry. What a relief that he was home! She hadn't had a chance to talk privately with him about Stone Face. She wasn't so worried about herself; it was those who were around her, the Finnelys, their safety was her concern.

Ben and Hawk were out the door when Lone Horse spoke. "Yellow Star, looks good."

"How—?" Promise was speechless.

"I raced you. I remember," he said, and he touched his clipped feather. "No worry. Stone Face not know. Your name has traveled through the tribes. You are looked on as a great runner. You saved Father Fox's tribe their ponies. You fed the poor. You bring light to those who see only darkness. You are called Giver of Light. Stone Face wants kills. All the people know of his hate for Yellow Star. No harm will come to you or to your friends. We stay."

Promise reached for his hand, held it and said, "Thank you, Lone Horse. I'm proud to have you and Hawk as friends."

He left to join Ben.

Promise couldn't look at Fanny. *What does she think of me now?* She stood and began clearing the table and putting things away.

Fanny put the twins to bed all the while arguing with them. "No. Say no more about it. The pup and kittens will stay in the barn. They will be just fine. Ben, Hawk, and Lone Horse will keep them company."

Any other time, Promise would be laughing as she listened to their banter. Right now, she felt like she'd never smile or laugh again.

Promise helped Fanny with the many dirty dishes and skillets. She didn't know if she was embarrassed for her secret to come out or ashamed that she was caught in an untruth. Either way, she was unable to look Fanny in the eye.

Fanny washed, and Promise wiped. Fanny broke the silence between them.

"Promise, I knew who you were when I laid eyes on you the first time. And if I was in doubt, when you first gave me a smile, I knew I wasn't. Giver of Light, and that's what you do."

Promise kept on wiping the same dish didn't say a word. She felt so guilty for not trusting Fanny. All that went through her head was: *Don't tell white folks you have lived with the Indians, for they will reject you.*

Fanny reached down to Promise's hand, stopping its movement.

"Promise, I don't think any less of you for being with Indians. I have met some really nice ones and some not so nice, but that's in both races. It's in any race of people. I have been waiting for you to tell me your story. I came to think you didn't trust me enough to share with me. I don't know why or how you ended up with Indians. In the stories that came my way, none mentioned you being with your father. I am glad to see you with him. Ben seems to be a good and caring father—"

Guilt made her lash out. "He's not my father! What do you think of me traveling with a man I am not kin to?" Promise's knees gave out and she dropped onto a chair she was shaking, the idea of Fanny disliking her because she wasn't honest with her was devastating to Promise.

"I am surprised. But if you are with him, there's a reason for it. And it's probably a good reason. I'm sorry you didn't trust me to be your friend. Get ready for bed. It has been a long, eventful day and we're tired."

Promise watched Fanny wiped out the dish pan and checked the coals in the cook stove. She suddenly appeared older and sounded old to Promise. "I'll tend to the hearth," Promise said.

"That would be helpful. Thank you, dear," said Fanny. The hurt Promise heard in her voice was so sad that the tears she had been crying for herself changed to crying for Fanny.

Before Fanny turned, Promise had her arms around her and was sobbing on her shoulder. "I am so sorry, Fanny. I didn't want you to know I lived with the Indians, and they were so good to me. I was told by different persons I'd be shunned by any whites if they knew. And Ben just about became my stepfather for real, but my mother died before they were able to marry. They are long stories, and I am tired also. I will rest easier knowing you know, and there will be no untruths between us now. Please forgive me."

"Dear, Promise, I was looking on you as a friend and daughter, of course I forgive you."

Promise gave Fanny a hard hug, stepped back, and saw the moisture in Fanny's blue eyes. "It's good to have you for a dear friend. I have made new friends on my journey only to say goodbye later, but they stay in my heart and give me warmth. "Now, why don't you settle in your rocker closer to the fire and read your letter and I'll finish up what needs to be done."

Fanny did what Promise suggested, and retrieved the letter Ben had brought her from her apron pocket.

Promise thought of her mother, how she missed her, and wished she was there with her.

The next morning, Promise sent Frederick out to the barn to fetch her parfleche. She felt like a weight had been lifted and she now could be who she was. Fanny was busy at the cook stove when Frederick came in carrying the parfleche, followed by Frieda carrying two kittens, followed by the new Spot.

Fanny, her hand on her hip, said, "Is this a parade?"

"No," the twins said together.

"My kittens need something to eat."

"And my Spot is hungry."

The twins stared each other down, their identical chins jutting out.

Smiling, Promise reached for the parfleche and retreated behind the screen. She had thought about dressing in her doeskin but remembered that Stone Face was close by. Be best for her not to give herself away by the way she dressed. She slipped on her old clothes and met the new day with a smile and thankfulness. She heard Fanny and the twins. "No, the kittens are for the barn to catch mice," said Fanny.

Frederick was holding out for Spot to be a house dog.

"But, Ma, they need real food," said Frieda.

"Yeah," agreed Frederick.

"It's not working, kids. Your pets have all kinds of meat scraps and bones to feast on lying about out there on the ground," said Fanny.

"Oh, Ma," echoed the twins.

Promise smiled, *I will miss this family.*

Fanny was frying ham steaks in one skillet, potatoes in another, and eggs in another. Under Fanny's instructions, Promise mixed up baking powder biscuits. The table was set, and everything was ready when Ben, Hawk, and Lone Horse entered the cabin. The food disappeared fast.

"Ben, can we fetch the root beer now?" Frederick asked.

"Not yet, son. After supper, when we have our chores done," Ben said. "There's things yet to retrieve from the crates and sacks. And we want your mother and Promise done with their chores too so we all can sit and enjoy our treats together."

Fanny put the finishing touch to the clean-up from the morning meal and took off her apron. When Ben entered the cabin, the crates and sacks had been pulled from the lean-to and were waiting to be emptied.

Ben handed Promise a pretty box. She opened it to find a toilet set. Red roses on mother of pearl designed the back of the hand mirror and back of the brush with the pearl going down the handles. It was also on the wide part of the comb.

"Ben, it's beautiful," she said.

He gave Promise a strange look as he handed a wide-eyed Frieda a child's porcelain tea set. For Frederick, he had a small knife with a sheath. When Ben saw Fanny's face, he said, "Don't worry. I'll show him how to use it. All young lads need a knife, and all mothers need a keepsake book." He handed Fanny a decorated, leather-bound book.

"Maybe I should keep you here and forget about Herb. That reminds me. Herb said in his letter that he should be home before the snow starts. I am sorry you will miss him."

"Is that right, Ma? Pa's coming home?"

Fanny nodded her head at her son.

"He'll sure be surprised when he sees little Spot." He paused. "And he's going to be surprised when he doesn't see big Spot, huh, Ma?"

Ben looked at the Indians and said, "Sorry. I didn't know you when I left here, and I'm really glad to meet ya, but I don't have anything for you."

Lone Horse reached up and lifted his own hair. With his knife, he pulled the dull side across his hair. Not a word was said, and then Ben began laughing.

"I'd rather give you the dried meat than my hair. Is that okay with you?" asked Ben.

Hawk patted his friend on the back and laughed with the rest of them.

That evening, Ben kept his word to the youngsters. Frederick and Hawk fetched the Tommyknockers Root Beer from the river.

Fanny found the popcorn popper and readied it. "Don't think this has ever been used," she said. Corn was poured into the popper and, using its long handle, it was put over the fire in the hearth. The twins were on the floor in front of the hearth as close as they dared, waiting for corn to pop.

"Is it ever going to pop?" asked Frederick.

Ben, holding the handle in one hand and slowly shaking the popper, reached over and ruffled Frederick's wild hair and said, "In due time. In due time."

About then, everyone heard, Pop! Pop! Pop! Pop! The braves even got a little excited. Using Fanny's largest bowl, Ben tipped the popcorn into it and added more corn to the popper.

Everyone ended up sitting on the floor in a circle with a full bowl of buttered popcorn in the middle and glasses of root beer in hand. Stories were being told. Hawk and Lone Horse had a few, and of course, Ben had some. Even Promise had a story. She told of the lemons her mother made her rub over her exposed flesh to lighten it and how her aunt said she smelled refreshing. The twin thought that was really funny, and they leaned into Promise and sniffed.

"You don't smell like a lemon now," Frieda said, and they both giggled again.

Fanny said she really didn't have any stories, but Herb did; and she shared his with the group. "Maybe someday he'll get tired of searching for riches and return home to stay."

It was a fun evening, and after everyone had their fill of popcorn and root beer, it was time for bed. The men left for the barn, Fanny put the twins down, and Promise put a kettle on the stove for tea. It was a good time to visit with Fanny.

Fanny said to Promise, "If you get your new brush, I will brush your hair." While Fanny brushed her hair, Promise told Fanny everything that had happened to her since her mother's death. "I don't know what lies ahead. I look at it as another adventure for me. I've read about adventures of others; now I feel I'm living one. I want to help Ben find his son. As far as my father goes, I don't have any desire to meet him. I do miss Aunt Hattie and feel in my heart I'll see her again."

Promise had to brush away tears as she told her story. Some of the tears were from laugher, thinking of good times, and some from sorrow. Fanny proved she was a friend indeed; she shared her tears with Promise.

Ben came back into the cabin and nodded to Promise and said, "Is there anything I should know about?"

"You mean about you and me, Ben?"

"Yes," he said.

Fanny spoke up and said, "Ben, Lone Horse gave Promise away when he called her by her Indian name and spoke of meeting her. And I had heard of her. I wasn't sure if Promise was her. And when Promise spoke of you or to you, she seldom called you Pa or any name. I had a feeling, Ben, you and Promise were not who you said you were. But it wouldn't make any difference if you were father and daughter or not. The situation that brought you two together isn't for me to judge. I knew you were good people. If I took time and tried to figure out your situation, the devil would come in and feed me all the wrong notions. We only have one judge, and that's our heavenly Father. And I'd rather be your friend than your judge. I feel we each will come in front of our Lord, and His judgment is the judgment that will count, not mine, not yours. So why waste our time judging others when we can befriend and help others and enjoy their company like I have enjoyed Promise's and yours? Promise is like a younger sister to me or an older daughter. I feel she is kin. And you might not know it, Ben, but you played a role for my children. What you have done will go a long way, and they won't forget your teaching even if you didn't realize you were a teacher. And Promise and I have something for you."

Fanny went to her trunk and pulled out the shirt. She held it behind her back as she walked back to Ben. "I am sure glad you took a liking to Promise's new clothes. We have one for you." She handed him the blue polka-dot shirt.

Promise tried to read the expression on Ben's face. He just looked at the shirt. He then held it up to his shoulders.

"Think it's going to fit fine. I was in need of another shirt. I've heard of mothers and daughters dressing alike but never fathers and daughters." He glanced at Promise, smiled, and said, "Or would-be daughter."

Promise, in good humor, said, "The Finnelys will all be dressing alike when Herb arrives home. Maybe we should come back for a visit at that time, huh?"

"I think there will be enough blue polka-dot in this cabin."

They all laughed. Ben gave Fanny and Promise a hug and thanked them for his new shirt.

Good-Bye Is a Sad Word

With the braves' help, Ben was able to process the deer hide. It was scraped and soaked in the river and stretched on a frame Hawk had built with scrap lumber he found. They took turns with the fleshing and removing hair. Ben related to Promise later how Frederick was underfoot and imitated what he saw Ben do. When they took a break, the braves went to the smoke house seeing to the meat. Ben and Frederick sat upon the top fence rail on the corral, where Ben taught the boy how to whittle.

"All the time I'm watching Frederick out of the corner of my eye," said Ben to Fanny and Promise. "He was holding his knife just like I was. He was very careful. I told him to never push the knife toward himself but always away from him. And we both whittled a point."

Ben kept a close eye on Frederick, making sure he was getting the hang of the right way to hold and use a knife.

"That's what men do, Ma, whittle a point on a stick," Frederick later told his ma.

While whittling was being done outside, a tea party was going on in the inside. Frieda had on her pinafore over her good, blue polka-dot dress. Even though it was hard to see, her fuzzy hair was tied back with a white ribbon. She insisted her ma and Promise dress nicely. Fanny dug deep in the trunk and came up with two bonnets and two lacey shawls for her and Promise and one pair of white gloves for them to share. The women left the cabin through the side door of the lean-to and walked to the front door and knocked.

Frieda was thrilled to see her company at the door. She graciously asked them in and asked to take their shawls and showed them to the table. One end of the table held the tea set. Its tiny, blue flowers seemed to float against the white porcelain. Frieda's rag doll was dressed in blue polka-dot. Her red yarn hair, held into pigtails with white ribbons, was propped up on the table. The fourth tea cup and saucer was sitting in front of it. Frieda served what she called 'cakes' on a small dish. She had taken a leftover biscuit, cut it in half spread preserves on the bottom half, and then put the top back on it and cut it in fourths. The tea in the little cups looked very strong.

The women, old and young, spread their white napkins over their laps. Frieda picked up her cup. She held up her little finger, as was proper for a lady to do, and her guests did also. She took a sip. So did the ladies. To their surprise, it wasn't tea but leftover root beer, very flat. Being a good guest, one didn't complain. They nibbled cake and sipped tea and had small talk. When it was time to go, the ladies thanked their hostess for the pleasant tea party. Everything was so good and tasty, and the ladies departed through the front door.

Fanny and Promise giggled as they went around to the side door and stepped lightly behind the privacy screen. They took off their bonnets, gloves, and shawls and returned them to the trunk. The first thing Fanny noticed after she folded the screen up and set it next to the wall was no Frieda in the cabin and the tea set still on the table, along with the rag doll, crumbs, and little spills.

She went to the door and called for Frieda; and when she answered, Fanny said, "Get your little behind in here and clean up your mess."

"But, Ma, the tea party is over."

"Not for you it's not," said Fanny, "until the mess is cleaned up. Then the tea party is over."

Over the evening meal of venison steak, boiled potatoes, gravy, and corn from the root cellar, Fanny asked Ben if he heard any news of the war.

"I didn't hear much at Dirty Pete's. But at Fort Robinson, I heard both armies were dug in around Petersburg, waiting each out, taking pot shots at each other. Thousands upon thousands have died on both sides." And he said no more on that subject. He did have something else to talk about: leaving in a few days.

That put a damper on the meal. Lone Horse spoke to Fanny. "If good with white woman, me and Hawk like to stay until your man comes."

Ben spoke up. "That's a good idea, Fanny. There's talk about Indians going on the warpath. With Lone Horse and Hawk here, you'd have a better chance of being left alone if any should come this way. If I didn't feel the need to move on, we'd stay here until spring. I want to be closer to Rapid Creek by then. I've heard my son is with Crazy Horse there. I heard of a cabin Promise and I can winter at past the hot springs area. If luck is with us, we can get an early start and be at Rapid Creek before Crazy Horse and his followers depart.

The next few days were busy getting ready to leave. Fanny was putting together supplies she thought they'd need. Ben tried arranging what Milkweed would be carrying. When he thought he had it figured out, Fanny came up with more items she thought was a must for them to survive the winter.

At night, the men retired to the hayloft; but the women were still busy sorting, changing, redoing, packing, and crying. Fanny took the time to braid Ben a headband for his new hat out of leather she had had rolled up in the trunk.

The last evening, Fanny fried three hens and made white gravy, mashed potatoes, peas form the root cellar, and baking powder biscuits.

"Ma, is one of these chickens Penny?" Frieda asked.

"Frieda, did I not tell you not to name our farm animals or fowl? If they cannot earn their keep, they go on the table," said Fanny.

"I don't want to eat Penny," Frieda said.

"Me neither, Ma," said Frederick.

"I'll tell you both what you can do. If you can pick Penny out of the platter of chicken, you don't have to eat that piece," said Fanny.

The conversation between Fanny and her children lightened the mood, bringing on giggles and laughter. When the peach cobbler was served with heavy cream, it was met with easy chatter between family and guests revealing incidents and bringing on laughter. The best incident happened between Moon, Spot, and Turk.

Spot thought he could chase Turk like he did the chickens. When Turk turned on him, the little guy whined and ran as fast as his little short legs could go, but he wasn't fast enough. When Moon came to his rescue—and it had to be Moon because Queen didn't have time for the pup—Turk's spread wings and his beak were all over Spot. Though Spot tried to run, he wasn't getting anywhere. Seeing Moon charging, Turk backed up, his long neck lowered, his red comb glowed, and his widespread wings made him look larger. He faced Moon.

Moon spread and braced her front legs and lowered her head, her teeth bared to face off with Turk. Spot, able to get his footing, scrambled out from under Turk, his little ears flapping and his tail between his legs. He ran up next to Moon, and then he turned and barked furiously at Turk. Turk took a hop forward, and Spot whined and scurried behind Moon and went under her belly. Moon stopped staring at Turk, peeked under her belly and spotted Spot. She started smiling and then, sneezing, lost her balance and fell on Spot. He yipped and crawled out from under Moon and saw Turk heading his way, and back under Moon he went.

By now, the laughter at the table couldn't be held back. Hawk rolled off the bench, hit the floor, and roared with laughter. Ben tried to hold his stomach in to calm it. The twins hit the floor with Hawk and rolled around with him. Lone Horse had tears running down his brown cheeks, and Promise and Fanny were leaning on each other to hold themselves up.

Taking a much-needed breath, Fanny wiped tears from her eyes and said, "Mercy. Mercy. I hurt from laughing."

"So do I," said Promise.

"I think we all are hurting," said Ben. "There are things yet to get done this night if Promise and I are to leave early. And, Fanny, I picked up enough staples for you and us, so you don't need to supply us."

"Well, Ben," said Fanny, "you have to hold up all winter. I am just trying to help Promise be prepared. It's not going to be a problem sending bread starter. It won't take up much room, and Promise knows how to use it. I can always make more butter for us. You need eggs, which can be protected in a bed of straw. Ben, there are so many things you need."

"Fanny," said Ben, "how is Milkweed to carry all this?"

"I am sure you'll think of something. Women come up with the notions, and the man's duty is to figure out how to make them happen," said Fanny.

Ben left the cabin shaking his head. The braves were right behind him.

Fanny and Promise got busy cleaning up. Frieda helped, and Frederick ran after Ben.

"The twins are going to miss you and Ben," said Fanny. "And so am I, but what has to be has to be. We have a lot to do ourselves tonight."

When Promise's head finally hit the pillow, she was exhausted, but her mind was busy. She didn't want to think about staying, and she liked the traveling; but most of all, she thought Ben, tough as he was, needed her. It's been grand being here, no doubt about that. But when Ben sees what else Fanny sacked up for him to load on Milkweed, he might just blow his new hat right off his head in frustration. Knowing Milkweed, if he thinks he's overloaded, he won't budge. It will be interesting.

Morning came quickly. Fanny was already up, busy at the cook stove. The aroma of bread baking was able to float a person right out of bed. Promise wrapped the shawl around her frame and joined Fanny. She heard the twins in the lean-to tending to the morning milk. She was going to miss the milk and cream and butter. She took a deep breath and set the table. She hoped to have time to bathe and wash her hair.

The men came in, and Ben said, "Fanny, I think I have it figured out how to travel with everything. With your permission to borrow your horse, Nelly, to use as another pack animal, Hawk has agreed to travel with us until we reach our destination. Then he will return with your horse."

"Ben, you can use or borrow anything I have. I knew you'd come up with a plan. There are a few other sacks and a crate or two to take with you also," said Fanny.

"No," said Ben. "There is no room on either your horse or Milkweed to add a stick, let alone more burlap sacks or wooden crates."

Fanny stopped stirring the oatmeal, looked at Ben, and said, "If you are taking the horse, take the buckboard, too."

She glanced at Promise and rolled her eyes, causing Promise to smile.

After the morning meal, the wagon was loaded. Promise did get a bath in the wash tub in the lean-to and was able to wash her hair with Frieda's help. Using the brush and comb, she was able to get the snarls out. She let it hang loose to dry while she dressed. From the parfleche, she put on her doeskin dress and leggings. She brushed her hair some more and then braided a scalp-lock on one side of her head and slipped the feather disk on and secured it. She felt at home in the doeskin dress. It was loose, not binding. From her neck hung the round, beaded emblem from Father Fox revealing the colors and insignia of his band that she was accepted into; and she rubbed her hand over it. Above it was the cameo locket. She slipped her knife and sheath over her belt. She packed her old clothes and her new clothes in the parfleche along with her new comb, brush, and mirror and also the nightdress and shawl Fanny insisted she take. She picked it up and delivered it to Ben. She saw Lone Horse staring at her; and she went over to him, touched his clipped feather, and then touched a half feather on her disk.

"Good race," she said.

Promise heard Frieda ask her ma if that was really Promise. About then, Frederick came running from the barn and slid to a stop, staring at the white girl in Indian clothes.

Fanny couldn't stop from staring at her either. She walked up to Promise and put her hands on her shoulders. "Promise, you are venturing on another journey. May all you see and all you hear be blessed to your heart. May you never know an enemy and all your friends be true." Then she gave Promise a long, hard hug.

Fanny turned to Ben and handed him the braided hat band. He seemed thrilled to receive it and slipped it over the hat's crown. Frederick saw the new hat band and took off. Terrible squawking could be heard from behind the barn. When Frederick returned, he was yelling, "Ben! Ben!" And running to Ben, he held up a long, white feather. "This is from Turk," he said, panting. "I had a heck of a time holding him down to pull out this feather."

Ben squatted down to be eye to eye with the lad and said, "Best feather I've ever seen, proud to wear it in my new hat." And he stuck it in the band. He ruffled Frederick's red mop of hair and stood up. "I hate saying good-bye, but our time is now."

Promise didn't have to carry any of her provisions except the usual bags hanging from her belt or over her head and shoulder or her neck.

Hawk noticed Promise's elk handle knife, and said, "Can you throw that knife?"

"Never was much good in throwing it, but I will tell you what. If you want to put up an object to test on, you throw your knife, and I will use this," Promise said, holding up her slingshot that was tucked into her belt.

"Can we all have a throw?" Lone Horse asked.

All eyes turned onto Ben. "A challenge is a challenge. Put a target on the smokehouse door."

Charcoal off a cold burned stick was used to make different size circles. A line was drawn in the dirt to stand behind.

Hawk threw first; his knife stuck the edge of the middle circle. Lone Horse's knife stuck above the mark, and Ben nailed the bull's eye. Promise stepped up to the line. She had a small stone ready and fitted it in the leather patch of her slingshot. She pulled both ends if the leather strings taunt, she twilled the slingshot above her head faster and faster. She let go of one strings, and the rock flew and hit Hawk's knife, knocking it off the target.

She turned to the standing men and said, "Looks to me like we are all pretty good at what we do."

Frederick yanked the fringe on Promise sleeve and said, "Can I have a turn, please?"

"Sure you can, if it's all right with your ma," said Promise.

Fanny looked at Ben, and Ben nodded his head yes. Ben drew up a shorter distant line for Frederick.

Frederick held his knife the way Ben had taught him. He lightly gripped the handle, moved his left foot forward, with his knees slightly bent. He held both arms straight out and pointed at the target, taking his time aiming. His right arm slowly swung up behind his head and ear. His left arm still out straight, he quickly lowered his right arm; and when it was even with his left, he let the knife go. It didn't hit the target, but it did stick in the door.

"Look, Ma! Look, Ben! Everyone look! I hit the door." Frederick beamed the biggest grin ever back at them.

Promise turned on the buckboard bench and waved back to the Finnelys and Lone Horse. She couldn't stop the tears, and she didn't want Hawk to see them. But it seemed he had his mind on the horse hitched to the buckboard. Moon was trotting alongside. Ben, Queen, and Milkweed were ahead. Promise could just imagine Ben still grumbling about their late start. It was Ben that delayed them. Couldn't pass up a knife throw. And she had to show off with her slingshot. She smiled, remembering how he pulled her away from Fanny and the twins, everyone jabbering and sniveling and Ben trying to talk to Fanny over the commotion. Finally he yelled, "Hawk should be back in about three or four weeks."

Winter Camp

The dried, yellow grassland crackled under the feet and wheels of the party crossing over it. The leaf trees had dropped most of their vivid autumn leaves. A few, faded in color, hung on for a stronger wind.

The air nipped at Promise's nose. The sky had shown its winter hues of blues and grays, and the darkness came sooner and stayed longer. Fanny had shared her concerns with Promise. She hoped the snow held back until they reached their destination and Hawk made it back.

Where they were going, Promise didn't know; past the hot springs somewhere. They had a river to cross and two creek crossings, and when they saw a finger poking out of the trees, they were to find their way to it.

Hawk wasn't much of a talker. He did ask Ben about them not going into the sacred land of his people. Ben told him he wasn't planning to enter the Black Hills.

Promise had offered Hawk the use of her cape the first night they camped. He thanked her, but he had his own blanket in the wagon. When they came upon the river, its banks were gathering ice. The chilly air seemed to make the animals frisky. The dogs chased each other, and Nelly and Milkweed had picked up their pace. After crossing the river, Promise was able to see steam coming from the hot springs. They made camp below the springs, and when Promise fetched water, it was warm. "This is the place to make winter camp," she said to Ben.

"Yes, I agree and if we camp up above where the water is hot, we'll have all the hot water we need. Tonight, we stay here. Tomorrow, we need to travel farther.

They followed a ridge, and the ground became rougher. Nelly had to work harder to pull the wagon. Everyone was walking now to give less weight to the wagon. They crossed a rocky creek, and the ridge leveled off until it met the ground. Ben kept gazing at the sky. Clouds were banking. He hurried his party along. When the next creek was crossed, the ridge showed itself again but this time on the east side of them. A dense timber line was on the west.

They had crossed a river and two creeks. Where was the finger that was to show them the way to the cabin? Ben and Hawk scanned the treetops. Promise studied the different trees: beautiful, full firs, rounded evergreens, and straight pines. Running her eyes up the trees where they connected with the pale sky, she spotted the finger.

"Ben! Ben, there it is the finger! Isn't that a finger, Ben?"

"Looks like a finger to me," said Ben. The timber line appeared to be compact, not opening an inch to pass through. The party kept moving alone, seeking a break to enter by.

A trail appeared wide enough for the wagon to enter. They followed the trial downward as it twisted through the forest. The wagon tipped this way and that way as it bounced over dead fall jerking Hawk about. He finally alighted and cleared what he could to help the wagon pull easier. Without any warning, suddenly, they were face to face with a rock barrier. Huge granite slabs and boulders towered over them. The trail followed the base of the barrier to the right. When it curved, it separated, like it had broken apart; and the trail went through an opening that led to a meadow. And the rock formation continued onto the meadow and curved back onto itself. And there was the cabin, tucked below the giant, finger-shaped granite.

Promise stopped, taking in the new sight. She had never seen boulders as big and oddly shaped as these, and the slabs appeared to grow out of the ground. She cocked her ear and thought she heard gurgling, and she walked toward the sound. She was thrilled. Water came down from rocks above, forming a waterfall, and it splashed into a creek. She followed the moving water to a small pond, and the creek picked up again at the other end of the pond and faded into the timber line. She turned to back to the cabin and saw it from a different view. She was surprised to see it was a fairly large cabin with two front doors facing south. It had two windows, one on each side of a door, and was protected in back by tall and wide boulders. The fireplace chimney was built about halfway up.

She saw Ben and Hawk unloading the wagon, and she ran to them.

"Ben, there's a creek close by and a small pond below. Wait for me. I'll help. Moon, where are you? You get back here." She yelled for her roaming dog.

The cabin was a surprise, period. One front door opened on a well-worn, wooden floor; a hearth on the north wall; two folded army cots hanging from pegs; and a table, small bench, and a chair were under the kitchen window. Promise couldn't believe she was looking at a small cook stove. Different-sized skillets and pans and pots hung on the wall next to it, and a shelf holding dishes and a bucket hung down from a beam. The second door was wider and opened onto a dirt floor, an empty space except for a rope tied from the south wall to the north wall, which separated it from the wooden floor. How crazy was this?

The place looked solid. She couldn't see any holes dug or chewed in anyplace. She wondered just how long the cabin was vacated. There were no signs of anyone returning, but would others like them show up to spend the winter?

Already, crates were stacking up and sacks lay against the wall. Where was one going to store everything?

Promise came up with a good idea, or a notion as Fanny would say. As the crates were being emptied, she stacked the crates on their side up against the wall by the cook stove. The top of the crates created a work area with storage shelves underneath.

Fanny had all kinds of surprises for the travelers that they didn't know about: canned vegetables, preserves, and honey from her root cellar; a big bowl; wooden spoons; and many candles. Seeing some material, Promise pulled it out; and it was an old, flannel sheet with big holes in the top. And twine was threaded through the holes and the ball of twine tied up with it. A note pinned to it said, "Everyone needs privacy. This is a privacy curtain. Love you both. Fanny."

This is great, thought Promise. She'd be able to have a wash now.

Tears sprang to Promise's eyes, and she thought: *What a wonderful, thoughtful woman.* Drying her eyes, she got back to unloading and finding places for everything. Rags were also stuffed here and there. Fanny once said, "You never can have enough rags." There were some rags large enough to use for toweling.

Hawk brought in Promise's parfleche and bedroll. She looked around, and she got another idea. With Hawk's help, they lifted down the cots from the wall. The one she'd be using was put against the north wall, next to the hearth; and the other cot was put alongside the rope on the other side of the hearth. She'd ask Ben to hang the privacy curtain kitty-corner. She set a crate next to the cot and put her toilet set on it.

While the wagon was being unloaded, the big animals grazed. Before she knew it, darkness was on them. After Ben and Hawk finished emptying the buckboard, they brought in firewood for the hearth and the cook stove. Ben said they'd take the animals to water. The dogs entered, panting. They must have been running all about. The other door opened; and Ben, leading Milkweed, walked through, with Hawk and Nelly behind them. Ben opened the oat sack and gave each a handful of oats.

Seeing her look, he said to Promise, "They need shelter, too. And when winter hits hard, we'll be glad to have the warmth that will come off of Milkweed."

That answered any questions Promise had.

Promise had Hawk take the bucket to the creek for water; and she started a fire in the cook stove, and Ben started one in the hearth. None of them realized how cold it was. Being so busy, they didn't feel the chill.

Promise began putting a meal together. In a bigger pot, she added water; and when it began to boil, she put diced potatoes in and added some of their dried venison and dried berries from her own bag. Hawk had his own bag, but he'll need his when he leaves. She mixed up dumplings and added them to the pot. Ben and Hawk, sat in front of the hearth, talking and having a smoke. Promise put out their utensils and plates and pulled up another crate to use as a chair. She had Ben open tinned peaches. But she asked him to cut the tin over a pan and make the cut about a half inch from the top and pour the juice and peaches in the pan and then cut the same off the bottom. She rinsed out the ends and used them as candleholders and set them on the table along with a sugar loaf and a sack of salt.

After they had eaten, Promise gazed at the dirty pot and dishes and wondered out loud if it was too dark to go to the creek. She'd do the dishes in the morning. Hawk jumped up from the crate and went out and came back in carrying a basin, a big smile on his face.

"Fanny woman gave me this and this"—he held up a bulging sack—"to give to you in new home."

The sack held soaps, and Fanny had written on each the purpose of it. Promise couldn't wait to start on the dishes. She poured water into the basin and set on the stove to heat. Promise sliced an amount of dish soap into the heating water. Ben walked through the door. He carried a new bucket, and it was filled with water.

"Will surprises ever cease?" asked Promise, smiling and taking the bucket from Ben.

Ben brought forth the hand hidden behind his back and said, "Not yet," and set a lamp base on the table. He trimmed the wick, added coal oil, lit it, and slipped a glass chimney over the flame; and Promise had light to work with.

Hawk laid out his bedroll in front of the hearth. Ben laid on his cot, his Hudson Bay blanket over him and Queen on the floor beside him. Promise, behind her curtain, undressed and slipped on the nightdress. She hung the doeskin up on a peg alongside her white-people clothes. The open end of the crate held her winter moccasins, leggings and her drawers.

Sitting on the cot, she brushed her hair and gave thanks for their safe travel and for Hawk's safe return trip. Pulling back the curtain enough to reveal the hearth and to receive heat, she lay with her head toward the hearth, using her capote as a pillow and her blanket over her. Her hand pet Moon on the floor beside her as she fell asleep.

Early the next morning, the men were already up and out. Promise dressed in her doeskin and thought she'd try her hand at baking biscuits in the small oven. Opening the oven, she found a tin sheet. Anything can be baked on that. She put back the skillet she had planned on using. She mixed baking powder biscuits and dropped them by the spoonful onto the tin. She wasn't sure about the oven's heat and checked it probably too often, letting too much heat out. She fried side pork, and when the men came in, she fried eggs. The biscuits were a little too brown and a little black on the bottom. After Fanny's butter was spread over them and preserves were added, everything tasted just fine. The dogs ate the extras that Promise made sure they'd have.

Hawk was ready to go. Promise had taken her knife and cut off a lock of her hair. She tied the lock with a fringe cut off from her sleeve and gave it to Hawk to give to Fanny.

"Tell her to put this in her keepsake book to remember me by."

"No one needs anything to remember you by," said Hawk sheepishly as he reached for the lock of hair.

"That's a sweet thing to say, Hawk. And thanks for all your help," said Promise, and she gave him a quick hug.

Nelly hitched to the wagon; Ben checked with Hawk, making sure the brave had all he'd need for his return trip to the Finnelys cabin. He crawled up on the wagon bench with Hawk to ride out with him to the edge of the timber. Queen rode in the wagon's bed. "Promise, I'm going to scout out the area, see what game is around. Be back later," Ben said.

Not one to sit and think, Promise had things that needed tended to. Supplies still needed a place to go. Tinned condensed milks were stacked in the shelves made by the crates. The other tinned foods like peaches and beans also went onto the shelves. Ben will have to think of something to keep what meat they had and the eggs and butter cool.

The dirt part of the cabin seemed cooler as she walked around in it. Milkweed was tethered outside to graze. If anything was to be put in that part of the cabin, it needed to be secured against Milkweed. Was that possible?

A pot of dried beans was simmering on the stove. Later, bits of side pork and diced onion would be added to the pot. Looking about, she found a sack of cornmeal. Cornbread would be good with the beans.

She washed the windows inside and out. She took a burlap sack and after it was washed and dried she cut it to make curtains. She hung the curtains on twine tacked across the top of each window.

Dressed warmly, she and Moon ventured outside. She checked on Milkweed, he was busy chewing grass, and ignored them.

Looking for something to use as a broom, she wondered which bough would work better, a pine or an evergreen? There were trees west of the cabin and at the meadow's edge. She browsed the closer trees like she was in a bookstore. On a lopsided evergreen she spied a promising looking branch. She pulled on it and looked at all sides of it, then whacked it off with her knife and gave it a shake. Her shopping done, she went back to the cabin to try out the new broom. She labored on it until it had a straight bottom, and it worked liked she had hoped. After heating a pan of water, she had a wash behind her privacy curtain.

Ben returned home to curtains on sparkly, cleaned windows, clean floor, and the smell of beans cooking and cornbread baking. The table was set with the usual, and a can of molasses was added.

He shared with Promise what he came across while scouting out the area: lots of deer tracks and small animal tracks, a skunk and a fox, a bobcat and a mountain lion.

"That tells me we keep a good eye out and make sure we know where our dogs are at all times. And Milkweed, of course, he'll raise a ruckus. But he'd still be in danger. You be alert and careful when you go to the creek. I know Moon will be with you, but even take Queen with you. If Moon or Queen begins acting strange and nervous, make your way back to the cabin. No running, just a steady walk."

"I'll keep that in mind, Ben. But do you have any idea were we can put our perishables? There's a cooler corner on Milkweed's side." Seeing the look she was receiving from Ben, she added, "I know that's out. Nothing is safe with him."

"I'll see what I can come up with, Promise, about keeping our perishables cooled down."

"This cabin was so well thought-out a person could walk right in and have mostly everything one needed right here except for food," said Promise. "It's like every time a person left, they cleaned the place up and left something behind for the next person. I am sure those pots and pans and the skillets were not all brought in at the same time. Some have been well used, and others show no wear. The hearth is the oldest thing here. The floor and this window are older than the other window. I am thinking that this floor was also dirt at one time."

Ben lit his pipe then said, "As you know, Buffalo Warrior, Isaiah, told me about this cabin. And it is old. Anybody and everybody are welcome here. There are two rules, you depart, leave a clean cabin behind and something useful for the next person. You don't need rule one because it comes down to entering a clean cabin and leaving a clean cabin and sharing. It seems repairs are done where needed. I haven't seen any signs of unwelcome varmints in the cabin. Very unusual for any cabin being left empty for any length of time, but then I don't know the time spread between occupants. I plan on looking over the outside and seeing if any repairs are needed. I want to do it before the snow. You look around inside and decide what we might leave behind."

"I think, Ben, we'll have a lot to contribute to the cabin, thanks to Fanny's generosity."

Ben did figure out a way to keep the perishables cool. He used a rope, a crate, and a burlap sack and a strong pine tree limb.

"If we have no tree-climbing animals close by, we'll keep our food in the tree I got picked out. I feel like I can go on a hunt and not be so wasteful now that we have a place to store meat and whatever you feel needs to be cooled, Promise."

She was happy with what she had accomplished that day; she was tired, a good tired. When she retired for the night, her thoughts buzzed around in her head like a busy bee. Promise took pride making the cabin more homelike. In this home, the mule was welcome and had his own space. She didn't know anything about mules, but she was pleased to learn they didn't mess where they lived, so she didn't have to be concerned about shoveling out Milkweed's space. Ben had told her she'd be thankful for the heat from Milkweed during the cold times, so she guessed they would receive heat off the dogs, also. She'd probably miss this place when they departed.

Ben was anxious to meet his son. Promise prayed Green Raven would forgive and accept his father. Her fear was he wouldn't. Then she thought she also should forgive her father. She couldn't say she hated him for not seeking her. She was just very disappointed.

She had to remind herself that she didn't know his circumstances at that time. There was still something she wasn't dealing with that infected her decision for not going to Fort Laramie when she had a chance. Was her father a good man, a decent man, a kind man? Would her living with the Indians—and that was sure to come out at some point—affect how he saw her, even after she'd been in his home? She said to herself, "He must have been a good man or my mother wouldn't have married him. Then she'd ask herself, "If he was a good man, why did his sister choose to follow her brother's wife out of his life?"

Promise had only had two men to compare him with: Father Fox and Ben. Father Fox would never forsake his daughter. Ben did forsake his son but was trying now to make amends and traveling all over this great land in his search for him. He wouldn't stop until he found his son. Her mother chose Ben to be her new father. She saw the good in him.

Promise missed her aunt, and she was sure she'd see her again some day, and she drifted off to sleep.

When Promise awoke, the fire was low and it was cold in the cabin. She wrapped the shawl around her shoulders, slipped on her moccasins, and put logs in the hearth. Queen opened an eye. Ben coughed and pulled his blanket over his head. Moon stretched and yawned, gave her body a shake, and stuck her nose under Promise's hand.

"Shh. Do you want to go outside?" Promise asked Moon. "Queen, do you want to go out too?"

Queen stretched, wagged her tail, and headed for the door. Promise opened the door to a white blizzard. Both dogs shot out the door, did what they had to do, and were quickly back inside.

Seeing Milkweed, his big head hanging over the rope, she knew if he tried he could have the rope down in a blink of an eye. She lifted the rope, retrieved his leash, tied it on his halter, and led him outside. He took off at a trot, pulling Promise with him; and when he stopped, Promise ran into him. He pulled her all the way back to the cabin, and both of them were glad to be in shelter.

Ben sleeping in was unusual for him. Perhaps he had a sleepless night. The weather change might have affected his bad leg. The coffee he bought at the trading post was already ground. She dropped a scoop into the coffee pot for Ben, and she planned on having tea on this cold morning. Leftover cornbread with molasses over it sounded good, with crispy side pork and a few fried potatoes. While she was thinking of good things to eat, she thought about mixing up bread dough using the bread starter Fanny gave her. By suppertime, they'd have fresh bread.

The smell of coffee brewing soon had Ben up. He didn't know why he slept in like he did. Promise noticed he favored his bad leg.

"No harm done, Ben, she said. Be a good day to read a good book if only I had one. Even a bad book would be good on a day like this."

She laughed at her wit.

They took their time eating, dropping morsels to the dogs, and reminiscing. For their short time together, they seemed to have a lot to reminisce about.

Ben wasn't sure how he was going to keep Milkweed fed if he was going to be cabin bound. A handful of oats once or twice a day was the limit on oats. It was embarrassing to watch Milkweed watch them. His head hung low over the rope. His ears even hung low. His big, brown eyes mournfully looked up at them as he watched them eat and watched them drop pieces to the dogs.

"Ben, you better think of something," Promise said. "I know he is sighing, and I think he groans every time the dogs get a bite. This is pitiful. Do you think he'd eat some cornbread?"

"Guess we can only try," said Ben.

Ben cut a hunk of cornbread and took it over to the mule. Milkweed raised his head and nibbled at it; and his ears perked up, he held his head high, looked at Ben, and lifted his hooves like he was going to dance, made a few turns, arched his tail toward Ben, and let out gas.

Ben glared at the mule. Waving his hand in front of his face, he tried to push the stench away. Like she had no bones in her frame, Promise slid off her chair and crumpled onto the floor. Her laughter was contagious. Soon, Ben doubled over with laughter. Milkweed came back to the rope to nibble more of the cornbread Ben had dropped after Milkweed gassed him. The dogs thought playtime was going on, and they got into the mix, barking and jumping on and over their masters. They were so weak from laughter they were unable to sit up.

Sitting on the floor, they wiped their eyes. Promise still giggled. She tried to stand only to fold over onto the floor again.

The blizzard blew itself out. Ben opened the door to bright whiteness. He told Promise he'd take Milkweed out and help him find grass and let the dogs run.

"Oh, by the way, Promise, you mind straightening my cot up for me? Thanks."

And out the door he went with the mule and dogs.

Promise put water on to heat and went to Ben's cot. *What is there to straighten up?* she thought. She took off his blanket, gave it a shake, and spread it back on the cot. He was also using his capote as a pillow. She picked that up to refold it and found a book under it.

"Ivanhoe! Where did this come from?" she asked nobody.

Opening it, there was writing on the first page. "To Promise with love. Frederick Franklin, Frieda Francis, and Fanny Finnely. P.S. And from Herb too."

Promise was speechless. She caressed the cover and thought, *Ben was just waiting for the right time to hand this over to me.* She glanced out the window; saw Ben, the mule, and the dogs; and said, "Yes, Ben, this is a good day to read a book."

Visitors

It was a long, cold winter; but Promise adapted like she always did. Ben's bad leg gave him fits. Promise offered and offered the willow bark powder from her bag to Ben, but he'd refuse. She got upset with him. It wasn't like he never tried the bark powder, and he acknowledged that it helped the ache. His leg ache worsened, and finally, he agreed to the tea. Promise mixed him up the tea with dried berries and bark powder. He sipped it.

Then he jumped up and said, "I feel better already."

If Promise was a man, she'd have hit him. She said, "Just drink it and hush up!"

The dogs were getting fat and sassy. Milkweed even had a temper and was mad all the time. He didn't like being shut in. And he was eating more and more people food. He even tried eating the curtains on his side, and that didn't help his gas problem. There were times when the door had to be opened to let the wind and cold air burst through to blow the smell out.

The meadow was pretty in white, and the boughs of the pines and evergreens looked like they were covered in sparkly sugar. The pond had iced over. The creek still ran, so there was no problem fetching water. Promise and the dogs played on the ice. It was so funny to watch the dogs hit the ice on a run and then try to stop. Promise had her tumbles too, and black and blue marks to show for it. Milkweed still didn't like the dogs; but he thought he should be able to do what the dogs did, and he wanted to go on the ice. Ben was fearful the ice might break under the mule's weight and didn't allow Milkweed on the ice.

Milkweed saw a chance one day, and he took it while Ben had his back turned. Like the dogs did, Milkweed hit the ice on a run. His belly hit, knocking the air out of him. *Whoosh!* His legs flew out, and he sprawled out on the ice. He spun around and around until he hit the opposite bank. Like he was in a daze, he didn't try to get up until the dogs started barking at him. He bared his teeth at them and tried to get his footing, and he kept falling down either on his rump or his nose. Promise tried calling the dogs away. She knew if Milkweed ever made it up, those dogs were in trouble. Even though they were just playing, he wouldn't be.

Between Ben and Promise, they were able to help Milkweed on his feet by sliding him across the ice to a better place to help him up. He never acted like he'd want to go on the ice again; and every chance he had, he'd try to nip a dog.

The days kept Promise busy and Ben hunting. The nights were long. Promise read *Ivanhoe* forward and backward and even read to Ben. Nights after she'd go to bed, she'd see him in front of the hearth, on the chair from the table, whittling and deep in thought. By morning, there was no sign of whittling from the night before; but the good smell of cedar was in the air. She always had tea with the willow powder on hand ready for him whenever he wanted it. He did tell her once again it helped with the ache in his leg.

They ate a lot of small game. Ben gave Promise rabbit pelts to do with what she wanted. She had everything she needed to process the hides from her bags. She scraped, rubbed, and stretched the skins; and she kept the fur on the last four. She knew Christmas had to be getting close. She felt it in her bones. She wanted to make Ben a pair of mittens using her rabbit furs. To find out the size of his hands, she kidded one evening about his small hands. He told her he didn't have small hands. She said they were not much bigger than hers. He held out his hand, palm up; and she laid her hand against his.

Then she said, "You really do have big hands."

Before Promise had a chance to finish the mittens, they received visitors. They were alerted by the ruckus the dogs were making and saw two riders coming in. The sun was bright and reflected off the snow. Ben shielded his eyes to see who was riding in. The riders came in closer, and Moon took off, her tail wagging in friendship.

"Well, look who's here, Promise," said Ben.

Lone Horse and Hawk alighted from their ponies. They both had black paint smeared under their eyes to protect them from snow blindness. Each held a hand up in greetings.

"Come in. Come in, you two," said Promise. "I'll get coffee going. That will help warm your innards."

Promise didn't notice what had ridden behind Lone Horse.

"Is that something you want to butcher here?" Ben asked.

Lone Horse nodded his head and said, "If that all right with you, Ben."

"I have just the right tree to hang your game from."

"Let them warm up first, Ben," said Promise. "Suppose the ponies better come in to get a hand full of oats and warm up, too. I hope that mule doesn't get snippety sharing his space."

Over steaming coffee, Promise and Ben were told what was going on in the outside world. Indians talked of gathering to rid the white man from their country when the snow thawed. Promise asked about the Finnelys.

"Will they be safe? And is Mr. Finnely home yet?"

"Yes," said Lone Horse, "the man's home." He went on to say, "Finnelys are well liked by all good Indians. It's the no-good Indians who will attack anyone. And Stone Face is getting his own followers that hate like he does. As long as he's alive, you, Promise, will never be safe."

"Well, we cannot do anything about that now," said Promise. "Let's enjoy your stay."

The men went to tend to the deer. Promise went through their supplies, seeing what they still had. Supplies were getting low. She had baked bread that morning. The cabin still smelled of it. Hawk came back in carrying a rump roast. She took it from Hawk, rinsed it off, seasoned it, put it in a pot, added water, and put it in the oven.

"Hawk, you met Herb Finnely?" asked Promise.

He nodded yes.

"What kind of man is he?" Promise continued to ask.

He put his arm out and said, "About this tall."

That made him shorter than Promise and shorter than Fanny.

Hawk then made a small circle with his hands and said, "About this big around," and then touched his hair and said, "No hair."

Promise pictured a short, skinny, baldheaded Herb next to a taller, heavier, bushy-haired Fanny. She had to giggle a little, and then Hawk laughed with her.

Still laughing, she managed to ask, "Are you planning on smoking any of the venison?"

Again he nodded yes.

"Is it possible to smoke four rabbit hides that still have the fur on them to make them waterproof without Ben knowing?"

"Can do for you, Yellow Star."

Promise retrieved the furs from their hiding place and handed them to Hawk. "Don't let Ben see them it's a surprise."

"No worry, Yellow Star," said Hawk slipping out the door with the furs.

It's been awhile since Promise was called her Indian name; it sounded good to her making her smile as she went about her work in the cabin.

Before long Promise saw a fire blazing outside and she guessed it was to cook ribs over.

When the men walked through the door and Promise was handed the cooked ribs, she sent them right back outside. "Use that snow and clean yourselves up before you sit at my table."

"She's getting bossy, isn't she?" she heard Lone Horse say.

"Think she's getting cabin fever," said Ben.

When they came back in, they were cleaned and their leathers had been rubbed down with snow.

The potatoes had started to sprout, and carrots that were getting soft and wrinkly went into the pot roast. She made gravy using the roast broth. The small table was crowded with four, but they didn't mind. Promise took the notion from Fanny and served thick slices of bread spread with preserves and poured tinned condensed milk over the slices for each person. It was a joyful meal, and it was good to share with others and hear other voices.

The Indians' ponies were brought in, and Ben had a talk with Milkweed like, "Mind your manners." The men stayed out keeping the fire going and tending to venison. Tired, Promise went to bed. Promise heard the cold wind blowing outside, shivered and pulled her blanket up to her chin. When the snow melts it'll be time for spring, and they will be moving on. She'd liked to see this place then. See the willows and cottonwoods leaf out around the pond. Cattails will come to life at the pond, their flowering heads that taste like corn on the cob.

Thinking of food made her hungry; instead of rising and prowling around the cupboards for something to nibble on, Promise thought about what she'd fix for the morning meal. Chops and skillet cakes served with molasses sounded good

Promise woke to the smell of coffee. She yawned and stretched and saw that there was no Moon to greet her. She just knew Moon was probably sitting at Hawk's feet, the little traitor.

She learned the men had spent the night smoking venison strips and smoking their pipes. They took turns napping. Still, their eyes were red from sleeplessness and smoke. The men took to the chops and skillet cakes like there was no tomorrow.

"Have to eat to get warned up," said Ben.

"You all must be frozen, then," Promise said, as she poured more batter in the skillet. She didn't mind cooking for them since a little banter with them was fun for her. After the meat was smoked and dried, the braves wanted to push on. They were heading for a winter camp of their people. Hawk slipped the rabbit furs to Promise. She thanked him, gave him a quick hug, and quickly shoved the furs under her cot. She hated to see the braves leave. She did give them cornbread and skillet cakes to take with them.

Everything went back to order in the cabin. While Ben kept himself busy outdoors chopping firewood or checking or setting traps, Promise worked on the mittens. She used her awl to poke holes around the cut edges and her bone needle to sew the mitts using sinew. She also had laundry to do, and that took time. She only had the dish basin and the buckets to use. She had Ben hang a rope in Milkweed's space to use as a drying line. As long as Milkweed wasn't in, the laundry was safe on the line.

She caught up with what she had gotten behind on while they had company. The mittens were finished. The fur was in the inside of the mittens to keep hands warm; and the outside had been smoked and was waterproofed. She was pleased how they turned out.

When Ben opened the door one morning not long after the braves had left, he yelled for Promise to come and see who was coming. She rushed to the door. The dogs were raising a ruckus, and Ben had a big grin on his face.

That big figure on that big horse couldn't be any other than Buffalo Warrior. Promise ran out with Ben to meet him. She turned back to the cabin, rushing in to put the coffee pot on; and then ran back outside in time to see the men hitting each other on the back. When Promise ran up, Buffalo Warrior grabbed her and swung her around, laughing. She laughed, and Ben laughed. The dogs barked.

It was so good to see him. Promise quickly put a meal together; and knowing Buffalo Warrior's appetite, she made sure there was plenty on the table.

"How you like the cabin, Promise?"

"This cabin is great. What a place to spend the winter. It's sheltered from the wind by the tall rocks in the back and surrounded with trees. This would be a great place to live year-round," said Promise. Then she nervously laughed. "I guess you knew all that."

"Many of the immigrants packed too much in their covered wagons, and the wagon trail is lined with what had to be thrown out to lighten the wagon load," said Buffalo Warrior.

Taking another spoonful of beans and a bite of cornbread, he nodded to the cook stove. "I brought that in. It wasn't that big enough stove that me and my horse couldn't handle. The stove pipe had to come later. What do you think you'll be leaving behind?"

"I've been thinking about that," said Promise. "I know we won't be able to carry the big bowl or the basin or the buckets. The big bowl is great for mixing and raising bread dough in. As bad as I hate to leave them behind, I know others will benefit from what we leave. And the crates will meet someone's needs, along with the burlap sacks. I think we could take a few of them. Don't you think so, Ben?"

A routine fell into place. Ben and Buffalo Warrior chopped firewood, went hunting, processed pelts, visited, and smoked their pipes. Ben had stopped whittling, but the pleasant scent of cedar was still in the air.

Ben said to Promise one morning, "I think this is Christmas Eve. Did you and your mom and aunt do anything special?"

"We'd have a small tree with a few decorations and go to the evening services at the Union Methodist Church on Fourth Street, where my mother is buried now. After we returned home, we'd have something special to eat like oyster stew with thin soda biscuits. On Christmas morning, we'd exchange gifts we had made for each other. Aunt Hattie roasted a duck and had yams, mince meat pie, fresh bread—"

Promise stopped speaking because she had to lick her lips. She knew she was drooling. "We enjoyed our time together, holiday or not. So, since tomorrow is Christmas, I better think on what we'll have to eat. But first I have our evening meal to plan."

Promise was excited. She'd be able to give Ben his mittens. What about Buffalo Warrior? She didn't feel right not having something for him. A nice meal tonight and tomorrow would be her gift to him.

Ben had risen from the table and went into his supply sack and returned with tinned oysters and a can of tinned milk and handed them to Promise and said, "I held out tinned milk in case we ran out before this day. I really like oyster stew, and I know our friend here does, too."

"And so do I," said Promise. "I hope I remember how Aunt Hattie made it, plus mixing up soda biscuits."

After the men left the cabin Promise mixed up dough for oyster crackers. Using a Mason jar as a rolling pin, Promise rolled out the dough thinly, cut it in small squares, and laid them on the baking sheet. When the men came in the soda biscuits were ready to crumble into the oyster stew.

Before Promise retired for the night, she mixed up bread dough and set the bowl on the back of the stove to rise overnight. She decided that small, individual loafs would go nicely with their meal the next day, whatever it was going to be. She fell asleep thinking of what she'd be fixing for their Christmas meal.

Christmas morning was bright and calm. Promise had a venison roast cooking on top of the stove. Buffalo Warrior surprised her by bringing in a wild turkey. He had plucked it, but it had taken Promise most of the morning working to get all the pin feathers out. Discouraged by the tiny, black pin feathers just poking up under the skin, she finally skinned it. She laid a few strips of side pork over the breast to keep it from drying out and put it in the oven. She was happy to have two meats.

She dressed up for the day, slipping on her blue polka-dot dress and the nice, white blouse. She brushed and brushed her hair and tied it back with a strip off of a blue polka-dot rag that was in with the rags Fanny had sent along. The cameo lay at her neck, and she thought of the gift that Grandmother had given her. She added the turquoise necklace and earrings. She pinned a toweling rag onto her dress while she cooked. Opening the last jar of canned corn, along with the last of the molasses, she set them on the table. The last jar of Fanny's peaches she used to bake a cobbler. She still had tinned peaches and tinned milk saved back for when they begin traveling again, along with other staples. Since it was Christmas, she'd let go of a tinned milk because it was so good over peach cobbler. Another idea came to her: fried dumplings.

When Buffalo Warrior saw Promise, he smiled and said, "The girl is really a white girl."

Ben said, "Sometimes I wondered. But today she really is." Then he walked over to his gear, and stepped behind Promise's privacy curtain. A few minutes later, he came out from behind the curtain, a hand behind his back. Promise just stared at Ben. She looked over at Buffalo Warrior, and his mouth was agape. Then he hit his knee, and the laughter boomed out of him. Promise was having trouble containing herself. A bubble in her belly rumbled to be let out. Ben just stood there, his hand still behind his back, the back that was wearing a blue polka-dot shirt.

Promise whipped off her apron and stood by Ben. To Buffalo Warrior, she said, "You'll probably never see this again, unless it's a dress up affair like it is today; a matching would-be-father and his would-be-daughter. The shirt does fit nicely, don't you think, Buffalo Warrior." Then she giggled.

"Here, Promise, Merry Christmas." Promise looked at what Ben had handed her. Tears filled her eyes. "It's beautiful!" She held in her hand a figurine carved out of red cedar of a standing girl, her long hair tied back, dressed in doeskin with a sitting dog at her feet. "Oh, Ben! Thank you! All these nights, I thought you were just whittling to pass the time." She turned and hurried to her cot. When she returned, her hands were behind her back.

"Merry Christmas to you, Ben," she said, and handed him the mittens.

"Why, this is nice," said Ben. "I can really use these mittens, and look how nicely they fit." He gave Promise a hug. "Me and Isaiah are hungry, and the aroma in this cabin is making our mouths water. And he wants to leave us after we eat."

"So soon, Buffalo Warrior?" said Promise. "Well, you have a Christmas gift after we finish eating."

Promise busied herself making the gravy and putting the meal on the table. It was joyfully accepted by the men. She could tell by them smacking their lips. She was a bit saddened that their friend would leave shortly. She rubbed her fingers over the smooth figurine she was holding in her lap. She was thrilled with it.

After the noon meal, Promise wrapped small bread loafs, slices of venison and turkey, and strips of smoked venison in cloths.

"Merry Christmas, Isaiah," she said and handed him the food sack. "I'm so glad you stopped even for a few days. I hope to see you again."

He picked her up and gave her a bear hug, and she hugged him around his thick neck. "I'll miss you both. Travel safe," he said.

He put Promise back on the floor, shook hands with Ben, took his sack, and left on his horse. Ben and Promise stood in the cabin's door and watched him vanish around the rock barrier.

Ben circled Promise's waist, and they entered the cabin. Promise looked at all the dirty dishes and gave a sigh. She went behind the privacy curtain and changed into her doeskin dress. She heard Ben go out; and Moon nosed in on her and sat, her big, brown eyes looking up at her.

"Merry Christmas to you too Moon," Promise said as she patted her dog's head. "Come on. Let's see what I can find for you and Queen. Hopefully Milkweed has found grass under the snow."

That night, under her blankets on her cot, Promise spoke to her mother.

Mama, this is Christmas night. It came upon me before I knew it, which probably was a good thing because I didn't have time to dwell upon it. It wasn't like our Christmases in Elfreth's Alley. The house would be filled with baking smells, a small tree decorated with gingerbread men, cranberry and popcorn ropes, and cutouts. You wouldn't have candles on it, and it was still pretty. We'd go to the Christmas service and be joyful in our Lord. Then we'd exchange our gifts. It wouldn't make any difference where I'd be. The Holiday would not be the same without you and Aunt Hattie. But to be in Philadelphia at this time without you would have increased my grief. It was a good day. I give thanks for our Lord, Jesus.

The days grew longer and somewhat warmer; and one day, Ben came into the cabin and said, "Promise, start getting your belongings together. We'll leave in a few days."

And they did. Packs and pelts and her parfleche went on Milkweed. Ben believed they shouldn't put all their eggs in the same basket.

"Aunt Hattie used to say that same saying," she told Ben.

So Promise carried her bedroll. She had added the flannel curtain and the twine to her bedroll; plus she had wrapped soap that she had been saving back in one of her rabbit skins, and she had her own box of wooden matches. Her survival bags she carried around her neck and hung from her belt, and that was the one she put the cedar figurine in. She wished the box her toilet set was in was in her bedroll, but it went in the parfleche. Promise, carrying her spear, slowed and turned around; getting a last look at the cabin that served them so well. She cleaned and readied it for the next lucky person that came upon it. When all their belongings were packed and Promise saw the oil lamp on the table alone, she became melancholy. She had done her best to turn the cabin into a comfortable home for them. It held good memories. There were a lot of laughs and the company of good friends.

There was still snow on the mountain's peaks, but at the foothills, it was melting and fading away. The sun was out, but the air was still chilly. They arrived at a Lakota winter camp at Rapid Creek. Ben visited with the chief. Promise stayed back with the mule and dogs. She could see where lodges once stood but were gone now. Crazy Horse and his followers had also departed. Stone Face and his renegades had been hanging around, making those still in the winter camp nervous.

Ben and Promise followed the creek north, where they made camp. Ben was in deep thought. Promise prepared a meal for them and cleaned up after it. Taking Moon, she went to the creek and filled up the canteens with the clear, cold water. Back at camp, Ben was drawing three arrows in the dirt with a stick. One pointed north, one south, and one west. He looked up and saw Promise. Promise saw a very sad, disappointed man looking at her. She wanted to cry for him.

"We have three choices, and each one is a guess. I have no idea which way they've gone: north, south, or west. But I do know all the Indians will gather at Mateo Tepee sometime in late summer for the Sun Dance. We can make our way there now and take our time. I hear it's beautiful country, and Mateo Tepee, or Bear Lodge as the whites call it, is something for the eye to see. I heard the legend from Father Fox many years ago.

"He told me there were maidens picking flowers not far from the Belle Fourche River and not paying attention. Suddenly a giant bear was upon them and they ran and climbed up on a rock and prayed to the Great Spirit to save them. When the bear jumped at them, the rock thrust upward higher and higher. The bear tried climbing it. And again and again, he fell backward, leaving his claw marks on the sides of the rock, causing deep grooves. Now it towers over everything. It could be used as a landmark because it can be seen for miles. If one took a hankering and thought about traveling, let's say, straight south to Fort Laramie, the tower will be at one's back for a long ways."

"Why even bring that up?" asked Promise. "I haven't changed my mind."

"Well, Promise, we're in country neither one of us has ever been in. It doesn't hurt us to know what landmarks are around. We might need them to show us where we were to where we're going and know we are going in the right direction. I just used Fort Laramie as an example 'cause once I heard it was about straight south of the tower. Also, there's another landmark closer to Fort Laramie called Register Cliff. Isaiah and I carved our names on the cliff when we went through there as young men with the Fremont expedition."

"All right," said Promise. "What are we doing now?"

"I'm cold and going to put my capote on. You want yours? I'll get it off Milkweed when I get mine. Then I'm going to begin walking. That's what we do best."

Devastation and Separation

The plains' rolling hills were beginning to green up. Every place Promise looked, there were different hues of greens. West of her, in the far distance, groups of gray, egg-shaped, granite boulders towered over the forest beneath them.

Ben didn't have much to say about anything. He laid his traps out when they stopped for the night. He checked them in the early mornings, and if an animal was caught in one, they stayed over until Ben tended to the hide. If the traps were empty, they traveled on. Ben was able to add on to the winter pelts he had gathered while at the cabin. He felt easier to have something to trade if the need arose.

When looking for water, they followed animal trails. This time, the trail led into the forest. One could see yellow-green buds on the aspen trees. The evergreens were bright after the wash by melting snow from their boughs. The trail entered between two cliff walls, opening to a small meadow and a spring. She was glad to be around water. She found a nice spot where she was able to clean up. After feeling clean again, Promise heated up tinned beans and mixed up fry bread while Ben scouted out the area. When he returned, he was quiet, again deep in thought. Promise knew that when he was ready, he'd share his thoughts. He didn't have much of an appetite, and the dogs benefited from the extra fry bread and beans.

Promise was awakened by Ben in the false dawn. He whispered to her, "Just get your things together. Put your extra moccasins and what you can of your personal possessions in your bedroll."

Promise waited for him to say more, and he said, "Want to lighten Milkweed's load."

That didn't make sense to Promise. It didn't make sense that Ben was being mysterious. But she's been around him long enough not to ask questions. She added what she could to her bedroll: her tin plate and cup. Ben told her to take some dried meat out of the food sack and put it in one of her bags. She had her knife and slingshot on her and carried her spear.

Ben led Milkweed, with Queen at his side. Promise and Moon behind followed him, but not the way they had come in. He led the party through a cut ridge and down a steep overgrowth bank to the floor below. Huge boulders, tall junipers, and pine trees shared the area with patches of snow. Soon, they were climbing up slick and rocky slopes and down to meadows. Promise had a terrible feeling that they had entered the Sacred Black Hills forest. But why?

They found and followed a trail down another hill full of tall trees and thick brush and into a canyon. Ben thought the trail would lead them out of the canyon back to the plains and out of the forest. Promise spotted a spring, and she and Moon went over to it. Ben, Queen, and Milkweed kept moving. She washed her face and cupped her hand and sipped the cold water from it, taking her time. Catching a second breath, she gazed at the sun through the limbs of spruce trees. It was like the sun was winking at her through the slight movement of the boughs.

A terrible roar bounced off the canyon walls. The hair on her arms and neck stood up and chills went up her back. Moon growled, and hair stood up along her back. Promise quickly rose. Her capote fell to the ground. She heard fierce barks coming from Queen. Milkweed ran past her braying and kicking, and the packs looked like they were about to come undone. She headed to where Ben went. She shielded her eyes from the bright sun blinding her from over the far tree line. She thought the sun was still playing with her eyesight. She couldn't be seeing what she thought she was. When Moon ran forward, barking, it brought her out of her trance, and Promise called her back. She saw Queen run to help Ben but was slung back, and she hit the ground hard and laid there. The roars came and came like a violent windstorm howling through the canyon. Finally, Promise was able to digest what was happening in front of her.

A huge, brown bear and Ben wrestled. The bear used his teeth and claws, and Ben used his Bowie knife. Blood flowed and flew into the air. Without another thought, Promise tightly gripped her spear and hastened to Ben's aid. Before she got to the bear, it was on top of Ben, pinning him to the ground. Ben stabbed the bear anyplace he could hit. Furiously, the bear roared. His massive head waved back and forth. Promise came from behind the bear and, with all the strength and might she had, she leaped. When she landed on the bear's back, she drove the spear into his thick neck. He screamed and shook his loose skin, throwing her off. She landed hard and had the air knocked out of her. Moon straddled her in protection and growled at the beast. Grasping for air, Promise noticed the bear wasn't moving. Neither was Ben.

She used Moon to help her up. She used caution and crept forward to the bear lying on Ben. She heard Ben moan and hurried to his side. His head, one arm, and part of his chest were visible and streaked in red. She didn't know whose blood was where, but likely it was blended together.

"Ben? Ben, can you hear me? Please, Ben, say or do something to let me know you're alive."

She couldn't help the tears falling, and they were falling on his bloody face. One of the dogs whined. Turning, she saw Queen pulling herself toward them. Moon went over to her and licked her face and, using her nose, tried to push her along.

"Promise," she heard Ben whisper, "you have...to get out of here now."

"I cannot leave you, Ben. You need help. Are you able to push the bear if I pulled so we can get him off of you?"

"No. Promise, I can't. I think I'm busted up pretty bad. Look. See that tree line at the edge of the plains. Do you see anything there?"

The canyon opened up at the edge of a tree line that held the plains back.

"I see Indians. Ben, they could help us."

"No. That's why I took this way, hoping to get past them." He coughed up spots of blood. "I spotted signs of them last night. I...believe that is Stone Face and his renegades." His breathing was shallow, and he coughed again. "I was looking for Indian signs, not paying attention to what was close to me until Milkweed jerked his leash from me. Then it was too late. You...you...cannot stay here, Promise. Your life is in peril."

Promise stood, and she cried and pushed and pulled at the dead bear.

"I cannot, cannot, cannot leave you!"

Anguish was eating her up. She knew if Stone Face got to her she'd be no help to Ben. She didn't know if Ben would live.

"Promise, let me go in peace, knowing you got away. Promise, do that for me," begged Ben in a weakened voice. "Help Queen over to me, please. I know she's unable to go with you."

It was all Promise could do to hold back her tears and the shakiness of her voice. She knew how an animal responds to the tone of one's voice. She carefully lifted Queen, and Queen looked her in the eye through her wet eyes and whimpered.

"I'm sorry, Queen. Don't mean to hurt you. I'm putting you next to Ben, where you belong."

"Promise, you'll have to go up the canyon wall, pick your spot. That's the only way you'll be able to get away. You can't outrun the horses."

He took a shallow breath. "Promise, you are a daughter to me. If you ever...see my son, tell him...I'm sorry...Are they coming, Yellow Star?"

"Yes," Promise said, sobbing. "Please, Ben, don't make me go."

"Go to Fort Laramie to your family. Give your father a second chance."

Ben had trouble keeping his eyes open. His one free hand lay on Queen. He slowly, with effort, raised it in a slight wave; and it fell back on Queen, who didn't move.

Promise trembled as she rose. She saw horses coming, not hurried. She studied the west canyon wall. It was steep, but one slim strip wasn't as steep as the rest. But it was higher, and more rocks jutted out and brushes grew out of crevices. She glanced at Moon, who watched her with trusting eyes.

Can Moon climb the wall? She gritted her teeth. Don't think! Do!

She reached behind her and adjusted her bedroll.

One rider out in front from the rest kicked his pony into a gallop, raised his spear, and yelled, "Kill! Kill!"

Promise knew who he was.

With one last look at the man she had spent months with and learned to love, she quietly said, "Love you too Ben."

"Yellow Star"—she heard Ben's faint whisper—"if by a slim chance I survive, I...I'll seek you. Go."

Moon beside her, they took off to the wall. Stone Face screamed at her, waved his spear, and whipped his pony to move faster. Promise helped Moon get her footing and pushed her upward; then she grabbed rocks or brushes whatever she was able to get a hand hold or a foot holds on. Moon loosened rocks that came down on Promise as she fought for holds for her paws.

"Go, Moon. Up. Up. Good dog. Keep going."

Promise glanced down and saw Stone Face climbing toward her. She hastened and deliberately loosened rocks to fall on the climber below. If her mind wasn't in such turmoil, she'd grin every time she heard a yelp. It did make her feel like she was closer to the top and away from danger. She witnessed with relief that Stone Face slid down on his stomach. He screamed at the other braves, who were milling around the bear and Ben. They had no interest in her. They might later if they decided to search for her.

She was ahead of Moon when she reached the top and was able to pull Moon up onto the canyon ledge. For Stone Face to get to her, he'd have to go back from where he started and make his way to the top of this canyon from the plains. If she traveled on the plains, she'd be caught out in the open. The only thing for her to do was stay in the forest out of sight.

She ran along the canyon's edge until she saw an escape route back down for her and Moon. She wanted to keep going. She didn't want to stop. To stop meant to think, and she wasn't ready to think or to remember. Tears betrayed her even when she tried not to think of Ben or poor Queen.

Run, she did, after stumbling over dead-fall and being easily tripped by the smallest things she realized she was exhausted and endangering herself, and Moon was laboring. Moon was going to be her anchor, her force to keep her mind on track to focus on what had to be done to survive. If she let her emotions take over and fall in a heap like she wants to, it could easily be the death of her and probably of Moon. Promise felt she was on the edge of her sanity. She realized she was exhausted. "Lead me to water, Moon."

Moon stared at Promise and gave her one of her silly smiles. Finally, Promise lifted the canteen up and shook it in front of Moon.

"Water. Where is the water, Moon?"

Moon took off. Promise had to run to keep up with her, and it was just a short distance to a brook. A secluded spot protected by evergreens, pines, and the mighty spruce and a shelter of rocks formed a hideaway. In a circle of stones she had arranged, she built a small fire using dry sticks for less smoke.

Promise took dried venison out of her bag for her and Moon who was stretched out next to her. Moon hardly raised her head to take the food out of Promise's hand. Promise couldn't swallow the meat. She unrolled her bedroll, slipped her cloak over her shoulders, and rested her chin on her knees, watching the small flames dance. She wondered if Stone Face even dared to enter the sacred forest. It wasn't like she wanted to; she had no other escape route. Suddenly, she thought of Milkweed and wondered what happened to him. Where was he? Then the sobs came, and she couldn't stop the tears. Her whole body shook. She had no control. She tried blocking the image of Ben in the bear's clutches, of Queen being thrown and hurt. She cried for days. She couldn't eat or sleep. She crawled to the brook, sipped the cool water, rinsed her face and sore eyes, and believed she had no tears left…and then cried more. Moon pushed her nose against Promise many times, and Promise wrapped her arms around her dog and sobbed into her furry neck. Finally, she fell into a deep sleep.

When she awoke, she was cold, and there was snow on her. She thought the fire had gone out. She reached for the blanket, and all she felt was her cloak. She opened her eyes and saw she was lying beside the brook, and she held the cedar figurine in her hand. She had no idea how long she'd been sleeping, and why by the brook? She felt refreshed and very hungry. Then she thought of Moon, how hungry she must be. She looked around, and Moon wasn't with her. She tried calling her, but her voice was weak. Did Moon leave her, too? Tears were building up when out of the brushes came Moon. Moon jumped around her and over her and did flips. She was one happy dog. Promise finally was able to grab her and gave her a long hug.

"Moon," she whispered, "I'm sorry for deserting you. I didn't mean to. Thank you for not running away. You must be hungry. I'll get us some dried meat out of my bag."

Promise tried to sit up but was too weak.

"Moon, help me sit up."

After Moon let Promise brace against her and she was able to sit up. "Moon you must be starving." Promise was close to crying again for her poor dog, until she saw evidence of food that once was there. Fur and feathers were scattered about. "You did find food."

She gave Moon a big hug. "God is good for putting a smart dog like you into my life. Help me to my feet, Moon, and back to my bedroll and I'll get a fire going."

It was a relief to see there was still firewood and she built a fire. She poured water out of the canteen into her tin cup and set it on the edge of the fire to warm the water. She still had a few dried berries and added them to the cup, and she tore up a slice of dried meat and put in the cup.

She offered Moon some dried meat and said, "When I get my strength back, we'll move on."

Pulling the blanket around herself she sipped her tea and ate the bits of warm meat.

After a few days of walking around their camp and resting, Promise was able to use the slingshot and down a rabbit. In a few more days, she felt up to traveling. One thing she had learned from Ben was that animal trails not only led one to water but also made traveling in unknown country easier to find one's way. The trails go the easier route if there is one, around the many obstacles in the forest. Mountains of rocks, clumps of boulders, cliffs, and limestone canyons and creeks all needed to be conquered by Promise and Moon as they made their way through the deep forest.

Animals were abundant. They didn't run when they saw her. They were startled at first, and then curiosity took over and they stared at her invading their domain. Moon made them nervous. Chipmunks followed Promise and Moon over layered rocks and hopped from rock to rock; and squirrels chattered from the treetops, jumping from tree to tree, following the intruders. A rabbit or squirrel was about all Moon chased since an elk chased her, as did a doe protecting her fawn. Moon went wild when flocks of birds were flushed out of bushes. She was able to catch the ones that were hesitant and supplied the meat for a meal. The nights were still cold. In the early mornings, Promise felt if she tried to grasp the crisp air with her hands, she'd feel slivers of ice crystals poking into her palms.

Promise knew where she was supposed to be heading, but she wasn't sure if she was on the right path. It was easy to get turned around when a trail leads back to where she once was. When a clearing appeared, she tried to get her bearings from the sun.

One day, climbing down a steep hillside, she heard water gushing. It sounded like a river or a nice-sized creek. The closer she got, the steeper the incline became until her and Moon were sliding down on their backsides. Promise's bedroll riding on her head, she tried to grab tree limbs, tree trunks, roots, anything to break her fall; and her bloody hands proved it. Moon was on her own, twisting, rolling, and digging her claws into the hillside. Promise landed first and was able to grab for Moon when she tumbled past before she hit the running water.

The limestone wall across from the creek looked solid from left to right. To Promise, she felt like she was facing old castle walls that had tumbled down in big hunks leaving jagged walls higher up with pines growing out of them. She had no desire to climb back up the steep, tree-studded hill she just tumbled down. Promise laid her arm across Moon.

"I guess it's time for us to travel north. Sooner or later, we'll come out of this canyon and hopefully be on the plains again, and we'll head west. And if Mateo Tepee is as big as Ben said it was, we should be able to see it from anyplace."

It was a beautiful canyon even though the trees hadn't budded out yet. The hillside was thick with spruce, evergreens, and junipers. On the canyon's pale pink and yellow limestone wall, black, yawning holes dotted it. The small, purple crocuses were in bloom next to snowy rocks. The ice blue creek foamed white as it pushed over river rocks and swirled as it moved on. Oh how she wanted to get into the creek and have a wash. She tried and tried to think of a way to heat up water, but she didn't have anything to hold water except her canteen. Promise and Moon followed the creek as it followed the curves of the canyon and had to cross it a few times. That's when she spotted fish in the creek.

"How about it, Moon, do you think you can snare a fish?"

Moon watched the fast-moving fish, and they slowed down when they swam into a quiet pool off to the side or in between rocks. She lowered her head with her mouth opened and tried snapping fish up. Promise decided she'd try too. She found a sturdy stick and whittled a point on it. She stood on another rock that was partly in the water and held her stick ready to stab a passing fish. After a lot of tries and much patience, Promise and Moon got the hang of snagging fish and soon had enough for a meal.

Promise searched for eatable greens. Moon didn't have any problems. She ate the grass. There were small ponds in a few of the meadow areas, but it was still too cool for the growth of wild food. Although it did take forever to cook, she'd cut out a square of the inner bark of a birch or juniper tree and cut it into small, thin strips and boiled it in water in her cup and ate it as noodles with fish or dried meat.

Promise and Moon made their way through the canyon with the water beside them. Small game and fish were handy. The canyon widened and opened up to the plains. They came out to open space and treeless, rolling hills and red buttes. Full, puffy, white clouds sat against the blue horizon. Promise closed her eyes and hoped when she looked west she'd see the tower. She opened her eyes and slowly turned and faced west to the view of low rolling hills, red buttes, and a scattering of trees. She realized going west was the only way she had to go. In all the open space, she'd be easy to spot. She didn't dare linger here. She wasn't in a run but more of a trot as she hurried over to the buttes in hope to find concealment in between them. Promise went behind the first butte and skidded to a stop. The hair on Moon's back raised and she braced her legs and growled.

Mateo Tepee

Time stood still. Promise missed her spear she had left in the bear's neck. Her hand went to her knife.

The tall, slim man spoke. His language was Lakota, and Promise understood what he said. "We are here in peace. I am called Lame Dog and my wife"—he pointed at a slim woman heavy with child—"is called Drop Leaf. We are taking buffalos to the Yellowstone in hopes of saving our buffalo."

In the dark shadow of the butte, Promise now saw five buffalos and a calf. She patted Moon on the head to calm her and said, "I am called Yellow Star."

The man nodded his head and made the sound, "*Ah.*"

"I belong to the band of Father Fox. I am heading to Mateo Tepee.

The man made the "*Ah,*" sound again.

"We know who you are," said Lame Dog, nodding his head. "Please sit and share pemmican with us."

Promise was so thrilled to see friendly faces that she wanted to hug them. She kept her composure and shared the last of her dried meat with them and they visited as if they were in one's sitting room.

Promise told them again she was traveling to Mateo Tepee but she didn't know for sure where it was.

"We'll be going by it," said Lame Dog. "Drop Leaf wants new lodge poles, and the best ones grew there. You and your dog are welcome to travel with us."

Traveling with people who knew where they're going was heaven-sent to Promise. She gladly thanked them.

Sadness hit her; and she said, "I might not be the safest person to be in your company. I don't want to bring trouble down on you. The one called Stone Face has taken it upon himself to kill me and all who are with me."

Drop Leaf leaned forward and laid her hand on Promise's shoulder and said, in her soft voice, "Lame Dog will protect you. You be safe with us. I'd like your company, Yellow Star. My baby coming soon, like for you to be with me."

The small group gathered their belongings and set forth for Mateo Tepee. Lame Dog on his pony kept the buffalos moving. Promise noticed that the other three cows were fat with calves and the big bull leading them made the rounds, checking on them and on the calf and its mother.

Drop Leaf pulled a travois behind her pony, and Promise walked beside her. They kept behind the buttes and the low side of hills. When they came across water, they stopped, watered the animals, and rested. When fires were to be set, Promise and Moon searched for firewood and whatever else that burned. Promise took over fixing the meals. She was happy to have a black pot and a skillet and dried berries and wild onions, and Drop Leaf had more dried meat and the needed staples. Promise thought hard about what to feed Drop Leaf. She thought the Indian woman was frail. She was small anyway; and she had large, dark eyes that gave Promise the impression that Drop Leaf saw all.

One by one, the cows dropped their calves. Moon took up looking after the newborn calves. The bull that chased Moon whenever Moon got to close to his family became used to her, and now Moon was able to be in the mix without trouble from the bull. After the red calves were born, Moon took it upon herself to herd them.

"Yellow Star, your dog much help to me in keeping my small heard together and close by."

The calves seemed to know when Moon was serious or in a playful mood. It was fun for the humans to watch the dog and calves play. Once Moon watched the two bull calves bunt heads in their play. She decided to join them. She ran with her neck stiff and head down and smacked heads with one of the bull calves. Promise saw Moon lying there on the ground, not moving, and ran over to her.

"Moon! Moon! Wake up, Moon!"

Lame Dog ran over and looked down at Moon and said, "Think dog is knocked out."

Moon opened her eyes and tried to stand up and wobbled. With Promise's help, she soon was able to stand without weavings. There were no more head games with Moon.

Early one morning, Promise woke to crying. She thought she was dreaming at first until the crying continued. It came from the small lodge of Drop Leaf.

The baby, thought Promise as she threw aside her blanket.

Moon, already by the lodge, came running to meet Promise, her tail wagging. Lame Dog came out of the lodge, a big smile on his face.

"A boy," he said. "Drop Leaf tired. Go in see baby and her." He went over to the fire and dipped out a cup of warm water out of the pot and added some dried berries and leaves. "Take this in to her, Yellow Star."

The group stayed an extra day at the birthing camp. Drop Leaf had most of what she needed for the new baby. When they moved on, Drop Leaf had a large shawl she wrapped around herself, which cupped the baby front of her. She had explained to Promise that the baby would ride this way until Lame Dog built a cradleboard for the baby to ride on her back.

The plains had greened up; grass was good, and the sun warmer. Still, snow flurries came now and then. Trees were budded out with their new leaves, and the buffalo preferred the plains to the timber. They made Lame Dog work hard to herd them into the timber where they didn't want to go. Moon also was being chased back as she tried to keep them going into the timber. Finally, man and dog won the day as the buffalo plodded through the timber.

They found a lovely spot to camp next to a nice pond with willows and cottonwoods and red ash trees mixed in with the greens. Moon quietly swam out into the pond's tall grass, and it was the rustling of grass that drew the people's attention. Moon emerged with a duck in her mouth. Lame Dog wadded out into the grass and found duck eggs and brought three back with him. Promise wadded into the cattails growing on the edge of the pond and cut down a cattail shoot and peeled it back and tasted the inner core and smiled with its sweetness. She then proceeded to cut down more shoots and carried them back to camp.

While the duck roasted over the campfire and the cattail shoots had been peeled away to the inner core, ready to eat, Promise mixed up fry bread and made extra to serve with fried eggs for their morning meal.

Promise had never been close to babies. She chatted with this new baby with its coal-black hair but didn't hold it. Lame Dog and Drop Leaf spoke to Promise one evening. They wanted Promise to name their baby boy. Usually, the baby was named by an uncle or grandfather, and Yellow Star was the closest family they had here.

Taken by surprise, Promise was speechless. What did she know about naming a baby, especially an Indian baby?

"That's an honor to be bestowed on me," said Promise. "I'm not sure I'd be the proper one to do that. I know you and your people take much acclaim on a name—"

"Think about it, Yellow Star. It would mean much to us if you named our child," said Drop Leaf. "Take your time, Yellow Star."

The terrain became harder to go over. Finding trails around the sharp ridges and steep red banks became a challenge for the travelers. The buffalo labored to get through the barriers. Moon was right on their hooves when they tried to turn around. One day, they came out of the trees and the Mateo Tepee loomed before them. Lame Dog had seen it before; but it was the first time for his wife and their friend, Yellow Star. Promise knew her mouth was open in wonderment. She didn't comprehend the imposing size when Ben had described the tower to her. They made camp next to the tree line, at a spring. Drop Leaf was very tired and welcomed the rest. Promise heated water in the pot and added onions and dried meat. Drop Leaf just wanted the broth; and Lame Dog, Promise, and Moon ate the thin soup. All retired for the night after a check on the buffalo.

In the early morning, Promise fixed a tea for Drop Leaf, and the rest ate the last of the soup. The herd was pushed down the bank of red clay and limestone rock and across the Bell Fourche River and up the other side. As they approached the east side, sagebrush and rocks mixed in with pine trees greeted them. Promise saw what Drop Leaf wanted and why. The trunks of the tall pines were very slim and straight and made good lodge poles.

Promise had to see for herself how big around the tower was, so she walked around the base of the tower; Moon went with her, and they stayed on a deer trail. The north side held snow in its gray rocks with lichens and velvety moss, and in its dampened soil, trees and shrubs grew thicker. The west side had aspens, scrub oak, bowed pine trees, and berry bushes. The south side had many pine trees and fallen trees and evergreens that were not thick-branched like the ones she was used to seeing. Different-sized boulders piled on each other circled the base of the tower. Promise thought she'd never get around it when she finally reached where she had started.

Lame Dog downed a deer; and while the women processed it, he picked out a few lodge pole pine trees and cut them down, scraped, and de-limbed them. After an evening meal, the people sat around the fire and chatted and the buffalos grazed and Moon looked after everyone. Lame Dog talked of the Yellowstone, where he was sure his herd would be safe from man. Drop Leaf spoke and told what her husband had revealed to her: streams of hot water and hot steam shoots out of holes and goes high in the air; many lakes and ponds and animals, some never been seen by man.

Lame Dog spoke. "Have you been thinking, Yellow Star, of a name for our son?"

Promise, her eyes closed, opened them and said, "Yes, I have. My feelings won't be hurt if you disagree to the name or how I came by it."

"Go on, Yellow Star," said Drop Leaf.

"I know names from your people come from visions, or from a famous person, or after an animal or bird to receive their power, strength, or wisdom. My mother told me when I hear a bird it's to remind me I am not alone. My mother had red hair. Father Fox put the eagle's meaningful symbols in my name. They represent strength and wisdom. I think the name for the baby gleaned from what I shared with you should be called Red Eagle."

No one spoke. The silence, to Promise, was deafening. *What have I done? Oh, what have I done?*

"Ah, I approve, Red Eagle good name." Lame Dog lifted his baby up high and said, "Great Spirit know this child is called Red Eagle. Keep him close to you, Great Spirit, and see no harm comes to him."

The day that Promise's new friends were preparing to leave, Promise asked Lame Dog if he knew what month they were in the English months. Drop Leaf had told Promise that Lame Dog, as a child, was put in an English school. He didn't care for it but learned many things.

Lame Dog nodded his head yes. "In Lakota moon, this month be called 'The moon when leaves are green.' In the English month, it is May."

Drop Leaf shared some of her supplies with Promise against Promise's will. Drop Leaf insisted. After all, Promise had helped in smoking the venison and finding some the early eatable wild foods and helped with the pemmican; but mostly, Drop Leaf, said, "It's because I like you and wish you were coming with us." Then she handed Promise a small, black pot. "For you, Promise, you need," said Drop Leaf.

"Oh, Drop Leaf, you cannot give me your pot."

"Yes, I can. You keep."

"While we're at it," Lame Dog, said, "I also have something for you. You need it, too." He handed Promise a spear he had fashioned after he had tended to the lodge poles and before he shaped the cradleboard.

Lame Dog and Drop Leaf, with Red Eagle tucked into a cradleboard on his mother's back, turned on their ponies and waved good-bye. The travois being pulled by Drop Leaf's pony stirred up the red dust. The new lodge poles were attached to it.

Sadly, Promise waved until the red dust faded behind a hill. "Good-bye, my friends," she whispered.

Sensing Promise's loneliness, Moon pressed against Promise's doeskin dress and nudged her nose into her palms.

Promise rubbed her dog's head. "Moon, we're on our own again."

Shifting her eyes from where her friends had vanished from her sight, she stared up at the towering rock beside her. The gigantic-sized Mateo Tepee dwarfed the hilly countryside, making her feel insignificant in this vast land. She didn't feel any bigger than the squirrels scurrying over the boulders at the tower's base. Knowing there was no turning back, she followed the winding animal path through the lodge pole pine and scrub oak trees to the south side of Mateo Tepee.

Like a gateway, a bright rainbow arched over the meandering Belle Fourche River, opening the Great Plains to view. Yellow plains spouting with new, green life rolled out before her as far as she could see until they touched the blue sky. The beauty hastened her heartbeat. The hidden hazards weakened her knees.

She kneeled and wrapped her arms around Moon's neck and shivered not from cold but from wondering if she had the ability to survive the plains crossing.

A shadow passed over the sparkling river, causing Promise to look up, an eagle, its wings spread, circled above her.

"Look, Moon! You suppose that's an omen?"

Eagles were one of the meaningful symbols in her given Indian name, Yellow Star, as she had told the parents of baby Red Eagle. Not only did they represent strength and wisdom, but were known to fly and to see at a great distance. She and Moon had walked a great distance. If only she could see ahead to the place she'd never been but must find to meet a man she'd never known.

A meadow lark burst forth with a chipper song. Promise hugged Moon.

"We'll be all right. A bird sings to remind me we are not alone. That's what my mama used to say."

The meadow lark also reminded her of the day she had left Philadelphia, a year ago in May, the moon when leaves are green, also the month she'd turn fifteen.

Promise spent one last night at the base of the tower. Wrapped in her blanket, Moon beside her, she stared out over the land that stretched out forever in front of her.

Ben's last words to Promise were for her to go to Fort Laramie, find her father, and give him a chance. She was still not ready for him, but she was anxious to see Aunt Hattie and would give her father a second chance.

During the time she spent with Ben, she'd learned a lot and grew in her thinking. And with what she had gleaned from Father Fox and Squirrel, she felt prepared for the Great Plains.

Squirrels woke Promise up by their chattering. Moon was chasing them. She called Moon over and shared dried meat with her. Promise rolled up her bedroll; slipped the small pot handle over her belt. Holding her new spear, she climbed down the steep embankment to the red banks of clay at the river. She double-checked her canteen to make sure it was full and then found a place to cross. She glanced back, assuring herself the tower was still there. Putting one foot forward and then the other, using her spear as a walking stick, she proceeded south.

Promise didn't even want to think how far she needed to travel. She didn't even know how far. One day at a time.

The Great Plains

The Great Plains and the sky became Promise's companions, along with Moon. Ben had told her once, "Always know where you're stepping and what the sky is revealing to you." She followed the river until she became discouraged with all the twists and turns. She wanted and needed more of a straight trail to keep the tower at her back for a long as possible.

The nights were still chilly. Snow was still on the ground in places, and Moon enjoyed rolling in it. Promise didn't worry about Moon straying far. And she had no complaints when Moon trotted back with a grouse or a rabbit in her mouth.

If water was close by, Promise used the pot and had a stew with dried berries, onions, and a few slices of dried prairie turnips in place of the potatoes from Drop Leaf. If water wasn't near, meat was roasted over the fire. Promise kept her eyes out for edible plants. She was craving greens, but it seemed like it was too early in the season for greens.

The plains had bluffs, rolling hills, gullies, and ravines. The sky showed her something new every day with its clouds. She was able to make out animals or birds and islands in the sky.

She thought they were making good time. They didn't linger, stopping only when the sun went down. They ate dried meat or pemmican as they walked. They saw herds of deer and antelope, and elk; and rabbits were abundant, as were grouse. Promise didn't think it possible for her slingshot to bring down a bigger animal.

From snow to rain; and if Promise read the clouds right a storm was coming. She didn't find shelter before the clouds let loose with their water, thunder, and lightning. Promise did find an indent in a hillside opposite of the wind. Taking the cape off the bedroll and the bedroll on her lap, she held the cape with fur side down over Moon and herself as she pressed them into the indent of the hill. She kept one arm around Moon. Moon whined and quivered, hearing the thunder boom and crack across the plains; and lightning revealed the sky's black clouds. Water ran down the hill and hit the cape and, like a waterfall, poured over it and splashed onto Promise's feet before it spread out in front of them.

After it was over, the sun came out and everything glistened. Moon gave her body a shake and smiled at Promise. Promise didn't smile back, but she used her to help unclamp her body. She was dry to her knees. From there down, she was soaked. Moon's legs were wet, and the rest of her was dry. Promise's thoughts were on how to make a fire with everything burnable wet and no dry place for the night. She decided to keep going and hopefully come across a shelter of some kind.

When night came, the sky was bright and clear; and the stars and moon were bright, making it easy for Promise and Moon to find their way. They came to a small creek, and Promise refilled the canteen and they went on. They traveled all night. Dampness followed them at every step. Moon was tired. Her head hung. Promise's legs ached, her moccasins were still soaked, and her feet were cold. Then the sun came out with welcoming warmth.

"I'll feel better now, Moon. My feet will dry, and my legs will quit aching once the sun warms me up. We'll find some dry brush or sticks for a fire and stop earlier today and get a good rest in. I think I'll make myself some hot tea. You like hot tea, Moon? I'd fix you a cup."

She patted Moon on her head. She turned just in case the tower was visible. It hadn't been visible for days. She felt like another friend was gone. The sun came up in the east; and it was on the left side of her, so she knew she was still heading south.

When the sun was right above her, she knew they had walked farther than she expected. She paused on a big rock and took pemmican out of her bag for her and Moon and noticed the bag wasn't bulging like it once did when it was full. She poured water in her palm for Moon to drink, and then she took a drink of it; and then they were on their way again.

Just before dusk, she saw an outcropping with a few trees around it. One was a cottonwood, and cottonwoods grow where there is water. Her spirit lifted, she hurried forward; and Moon noticed the different in Promise's walk. It showed happiness. So Moon was happy now; and she was running back and forth, tail wagging.

What more could a person ask for? The outcropping held a ledge over a small cave, firewood lay on the ground, and there was a spring at the base of the big cottonwood.

Promise was so happy she wanted to bawl. She told herself to snap out of it. She was just overly tired. She gathered sticks, many sticks, just to have them near. She had Moon nose out the cave to make sure there weren't any varmints in it. Promise made a rock ring up close to the cave entrance and set her fire. The heat felt good on her hands. She took the pot and the canteen and her tin cup and filled them all up at the spring and went back to their new camp. Moon had disappeared. She hoped Moon would land a grouse or another type of prairie chicken. She felt she was in need of chicken broth. Her throat was itchy, and her body ached. She didn't want to get sick like Ben did; and if it wasn't for the old Cheyenne woman, he probably wouldn't have made it. She didn't have anyone to aid her except for Moon, and she didn't figure Moon would be much help to her; but in her own way, she'd be a great help.

Promise mixed herself some hot willow bark tea, and she added sagebrush leaves to it in the tin cup. She had the black pot of water over the fire; and she added dried onions, berries, anything she could find. She remembered she had rose hips in her bag and added those into the pot too. She laid out her bedroll; putting the cape under it, skin side down, to block any dampness from the ground. She shivered and put her cloak on and wrapped the flannel sheet around her. She leaned back on a rock and sipped her tea, waiting for Moon.

When Moon showed up, she dropped her prize at Promise's feet. When Promise didn't move, Moon nudged her. When that didn't work, Moon put her paw on Promise's shoulder, and that awoke Promise.

"Sorry, Moon. Ah, you're a good dog," said Promise, eyeing the grouse. "Give me a hand up, and I'll pluck and clean it out. Let's go elsewhere to do that."

Promise rose and felt dizzy. She waited a moment until that passed and took the grouse to another spot to clean and rinse it. Back at the campfire, she cut it up and put it in the pot of hot water to boil. She felt like she had better have things close at hand and ready for her when she'd need them. She didn't have mustard or flour to mix a mustard pack for her chest. Nor did she have a cocker burr to swallow to bring up any blockage in her throat.

She looked at Moon. "I know what I'll do. I think I'm going to need the hot tea. And to have enough on hand for me, I'm going to add willow bark powder and sagebrush leaves to the pot of chicken broth and more rose hips. That won't hurt you, Moon, if you should swallow any of it. You can help yourself to the bird. I just want the broth. And we need to keep the fire going."

Promise sipped the tea in her cup and watched the pot boil. When she thought the bird was done, she dipped her cup into the pot. While she was able, she added more water to the pot and more sticks into the fire.

"Moon, I know you've gathered firewood with me, but can you do that without me? You're a smart dog, Moon, but I don't know if you understand what I'm saying now. I'm tired and going to go to sleep. I do know one thing for certain you will protect me."

Before she lay down, she took both grouse legs out of the pot and laid them aside for Moon. Promise remembered little after that.

She saw herself dip out of the pot with her tin cup. She wanted cold water. Thirsty. So thirsty. She felt the presence of someone. *Moon? Where are you, Moon? Protect me! Oh, that feels so good on my forehead. So cool. Do I know you? Moon, are you doing this to me? Are you helping me? You are such a smart dog. Please let me go back to sleep.*

Promise felt her head being lifted and liquid on her lips. She licked her lips, wanting more. More liquid was dribbled on her lips and then into her mouth. Her lips and mouth were so dry. She tried forcing her eyes open; and through a slit, she saw black hair hanging down over her.

She wondered, *Who is that?* She didn't feel any fear. She then felt a lick on her hand. She tried moving her hand, and just her fingers moved. She tried to see who was in her bedroom with her. It was so hot she tried to open a window, and it wouldn't open. Then she was cold and tried to shut the window, and it wouldn't shut. She wanted more liquid, water. She tried to speak, but her throat was closed to words.

Swallowing hurt and something was pressing on her chest. Breathing was hard to do. She felt a hand on her chest. Moon's paw turned into a hand, and the hand was rubbing something on her chest. Then something was laid on her chest.

Too hot! Too hot! Take it off, Moon! Her mind screamed.

Promise's head was lifted up, and something was pressed to her lips. She opened them a little, and some terrible-tasting stuff went down her sore throat. She gagged, and someone held her close and rubbed her back. She hurt. She hurt all over. She tried to open her eyes.

All she managed were slits, and she thought: *Windows wouldn't open, and they wouldn't close, and my eyes won't open now.*

She was laid back down, and she saw black hair over her; and the hair moved, and she saw a green eye.

That eye is open, she thought. *Why not mine?*

No!

She didn't want any more of that awful tasting stuff.

No!

She felt herself go limp.

Promise felt warmth. It felt good. She opened her eyes and saw the sun shining on her, giving her the warmth she felt. She rolled over onto her side, facing the campfire, and saw it had a small fire under the pot. She thought she had a nap longer than she planned on.

She sat up and felt dizzy; and speaking to no one, she said, "I think I swooned. I have never done that before."

Feeling hungry, she tried standing and had to use one of the rocks that formed the small cave to stand up with. She couldn't figure out why she felt so weak. And where was Moon?

"Moon, Moon, where are you? Come on, girl," Promise called out.

She saw her cup lying by the fire and wondered how that got there. Then she heard rustling in the grass. Something was running through it, and that something came around the cave with a big grin on her face and a wet tongue for Promise's face.

"Hey, girl, you act like I've been gone, not just taking a nap. I know I overslept. I feel pretty good. And my moccasins are dry. That was quick. That was a soaking rain. I can't believe how everything dried up. You don't know how wet moccasins feel on your feet. Is there any bird left in the pot?"

She rubbed Moon's neck and then patted on her back and leaned into the pot with her cup.

"Moon, you ate the whole thing? That's all right. The broth will be filling." Promise looked into the pot and said, "Moon, what those strange leaves are floating around in the pot? I didn't put them there. Maybe I did and don't remember. I was really tired, but I don't remember what they are."

She dipped her cup in the pot and tasted the broth. She made a face of disgust; but then something about it was familiar, so she drank it.

"We'll have one more night here and leave in the morning."

She noticed her one bag that was pretty empty was filled with dried meat and pemmican, and her canteen was full.

Turning to Moon, she said, "I must have been really tired and thought we were low on food. I'll tell you, Moon, I really had strange dreams. You were in it, and someone with a green eye. Heavens, the only ones I know who have green eyes are Ben and Green Raven, so one of them was in the dream. Maybe I'm just missing Ben or wishing to see Green Raven."

Promise hated to leave the small cave and the cold spring. She felt some stronger, but she knew she wouldn't be pushing herself like she did until she felt stronger. She was thankful to have the spear, and she used it as a walking stick and to keep her balance. Moon was ready to go forth. There was new territory to sniff out.

The terrain was pretty much the same. Here, though, there were interesting and weird sand rock formations, and finding shelter for the night was easier. Promise felt good. Her stride was longer, and she was feeling anxious about reaching Fort Laramie. The thoughts of her father were getting to be more positive.

She checked the sun, making sure they were heading south. The sun being up longer meant the travelers were able to walk farther. She saw a herd of elk off to her left. She teased Moon about going to get one. Moon seemed happy just where she was. Rabbit and grouse were still most of their diet, and Promise was thankful for that; and she was able to find some edible greens to add to their diet.

When dusk was upon them, Promise began looking for a decent shelter hopefully by water. Water was getting harder to find. Pine, evergreen trees, and sagebrush were about, so fuel for the camp fire was handy.

One evening, Promise found a bank that had a large log across the top of it. So she set up camp next to the bank. She shared the dried meat with Moon and the water from the canteen. She had a small fire going only to keep away any animals that might be curious.

With her back next to the bank and Moon in front of her, Promise snuggled into her blanket and fell asleep.

She awoke to Moon's whining. Moon was pacing and very nervous. She kept sniffing the air and looked at Promise and whined more.

"What is it, Moon?" Promise asked in a soothing voice, trying to calm her dog.

Then Promise smelled what Moon smelled. Smoke!

Promise jumped up and looked over the log, and then she heard a sound that stopped her heart. Thundering hooves headed her way, leaving a dust storm in their wake and behind that, smoke. She saw a black mass of heads and horns. She knew there was no way to outrun the panicked buffalos. She pushed her belongings tightly into the bank and kicked dirt onto the fire. She grabbed Moon, holding her tightly, and pressed her frame into the bank. The thundering herd was right above her. Some jumped over the log and landed ahead of Promise while others came down beside her, kicking up dust as they went on. Promise, holding a shaking Moon, stayed where she was, making sure there were no stragglers to come down on them.

The smell of smoke was heavier, and Promise had to take the chance. Still holding Moon, she stood and looked over the log. More animals raced ahead of a huge flame that was blackening the sky. Promise quickly rolled up her bedroll, slipped it over her back, and was glad she kept her stuff always close to her.

"Come on, Moon! Run for your life!"

They had just taken off when the first of the scared animals went over the bank and soon passed Promise and Moon. Promise knew she had a steam of energy going for her, and she knew Moon was able to outrun her; but Moon stayed by her side. Deer bounded past them. Little animals scurried under her feet but never tripped her. Coyotes raced past her, as did wolves. There was no prey or hunter at this time. There wasn't a break in the long line of fleeing animals that had spread out on both sides of Promise and Moon. The fiery beast charged and destroyed anything in its way. Cries of terror and pain could be heard over the fire's roar. Terrible heat catching up on them drove them all faster; and some just didn't have it in them anymore.

Promise didn't dare turn around to see how close the flaming monster was. She could feel its heat, and she could hear its roar. Smoke thickened up ahead of her. She couldn't see Moon. She couldn't see if anything was in front of her. Her lungs ached for fresh air. All she could do was keep going.

Suddenly, a horse appeared next to her, and a hand reached out for her. Without thinking, she dropped her spear and reached out for the hand. She was swung on behind the rider; and then she thought: *Stone Face!*

And Moon? Where is Moon?

She tried to call Moon, but her voice was weak. The horse she was on took off from the direction they had all been running to and crossed in front of the fire. Promise hung on for dear life. Her head lay on the rider's back, and tears of worry about Moon dripped down her face. She couldn't lose Moon. She just couldn't.

She noticed the smoke had lessened. The horse had outrun the flame.

Thank you, Lord.

Now if only Moon was able to appear. Then she heard it, a bark.

Moon! Thank you, Lord.

She was scared the rider was Stone Face. Why would he risk his life to save her when he wanted her dead? Because he'd want to do the dirty deed himself?

The rider jumped off the black-and-white pony and rubbed its nose and whispered in its ear. He then came and lifted Promise down. She finally saw who the rider was and her heart beat faster not because of the danger they escaped but from gazing into piercing green eyes.

Promise spoke up, "Where did you come from, Green Raven?" Promise asked in Lakota. "Did you know Moon and I were in the fire's way? Have you been following me?"

Surprising her he spoke back in English. "You ask a lot of questions. Can't you be content with being saved without a lot of questions? There's a river up ahead. That's going your direction."

"And what direction is that, Green Raven?"

"My guess would be Fort Laramie. We'll talk later."

Later! He wants to talk later! I want to talk now! Before Green Raven was able to lift Promise back on his horse, she sneezed and sneezed again.

"I'm sorry, Green Raven. I cannot ride your pony with you. I'll walk beside you."

"I'm sorry too Yellow Star. I forgot about you and horses. It'll do me good to walk."

The travelers walked. Green Raven told Promise how, although Indians set grassfires so the land could have new and healthy growth for the buffalo, he was sure this fire was caused by lightning.

When they stopped for the night, they were a very tired group. Dried meat and water was the fare that night. They were ready for sleep. Although she was exhausted, Promise had a time getting to sleep. Smoke was still in her nose, and they all were sooty; and every time she closed her eyes, she saw the fire and the hand that reached down for her. She felt Moon lay beside her.

Morning came early, promising a clear, warm day. Clouds floated across the pale sky like they had a place to go. Green Raven told her he knew she could make it from here on without him. She wanted to tell him, *No, I can't.* But she was sure she was able to finish her trek.

"I'll walk with you to the river," he said, "we all in need of a wash."

She'd wait until after they cleaned up and had a bite before she'd let her questions fly at him. They left behind them destruction and the loss of life. Now they were walking to a river through tall grease wood, pines, and new growth of grass, and again life was around her. Herds were grazing, unaffected by the fire north of them.

Green Raven's pony grazed as they walked along. He and Promise were quiet, both in deep thought.

Ahead of her, she witnessed the sparkle of a river and took off running. Moon ran beside her. Green Raven had to leap on his pony and spur it on to catch up with them. When he reached them at the river's edge, Promise had her hands in the water, splashing it back on her. She stared at Green Raven like she was just seeing him now.

"Am I as dirty as you?" she asked.

He laughed, jumped off his pony and rushed at Promise. Picking her up, he threw her in the river and jumped in behind her. The water was cold but felt so good and clean. Promise got her feet under her quickly. She didn't mind being wet. She and her clothes needed to be rid of the smoke that covered them. But she didn't want the items in the bags to get wet. She waded to the riverbank and took off her belt and all that was hanging on it: the bags, slingshot, the pot, her knife, and the beaded bags and emblem from around her neck. She left the cameo necklace on. In the one bag, she lifted out a piece of soap. She looked at Green Raven and told him it was a good thing her bedroll was on his pony. She plunged back into the water. Moon splashed in by her. Green Raven gladly accepted Promise's offer of the soap. Chilled after leaving the water the second time she cut sage and grease wood for a fire.

She retrieved her bedroll from the pony and unrolled it and laid it all out on top of the grass to air out. Took her cloak to the river and washed it the best she could and laid it out along with her moccasins close to the fire to dry, she wished she could with her doeskin dress. Her fingers spread her wet clean hair for the sun rays to dry.

When Green Raven emerged from the river, he stripped his leathers off, leaving his loin cloth on, and said, "Anything to eat?"

"I'm fixing a pot now for us, it won't be long," said Promise.

She had the pot over the fire added dried meat to the water and slices of prairie turnips. She had found watercress by the river and added some of its leaves to the pot.

"While we wait for our meal to cook, I have questions for you. And I have a message for you from your father," Promise said.

His frame stiffened, and a shadow passed over his face, freezing his expression. She was determined not to let that dark look stop her. First she told him about Ben, about the bear, about the love he had for Green Raven's mother, the devastation he felt when she died, and the devastation he felt when he heard his son thought his father blamed him for his mother's death. She told him how Ben searched for his son to ask for forgiveness and a chance to know one another. How Father Fox forced her on Ben, how she found out Ben had met her mother, and how they fell in love.

"They wanted to be a family with all four of us," she said. "You were included in the family plans, Green Raven, as I was. Ben told me in his last breath to tell his son he was sorry." Promise had tears rolling down her face, but her voice was steady. Green Raven's back was to her. "All right, Green Raven. You heard my story. Now tell me yours. How and why are you here?"

Promise didn't think he was going to turn around and face her. When he did, the dark look from his face was gone.

"Father Fox sent me. A truth rider rode in to camp and told Father Fox you were alone, and Stone Face was searching for you. Didn't have any word about Ben or why you were alone. Father Fox thought you had a change of mind and decided to go to Fort Laramie while Ben went searching for his son, me. We know you and Ben stopped at the camp I wintered at but had left before you showed up. All the camp knew was Ben was going to try and follow us by heading north. Father Fox thought Ben would aim for Mateo Tepee and wait for me there. So Father Fox sent word to me to start at the tower and head south. That's how I came upon you when you were very sick. I nursed you." Here, Green

Raven turned red in the face and cast his eyes down. "I had to do what had to be done."

"What do you mean, you had to do what had to be done?" asked Promise.

"You were very sick, Yellow Star. I had to put the healing herbs on your chest to draw out the sickness in your lungs. You could hardly breathe." He tapped his chest and said, "I just touched your chest and rubbed the heated herbs into your chest and neck. Yellow Star, I would've given you my last breath if that's what it would've taken. But you couldn't breathe even to take my breath. Forgive me if I have offended you or embarrassed you. That wasn't my purpose. Healing was what I focused on, nothing else. When I saw you coming around, I placed dried meat and pemmican into your bag. I was saying good-bye to Moon when she heard you call her. She's a very good dog. If she hadn't known me, I wouldn't have been able to get close to you. And, yes, I followed to make sure you didn't have a relapse. Then I left you alone until I spotted the smoke and rode back."

"When I woke, I had no idea I had been sick. I had weird dreams. I was miserable, hot and cold and thirsty, and thought someone with long, black hair was with me. And I saw a green eye. Now, I understand that all happened when I really was sick. How can I ever thank you, Green Raven? Three times you have saved me." She walked up to him and said, "May I?" and gave him a hug. She felt his arms hug her back. She didn't want to let go, but knew she had to. She backed up. "Where are you off to now?"

"Join Crazy Horse. Where that leads me, I don't know," he said. "But like you, have to do what I have to do."

The meal was eaten in silence. Promise felt drained and had no more questions; but she was sure after Green Raven left, more unanswered questions would come to her mind. She reached into her bag and brought out the cedar figurine of her and Moon and held it out to Ben's son.

"Your father carved that for me. That should show you what type of man your father was. He was caring, giving, and helpful.

He loved your mother, and he loved my mother, and he loved me. Because of him, I'm going to give my real father a chance."

She held out the figurine to Green Raven. He took it and ran his fingers over it and felt its smoothness. He handed it back to Promise and looked her in the eye. With a shake of his head, he turned. He leaped on his pony, gave her a long, lasting look, and then galloped away.

Sadly, Promise watched Green Raven until he was out of sight.

She and Moon continued their journey. Moon hunted for their meals. Promise had no idea where they were or how much farther they needed to go. By the sun, they were still going south and should be coming up on something to let her know where she was. Moon had taken off on her own, nose to the ground. When Moon came back all wet, Promise got excited.

"Take me to the water, Moon. Show me. Now, please," Promise begged her dog.

When Moon took off, Promise was right behind her. They crossed a well-traveled red-dirt road. It went out of sight, heading west into the timber and white rock. Moon lead her to a river, and across the river was a long, sandstone cliff. Promise had never seen it before. Why was there a memory or even a thought of it in her mind? Why? Then she remembered Ben had told her about a cliff that he and Buffalo Warrior had carved their names in when they were with the Fremont Expedition. Could that cliff in front of her be it? She didn't remember anything said about a river. If it was the same cliff, Fort Laramie was just past here.

Promise looked around to see if there was a crossing over the river, and there was one.

Like the White River, there was a wider spot where the river wasn't deep. She took off her moccasins and tucked them under her belt. She wasn't having wet moccasins again if she could help it. Moon beside her, Promise waded across. She walked up to the cliff and searched for names. Many of the names the weather had worn down. She came across a "J.W. Robb, 1857, US Post." There was an "I.J. Marsh, 1857." Promise wondered if they were traveling together. There were a lot of names. She ran her fingers over them as she searched for Ben's name, and there it was: "Ben Reed, 1842." Promise felt like crying. She missed him so. Above his name was "Isaiah Jefferson, 1842." What young men they were. She remembered their talk when they had reunited that day so long ago and told how they both had lied about their ages. Both were big and strong, and that was what was needed for the expedition. She'd have to tell Green Raven about this cliff and his father's name on it.

"Moon, you ready? I think our journey is about over. That road we crossed probably goes to the fort. I've got to think how I'm entering the fort without looking like a white Indian. If only I had my parfleche. It has my blue polka-dot garment. I wonder what happened to the parfleche or Milkweed. Maybe an idea will come to me as we walk."

Promise decided to stay on the right of the river and follow it, keeping away from the road. She didn't want to be spotted at this time. She didn't realize her pace had really slowed down. She had to come to terms with herself.

She was pretty sure Aunt Hattie was at the fort: But what if she isn't? Well, there was only one way to find out, unless she wanted to wander around the fort forever.

Fort Laramie

The late morning sunrays broke through a cloud and like an upside down bowl gleamed over the fort and surrounding area. Wild flowers popped up in an array of bright colors, grass appeared greener and the river bluer, and the roofs had a shine on them. On a bluff overlooking Fort Laramie, Promise lay on her stomach and studied the situation. Below her were a few covered wagons, and she watched the women, wondering if they were willing to give her a dress or looked down on her for wearing Indian clothing. Closer to the river were small, tattered lodges. She had heard they were called loafers: Indians who depended on the charity of the fort. The road went by them to a wooden bridge over the river; then it curved into the fort. There was no stockade around the fort. It was all an open arena.

Sharing pemmican with Moon, Promise pondered her dilemma. She remembered her aunt's words: "you must not embarrass your father."

"You know, Moon, if I still had my capote, I'd wear it over my doeskin, and no one would be able to see it, and I'd be able to just walk by the emigrants and the loafers. But where to walk to in the fort, I don't know yet. I may not have my capote, but I do have my cloak!" She slid back from the edge of the bluff and down to the ground where she unrolled her bedroll. As she was preparing, she remembered the trunks that were sent ahead when she left Philadelphia; she'd have clothes at the fort. She must find Aunt Hattie first. She shook out her cloak and frowned at the wrinkles. She rolled the bedroll back up with the cape inside and the Huston Bay Blanket on the outside. With the rope, she tied it on an unwilling Moon. After Moon accepted her fate, she settled down. Promise donned her cloak, which concealed her doeskin dress and what she wore around her neck and on her belt. She pulled the hood over her head as far as she could to hide her hair and face. She carried the pot and forced confidence in her walk as if this wasn't her first trip to the fort. She didn't look left or right. Eyes straight ahead, Promise strolled over the bridge with Moon at her side and followed the road as it curved in to the fort area.

Buildings were around the perimeter. Where would she begin to look? Her false confidence was slipping. She paused, trying to take it all in. Across from her she saw people entering and leaving from a long building and others were sitting in front of it. "Well, why not?" she asked herself. "Come on, Moon, stay with me."

On the stone and adobe building, a sign read *Post Trader*. The white men and a few Indians who were sitting on the benches in front of the store stopped their chatter when Promise and Moon walked by them and entered the store. Coming in from the brightness of the day, Promise couldn't see. She stopped until her eyes adjusted to the dimness. There was a long counter before her, and behind it were shelves that went onto the next wall. There was a person behind the counter tending to a customer, so Promise browsed. After the customer left, Promise went up to the counter; head bent enough to keep the hood forward.

"May I help you?" asked the women. "Is there…something…do I know you?" The voice, Promise knew that voice. "Promise…is that you?"

Promise's head flew back, and she was staring at her Aunt Hattie. "Oh, Aunt Hattie," she cried. "I found you!"

Hattie flew from around the counter and grabbed her niece. All she could say was "Promise! Promise! Promise! Let me look at you," she said, crying. "Let me look at my precious niece. I've prayed for this day!" She pulled back and said, "Oh, my." Hattie quickly glanced around then pulled Promise into a storage room, and she lit the lantern. That was when she noticed a dog. "Oh, my."

The two stared at each other. Promise thought her aunt looked older and thinner. "Promise, what has happened to you? You look older and taller, slim, your hair, your poor hair—when's the last time it had a brush to it? What in the world do you have on under your cloak?" and she pulled it open. "Oh, my, we have to do something with you before your father sees you! Why are you carrying a black pot?"

"Too many questions, Aunt, and I thought you'd have my clothes for me from the trunk."

"I do. I do. The trunk is in Oliver's room. I have a cot there. I have to get past Mrs. Amrose first."

"Who?"

"Your father's wife."

"You have to call her Mrs. Amrose?"

"She's very proper. Just because we live away from civilization does not mean we cannot be civilized here. We do not have time to waste; I have to get you in proper clothes. What can we do about your skin and hair? Oh, my." Hattie then looked like she saw a ghost. She pulled at some crates. Reaching behind one, she said, "Awhile back while I was tending the store and I had to come into here for something and when I went back out, there was an odd package. I guess I have never seen a package like that. Here it is." She lifted it up. To Promise's amazement, it was her own parfleche!

"Where did it come from, Aunt Hattie?" Promise asked as she reached for it. "Did you look in it?"

"I was going to, and when your father came in, I felt I should hide it, and I forgot it, until now."

Promise opened her parfleche, and there was her toilet set and her blue polka-dot dress. Everything was still there.

Seeing the brown and yellow gingham dress, or part of it, Hattie asked, "Is that yours? Your brown and yellow gingham dress you had on when those awful fellows took you?"

"We have a lot to talk about, Aunt Hattie. But first let's get me properly dressed. I can wear the blue polka-dot. I had a wash in the river; my hair is clean. It's just that everything is wrinkled—"

"I can fix that. You tend to your hair the best you can, and I will be right back. Oh, stay in here." Aunt Hattie gave Promise another hug, patted her on her face, and kissed her cheek. Bundling the polka-dot dress and the white blouse, she scurried out. She yelled, "Mrs. Amrose, I am running an errand. I will be back shortly."

Promise heard a woman answer back to Aunt Hattie, "See you are not gone long. I do not have time for the store today!"

Promise glanced down at Moon and whispered, "Sounds like a fun household. I knew my aunt wouldn't look down on me, but I think she knows if my father sees me in doeskin, I'd be living in the loafer's camp."

Trying to run the brush and comb through her tangled hair, Promise moaned and groaned. She gazed into her mirror, studying her face. Her skin was still a little too dark for a lady, but it wasn't as dark as it was last summer; it had faded without the sun on it, and she had color to her eyebrows and lashes. Also, her hair had more color to it now, being out of the hot sun.

Aunt Hattie came bustling in, carrying a sheet, which hid the newly ironed dress and blouse from everyone's eyes.

"Didn't the wife notice the sheet?" Promise asked. "Didn't she ask you about your errand?

"No, as soon as she saw me coming in she left for the living quarters. My, you are going to be a shock to her—and your father. And you know you mustn't—"

"I know I mustn't embarrass him."

"Promise, I'm so sorry we cannot sit and catch up over a cup of tea, which I would love to do, and just hold your hand and gaze at you. Oh, Promise, I've missed you so! I'm having trouble comprehending that you are really here right now. My mind is busy trying to work this situation into our favor… This is a nice garment."

"A friend, Fanny Finnely, made this for me. And I helped her, and she gave me that blouse to go with it and those drawers. But I don't have a petticoat, and I just have moccasins."

Hattie pulled off her petticoat and handed it to Promise, saying, "I can get another one. Promise how did you get here? One of the wagon trains?"

"I walked, Aunt Hattie," Promise said, as she tied back her hair.

"Oh, you mean you walked across the bridge. The covered wagons are not allowed inside the fort. Stagecoaches are, though."

Promise thought there'd be another time to tell her aunt how she arrived when she'd have her aunt's full attention. "She lifted the cameo of the necklace so it would lie over the high neck of the blouse. When Hattie saw the cameo she nearly fainted, Promise caught her before she fell. "Child where did you find that or how did you find that?" Hattie said, fanning her face with her hand.

"Oh, Dear Aunt, a lot to tell you, but now you better take me to my father."

"What about that dog?"

"That *dog* stays with me, Aunty."

"Oh, my, oh my."

Both women took a deep breath and stepped out of the storage room. A small framed boy stood at the door like he had been waiting for it to open. "Aunt Henrietta," he said, "I have been watching the store for you. "And I made a few sales, while you hid out in the storage room with this pretty lady," and he bowed to Promise. "My sister probably will not like you but I like you already." He turned and walked away and Promise couldn't help but notice his limp. She looked at Aunt Hattie for an answer.

"He was borne with a leg shorter than the other and your father refuses to buy him shoes with one built up so he could walk without a limp, and it would be better for his back, too. Your father always wanted a boy and he gets one but he's marred, he's tainted, he will not be manly—if he had been a horse he'd been shot."

Shocked, Promise had never heard her aunt speak against anyone, and this was her brother she was talking about. *Am I going to have a chance here?*

"Before we go in, I need to tell you, watch your language; you are shorting your words. Mrs. Amrose will have your head." Then Hattie gave Promise a big smile, "Come and get your welcome."

Pushing the curtain hanging in the door frame back they stepped into the kitchen; an Indian woman was at the stove, her head down, as Mrs. Amrose shook a finger at her. "Now you do this right, or you will not work here anymore. There are more of you out there waiting to get into my kitchen to work." She turned and saw Hattie with a young woman, "Henrietta, you know how I hate having extras at the table, it throws my settings all off. You must let me know ahead of time." She looked at Promise and said, "I do not blame you, it is Henrietta's fault, I think she must be losing her mind. She cannot remember anything. Maybe some other time you can join me and my little family." Giving Hattie a hateful look she left for the other room.

Hattie turned to Promise, said, "I did not think it would be that bad. And poor Broken Wing," she turned to the Indian woman. "I am sorry; I should have been in here to help with dinner. I want you to meet my niece who, arrived—Oh my—"

"I came from the wagon train camped across the river," Promise said. She felt bad for telling lie, *Please forgive me, Lord.*

Broken Wing smiled slightly and said, in Lakota, "Greetings, Yellow Star,"

Without a second thought, Promise said, "Greetings to you, Broken Wing," in Lakota. Again, Promise wondered how others knew her when they never met her.

"Wow," said the boy sitting on the floor with Moon. "Things are going to be fun around here now, huh, Aunt Henrietta. In case you want to know, Father is in there reading the post."

"Promise, where did you learn—another language?"

"In due time, Aunt Hattie." Promise then said to the boy, "Would you mind taking my bedroll off of Moon. And, Moon, you stay where you are. Well, Aunty, are you ready, let us face the music."

Butterflies in Promise's stomach were ready to lift her; she took deep breaths, held her head up and followed her aunt.

"Henrietta, I told you we are not having a guest for dinner, and I been thinking she must be a half-breed and I cannot have her in my home. Please tell your friend to leave."

Hattie said nothing nor did Promise. She was watching the smoke coming from a pipe from a person setting in the chair before the hearth.

"Stewart! Do something with your sister. She has lost her mind. Escort this half-breed out of my home! Stewart, I insist!"

The man stood up. Promise saw a well built man with a full head of hair and a bushy mustache. When he saw Promise his face turned white. "Carolyn, it can't be! Henrietta told me you died."

"She did, Father, I am her daughter and yours," said Promise.

"Stewart, you told me your daughter was taken to Mexico! How am I going to have her in my home? We do not know where she has been this last year or whom she's been with! She will bring disgrace upon us, Stewart what are we to do?"

"Not much we can do, she's here. Find a place for her to sleep, Hazel. Mary should be home soon, she will console you."

"Where is she to sleep? Mary will not share her bed and Oliver has Henrietta in his room and that room is too full now. We have the storage room in the store that a cot could be squeezed into—"

"Whatever you think, Hazel." Stewart said.

"Come, brother, "said Hattie, "you do not want to put your child in the storage room, it's dingy and dusty. Mary has a big bed; it would not put her out."

About then Moon made her appearance to the screams of Hazel. "Get that flea bitten cur out of here, now! Out of my house!"

Promise said, "No, the dog stays with me. I have no problem sleeping in the storage room. Moon is a good guard dog, she'll earn her keep and so will I. If she goes I go."

Promise was surprised at her disrespect to her elders and the sternness in her voice but she didn't care, anyplace but here was sounding better to her.

Hattie advocated for her niece, said, "That would cause a stir in the fort if your daughter walks out of here and goes back to the wagons across the river. It would be a shame if the word got around that you did not make you daughter, your missing daughter, welcome into your home."

"Oh, Stewart what are we to do," said Hazel, sobbing.

Stewart shrugged his shoulders turned back to his chair and said, "Put her in the storage room. We can get rid of that Indian cook and the girl can take over the cooking."

Promise felt bad Broken Wing was being let go because of her. "I am not a good cook, Father. It's probably best to keep the Indian woman on. I bet she's a good cook, is she not, Aunt Hattie."

Before Hattie had a chance to speak, Hazel popped into the conversion, without her sobs, "You listen to me, your aunt's name is not Hattie but Henrietta, and she will be referred to as so. You may call me Mother Hazel."

"I prefer Mrs. Amrose, if you do not mind. You may call me Promise."

"That is no name it is a verb. I will call you by your middle name, which is—"

"I do not have a middle name."

"Everyone has a middle name."

"No, Hazel, she does not have a middle name," said Hattie

"What fool would give a name like that to anyone!"

"My mother," said Promise. "I was named after my great grandmother and I like it."

The front door blew opened and in walked a young lady with wavy brown hair and wearing stylish riding clothes, "What is going on in here you embarrassed me in front of Lieutenant James." Looking at Promise she said, "And who are you?"

Promise was unable to hold in her reply, "I am your sister, Promise."

"Father, how could you bring her here? I am not, not, not, sharing my room or my bed with her! And a dog! Not a hairy dog, too!"

"It is all settled, dear. Oliver, bring a chair up for the girl to set on. Our meal is getting cold," said Hazel with a sigh.

Promise could not leave well enough alone. She had a few questions for her father, like why he did not try to find her. His reason was he did not know where to look. That pretty much said it all for Promise. She'll stay and make the best of it for Aunt Hattie. She had a feeling her aunt had not had it easy living here in this household. The only one that was likable was Oliver. She was going to help her half-brother somehow. And thank goodness Mary was no relation to her, and considering how Mary responded to her, she's glad, too.

The household settled into a truce of sorts. Promise did try extra hard to not hold a grudge and to be helpful wherever she was needed. She mentioned to Mrs. Amrose how pretty the red geraniums were setting in a windowsill in their pot. "Her mother liked geraniums, too." The next time Promise looked at the windowsill it was empty. Broken Wing was still cooking, to Promise's relief; she did not want to be the reason for someone losing their job.

Moon made good on being a watch dog, she alerted the house that someone was trying to break into the store late one night. By the time Stewart arrived at the store's door with his pistol the would-be intruder was long gone. Promise thought maybe her father would hang back and they might chat. All he had said was, "Guess the dog was good for something."

Promise kept asking herself, *Why do I even care?* She was going through what she went through when she was at Father Fox's camp. Everyday wondering if her father would show up, was this the day? Now she wonders if this *is the day* he'd acknowledge her.

She knew her aunt was thrilled to have her back and safe. They had not had their talk yet, never the time. She was receiving an education from Oliver on the ins and outs of the running of the fort. Promise asked one day how old he was, he told her nine, but his sister was old, she was seventeen! Then he asked Promise how old she was. She had to think, what month is this she asked, he said June. "Last month, the moon of when leaves are green, I turned fifteen." Oliver loved it when Promise talked like that. He was always after her to teach him Indian words, and he'd keep it a secret. Promise had no doubt that he would. She enjoyed the little imp's company. She stayed away from the loafers, feared of being recognized, she didn't know how many people Broken Wing might have told.

When Promise was able to get away, she walked beside Oliver on his pony, searched the prairie and surrounding hills for greens and herbs that Broken Wing could use in her cooking, or just to take back to her lodge. Broken Wing was allowed to take scraps home but it was deducted from her pay. She had told Promise she'd just as soon Moon received them.

She did help Broken Wing with clearing and doing dishes until she found out Hazel docked her pay, because Promise did half her work. Promise tried to keep busy. She rearranged the storage room to make a little more room for her and the cot her father furnished. Then Hazel thought Promise should pay some rent. Again, Hattie championed for her niece. She said to her brother, "Like pay with what? She receives no wages for what she does around here; you know she works for room and board. Your stepdaughter may have to start making beds again if you run Promise off. Or have you forgotten what she was like when it came down to her doing her chores." Hattie did slip Promise a penny candy now and then, saying, "You earned it."

The Post Trader was where the emigrants, passing through on their way to California or Oregon, picked up supplies. What the fort didn't provide to the military, the soldiers bought from the Post. Promise helped Hattie by stocking shelves or sweeping. It seemed Hazel did not feel Promise was able to use the register or handle money.

One day Hattie told Hazel she and Promise had an errand to run and will not be in the store, it will have to be either Stewart or her to tend to the store. Hattie had packed a basket with a blanket on top and they, with Moon, left the fort and found a nice spot by the river.

While Promise and her aunt visited, Moon was able to explore and wade in the river.

What Hattie told Promise was a big surprise? Aunt Hattie had been courted by Stable Sergeant Pauly Martin. That was who Moon thought was breaking into the store. She forgot he was coming over later that night and forgot to leave the store door unlocked, that's about the only time they get to see each other. They plan to marry as soon as a house is available for them. Hattie learned forward, "Promise you are welcome to come and lives with us, it is all right with Pauly. He is a nice man and a caring one. I have never been in love before but what I feel when I am around him must be love. I will let you know now, as far as your father and his wife thinks I am marrying below their station. They have told me they will disown me. What they think I really don't care. I don't want you living there without me. Think about it. Now you have a story for me and I bet it is a dilly."

"Do we have time?" Hattie nodded, yes. Promise didn't know where to start, might as will at the beginning with the Squirrelly Girly Brothers. So Promise began to talk—

Hattie interrupted a few times by asking questions, but mostly saying, "Oh, my!"

Promise took a breath and drank water out of a jar. Picked up a berry preserves sandwich and began eating. She looked at her aunt, who was just setting there looking at her. "I have not had a sandwich like this since our train ride.

"Promise, if I didn't know you I'd say you told the biggest whooper I have ever heard. And I have heard some great ones at the store. No wonder you seem older than your fifteen years."

The women ate their lunch watched birds felt the cool breeze, yelled at Moon for shaking water off over them.

"Your father had just mustered out of the army just before I arrived and had taken over the Post Trader." said Hattie. "I found out later he did receive the telegram I had sent and didn't send one in return. After I had heard Penelope Rogers had been picked up by troopers from Fort Kearny I stressed with your father to contract Fort Kearny. I had hoped they might know where you were at. His excuse was he wasn't in the army any more and he had no say. And while I'm on your father and I know you wanted to know why he didn't keep in touch with you, was because you were born a girl. He had no use for a girl and tried to talk your mother in trying for a boy. She knew if she had another baby girl that she'd be treated as you were. If by chance it would had been a boy, you'd still been ignored. There was no winning for you. You would be better without a Father, than one like him. Your mother told me that when she decided to leave him and I went with her. I loved you the first time I had laid eyes on you, and your mother was like a younger sister to me, I loved her so. With her I was able to stand up to my brother, without her I couldn't until you came."

"To be honest, Aunty, I came because of you. My biggest dread was you might not be here. And I thought I'd give him a second chance. I Promise Ben I would. A thought every now and then revealed itself, telling me once he sees me; he'd like me or at least learn to know me. That was a fairy tale, huh.

Through the summer months nothing changed except for Promise tried to find somebody who worked on shoes. She went to the stables to see Stable Sergeant Pauly Martin. She had met him shortly after her aunt and she were on the river bank. She liked him right off and thought he would be good for her aunt. This day she needed some help. He was in the stable looking over the horses for welts, bruises and sore spots. Horse and hay smells drifted into Promise nose as she watched him and when he came to what appeared to be older horses with old scars and they all had a C branded on their cheek, she had to ask what the C was for. The look he gave Promise told her he didn't want to answerer that question, under her persistence, he told her.

"These horses are branded with a C because they are condemned, meaning when the artillery wagons go out of the fort it's these horses pull the wagons. The enemy will try to take out the artillery wagons first and then the horses are history. I know what you are thinking, Promise. I have thought the same thoughts. These horses have seen battle and they have the scars to show it and still brought their riders through the battle. As long as they are in the army, like the rest of us, they have to earn their keep. I do the best I can to keep them fed and comfortable. And that is the end of this discussion. What is it you wanted to see me about?"

What Promise wanted was a cobbler or maybe a blacksmith.

"Someone, who's capable of building up a shoe. Oliver likes riding his pony but sometimes he likes to walk and run a bit with me when were out on the prairie. But over uneven ground it bothers his good leg and his back. I even thought if I had the right size wood block I might be able to nail it on but I am fearful of doing more harm than good. I want some one with knowledge."

"Good idea, I'll think on it, Promise. Your eyes are turning red with all the stables smells. Better get yourself out of here. Talk with you later."

Late one night all the horses branded with a C escaped out of the horse barn. The talk around the fort was Indians took them or emigrants that were outside the fort needed horses and took the condemned ones. Stable Sergeant Pauly Martin had his bet on a certain girl, but he had no proof. He didn't feel upset either, he was glad the old war horses was given a chance to be free

He kept his eyes and ears opened to find a person who was able to help Oliver with shoes. He liked the ladies also and he was welcome to live with him and Hattie when they marry.

In the store Promise met some of the Galvanize Yankees Mr. Glenn Potts had told her about; she learned most of them were Kentuckians. She did ask one Kentuckian why he was still here at the fort now that the Civil War was over.

"Don't have no kin to go home to," he said. "Some of the boys have already skipped out. I'm a waitin' to be mustered out. I didn't desert my beloved South when I was in the Confederate army an' I'm not desertin' this army. Thinkin' of signing on again, been treated pretty good here."

The Indians wars were picking up. With all the Indian menacing activities going on troops were marching out daily, coming back late, or staying out for a few days. Still emigrants keep arriving and moving on to California or Oregon.

Promise's concern was over her Indian friends. Father Fox had said the elders can't keep the braves from going on the warpath. They were fighting for their freedom and their rights.

One day Promise spotted Oliver coming from the loafer's camp and when she caught up with him he acted nervous. "Please, Promise, don't tell on me."

"Not tell what?" she asked.

"I'm not to go to the loafer's camp. Father will have my hide. But I like going there. That's where Broken Wing lives with her mother. I like her mother, I don't understand most what she says but she can make me laugh. The other Indians there are nice to me, most of them are old. Please don't tell."

"I wouldn't tell a fly," said Promise. "You probably will learn a lot from that camp. Just because you don't speak their language doesn't mean you can't learn from them."

"I like you, Promise, glad you're my sister."

"I'm glad too" she said, throwing her arm over his shoulders and they walked together.

After the simmering heat of summer the snow was welcomed until there came too much of it and it became too cold. Promise allowed Moon on the cot with her so both of them were able to stay warm.

Christmas was around the corner. Hattie insisted Promise will have a ball gown. Promise did not care a hoot about the ball being held in Old Bedlam house Christmas Eve, even if there was a special guest coming to be part of the entertainment. She finally bowed down to her aunt's wishes. Neither one of them had the funds to buy material from the store.

They checked the trunks and nothing was presentable for a ball. Promise's choice of clothing was limited, even for everyday use. She did notice items that had belong to her mother. Hattie told her she did not give everything away because they could use it someday, like now with these petticoats and these slippers that will fit you and long stockings.

Somehow Hattie convinced Hazel to let Promise have one of Mary's discards. The one Hazel chose for Promise was a plain turquoise dress without frills; it fit, except the bodice was too big.

Promise found her gold fan in one of their trunks and Mary saw it and insisted she would take the fan. When Promise told her no, Mary wailed and called her mother in and told her mother to make Promise give her the fan for the ball. Hazel asked nicely but Promise told her no, her mother gave her that fan for her birthday that she did not live to see. Hazel threatened that she would kick both of them and the dog out if she did not give Mary the fan.

Promise looked her in the eye and said, "Do you remember saying to anyone who listen, that you didn't know who I had been with or what I had done? You left one out, things I learned to survive. I will show you if you what I learned if you try to harm my aunt or my dog in any way." Hazel stormed off in a huff. Mary threw herself into a chair and wailed, "You are mean, mean, mean! I hate you! You should not be allowed in the ball! And she wailed some more.

Good smells from the living quarters floated into the store causing Promise to remember the Christmas's in Philadelphia. She thought of the one in the winter cabin, it was sad thinking of both Christmases. Hattie came to her and brought her out of her melancholy mood by telling her that they have permission to pulled taffy and Broken Wing was staying over to pull with them and Oliver, too. Promise found out why Hazel was so generous with her kindness. The family was invited to take supper with Lieutenant James and the invitation was just for the main family. Then, she added, Oliver was too young to go since it was just for grown-ups.

It was so nice and peaceful having the kitchen to themselves. They made and pulled taffy and Oliver had the best time. Christmas carols floated in and they all ran to the frosted window. Outside in the falling snow was the fort's glee club. And Pauly was one of them! Hattie swooned; laughing, Promise and Broken Wing helped her to a chair. Then there was a knock at the side door of the kitchen. Promise opened it, and the glee club wanted to come in and have something hot to drink.

Hattie, with Broken Wing's help, mixed up hot cocoa for the group. One of the members had a little something in his great coat pocket to lace the cocoa with. Taffy was shared with them. Hattie asked if they had been to all the houses and living quarters. Stable Sergeant Pauly Martin said, "All but one. Men, we missed one, Lieutenant James. Do you want to go back and serenade him and his choice of company?"

They all agreed they were too cold, but if there was more cocoa left, a little more warm-up would be acceptable here. When the group left, Stable Sergeant Pauly Martin held back, saying he'd catch up with them.

He reached in his great coat pocket and brought out two boxes, he handed one to Hattie and one to Promise. The women looked at each other, smiled and opened the boxes. Both slim boxes held a pair of white gloves.

"Oh, Pauly, how did you know neither of us had any decent gloves to wear tomorrow night?" Hattie said.

"I remember your gloves from the last ball," he said with a laugh. "And I guessed Promise probably needed them, too."

"I cannot believe Mr. or Mrs. Amrose sold you gloves knowing who they were for since they had to know you were buying them for us," said Hattie

"You are right, but the young Mr. Amrose was glad to sell them to me, even with a discount," and he winked at Oliver. "And Oliver, I have something for you from Hattie, Promise, and me."

He handed Oliver a box he had set on the floor. Oliver tore open the box, as if it might escape him, the look on his face was pure shock. He lifted out the new shoes and quickly took off the shoes he was wearing, to try on the new ones. He stood and both his legs were even, sitting down on a chair, he laid his head on the table and sobbed. Then the women sobbed and, even Stable Sergeant Pauly Martin wiped his eyes a few times.

He turned to Broken Wing who also was crying and said, "Ma'am, do not think you were left out, I do not forget anybody."

He handed Broken Wing a box, she just stared at it.

"Open it, it will not bite you."

Her hands shook so she hardly was able to hang on to the box. Oliver stood and went over to the cook his back straight and without a limp helped her open the box. He had to hold the box while she lifted out warm, red mittens.

Promise got Pauly aside and asked him how he got the shoes? He told her he had talked with a drummer off the stage awhile back after she had talked with him about shoes for Oliver and the drummer knew where to get those built up shoes. Hattie was able to get the shoe size and the inches that were needed and they arrived with the last stage today.

"We weren't sure if we'd get the shoes," said Pauly watching Oliver strut about with his new shoes. "That's why we didn't say anything."

Promise gave Pauly a hug and thanked him for telling Oliver they were also from her. Pauly told her the idea was hers, and it was a good one.

"Look at that kid now."

Oliver strolled from one end of the living quarters to the other. He now didn't appear small for his age. Promise did not know what Christmas day will bring but it couldn't beat this.

Christmas Eve was a madhouse in the store and in the living quarters. Hazel and Mary took so much time getting ready they were no help in the store, which was busy because it was Christmas Eve. Stewart brought a wagon around for his wife and step-daughter to protect their slippers from the wet snow on their way to the ball. When they left Hattie and Promise still had the store to clean and themselves to get ready and their hair to do.

When Promise went into the storage room she saw her belongings had been moved about. Quickly she looked behind the flour barrel. The box with her fan had not been moved but she checked it anyway and was relieved. She wondered how many more things Mary had gotten into without Promise knowing. She quickly checked her bag for the turquoise jewelry, and it was there.

Hattie came into the storage room with Broken Wing behind her.

"Look who came to help us get ready—I told her how glad I was and knew you'd be, too. She does dress hair nicely."

While Hattie and Promise cleaned themselves up, Broken Wing cleaned the store. Hattie helped Promise into her grown. Hattie did wonderful work on it. The plain silk turquoise dress was simply accented with silver and white stripes from an old dress of Hattie's. Broken Wing had helped with the sewing. From the waist two wide and long silver and white stripes with white tassels on the bottom of them flowed over the wide skirt in front stopping above the hem. There were silver and white stripe bows in the middle of the scooped bodice and on both short and slightly puffed sleeves, with a silver and white flounce on the bottom of the skirt. Promise put on the silver and turquoise jewelry and tried to see herself in the small hand mirror. Hattie told her to go into Mrs. Amrose's bedroom and look in the dresser mirror. That's where Broken Wing found her.

"Oh, Promise, you beautiful. Sit. Let me do hair. We do it here." Broken Wing played with Promise's long hair. "Let's go kitchen, curling iron there."

Broken Wing parted Promise's long blond hair in the middle and loosely pulled it back where it slightly fell over her ears and using the curling iron heated on the coal stove proceeded to curl the hair into a mass of curls, then lifted it up high with a white ribbon letting it cascade down her back. Promise's eye brows had a trace of match ash over them and her lips had a touch of rouge. With her coloring and the colors she wore, one would think the sun was shining on her.

Hattie had her dark hair rolled and twisted at her neck and covered with a white hair net with a blue ribbon threaded through it and tied into a small bow towards the back of her head. Broken Wing had helped Hattie with her gown. The last year's gown had been restyled. The smoky blue, dotted, Swiss gown had the neckline changed into a wide V that came off the edge of her shoulders The flounce was a light blue silk, as were the bands of her short puffed sleeves. She wore Carolyn's cameo necklace and matching earrings.

Oliver stepped into the room wearing his Sunday best and asked if he could go with them to the ball. About then there was a knock on the door. Oliver opened it to Pauly. "Well, look at you," he said to Oliver. "Glad to see you are coming with us. I borrowed a covered buggy from an old friend to take you gals in style to the ball. I wished you were able to come, Broken Wing, but you are probably glad you're not."

That brought a smile to Broken Wing's face.

The ladies gathered their wraps and slipped on their new white gloves. Promise slipped the fan loop over her wrist. They were ready. Pauly helped them into the buggy, and Promise heard him whisper to her aunt, "Remember to mark me in for all dances in your dance card."

The Old Bedlam house was decked inside and out with boughs of evergreens. The smell was lovely. The fort band was playing, and then an angel began singing. Promise knew that voice. There was only one who could sing like that. She rushed to the hall's wide doors, and there, on stage, was Penelope Rogers. Promise was so glad to see her friend that she thought her smile was going to divide her face. Penelope finished her song to wild clapping. She did a slight bow and began singing "Come home to me my darling." When she was done, there wasn't a dry eye to be seen. Promise wanted to get over to her, but admirers quickly surrounded Penelope.

Promise glanced around the room trying to spot Mary and the Mrs. Amrose. They were standing by the great hearth and by her look, Promise bet Mary's lieutenant was one of Penelope's admirers. Jealously distorted any prettiness about her, it even took the beauty from the gown she wore. Dance music played, and although Penelope was only able to dance with one soldier at a time, they stayed in line for her return. Pauly had Hattie out on the floor and Oliver shyly asked Promise dance with him.

"I will be most pleased to dance with you."

She laughed. Neither she nor Oliver had ever learned to dance. It was the new shoes that gave him confidence.

"I am glad and honored to be your first partner," said Promise.

She got a glimpse of Oliver's mother as they danced by. Promise reminded herself to tell said mother not to stare and gape with her mouth open. Not proper at all!

After Oliver's dance with Promise, she was swarmed with soldiers wanting a dance. All she was interested in was seeing Penelope, but she also was swarmed. They danced by each other and it took Penelope a few turns before she realized Promise was there.

Before the next dance began, Promise and Penelope left the ball room and found a quiet room. "Promise you are so beautiful."

"Never, never as beautiful as you, my friend," said Promise and they hugged.

They talked until an orderly found them and told Penelope she was due on stage. Back in the ball room Promise found Hazel and asked her if she could invite a friend over after the dance. Hazel wanted to know who? Promise said, "My good friend, Penelope Rogers's the singer."

Hazel rolled her eyes, "You cannot bring an entertainer in our home!"

Promise was so mad her face felt on fire. All joy had left her. Perhaps tomorrow after church services at the fort chapel and Christmas dinner at the Officers' mess hall she and Penelope could find time to visit. That didn't happen with Penelope admirers crowding around her, and hanging on to her every word. Then Penelope was gone, left on the afternoon stage. Promise felt she must had dreamt seeing Penelope it all was over so quickly.

Hattie and Pauly were still not married but a house was coming available soon. Promise and her aunt were going through the trunks sorting what Hattie wanted to take and what she wanted Promise to have. Why, Promise thought. She didn't plan on staying on at the fort. She didn't know when or how or where she'd go. When she knew her love ones were away from the grip of Mr. and Mrs. Amrose there was no reason for her staying on. She told her aunt to keep everything together in the trunks. She didn't have anyplace to store what her aunt wanted her to take. Hattie tried to talk Promise into move in with her and Pauly, and then Promise would have room to store all her belongings.

Promise thought her place was with Oliver for now. She was still upset with her father, not for what he did or didn't do for her, but because he had not said one word to Oliver about his new shoes. Oliver was never asked where he got them. It did not seem to bother Oliver, and he had told Promise not to let it bother her.

Pauly and Hattie set their wedding date. Promise tried to convince her father and Hazel to go to his sister's wedding. "Hazel doesn't want to go," he said.

"Well, then you go," Promise said.

He declined again.

"You know, Father, I blamed Hazel being the cause of your refusing to recognize or accepting your own family. It isn't Hazel. It is you, Father. You use her as your excuse all the time in the way you treat your son Oliver, your own sister and me. And it's your own doing. I feel sorry for you."

Promise didn't tell her aunt about the short conversation she had with her father.

Hattie and Stable Sergeant Pauly Martin were married February 14, 1866, in their new home. Hattie held a small bouquet of dried flowers from Broken Wing. Her wedding dress had a high neck and long sleeves with pearl buttons and pearl buttons were on the high neck down to her waist. Two flounces were added to the skirt with many pearl buttons sewed on them and she wore a short white lace veil. Promise stood up for her aunt and a friend of Pauly was the best man. It was small ceremony, with Oliver and Promise being the only family on Hattie's side that came. Broken Wing and a few other close friends and many troopers were there to harass and cheer Sergeant Pauly Martin on.

A reception was held in the Officer's mess hall. Broken Wing didn't want to attend the reception, feeling she'd be shunned.

Hattie set her straight on that, "None of our friends or family are like that."

The mess cooks baked a lovely, three tier white cake with white and blue frosting for the newlyweds. Punch and coffee were served. It was not long before the punch was spiked and soon music and dancing began. Promise was pulled out onto the floor more than she wanted to be but this was suppose to be happy time and for her aunt she would be happy! Broken Wing also was being pulled on to dance. Oliver danced when he could find a partner. Women were not plentiful in the fort.

Promise went back to the storage room, feeling better. She did have fun and her aunt looked so lovely in her dress. Broken Wing had helped, cutting and sewing, using two white dresses to make one fashionably proper wedding dress. It was lonely going back to the store until Oliver caught up with her. "That was a great party, huh, Promise" Promise draped her arm over the lad's shoulder and agreed with him.

Hattie was still working at the store but since she was not living there she received a small wage. Promise was happy to see her every working day and she went to their house on Sundays after services and Oliver was usually along. She knew Pauly had told Oliver he had a bed anytime he wanted one. That told a lot to Promise about her aunt's new husband.

One day, in fact it was March 8th, that Oliver came running into the store," You have got to see this," he said, pulling Hattie and Promise outside with him. "An Indian girl died and she wanted to be buried in the fort cemetery on the hill."

"Do you know who the girl is?" Promise asked.

"Well, no, but her father is called Spotted Tail." Promise's legs gave out and she slumped to the ground.

"Do you know her, Promise?" Hattie asked. She and Oliver were helping Promise back on her feet and she nodded her head, yes.

"Oliver, go get water for Promise."

The loafers were lined on both sides of the road as Colonel Maynadier rode beside Spotted Tail and his wife ahead of the horse pulling a travois with a body on it across the bridge, Spotted Tail's band, dressed in their finest garments, followed. Women were crying and keening. Troops, in dressed uniforms were lined up in the parade ground. The flag on the pole in the center was half mast. A scaffold was erected at the cemetery and a coffin had been built. Promise noticed the sky was blue and clear.

"I have to go, Aunt Hattie," said Promise.

Promise joined the mixed group on the parade ground. The respect that was being shown to Brings Water, Spotted Tail's daughter and family and his band from the military amazed Promise. She scanned the Indians as they arrived, seeking Father Fox and Squirrel. She never saw them, perhaps they couldn't come. She thought maybe they didn't hear about it. No, news travels fast between the tribes. Whatever the reason, it would have to be something more drastic than Brings Water burial, to keep them away.

Just before sunset the drum beats began, low and steady. Soft soulful sound of flutes could be heard coming from somewhere outside the fort. Bring Water was carefully lowered into the coffin and carried to the scaffold followed by her father and mother, the chaplain, the colonel and officers and soldiers of the garrison and many Indians, and Promise, who was numb. Brings Water had a Christian burial service; Promise knew Brings Water would like that.

After the chaplain was done a line formed and everyone was able to pay respects to the departed as they passed by the coffin. Brings Water was covered with a buffalo rob and she had her garments and her own treasures, and her mother laid a little red book inside.

Colonel Maynadier laid a pair of gauntlets in the coffin, saying, "To keep your hands warm during your journey."

Promise glanced around her until she saw one who had a knife and she asked to borrow it and she cut off a lock of her hair. Using a few strands of hair she tied the lock together. When she went by the coffin, she laid her gift in it, and said, "To remember me by."

Looking at the scaffold, she saw a beautiful red blanket nailed to a post to keep it from blowing away. What else she saw turned her stomach but it was done in respect for Brings Water. The heads and tails of her two white ponies were nailed to the posts for her to have transportation into the next world. The coffin was lifted and set on the scaffold. Some stayed, others departed and Promise was one of them, she wanted quiet time. She felt a nose bump her hand, looking down she saw Moon looking up at her. "I'm sorry, Moon, I forgot you. But it was just for a little bit." That was all Moon needed to hear, not so much the words but the tone they were set in. Oliver joined up with her and they walked back to the store together.

Hattie met her at the door and gave her a hug and a shoulder to lay her head on, and let the tears come. Hazel came into the store paying no attention to the crying girl. She wanted to know why Henrietta was not doing her work.

"Please," said Hattie, "can you not see this child's heart is broken."

"It will heal without you."

About then the store door burst open and in walked the biggest man either woman had ever seen. "Stewart! Stewart! You better get in here, fast, bring your gun," yelled Hazel.

Promise had a big smile, and she ran over to that big man in his buffalo robs jumped up and he caught her and twilled her around. That's when Stewart entered the store, his pistol pointed at the big man. "Unhand her, you heathen," he said.

"It's all right, Father I know him," said Promise, hanging onto Buffalo Warrior's arm.

"Get him out of here, Stewart," said Hazel. "We do not need his business now or ever."

"I came for the girl," said Buffalo Warrior.

"What in the world you want her for?" said Mr. and Mrs. Amrose together?

"Father Fox wants her to come to the Yellowstone.

Promise didn't ask why and she didn't pause. If Father Fox wants her she'll go. She turned and went into the storage room and when she returned she was wearing her doeskin dress, her leggings, her beaded belt with her knife and beaded bags, and bags around her neck along with Father Fox's beaded emblem. She had braided a scalp lock in her hair and she adorned it with the feather disk. Her bedroll was on her back and she carried her parfleche and the small black pot.

"Promise, are you sure you want to go with this man," said Hattie crying.

"Yes, Aunt Hattie. Chief Father Fox was a father to me. I won't be in any harm with Buffalo Warrior. You have Pauly and Oliver and when I return, I'll find you."

Buffalo Warrior led her and Moon out the store door, her aunt and Oliver behind them. The sky was adorned in a beautiful sunset, fitting for Brings Water, Promise thought. Then she saw him: a ghost! No, it was, Ben! She ran to him and they hugged.

"Ben, I thought you had died," Promise said with tears in her eyes.

"If it wasn't for your spear in the bear's neck and for Buffalo Warrior showing up when he did I would have. "Smiling, he handed Promise back her spear. When he took her parfleche from her that's when she saw Milkweed. And she was glad to see the ornery mule again. Then she saw Queen, "Oh, Queen you made it, too! We're all together again!

"Aunt Hattie," said Promise, tears of happiness was flowing down her cheeks. "This is Ben the man I told you about. The one Mother was planning her future with, our future," tears blinding her.

Hattie walked over to Ben and stood before him. She had to look up to see into his eyes and without warning, she grabbed him around his waist in a big hug, and said, "Thank you, for caring and loving my family. I trust my niece in your hands."

Then Promise saw *him*, and her stomach got that funny feeling. He was on his black and white pony next to Buffalo Warrior. And seeing Broken Wing on a pony was another pleasant surprise, but why was she there with them?

Broken Wing spoke up and said, "I and Buffalo Warrior have walked under the blanket after he began coming here to check on you, Yellow Star. It was he who brought your parfleche and it was Oliver who got it into the store for Hattie to find."

Finally Ben was able to speak. He told her he wanted to make sure she wanted to go with them. He didn't want to influence her in anyway if she wanted to stay here. That's why he didn't come in for her, or have her told that Father Fox was ill and wanted to see her. She had to come of her own free will.

Buffalo Warrior and Broken Wing led the party out of the fort. Ben, with Milkweed followed. Queen, Moon and Promise were bringing up the rear when the third rider rode up beside her. He jumped off his pony, "Yellow Star, we're taking another long walk."

"Yes, Green Raven, it looks like we are."

Promise felt like she was home.

AUDITING THE DATA PROCESSING FUNCTION